LINDA

For Whom the Stars Shine

CHAIKIN

Books by Linda Chaikin

Endangered

THE GREAT NORTHWEST SERIES

Empire Builders
Winds of Allegiance

HEART OF INDIA SERIES

Silk
Under Eastern Stars
Kingscote

JEWEL OF THE PACIFIC

For Whom the Stars Shine

ROYAL PAVILION SERIES

Swords and Scimitars
Golden Palaces
Behind the Veil

LINDA

For Whom the Stars Shine

CHAIKIN

BETHANY HOUSE PUBLISHERS
MINNEAPOLIS, MINNESOTA 55438

Published by Bethany House Publishers
A Ministry of Bethany Fellowship International
11400 Hampshire Avenue South
Minneapolis, Minnesota 55438
www.bethanyhouse.com

Printed in the United States of America by
Bethany Press International, Minneapolis, Minnesota 55438

ISBN 1–55661–647–3

HAWAIIAN ISLANDS

NIIHAU

KAUAI

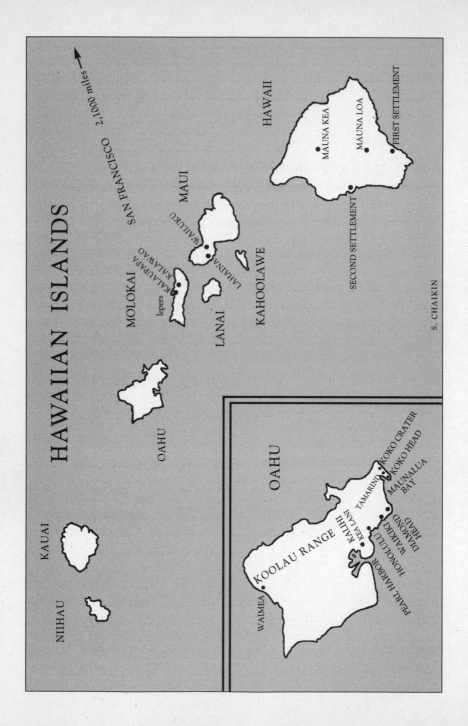

OAHU

MOLOKAI

KALAUPAPA
KALAWAO
lepers

LANAI

MAUI

WAILUKU
LAHAINA

KAHOOLAWE

HAWAII

MAUNA KEA

MAUNA LOA

FIRST SETTLEMENT

SECOND SETTLEMENT

SAN FRANCISCO   2,1000 miles

S. CHAIKIN

OAHU

WAIMEA

KOOLAU RANGE

KALIHI

KEA LANI

TAMARIND

KOKO CRATER

KOKO HEAD

MAUNALUA
BAY

DIAMOND
HEAD

WAIKIKI

HONOLULU

PEARL HARBOR

Declare his praise in the islands.

ISAIAH 42:12

———————

Ua mau ke ea o ka laina i ka pono.

"The life of the land is perpetuated by righteousness."

KING KAMEHAMEHA

Restoration Day, 1843

PART
I

SEPTEMBER 1888
HAWAIIAN ISLANDS

On Oahu, near Honolulu

Pearl Lagoon,

Kea Lani Plantation

White moonlight filtered through the palms and reflected from rain beads, illuminating the distant wooden cross on the small mission church founded by Eden Derrington's parents. Nineteen-year-old Eden galloped her horse along the wet sandy beach as leafy fronds shook overhead. She must hurry! Would Ambrose still be at the church?

It was after ten. The night was full of wind, shaking trees and raising ocean waves that inched closer toward the narrow dirt road.

Not far from the little church a golden light glowed in a window of a thatched-roof house built on stilts. Nearby, heaps of coconuts, bananas, and mangoes shone with pale muted tints of yellow-golds and browns.

Eden urged her mare onward, its dainty hooves kicking up sand. She had just left a prestigious dinner at Kea Lani Plantation House, and there hadn't been time to change into her riding habit. As she raced along, her silken frock flowed in the moonlight, the stylish Victorian eggshell lace at the high neck and wrists fluttering like nervous bird wings. A strand of her ebony hair had come loose from its sedate chignon and whipped over her shoulder. Eden's eyes, like two green peridots, shone in the moonlight. She breathed gulps of warm, moist, salty air mingled with a strange potpourri of sweet-scented flowers that shook on tall bushes and robust vines.

The lull in the rain was only temporary. Soon, swollen thunderheads tumbled across the Hawaiian sky and the face of the full tropical September moon once again became obscure. Steamy drops sputtered down the leafy banana trees. Her silk dress would soon be ruined—not that it mattered compared with the urgency at hand. Her mind was on the women and children in the Kalihi area down the coast and on the villagers' fishing boats and grass huts. Eden must deliver a troubling message that Moana, the seventeen-year-old daughter of a Hawaiian chief, had brought her at dinnertime over an hour ago.

Moana had arrived at the plantation house on foot—exhausted and searching for Eden, her Sunday school teacher at the mission church. Eden, with her grandfather Ainsworth's guests in the large parlor of the mansion belonging to the Derrington family, had been told by the house-keeper that Moana was on the back porch. Eden had gone there at once to find the pretty Hawaiian girl distraught, her brown eyes reflecting fear.

"It is the *kahunas*," she had said. "They swear by Kane that his wind and rain are coming to destroy our boats and children! Like Pele, Kane is angry that we serve the Christian God."

The kahunas were self-proclaimed priests of the many Hawaiian gods of earth, water, and sky. The first missionaries to the islands in the 1820s had labeled these priests "witch doctors." Even though the ancient wor-ship had been officially disbanded in the islands by King Kamehameha II in 1819, there remained a remnant who wanted to restore the worship of the Hawaiian gods.

"There are demons behind the Hawaiian idol-gods," Ambrose Easton would calmly insist to his Hawaiian congregation whenever the priests frightened them into believing that the old gods still had power over them. "You must stay away from serving Kane or listening to his priests."

On hearing that the kahunas were causing trouble again, Eden had left Moana in the care of the housekeeper and immediately set out on horseback to ride the two miles along the coast to find and alert Ambrose, the lay pastor of the mission church and her dear friend. As she rode she prayed that he could convince the church elders not to turn from the Christian faith and sacrifice to Kane.

The church was closer now, and so was Ambrose's house. She could see a lantern glowing in the window. She hoped to find Ambrose still up preparing his Sunday sermon. He usually studied at the church in a small cubicle that contained his pulpit commentaries and provided a quiet place to pray. His wife, Noelani, had so many Hawaiian brothers and sis-ters, nieces and nephews, that during the day the little house was always astir with comings and goings.

Eden brought the mare to a halt and anxiously scanned the wooden church building for sign of a welcome glow from the cubicle. A dim light moved beside its window. With relief she dismounted and tied the reins to the tall, slim trunk of a palm tree. She picked up her hem and ran along the flowered path to the front door, calling out above the whining wind, "Ambrose! It's me, Eden!"

Fingers of wind pulled at her hair, loosening more strands. At the door of the church she reached for the handle and called out again, then heard a door thrown open behind her and a booming voice shouting out, "Eden, child, what are you doing over there? Come indoors at once!"

She whirled, facing the ocean wind, and saw Ambrose's stalwart figure on the steps of his house, a swaying lantern in his hand.

With relief she ran across the yard toward the tossing Hibiscus bushes growing beside the steps and climbed up toward the precarious little porch, breathless and grasping Ambrose. He was a big man, and heavy, and his solid stance brought her a sense of fatherly comfort. His usually sleek silver hair was tousled. He drew her inside the room and shut the door against the snarling tropical wind.

Eden stood looking up at him, trying to calm her breathing. He waited as patiently as ever. The wooden house creaked and moaned on its stilts, making unearthly noises. Eden stood on the woven rug made from palm fiber that was stained blue-green. There was some rattan furniture with indigo cushions, and on the warped wall hung one large, out-of-place painting of a fox hunt in Tudor England with ladies and lords wearing massive white wigs. On a small stand under the painting, coconuts and bananas were piled in woven baskets next to a coffeepot and a stained brown mug. A low wooden table held a sheaf of papers, a writing pen, and a worn black Bible smudged with thumbprints on the yellowing margins.

She did not see Noelani, who had been Eden's nanny during child-hood. Noelani and her relatives worked long hours mending their nets, cracking oysters from the pearl bed in the lagoon, or drying ocean fish, seaweed, and coconuts to sell in the Chinese district in Honolulu. Some-times Noelani traveled miles inland with the younger Hawaiian women and boys to gather mountain taro roots to store and sell for *poi*, the staple food of the Hawaiians. She had been the only mother Eden had known.

Eden decided that Noelani must have already retired to her bedroom in the back of the house after a long and tiring day. Did she know about the concerns of the Hawaiian elders? Eden thought Noelani might but had decided to say nothing to her husband. It had been left to the young Moana to deliver the message to Eden.

"What ails you, Eden?"

"It's the kahunas. Moana brought word tonight. After what happened last year, many of the village elders are frightened of the coming hurricane."

Ambrose let out a deep breath, but his black eyes remained calm. Eden knew that Ambrose was used to having trouble with the kahunas. While they appeared to respect him and often called on him, sitting about outdoors near the church sipping Kona coffee and debating Christianity, they never ceased to defend Kane or to work tirelessly to overthrow Ambrose's hold on the small Hawaiian congregation. The kahunas had practically given up on the old men, but they still sought secret meetings with the young boys, urging them to abandon the ways of the white *haoles* and return to the beliefs of the *alii*—the Hawaiian warrior king race—and their island gods. It was unfortunate that the young Hawaiian church members attended night meetings with the kahunas near the inland volcano.

"Ah yes, the storm," Ambrose said, rubbing his short-bearded chin. "I expected this."

Eden remembered what had happened the year before. Two Hawaiian fishermen and a lad drowned and many fishing boats were destroyed.

"Unfortunately this sort of natural disaster gives the kahunas' warnings more credence with the villagers." Ambrose sighed. "Where are the elders now, my dear? Did Moana say?"

"They're keeping watch on their boats. They're asking for you to come tonight to pray. The kahunas are there, too, insisting it will do them no good."

"I don't want to argue with the kahunas," he stated. "But if I don't go, they'll think I'm conceding defeat to Kane. If only something could be done to stop them once and for all from believing that the church is angering Kane. Nevertheless, I'll go."

Eden's dark brows furrowed as she watched him take his worn frock coat from the peg and slip into it.

Noelani had recently told her that Ambrose hadn't been well. Eden could recognize the signs of his deteriorating health, and she worried almost as much as Noelani.

What would befall the mission church and its little Hawaiian congregation if Ambrose was forced to give up his work here? There was no one willing to take his place and certainly no one spiritually capable. Ambrose had hoped to turn the pulpit over to the Hawaiians, but sadly, he doubted if any of the elders were spiritually ready and prepared.

Though she did not want to admit it, after tonight she was beginning to agree. Without Ambrose to rally them, they were all likely to scatter and give way to the kahunas' demands.

"Noelani is asleep," Ambrose said. "I'd better not awaken her. Keno can tell her in the morning where I've gone," he said of her nephew. "He's bringing her a chicken for her birthday."

"Moana said Keno is with the elders. He's trying to convince them to stay calm."

"His friendship with your cousin Rafe has done much to add to his wisdom. I had high hopes for Keno becoming a pastor, but unfortunately he is bent on an excursion with Rafe to Bora Bora."

Eden hoped her expression did not reveal her shock and disappointment. Bora Bora! Rafe was leaving Hawaii? This was the first time she had heard of it. She had seen Rafe briefly tonight at the mansion, but he hadn't mentioned a trip. He had seemed preoccupied, however, and left before the gala dinner.

There was no time to think about the news now. Since Eden had been working at the mission church and teaching the women's Sunday school class, she was determined to go with Ambrose tonight. While he wrote a note for Noelani to find in the morning, Eden rushed to the closet and flung open the wicker door. She visited the house so often, often staying the weekends, that Noelani allowed her to keep some of her common working clothes at hand. Eden sometimes helped with the fishing boats and with the gardening work about the church, tending the flower garden begun by her mother, Rebecca, years ago.

She dug out her old pair of shoes and a hooded cloak to wear over her pretty dress—not that it could do much to save it now.

"I'm going with you, Ambrose," she called.

His brows shot up. "And have the Derrington family take me to task?"

"I'll take full responsibility. While you speak with the elders, I'll try to encourage the women. They're my little flock too, you know."

"If the storm moves in tomorrow, we may not get back for several days."

Eden walked up, wrapped in the weatherworn cloak. His eyes softened.

"You're just like your mother was. Your father found it nearly impossible to keep her from showing mercy at the leper camp on Molokai."

Eden watched Ambrose collect his Bible and hat, then followed his tall frame out into the night.

———

The wind impeded them, and travel by road took longer than it would have by boat. They didn't arrive at the fishing village farther down the coast until the moon had disappeared behind the racing clouds.

Keno was waiting for them on the beach, his white shirt flapping in the wind. He ran up—a strong, handsome youth of perhaps twenty-two. He didn't know his age exactly and neither did anyone else.

"Where are they?" Ambrose asked.

"In Kinau's hut. They're coming now."

Eden saw the burning torches dancing in the wind as the kahunas came out of the hut and walked toward them in the darkness. The Hawaiian church elders followed a short distance behind.

"How did the church elders know I'd arrived?" Ambrose asked.

"The kahunas told them."

"How did the kahunas know?" Ambrose asked suspiciously.

"Kane must have told them," Keno said with a grin.

Ambrose's eyes narrowed. "Kane cannot tell them," he insisted. "You know that, Keno."

Keno sobered. "Yes, *Makua* Easton. I know, but they do not know."

"They should know by now," Ambrose said. "They've been church elders for two years."

"The old ways are hard to forget. Look at the haoles. They stray back into their old ways too."

The five Hawaiians were all members of the ruling alii who had given their allegiance to the Christian faith and now served as church elders to the small Hawaiian congregation. They walked up, grave and dignified, greeting Ambrose and Eden with a warm *aloha* while a young boy led the horses to shelter. Kinau, the chief elder, gestured to the kahunas. "They will listen to you, Makua Ambrose."

Ambrose faced the kahunas, his Bible in hand.

The kahunas all wore feathered helmets, carried feathered staves, and wore ankle-length ornate feathered cloaks over their strong, muscled bodies.

"Aloha, Makua Easton," they said gravely, politely.

Ambrose bowed his head with equal gravity and respect. "Aloha, friends."

"Kane is unhappy. Kane brings a storm because of the Christian church on his land. All Hawaii belongs to Kane."

"Jesus Christ is stronger than any hurricane. He created these islands long before there were Hawaiians. When your ancestors came in canoes, perhaps from New Zealand, these islands were here, a work of His hands."

Eden glanced from face to face and saw their smiles.

"Yes, Makua Easton. We know the story. Ask us. We know it well. We also believe in your god too. Your god and our Kane are the same."

"Kane is not God," Ambrose said patiently. "As for the hurricane, Christ was in the boat when the storm arose on the Sea of Galilee. The waves and wind threatened to sink the boat with the disciples on board. The Son of God stood up and rebuked the winds and sea. 'Peace, be still,' he said, and the wind ceased, and the sea became as smooth as glass."

"But Jesus is not here now," said one old kahuna. "He is not in our fishing boats. Kane is unhappy and will sink our boats."

"Jesus knows all things," Ambrose explained. "He knows when a little bird falls. He knows the hairs on your head. He knows if your fishing boat is threatened by wind and waves. You must not pray to Kane but to God."

"They are the same, Makua Easton. Kane is the same as the Christian God. You call him Father. We call him Kane. He told our people his name long ago."

"Kane is not God. Kane is not called the Father."

"True, he is called Kane. Kane sends the storms. Kane must receive sacrifices."

"God alone controls the storms. He does not ask for our sacrifices. It is not God to whom you give your blood offerings."

"You are wrong, Makua Easton. Kane *is* god. The Holy Ghost we call Ku. Jesus Christ is Lono. And the devil is Kanaola, king of the underworld."

"You must be careful what you say about the one God who made the islands and the sea and all people," Ambrose reasoned, opening his Bible.

Eden held the lantern steady, and when Ambrose found the book of Isaiah, he read from the forty-fifth chapter: " 'I am the LORD, and there is none else, there is no God beside me. . . . That you may know from the rising of the sun, and from the west, that there is none beside me.' "

The kahunas listened, but when it came time for them to answer, it was as if they had not heard. They said, "When Kane wishes to punish us, he sends a storm to kill and ruin and destroy." They pointed to the elders who stood some feet away, soberly listening. "Kane is sending this storm because his Hawaiian children have forgotten him and pray at the Christian church. Kane does not like that church, Makua Easton. He is telling us not to go there anymore. These elders must not go there anymore. If they do, Kane will send the storm to destroy their boats and huts."

"But God wants the Hawaiian people to worship Him. I just read His words to you. He already punished His Son, Jesus Christ, on the cross for the sins of all people—the haoles and Hawaiians," Ambrose explained quietly. "God is happy with what Jesus did. Jesus' work for our sins is finished. Now there is no need for you to be punished. God's arms are outstretched toward us in love, forgiveness, and blessing. You need only accept His great love in faith and you will be welcomed as one of His own."

"But Kane cannot be happy. He sends the storm to destroy our boats and huts."

"Kane cannot send the storm. Kane is not God."

"If Kane does not send the storm, then he tells Pele, the Woman of Whiteness, to send it. So we will travel to the volcano to bring a sacrifice. We will pray to her and ask that she not destroy you because of the church on Kane's land. Maybe she will save the boats and huts too."

"You must not offer a sacrifice to Pele either. Jesus Christ was the only true sacrifice. God raised Jesus from the dead, and He sits at God's right hand as Lord of Lords and King of Kings. All other sacrifices offend God."

"But Kane is not happy, Makua Easton. So Kane sends the wind. . . ."

A strong gust of wind whipped through Ambrose's Bible, causing him to lose his place in Isaiah and blowing out the lantern that Eden held. She felt her heart sink to her stomach. *Lord, help us.* She fumbled for the spare matches in her cloak pocket to relight the lantern, but her fingers trembled and she dropped them onto the sand. She could feel the kahunas watching her. Eden calmly stooped, her shaking hand searching across the dark sand for the matches. Fear of failure gripped her heart. *I can't find them.* The silence grew uncomfortable. The wind kicked up the sand and shook the palm trees.

The kahunas turned toward Ambrose. "Kane is not happy," they repeated more firmly, looking over at the church elders. The elders stood motionless as they glanced at Ambrose.

Through clenched teeth, Eden gritted, *Father God . . . for your glory, for the sake of your truth, and the honor of your Son, Jesus.*

Then her cold fingers brushed against the matches. Quickly she struck one, praying that the wind wouldn't blow it out. The wind continued to gust, but the tiny flame sprang to life and held as Eden's fingers quickly brought the flame to the wick. She felt the wind cast grains of sand against her face as she blinked her eyes.

A moment later she stood with the golden lamp burning brightly.

Ambrose, with humble dignity, went on as though nothing had happened, and Eden held the lamp toward the Bible. Again he turned calmly to Isaiah and read patiently.

" 'I am the LORD, and there is none else. I form the light, and create darkness. . . . I the Lord do all these things. . . . There is no God else beside me; a just God and a Savior; there is none beside me. Look unto me, and be ye saved, all the ends of the earth: for I am God, and there is none else.' "

"Yes," the kahunas said, "but we know that there is Kane. Since Kane and God mean the same thing, we will sacrifice so Kane does not destroy the fishing boats, the huts, and the young men, women, and children."

The patient discourse went on and on until Eden wondered if they would stand there until the sun arose in the east. At last two of the five church elders stepped forward. They had been silent until now. "We speak for all of us, Makua Ambrose. We ourselves will not sacrifice to Kane, nor seek to appease Pele. We will not make the trip to the volcano. We believe that Jesus Christ is our sacrifice, as you have taught us from the Bible. We accept that He is the one true God who controls all things— the hurricane, our fishing boats, our wives, our children, our pigs, our chickens, and the taro roots. So we ask that you come instead of the kahunas and pray over us."

Eden glanced at Ambrose, and although he kept his demeanor and was looking down at his open Bible, she saw the satisfaction of spiritual joy in his face. His congregation had stood for the truth as he had been teaching them for years! They had taken a step forward into spiritual maturity. Eden swallowed the lump in her throat. A victory had been won. And God had given her the privilege of standing beside Ambrose to hold the light.

"I will pray," Ambrose said simply, closing his Bible.

"We will begin with Kinau's boat, then his hut," said an elder. "His wife and children will also pass before you, and we will bring his pigs, his chickens, and his taro roots for you to pray over."

Ambrose nodded soberly.

It would be a long night, thought Eden.

The elders led the way toward the boats. Ambrose followed, his coat flapping behind him in the wind. Eden looked at the kahunas, the feathers in their staves whipping. She saw the look of sadness in their faces; then they turned in unison and walked in the opposite direction. Eden's breath escaped with relief. *Thank you, Lord*, she prayed silently. She looked down at the lantern in her hand. The flame continued to burn clean and strong.

Through the long night Ambrose followed the elders from boat to boat, praying audibly for the safety of each one, evoking the name of the Redeemer and asking God to have mercy and spare the livelihood of His Hawaiian children. As the hours inched by, the elders brought him from hut to hut, insisting he stand before each one and pray while wife, sons, daughters, and even the family hogs and chickens were brought before him one by one. Eden, too, spoke words of comfort and courage to the women who attended her Bible class, assuring them, as the psalmist had written, " 'My times are in thy hand.' "

It was nearing dawn when Eden, covering a yawn, heard Ambrose's last "amen."

The sky was a hazy, murky yellow-red when, bleary eyed but happy, she and Ambrose mounted the horses to ride back to his house.

Keno came running with a gunnysack, tying it to the back of Ambrose's horse.

"What's in there?" Ambrose asked.

"Noelani's chicken," Keno said with a grin. "Tell her I'll be over tonight for supper. Me and Rafe both. And Rafe wants plenty of bananas and coconut in the dessert cake—and lots of Kona coffee, strong and black."

Ambrose, usually dignified, broke down and laughed a merry, ringing chuckle that echoed among the palm trees. "I'll tell her."

Eden smiled and waved good-bye to Keno. "I'll tell Moana to meet you there," she teased.

Keno flushed. "Aloha."

When Eden and Ambrose reached home, Noelani took one look at their soiled condition and wailed, "Your church frock coat is ruined, Ambrose, and where will we ever get money for a new one? And you, Eden, your pretty dress—look at it!"

"We had quite a night, Noelani" was all Ambrose said.

Eden, going back out on the steps, shaded her eyes and looked east toward the golden Hawaiian sunrise. "Ambrose! Look." She whirled, smiling, clasping her hands together. "Come see for yourself."

Ambrose joined her, looking tired, worn, and perhaps more surprised than anyone else when he stared out at the ocean and saw a rolling blue sea. Turning inland, his eyes swept the sky and he saw only some fluffy, pearly gray clouds disappearing over the volcanic mountain range. His black eyes were lively as they met hers. "The hurricane must have blown back out to sea. It's a clear September morn!"

"Yes," she breathed and looked with new wonder at the humble little mission church. "I wouldn't have missed last night for all the silk dresses in Paris."

TWO

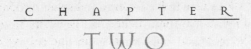

After breakfast Ambrose went off for a few hours of well-deserved sleep, but Eden lingered drowsily at the sunny table over Noelani's fresh pineapple hot cakes. Noelani poured her a cup of steaming coffee. The handsome older woman with white hair and a pleasantly creased round face was a *hapa-haole*—half-white—whose haole father had worked on a New Bedford whaling ship. Noelani had never seen him but had grown up on tales of how the American whalers had furiously resisted the missionaries.

The whalers had become angry with the missionaries who interfered with the seamen who encouraged the native women to come on board their ships to sell themselves for cheap trinkets. The missionary influence began to change all that as churches and schools were established. One day some seamen from a whaling ship came and tried to harm Hiram Bingham, attacking him with knives and clubs. They might have murdered him had not some Christian Hawaiians come to his rescue. Afterward the missionaries continued to insist that the Hawaiian girls wear muumuus and live sexually pure lives.

The first time Eden heard the story of the whalers she became angry at what they had done and more determined than ever to honor the first American missionaries who had arrived on the islands.

She sipped her coffee while Noelani wove the green palm leaf in her lap into a basket as Eden had often done as a child. Noelani had taught her to weave baskets, small rugs, and the leafy head crown that the Hawaiians also wore during their hula. Noelani's strong arms had often embraced her, consoling her after the loss of her mother, whispering comforting words in Hawaiian. On Eden's fourteenth birthday, Noelani even translated an English hymn into Hawaiian from the *Foundling Hospital Collection of 1796* and had taught it to her on the ukulele:

Praise the Lord! you heavens adore Him;
Praise Him, angels, in the height;
Sun and moon, rejoice before Him;
Praise Him, all you stars of light.

Praise the Lord! for He has spoken;
Worlds His mighty voice obeyed;
Law which never shall be broken;
For their guidance has He made.

Praise the Lord! for He is glorious;
Never shall His promise fail;
God has made His saints victorious;
Sin and death shall not prevail.

Praise the God of our salvation!
Hosts on high, His power proclaim;
Heaven and earth and all creation;
Laud and magnify His name. Amen.

The door stood open, airing the kitchen of the smoking coconut oil. A flight of narrow wooden steps wound down a little hill, where a passionfruit vine meandered to the beach below. Through the open doorway Eden watched the waves. They were still rough this morning, foaming and curling a lacy edge along the sand. She was unprepared for Noelani's next words, which jarred Eden from her lazy reverie.

"Ambrose won't listen to me, but a revolution will come if the haole planters and businessmen refuse to support Liliuokalani as Hawaii's queen—if they insist on annexation."

Annexation, Eden thought wearily. That was the topic on everyone's tongue, as it had been for months, especially at the breakfast and dinner table at the Kea Lani mansion. Her grandfather, Ainsworth, was one of its strongest proponents and had recently returned from a voyage to San Francisco and Washington, D.C., where he'd tried to influence Congress to take up the issue. She recalled their first meal together after his return. No sooner had her grandfather ended the prayer of thanks for their food than the conversation had turned to Hawaii becoming a territory of the United States.

"Keno told Ambrose they've bought up every rifle in Honolulu," Noelani said gravely.

Eden looked at her sharply. "The Hawaiians?"

Noelani's brown eyes were troubled. "No, the haole planters, all those in what Makua Ainsworth calls the Hawaiian League."

"Oh, Noelani, it mustn't happen. Not fighting. The haoles and Hawaiians mustn't turn against each other. May God save us from bloodshed!"

"It's the young Hawaiian men, child. They love their kings and queens, their noble alii."

Eden stood and went to her, stooping beside her chair. "Of course they do. They should! And Liliuokalani should become queen after King Kalakaua. I, too, will support her."

Noelani's sad countenance remained as she covered Eden's hand with her own. "Be careful of making pledges, little one. You don't know yet what you'll do until the awful moment to choose comes. The Derringtons will have much sway over you. It is right they should. Makua Ainsworth is a good man in his way, a child of the missionaries, and he loves Hawaii. As his grandchild, you cannot turn against him."

"But neither can I turn against you and the native Hawaiians!"

"No matter who wins politically, in the end, many will be hurt. Our hearts will be torn from us."

Until this moment, Eden had viewed the annexation question unemotionally, but seeing the pain in Noelani's eyes over the prospect of the rejection of her future queen personalized the political debate.

Eden grew silent as they looked at each other. *Noelani is the embodiment of native Hawaii*, she thought. *And I'm the granddaughter of one of the richest and most politically powerful haole planters on the islands. How will this end?*

A kingdom divided—a house divided—could not stand. Some would win; some would lose. All would be affected. The heart of Hawaii would be divided and the feelings of betrayal would leave scars that would last for generations. Not just among Hawaiians and haoles, but between blood brothers and sisters.

A lingering cloud darkened the sun as a gust of warm, moist wind from the Pacific blew into the small sunny kitchen, causing the cane shades to rattle.

Eden left Noelani in the kitchen and walked the short distance across the red earth toward the mission church. It would only take her a few minutes to pick up her teaching materials for Sunday's Bible class. If she hurried, she could be home before eleven o'clock with good news to share with Moana about what happened last night. Moana would be proud of her uncle Kinau for siding with Ambrose against the kahunas.

Eden neared the church built beneath the palm trees, a plain-looking structure with a white cross and a door that was a little off center. Inside, there were no stained-glass windows or elaborate furnishings, only some hard wooden pews and plain windows. As she stepped onto the bare wooden floor, the inevitable beach sand greeted the soles of her shoes. Somehow the sand always got blown indoors or was tracked in. Yet it was here, in this little church amid the soft rustle of the palms and the distant breaking of waves, that Eden felt close to the gate of heaven.

She suspected that she was sentimentally inclined toward the church because her parents had established it before her birth. When several Hawaiians who worked for the Derrington family in the pearl fishery had made professions of faith and were baptized—in, of all places, the pearl fishery!—her father, Jerome, had requested land from his father, Ainsworth Derrington, to build the church. A missionary friend of Jerome had served as the pastor until the American mission board transferred him to the Big Island.

The ministry of the little church bore fruit when a nearly blind eighty-year-old Hawaiian became the first female convert. That woman was Noelani's mother.

After their missionary friend left, Eden's parents had managed to keep the church open until her mother's sudden death and her father's departure from the islands. Ambrose then had stepped in to carry on the work as lay minister while continuing to manage the pearl fishery for the Derringtons. Though Ambrose Easton was not an ordained minister, he had a heart for the Lord and for the dozen Hawaiian families that made up the congregation, and the Hawaiians respected him.

Eden had grown up on Ambrose's missionary tales about her parents and how the independent church had been started and continued to thrive over the years. The church remained a link that joined her heart to her parents. Though her mother was now in the presence of the Lord, her father, Jerome, had immersed himself in his work of finding a cure for leprosy after his wife's death. His dedication to the lepers on Molokai spurred him on to travel the world doing his medical research for Kalihi Hospital.

Her father, though he did write to Eden frequently, was like a beloved stranger. She had seen him only three times since her mother's death fourteen years earlier. Despite his prolonged absence, there was a special connection between them. His letters, speaking of the world's medical needs, were anything but dull, and Eden found his fiery John Brown–style passion for his cause inspiring. She admired his relentless dedication to medicine, though she sometimes secretly worried about what appeared to be a driving obsession. She did not resent his prolonged absence or view his research as a thief that robbed her of his presence. Instead, she imagined following in his lofty footsteps.

Perhaps it was his fascinating letters, written from steamy jungles in the Far East and South America, that had helped forge her decision a year ago to enter nursing college rather than seek teaching credentials and work at the public school in Honolulu. The public school was a safe place to work, but joining the staff at Kalihi Hospital to aid the leper camp at Molokai was another matter.

Eden walked the narrow aisle to the cubicle that Ambrose used for his office and found her teaching materials in the cupboard where she'd left them last Sunday. She turned to leave when she saw that the candle on the desk had burned down to the wick's end. It wasn't like Ambrose to leave the candle burning. Then she saw an envelope with her name on it propped against the *Pulpit Commentary*. *Eden Derrington* was written in bold black ink.

Odd . . . she thought, picking up the envelope.

She removed the single sheet of paper and read the brief message carefully printed in block letters:

WHY DON'T THE DERRINGTONS WANT TO DISCUSS YOUR MOTHER'S DEATH? WHAT ARE THEY CONCEALING FROM YOU?

Surprised, Eden continued to stare at the words, deeply shaken by their suggestion. The message was unsigned.

The silence of the cloistered cubicle became smothering as she fought the compulsion to turn and flee into the bright morning sunshine.

Lord, I don't understand. What could it mean? Is someone playing a cruel joke? She rejected the thought. She had no real enemies that she knew of; nor was this carefully worded message the work of a young, mischievous mind. The dark undertone of the questions reawakened her own, buried since childhood, that all was not right when it came to the subject of her mother.

Who had left this note for her to find this morning? Someone outside the family? A Hawaiian worker who might know something long forgotten by everyone else? A servant at Kea Lani Plantation? Or someone in the family?

Someone had known her schedule well enough to risk being seen coming here. Had the note been left this morning or last night? There was no way of knowing, since the church door was never locked. Anyone could have slipped inside and left again unnoticed.

Then she remembered. Last night! When she had come for Ambrose, she had seen a dim light in the cubicle and thought it was him, but Ambrose had called to her from the house. She'd been so upset then and so anxious to tell him about the kahunas that she hadn't paid much attention. She looked at the burned-down candle. Someone had planted the envelope and left before being noticed.

She reread the questions alluding to concealment of family wrongdoing. While this seemed to Eden to be preposterous on the surface, she did not know whether there was at least some truth behind the innuendo.

What did she know for certain about her mother's death? The particulars had always been cloaked in obscurity. In recent years any of her questions to clarify the details were met with uncomfortable attempts by the family to avoid discussing the tragedy. Eden had always thought that they didn't want to talk about Rebecca because they had never fully approved of Jerome's marriage to her. Even her death had somehow seemed an embarrassment to them, though why Eden thought this was unclear. She only knew that she had never received the same acceptance as the others in the family, even though she was Ainsworth's granddaughter. No one had come out and said so, but there was the intimation that there was Hawaiian blood in the family somewhere.

Eden glanced up at her dim reflection in a small mirror on the wall near the desk. She smoothed a strand of dark hair from her neck and tucked it into her chignon. As she brought her hand near her temple she could still see the scar she bore as an ever present reminder of a foreboding childhood incident when she'd taken a fall on the night of a storm. She felt the scar, running from her left temple into the hairline past her ear, and shivered. She usually managed to cover it through careful arrangement of her hair, though she was often aware of it, especially as she grew older and it was fashionable to wear one's hair up off the neck.

She had her father's lucid green eyes, and there was little use in denying she looked as Irish as the painting of her great-grandmother Amabel Bancroft standing on the porch of her southern plantation home in Vicksburg, Mississippi. Nevertheless, the veiled suggestion of Hawaiian blood persisted from some of her cousins.

As for her fall, the family seemed embarrassed by it, as though what had happened to Eden afterward was a matter that she herself should seek to conceal. Eden's memory of that night remained obscure, and it had not been something she had sought to dwell upon.

Eden was told she had been sent away from Kea Lani Plantation a few months after her fall because there'd been no one in the family to properly care for her after Rebecca's death. Jerome had taken the loss extremely hard, it was said, and he had left Oahu to voyage to Tahiti, Bora Bora, and eventually the Far East. At first it wasn't clear to Eden whether his departure had been motivated by deep-seated grief or for some other reason. As she grew older and her father returned on a few occasions to Kea Lani to visit her and his colleagues at Kalihi Hospital, she understood that his prolonged absence was motivated by his medical research.

When she was a child, the family had told her that she was better off being cared for away from the plantation house by Ambrose and Noelani—that she had "special needs" after her accident, which Jerome was paying Noelani to take care of.

It was true that for the first two years Eden had needed care for a minor difficulty in walking. And Noelani, who had worked for Rebecca at the public school, had been very patient while Eden recovered. Thankfully, except for the scar, there was no visible evidence of the fall.

Her cousin Rafe had encouraged her during those early years, even telling her what he'd learned about the Bible from books by Spurgeon, Moody, and Wesley. Even so, the family had appeared in no hurry to bring her home to Kea Lani. "She fits in so well with 'Uncle' Ambrose and 'Aunt' Noelani," they had commented. For a few years Eden wondered if she would ever return to the plantation house.

Then five years ago, without warning on her fourteenth birthday, Grandfather Ainsworth had sent for her by carriage and brought her home to Kea Lani as a rightful member of the prestigious Derrington family. Eden hadn't resented those years spent with Ambrose. It was through Noelani that Eden learned to love the Hawaiian people and to understand their Polynesian culture. And with Ambrose filling in like a father, she had grown up around the small church, appreciating the missionary endeavors as well as the work with the fishing boats and the pearl fishery.

Eden then settled down into the comfortable life at the plantation to become one of the wealthy Derringtons, receiving her higher education along with her cousins. For the last two years she had moved among the elite families of the influential planters and members of the Hawaiian monarchy. Through her great-aunt Nora, who was a friend of the royal family, Eden had even attended dinners and balls at Iolani Palace in Honolulu and had met dignitaries from around the world.

Now, standing in the small cubicle holding this strange and mysterious message, Eden wondered if she even wanted to delve into the murky memories of her childhood. Especially when the person that left it for her had not signed it.

Her heartbeat quickened. *Destroy the note. It could be the work of a prankster. Let the past stay buried.* But could she? The old questions were stirring to life again—her wish to know the truth.

She squashed the small inner doubt that questioned her wisdom. Her eyes flickered a warm green. Yes, of course she wanted to know—and she would.

Eden left the church and followed the palm-lined road past the pearl fishery back toward Kea Lani.

The sun was warm, and she tied the ribbon on her fiber sun hat beneath her chin as the trade wind toyed with it refreshingly, smelling of the sea, weaving mysterious enchantments throughout her imagination, telling of many adventures yet to come.

On that long-ago stormy night before she had fallen, she remembered hiding under someone's bed in an unfamiliar room with her cousin Zachary. It was a matter she'd deliberately put off discussing with him. Zachary was rather shallow and flirtatious at times—in spite of being a cousin. She found him embarrassing and feared he would make something of the incident of the two of them hiding together under the bed "with his arm around her."

She frowned and quickened her steps. Strange that Zachary hadn't mentioned it. It was the sort of bizarre incident that he would find amusing. And he always seemed to be at odds with Rafe, who warned her to avoid him.

Could it be that Zachary didn't remember that night when they were children? It hardly seemed possible. He'd been around fourteen at the time, and she had been five. Again she touched the scar, almost grateful that the fall had blocked out her memory. If it weren't for the note, she could be content to let the matter remain hidden.

Her frown deepened. Zachary had grown overly confident and careless recently. Even so, she must learn to deal with him, since he was likely to become the heir that Ainsworth would leave in control of the Derrington sugar enterprise. Recently Grandfather hadn't been pleased with Zachary's behavior. Her grandfather was a moral man who had not forgotten his missionary family roots. He was also one of the most politically influential planters in Hawaii and a comrade to both the pineapple king from the Dole family and the California sugar king, Claus Spreckles. He expected Zachary to be mature enough to follow in his steps.

Perhaps she should show the note to her grandfather. What would he say? She could imagine his white brows bristling and his dignified face forming a scowl of displeasure. He might even toss the note into the fireplace.

Would he suspect who might have left it for her? One thing was certain. He would not want any scandal attached to the proud Derrington name.

Eden's steps slowed. Was it possible that someone wanted her to go to him with the note, perhaps just to upset him? Eden was not particularly emotionally close to her grandfather, but she didn't want to hurt him. Recently they had begun to grow closer. The thought of risking that relationship with suspicious questions made her heart recoil.

She must be careful not to fall prey to anyone's trap. Perhaps she should keep the note a secret until she had time enough to ask questions on her own without appearing to threaten anyone at Kea Lani.

Ambrose would be the one she should ask first, and then Noelani.

With that firmly resolved, she hurried on her way. She would see Ambrose again on Sunday. Noelani always asked her to stay after church for Sunday dinner.

THREE

Sunlight filtered in through leafy banana trees as Eden walked along the dirt road. A bird songfest was underway in the shady branches while tiny jewel-like hummingbirds of crimson and lime green hovered among deep-throated pink trumpet flowers. Perhaps a hundred feet from the dirt road the sand glistened like white sugar while waves dissipated gently at the shore. Small ivory clouds in an otherwise blue sky formed endless fluffy trails, mocking yesterday's fear of a hurricane. The ominous insinuation of family wrongdoing toward her mother struggled to coexist with the glorious morning. Yet as a distant bird shrieked in unexpected fright, Eden was reminded of an even more beautiful setting . . . a truly perfect lush environment, a garden without decay until evil entered, bringing physical death and spiritual separation from the Creator.

Thinking of the serpent in the Garden of Eden, she automatically quickened her steps in the dusky warm shadows of a row of palm trees but soon emerged into the warm sunlight again. *Lord, how beautiful that garden must have been! For even now, with thousands of years of the curse of thorns and thistles and death and decay, the beauty of your creation remains unrivaled.*

Eden cast aside her gloom and firmly tied the ribbon of her sun hat beneath her chin. She reflected, "*Be careful for nothing; but in every thing by prayer and supplication with thanksgiving let your requests be made known unto God. . . .*"

If that faithful promise were not enough to sweep her heart clean of dark concerns, her heavenly Father had graced the morning with mammoth crimson butterflies, their wingspan six inches across, and they were sailing among wild white orchids.

Farther down the road her footsteps slowed. A group of young Hawaiian men were gathered on the beach with canoes. It looked as though they might be preparing for tomorrow's pearl-diving contest. Their shirts were off and their white trousers were cut off at the knee. They glistened brown and muscled in the sun. Eden had already heard that Uncle Townsend had arranged for a publicity stunt for the newspapers back in the States. At tomorrow's ceremony he would toss a large black pearl into the Derrington pearl bed. Whichever diver was able to find it and bring it up could keep it and show it off amid clicking cameras and newspaper reporters that would declare the Derrington generosity. The prize was unprecedented! Naturally there was great excitement among the young Hawaiian divers.

Eden heard horse hooves trotting toward her and turned her attention back to the road.

Her cousin Zachary rode a new stallion that his father, Townsend Derrington, had bought to strengthen the bloodline of Kea Lani horses. Townsend, who had many interests—most of them lasting only a short time—was now enthused about the possibility of expanding the Derrington enterprises to include raising cattle in the Waimea area where there were ranches. His son Zachary rode toward her, dressed stylishly in a fawn-colored riding habit, but she noticed that he didn't look as pleased with himself this morning as he usually did.

Eden thought she knew why. When their grandfather returned a week ago from a tour to San Francisco promoting the annexation of Hawaii, he'd been greeted by a stack of bills from Zachary's lavish luaus and hula parties with friends in Honolulu and Waikiki. Their grandfather was a stoic man who had no patience for the carnal excesses of either his grandson or Townsend.

Zachary slowed his horse to a trot. "Hello, Eden."

She stepped back from the road and waited in the purple shade of thick foliage, surrounded by sweet fragrances.

Zachary climbed down, tying the reins to a coconut palm.

He was gloriously fair, and his white shirt rolled up at the sleeves displayed strong, tanned arms. He had a cleft in his chin, not as pronounced as his father's, and a brash, toothy smile. His bold eyes were a pale blue, as cool as a glacier, dusted with gold lashes. Eden lamented that Zachary, like his scandal-ridden father, had a similar propensity for women, including the gullible Claudia Hunnewell, who was no match for his wit.

The Hunnewells were "husband hunting," and Zachary was near the top of the list because of the Derrington plantation holdings.

"You've got Grandfather plenty riled, taking off during dinner and disappearing all night."

"I left a message with Moana. Didn't she explain to him?" Eden asked worriedly.

"Oh, she explained about the old witch doctors, all right. That didn't help calm him, though. He's blaming everything on that missionary church. He hinted he wouldn't be disappointed to see the old place eliminated entirely."

"Oh, but he can't allow that," she cried. "He wouldn't. He knows what it means to the Hawaiians, to my father, to me!"

Zachary shrugged rather impatiently. "Well, I didn't come about that anyway. Moana thought you'd be back late last night, so I looked for you at breakfast this morning and you weren't there" came his mildly complaining tone. "I was on my way just now to Ambrose's hut to find you."

So Zachary had expected her home last night. Then he wouldn't have been the one to have left the note in the church . . . not that she had suspected him. He'd been at Kea Lani with their grandfather when she'd ridden to find Ambrose. If that dim light she had noticed in the cubicle window had been someone leaving the note, it couldn't have been anyone at the dinner. However, Zachary did seem unpredictable at times.

"Well, I'll have to admit your dash to find Ambrose must have done something to thwart the kahunas—the sun's out," he said. "It's a perfect weekend for a luau."

"What did you want to talk to me about?" Eden asked, troubled by the turn of events.

Zachary bloomed as excitement warmed his eyes. "Did you hear the news yet?"

She assumed he meant the family *hoolaulea*, the weekend-long festive celebration with a daily luau on Kea Lani. Everyone of importance in Honolulu would be dropping by. Their grandfather, Ainsworth Derrington, intended to use the gathering to talk about annexation with his fellow planters and businessmen.

"I heard about your father's black pearl," Eden admitted. "I expect every diver in Oahu will be converging on the pearl fishery this weekend. I'd think that even you would want to dive for it."

His lip twitched as though some thought he wasn't sharing amused him.

"I wouldn't waste my time," he said. "But I wasn't talking about the luau. Haven't you seen the front-page stories in the *Gazette* and the *Advertiser?*"

She thought of her cousin Rafe, who was a journalist for the *Gazette*. "I haven't had time to read the newspapers this morning."

"King Kalakaua's ill health may force him to abdicate the throne."

Gossip had been buzzing for months about the king's declining health, but Eden had paid scant attention.

"Grandfather is furious with Rafe," he said, a note of satisfaction in his voice.

"Furious . . . why?"

"Because Rafe supports the monarchy, of course. And that's why he debated Rafe last night before the dinner guests, but Rafe held his own in the match. Then at breakfast this morning, my father opened the *Gazette*. What do you think was staring up at him from the front page? Rafe's editorial! I wonder if he had time to go to the office last night and write it. He openly endorsed Liliuokalani as the new queen and criticized the Hawaiian League."

"And naturally your father read it to Grandfather over breakfast," she said shortly.

He grinned. "Naturally. Grandfather was livid. He got up and left the table. Now Father is threatening to run Rafe out of Hawaii." He laughed. "He went down to the *Gazette* to rough up the editor in chief. Old Thornley will be shaking in his beach sandals before it's over. Everyone's afraid of my father. The last man he confronted in a waterfront tavern is still nursing a fractured jaw."

Eden's lips tightened. "I don't see anything impressive about your father's lack of self-control. And as a journalist, Rafe should be able to report what he believes is the truth without fear of family reprisal. Especially from your father. I hope Mr. Thornley and Rafe stand their ground."

Zachary's smile froze. "Always defending poor little Rafe."

"Poor little Rafe" didn't need her defense, but saying so to Zachary would only irritate him.

"I happen to think Liliuokalani will be a good queen for her people," Eden admitted.

Zachary looked scornful. "If she does become queen, my dear, there'll be a Hawaiian revolution of independence for sure."

The 1887 Constitution was called the "Bayonet Constitution" by King Kalakaua's disgruntled supporters. Many of the same haole businessmen who were now working with her grandfather for annexation of

Hawaii to the United States had been members of the "Honolulu Rifles" the year before. Eden remembered how her grandfather and the haoles with him had marched grimly to Iolani Palace and demanded King Kalakaua form a new government. Kalakaua had cooperated and signed the new Constitution of 1887, limiting his authority and granting more power to the new legislature, but Princess Liliuokalani had been furious that he'd given in too easily to the haoles' demands. There were many among the king's supporters, as Zachary said, who were quietly threatening a counterrevolution. Whether or not the controversy would end in fighting, Eden didn't know. She was distressed at the thought and torn between loyalties. She remembered what Noelani had said to her earlier that morning.

Eden admired Princess Liliuokalani and took pride in knowing that her mother, Rebecca, had been a respected teacher at the Royal School, where the Hawaiian princess and the other royal children had attended.

She frowned. "I don't see why there must be a revolution if she becomes queen. Some think she'll be a better ruler than David Kalakaua."

Zachary impatiently slapped his riding crop against his palm. "The planters like Thurston and Bingham aren't going to put up with her meddling in our affairs. And if she thinks she's going to stack her cabinet with Hawaiians in favor of tossing out the Constitution of '87, she'll have a war on her hands."

"Level heads will prevail," Eden insisted. "They'll come to some compromise so everyone can live in harmony. They always do."

"You're like others in the old Missionary Party—always ready to back down for the sake of what they call peace."

"We all want peace," Eden protested. "True peace."

"Peace at any price," Zachary scorned. "The price of haole dignity and what belongs to the planters. It's our tax money that built Hawaii, and the monarchy spends it on lavish parties and fancy dress. We—the haoles—built Hawaii, not the natives. The planters won't back down this time. We don't want a monarchy telling us what to do. We want a republic. Grandfather said so at breakfast this morning. You should have heard him. It was splendid. A true Patrick Henry speech."

"I can imagine it all very well," she admitted wearily, but Zachary wasn't to be put off.

"The planters are determined, all right. Even some of the Englishmen and Germans." He lowered his voice. "The Hawaiian League is talking about buying up every rifle in Honolulu just in case things blow up. They say some of Kalakaua's supporters may try a revolution of their own to end the '87 Constitution. I already have two rifles myself—and enough ammunition stashed away in the old rum house to hold out for a month. We'll teach 'em a few lessons if we need to."

"Do you think the Japanese and Chinese will just stand by while . . ."

He waved a hand. "Look, my dear, any uprising among the coolies in the cane fields and they'll end up six feet under."

"I wish you wouldn't speak of death so lightly."

His eyes laughed at her. "Now you're worried about the poor coolies. Don't you know there's millions of 'em to spare in China?"

"They're all human beings, made in the image of God—just like the haoles."

"The 'Yellow Peril,' America calls 'em. They don't want hordes of 'em immigrating to America. Too many were already brought in to build the U.S. railroads."

Eden unloosed her hat and fanned her too-warm face. His words could become like fire to dry thorns, and she had no doubt of the outcome among folk already seething with racial resentments and fears.

Zachary scowled unexpectedly. "You're all upset with me again. Why can't you show a little concern for me getting shot in the war instead of *them*?" he asked shortly.

War? Startled, she looked at him. Sometimes his emotions went off in every direction like buckshot.

"Of course I'm concerned," she said, cautious lest he make too much of her remark. "But I don't think there's going to be any war. Grandfather said the U.S. Navy secretly promised the Hawaiian League that they'd land marines if life or property of any American appeared to be in jeopardy of rampaging Hawaiians. Anyway, the Hawaiians won't rampage. They've learned restraint from the missionaries far better than the haoles themselves."

He smiled. "Maybe. Oahu could use a little excitement for the right cause, and so could I."

"So I've heard. You've been getting into fights at the waterfront haunts like your father. Grandfather must have been upset when he came home from the States and found out."

His friendly smile vanished. Temper flashed in his eyes. "So Rafe's been talking about me."

"You're rushing to conclusions," Eden said, trying to avoid trouble between her two cousins. "I haven't spoken to Rafe. As you said, he's been consumed with his work at the *Gazette*."

"Father's talking about disinheriting him for treason."

"Disinheriting him? He can't do that!"

Zachary's father, Townsend, had married the widowed Celestine Easton, Rafe's mother, and there'd been trouble ever since between the Derrington and Easton families. The fierce rivalry between Zachary and Rafe—now stepbrothers—flamed from time to time as tensions over the family inheritance smoldered. Her family reminded Eden of Jacob's twelve sons in the book of Genesis. There was envy, jealousy, rivalry, and anger. The Derringtons were in need of God's touch in their hearts.

Eden knew that her uncle Townsend couldn't keep Rafe from inheriting the Easton land on the Big Island unless Celestine agreed, but Zachary apparently wanted Rafe thrust out of Hawaii.

"So you didn't speak to him last night?" Zachary asked doubtfully.

"No, he left Kea Lani before Moana arrived. When I do see him, which is seldom, he has little, if anything, to say about you."

Zachary showed his disbelief. "Little, if anything good, you mean. He's jealous. He thinks he can have any woman he wants. Including you."

She managed to keep her poise. "I wouldn't know what he thinks. Anyway, I don't go to the riding clubs he attends in Waimea." She had heard that Rafe went there often. "I'm usually helping Ambrose on the weekends. Something I wish to do."

"I don't know why you waste your time at that little church, Eden. The Hawaiians who go there could attend services in town just as easily—at Kawaiahao Church, for instance."

Kawaiahao Church was across the street from Iolani Palace and was attended by royalty and government officials.

"I would think they'd get a better sermon there than old Ambrose can muster up anyway."

She gave him a sharp look. "Ambrose does well. And he has a heart for the Lord and the Hawaiian people."

"They don't appreciate him enough to pay him."

"He wouldn't need to be paid if the Derringtons hadn't taken Easton land, including the pearl fishery. Rafe's father discovered the lagoon and cultivated the oyster bed. Those rare black pearls are from oysters he brought in years ago from Marutea in the South Pacific."

Zachary laughed, bored. "If Rafe isn't out with his vicious dogs prowling the plantation at night or writing propaganda for the monarchy, he's hatching tales about black pearls first discovered nine hundred miles from Tahiti. It's amusing, really."

What did he mean, "prowling" Kea Lani at night? She thought of the note. Rafe *had* left the plantation perhaps an hour before she did. But Rafe wasn't the sort to resort to sneaking about leaving mysterious notes. If he wanted to confront her about an issue, including her mother's death, he would do so openly.

"Those dogs in the kennels are pets," Eden countered. "Rafe's interested in breeding animals strong and big enough to round up cattle at Waimea. I would think your father would be interested in what he's doing, since he's thinking of a ranch out there." She realized her mistake in defending Rafe.

"So that's his excuse. He has big plans, doesn't he? First, a newspaper journalist, then a defender of the Hawaiian monarchy, now a cowboy. Anyway, about that fancy riding club at Waimea." He patted the new stallion's strong brown neck. "I've asked you to go riding with me more than once. Last time a month ago, to be exact. You refused. I was going to take you all around and show you off."

Zachary's notorious late-night parties with his rich planter friends usually ended up in drinking and fights on the moonlit sands of Waikiki Beach—which was the last place Eden wanted to be with him, even if he was a cousin.

She changed to a safer subject. "I suppose you know that Miss Hunnewell is back from England. She's a nice girl, Zachary. Aren't you supposed to be at the mansion to welcome her today?"

He looked bored. "Yes, Claudia's back. And already at the house. She came yesterday to spend the night with Rozlind," he said of their other cousin. "They're both full of tales about England. They even met the old dowager."

"Queen Victoria! She's a great woman, Zachary. I can't wait to hear what they have to say. Did they go to the palace?"

He shrugged. "I suppose . . . they all do. They met Princess Kaiulani."

The Hawaiian princess Kaiulani was going to school in England and was the younger niece of Liliuokalani.

"Liliuokalani can't wait until King Kalakaua dies so she can sit in his place at Iolani Palace," Zachary taunted.

"I can see why she wishes to rule after her brother. But I think it's dreadful of you to say she can't wait until he dies. She's not overly ambitious at all."

"You would know that, of course?" Zachary teased. "Perhaps you've had tea with her recently?"

She hadn't, of course, though her mother had been on friendly terms with Liliuokalani. "Liliuokalani wants to do something just and fair for her people. Can you blame her? After all, Hawaii does—"

He held up a hand. "Yes, yes, I've heard it all too many times from Great-aunt Nora: 'Hawaii for Hawaiians!' Well, Nora can go ahead and write her books and go on author lecture tours in all the hotels in the States. She won't stop Grandfather's influence on members of Congress. Hawaii will be annexed to the United States one day. There's no one able to stop it. It's the call of Manifest Destiny."

"Spoken like Grandfather himself," Eden said with a smile.

Zachary turned grim. "I'd better, hadn't I?"

She looked at him, curious, detecting a serious note. "What do you mean?"

His eyes sobered. "If I didn't agree on annexation I'd be disinherited from managing the plantations after his death. Nothing means as much to me as that."

"Why, Zachary Derrington," Eden fumed. "After all your hard speeches against the monarchy, are you saying you're only for annexation so Grandfather will leave you in control of Kea Lani?"

"Kea Lani, the steamships, and everything else in the family enterprise—what did you think?"

She didn't dare tell him.

"Rafe's a fool for supporting the monarchy," he said. "He's losing everything."

"He has convictions. His principles mean more to him than Grandfather's support."

"Really, if I needed inspiration we could play the Hawaiian anthem."

"I don't see why you think you need to worry about being left heir."

"Grandfather says Kea Lani needs a level head. We need the old Puritan mindset of our missionary relatives, bless their hearts."

"You've always been his choice. He has no one else."

He turned thoughtfully moody and played with his riding crop. "You forget Rozlind."

"He wouldn't leave the business decisions to a granddaughter, even if she is his pride and joy."

"Maybe, but there's Rafe too. Stepbrother or not, he'll have some say."

"He should. When your father married Rafe's mother, he took the Easton land. Rafe should at least get that back."

Zachary looked at her. "And you, too, will have a say."

She didn't think so. "He still hasn't forgiven my father for marrying a missionary schoolteacher."

Zachary didn't look convinced. "He still considers you a Derrington, of sorts."

"Of sorts?" She smiled ruefully.

"Anyway," he said, "Father enjoys reminding me there are others Grandfather *could* leave Kea Lani to."

Eden didn't appreciate her uncle using her to threaten Zachary with losing his key position in the family.

"He mentions Rozlind more than either you or Rafe," Zachary went on. "My father likes to point out that she was always Grandfather's favorite. His little 'Bonny sunshine with dimples and golden curls.'"

Eden looked at him, troubled. She had thought that Zachary was emotionally close to Cousin Rozlind, but now his words sounded vindictive.

"I think he enjoys seeing us all grovel," Zachary said. "And sometimes I think Rozlind and I compete for Grandfather's approval."

"If you both allow it, it's your own choice," Eden said quietly.

Zachary leaned his elbow into the saddle as he brooded over the riding crop. "Yeah, sure. We should be more like Rafe, right? Stand up to the old man, like he did with that editorial in the *Gazette* this morning."

"I didn't say you needed to go that far. Rafe is—well, he has his convictions. And he really isn't a blood Derrington."

"He has his resentments, you mean. Regardless, though, you're a daughter of Uncle Jerome, so Grandfather is bound to leave you plenty. We all know Jerome was once his favorite son. Being the younger and all, Jerome was the beloved—like Rozlind is now. Grandfather certainly favored Jerome more than my father, who has always upset him."

So she had heard, but Eden wondered if the story was actually true.

He went on. "Uncle Jerome was quiet . . . a decent sort, I'm told." He frowned thoughtfully. "That's what I don't understand."

Alert, she scanned his face, watching the breeze toss his blond hair. "What do you mean?"

"Since Grandfather loves Jerome so much and grieves over his absence from Hawaii, why doesn't he transfer some of that affection to you, Jerome's only child?"

Eden reached over and plucked an orchid. She thought of the note. *What are the Derringtons trying to hide about your mother's death?*

"Did Grandfather ever mention how he felt about my mother?" she asked.

She sensed that he watched her now, as alert as she was. She lifted the orchid and enjoyed the fragrance.

"Not that I ever recall, and Great-aunt Nora won't even discuss your mother."

"I don't see that Nora has anything to do with how the Derrington fortune will eventually be divided up."

"She may have more to do with it than anyone thinks."

He sounded secretive and Eden studied his handsome face. Would he even tell her the truth if she asked him about that night she had fallen down the stairs?

"Look, Zachary, I want to talk to you about something important." She glanced about. "I'm glad we met on the road today. I was going to wait until the hoolaulea, but it's easier to discuss the matter here away from all the noisy guests. I was worried how I could get you away from Claudia Hunnewell."

"Were you?"

She pretended not to catch his innuendo and rushed on.

"You know how people talk."

"Let them."

"Do you think we could walk down on the beach for a few minutes?"

He grinned, the dimple in his cheek adding to the masculine mystique that drew so many mindless women.

"Why not?"

She frowned at the crafty glint in his eyes.

He laughed at her. "Little Eden and her missionary piety." He shoved his tanned hands, flashing with gold rings, into the pockets of his riding habit. She had to admit he looked debonair and very much a member of the old social school that sipped drinks on acres of spotless lawns and discussed golf and the latest prices of sugar.

They left the road and walked onto the sand. Eden breathed in the salty air.

"You know you're just a holdover from the old days of your New Bedford ancestors," he told her, tipping his golden head to one side and scrutinizing her as they strolled along. "Do you know who you remind me of right now?"

"No," Eden said reluctantly, "and I'm not sure I care to hear."

"I'll tell you anyway. That painting of Great-grandfather's sister hanging on the wall of the little-used bedroom. Remember it?"

Eden did remember.

"She was the family Puritan from the Congregational Church in New England," he said. "The one with the black dress and high collar. Looks like she's choking on a pickle, just like Rebecca."

Her eyes swerved to his. "I don't find that funny. Please leave the memory of my mother out of your jokes. You're being very unkind. I happen to be proud of my Christian roots. That Jerome Derrington chose to marry a missionary schoolteacher speaks well of his discernment."

"Something I'm lacking in?"

"Even if my mother does remind you of Great-grandfather's sister, they're not related, since she was a Stanhope. Jerome saw something valuable in my mother or he wouldn't have married her. I don't care what she looked like on the outside."

"No harm intended, little cousin. You can calm down. It's just that I don't like prudish dresses or self-righteous girls. You're a little too standoffish, if you ask me."

"In my mother's case, her manner of dress was more likely to have come from modesty," she went on, fuming. "If you can't appreciate that, you'll probably keep visiting Waikiki Beach and wonder why you can't find a decent mate. And you'd best leave Miss Hunnewell alone too. You'll end up breaking her heart."

"Ah, lectures!" He looked down at her as they walked toward the dry beach. "I've been reading British history. . . . In the old days cousins used to marry."

She kept her eyes on the waves rolling gently to shore. "And they produced more birth defects, I'm told." She hoped this would deter him, even if it meant she must be blunt. Her past experiences with Zachary had proven he rarely took a polite hint. "Anyway, I think of both you and Rafe more as brothers than as my cousins," she said.

"Rafe? A brother?"

She expected him to laugh. She didn't know why she had included Rafe. She was taken aback, however, by his rush of temper.

"A white lie!" His eyes gleamed unpleasantly. He stepped in front of her, impeding her stroll on the beach. "A brother!" His lip curled.

Surprised, Eden stood her ground, but things were not going as she had intended. She couldn't even introduce the topic of the night when they were children. It might be wiser to call it off for now.

"Rafe ignores you, doesn't he? You'd like to get his attention—his full attention."

She flushed. "You're behaving rudely. I don't need to put up with this. I'm going back." She turned toward the road, lifting her skirt as her sandaled feet sank into the warm, dry sand.

Zachary cut in front of her again, tall and broad shouldered, blocking the sunlight so that all she could see was a golden halo over his hair.

"Yes, it's true," he stated. "I have an affinity for picking these things up."

"These things! What things?" She laughed with an attempt at lightness. He was taking this much too seriously.

His eyes narrowed thoughtfully. "You know. I've been watching both of you recently."

She raised her brows. "Watching? I don't think I care to be watched."

"Rafe stays away from you as though you've got poison ivy. And you do the same with him. Why? It's so obvious. There's a slow fire growing between you two, and neither one of you likes the idea. Especially him."

She tried to go around him. Again he blocked her.

"I'm right," he accused, his mood swinging between despondency and sudden anger.

"You sound rather bizarre," she said stiffly. "*Watching* Rafe and me? What do you mean? There is nothing to watch," she said with exaggerated calmness.

"You're blushing."

"Because you're making me feel like a fool, that's why. Step aside. I'm going back."

He wouldn't move. She had known Zachary's moods could vary widely, but she'd never seen him this intense before. When they were younger, he'd been gentle and protective—much more so than Rafe.

"You've always been attracted to Rafe instead of me." His tone came close to being petulant.

She hadn't always been attracted to Rafe ... the attraction had emerged slowly, awakening from its cocoon against her will. She hadn't realized anyone knew. She had fought against it. Her heart blanched. Did Rafe notice, despite her casual attempts to appear utterly indifferent? If he did, perhaps that was the real reason Rafe was staying away. No ... Zachary was wrong. Rafe didn't care.

"Rafe isn't even a true cousin," Eden said with some justification and an attempt at dignity. "There's no bloodline between us. Even so, he's simply a friend."

He looked at her a long moment, then smiled suddenly, his intense mood ebbing like a wave rolling backward. He laughed and threw up his hands. "All right, I apologize. I've gotten you upset, haven't I?"

She was more than upset—she felt frustrated and angry with him. She disliked being accused and forced into a corner. "Sometimes you act as if you own me. You don't, Zachary. Please understand that."

He laughed again, this time merrily. "Maybe I will own you one day."

He reached and took her arm and looped it through his, smiling down at her.

She might have pulled away, but his smiling mood was easier to deal with than his emotional extremes. She gave in, perhaps unwisely. There were times when, despite her denials, she felt willing to placate him because she feared his outbursts.

"All right, I promise to be good," he said. "Let's walk on."

She remained silent and troubled as they strolled along the edge of the sand, the waves coming in closer about her feet. She felt the sea breeze cool her skin. She remained silent. The waves were like events, like the strong currents of other people outside her control, threatening to sweep her away.

"I have more news," he said.

High tide must be coming in, she thought as she watched the young Hawaiian men gathering with their canoes and surfboards.

"You're not listening."

"I'm sorry. Go on. You mentioned news. Is it about my father?"

Zachary's face colored with impatience. "Good heavens, Eden! Why ask that out of the blue? No. Uncle Jerome's not coming home to Hawaii. When will you give up on your father?" He dropped her arm and shoved his hands into his pockets again. "By now he's probably fallen from his canoe into some crock-infested river."

She stopped and whirled. His impatience with her father's prolonged absence irritated her like fingernails scratching along a blackboard. "I don't find that amusing!"

"It wasn't meant to be." He stopped. "It's probably the truth, though. You ought to give up on him. How long's it been since you've seen him? Ten years?"

"More like four years and you know it. He came home on my fifteenth birthday. And I'll never give up on him. He's dedicated to medical research. A noble, self-sacrificing endeavor. Why—even William Carey sometimes had to put his missionary work above his family. I can understand why my father doesn't come home. He's out in the jungles somewhere—unaware of the passage of time."

Zachary laughed, almost a yelp, as though they were having a merry time lingering on the beach. She fumed. She saw the young Hawaiians look in their direction. She and Zachary had unknowingly been walking toward them. Embarrassed, she imagined the worst—that they thought she and Zachary were enjoying a pleasant stroll together.

"Don't laugh," she urged in a low voice. "You'll draw attention to us.

I have my reputation to think of. They all know I teach their women the Bible on Sunday mornings."

"So why can't I walk with the pretty Sunday school teacher on the beach near Kea Lani?"

It was no use; he was impossible. Discussing anything as serious as that night so long ago must wait. And she didn't care what his news was. "I think we'd better start back, Zachary."

"All right. I'm sorry," he repeated. "Wait, Eden—don't march off like this—not until I can tell you the news."

She looked at him, almost with pity. "Oh, Zachary," she said with a sigh, like a mother to a frustrating child.

He had lost his smile and looked genuinely miserable. "Grandfather says he's sending you to San Francisco, as you've been wanting him to do since last year. You're leaving next Wednesday."

Stunned, she stared at him. "What?" she breathed.

"You got your wish about the nursing college in San Francisco. Grandfather must have taken a look at the school when he was there recently. He's come home prepared to send you." Zachary winced. "But must you follow in the steps of Uncle Jerome? The next thing I know you'll be off in the jungles chasing mosquitoes in the swamps. Then we'll never hear from either you or your father again."

San Francisco! Chadwick Nursing School! Her grandfather had decided to take her plea seriously. Her heart beat faster and a smile crossed her face. "You're certain of this? Why didn't you tell me at once!"

He shrugged. "Because I'm not happy about it."

"Then be happy for me, Zachary. This is what I want more than anything."

"Yes, I know." He frowned and looked out toward the sea.

A gust of tropical wind billowed her skirts. She hardly noticed that storm clouds were moving back in toward Diamond Head. *San Francisco!* "Oh, thank you, Lord."

Zachary looked embarrassed by her display. "It was Grandfather who allowed this."

She laughed at his simplistic conclusion. "Yes, and bless his heart. But I've been praying about this for a year. And it was the Lord who moved upon Grandfather's heart to approve it. Oh, Zachary, you just don't understand how much I want this."

"I don't agree with his decision. Neither will Rafe, is my bet."

She didn't think Rafe would care one way or another. *San Francisco,* she thought again. She weighed his words, looking at him carefully.

"You're not just teasing me, are you?"

"I wish I were. The arrangements are all made. I overheard Grandfather telling Aunt Nora this morning. Someone will explain to Ambrose and Noelani. You'll depart from Pearl Harbor on a steamship. I won't be there to send you off with cheers." He frowned. "I'm being sent away too—to London, then Japan. I'll be gone for two years. Grandfather wants me to enter Hawaiian politics, and he thinks foreign travel will benefit me. I'm sure it will."

"Congratulations," she said warmly. "I hope you'll be happy, Zachary."

"Look, Eden, I want to see you alone before I go. Will you meet me tonight down by Ambrose's boats? We can take a ride on the lagoon. We need to talk, Eden—about us."

"Oh, Zachary, no. There's nothing between us. There *can't* be. We're cousins."

"What if you were related to the Eastons instead of to the Derringtons?"

The Eastons? The thought brought dismay. Rafe her blood cousin instead of Zachary?

"That's not possible. Please . . . let's not talk like this anymore." She looked back toward the quiet road. "I've got to get back, Zachary. I want to see Grandfather about San Francisco."

He caught her hand, holding her back, his eyes burning. "I may not see you again before either of us leaves Hawaii. You can at least kiss me good-bye," he said stiffly.

She assumed he meant nothing by it except a friendly peck on the cheek, but it was soon clear he had other intentions.

"No!"

His arms wrapped around her as he tried to reach her lips. She resisted, pushing him away. "The Hawaiians are looking at us," she gritted. She turned and started to walk briskly away. He caught up in a few forceful strides.

"I thought by now you'd know I have feelings for you, Eden. I don't care who knows it. I'll come back to you one day. Wait for me."

She avoided his gaze.

He grabbed her arm and his eyes became angry. "Don't play coy. I've wanted to kiss you for a long time. You're not my cousin and I'll prove it, if that's what it takes."

"You're wrong. My father is your uncle. Even if the family didn't approve of his marriage, I'm a Derrington as much as you are. No one has ever denied that."

"Maybe they have reasons to cover it up."

"What do you mean! What do you know?"

"Nothing yet, but I'll find out what those reasons are myself."

"Did *you* leave that note?" she demanded.

"Note? What note!"

She caught herself and stopped before giving away too much. She wasn't sure about Zachary.

"What note?" he repeated, his pale blue eyes watching her.

She shook her head. "Nothing. Never mind. I'm leaving now."

But he took the orchid she still held in her hand and stuck the stem into her chignon. "I'll write you in San Francisco during all my travels. Keep the orchid. Remember what it means to us."

Suddenly, Rafe Easton's mocking voice interrupted from behind them. "How touching! Where are the ukuleles?"

FOUR

Rafe must have walked up the beach from where the Hawaiians were gathered. Eden remembered that he'd always been friends with the pearl divers. He was wet from swimming and his faded blue shirt was unbuttoned, as though he'd just slipped it on. He wore dry white trousers and stood barefoot as the sun sparkled on his tanned skin. He had the splendid looks that once belonged to his rugged father, Matt Easton. Rafe was dark haired and earthy, and his swimming and diving had muscled his form. At the moment his rich brown eyes mocked beneath wet lashes as he held his stepbrother's gaze.

A wave covered Eden's feet and splashed cool against the edge of her skirts, startling her.

Zachary, too, came awake. Like a guilty child, he dropped his hands from her sides.

Rafe stood, hands on hips. "Trouble with you, Zach, is you take after your family. You think everything in Hawaii is yours for the taking."

Zachary flushed angrily. "Where'd you come from? I'd expect you to be prowling about the flora with your mad dogs."

Rafe took a step toward him, but Zachary laughed carelessly. "They're sending you away from Hawaii, you know. They say your mind is on edge, Rafe."

"No one is sending me; I'm leaving on my own."

"Stop. What's going on?" Eden's voice tremored.

"Go back to Noelani," Rafe said. "Can't you smell Zachary's breath?

He's been drinking." He turned to Zachary. "Prowling about is more in your line. I warned you last night."

"So you did, and I chose to ignore you. What concern is it of yours?"

"I've made it my concern since Ambrose isn't here."

Alert, Eden looked from Zachary to Rafe. "What about last night?"

Zachary caught her wrist. "Stay here, Eden. You needn't obey *him*." He looked sharply at Rafe. "All your self-appointed concern is misplaced. Eden just wanted to kiss me good-bye."

Eden caught her breath and looked at Rafe. She could see a momentary hesitation. He glanced at the white orchid. Eden reached a hand to impulsively tear the flower from her hair but decided she needn't react too defensively just to convince Rafe. He should know what kind of woman she was. Her hand lowered to the side of her long cotton skirt. She felt her skin warming under Rafe's steady gaze as though he searched her mind.

"You're not jealous are you, Rafe?" Zachary goaded.

"I don't know, could be. I'll need to think about it. It's clear you have—too much."

Zachary's mouth curled maliciously. "So you haven't thought about it."

"Oh, please stop it!" Eden's hands formed fists in exasperation. She refused to look at Rafe.

"The only things I'm jealous about are those that will become mine," Rafe was saying nonchalantly. "The pearl fishery and Hanalei Plantation on the Big Island both belong to the Eastons."

Zachary laughed. "Hear that, Eden? Notice he didn't bother to include you."

Rafe tilted his dark head, hands still on hips, and looked at Eden for a moment. She tore her eyes away.

"I wasn't expecting Eden to come with them," Rafe said, "but I'll give it more thought, Zach."

Eden turned with dignity and started back toward the road. "I'm going back."

Zachary's smile vanished. Temper flared in his eyes. He caught up with her, taking hold of her wrist. She knew if she resisted, Rafe would confront Zachary physically and she didn't want that.

"I wouldn't have either one of you, the way you're both behaving," Eden protested.

"Smart woman," Rafe said, walking up. He looked down at Zachary's hand holding her wrist and gestured his head. "I'd advise you to let go, my brother."

Zachary's jaw muscles flexed. He deliberately waited but slowly released her.

A moment of silence passed and the wind blew against them. Then Rafe walked over to Zachary's horse. He took the reins and flapped them against his palm. "You know I've been wanting to ride this one since it arrived last week." He whistled softly, carelessly, and swung himself into the saddle. "Nice horse," he smiled. "Real nice. Perfect for Waimea cattle country. Say, I'm thinking of retiring Ambrose and Noelani there. What do you think? They deserve a few good years."

"I . . . um . . . think they'd be very pleased," she said quietly, her eye still on Zachary. A mottled anger was darkening his cheeks. Eden stood tensely waiting for Zachary's explosion. She suspected Rafe was waiting as well.

Rafe gave a flip of the reins and rode forward, stopping beside her. He sat there with his shirt blowing in the warm wind looking down at her, ignoring Zachary's glare.

His eyes softened. "You look exhausted. I'd better ride you home to Kea Lani. I hear you and Ambrose were up all night confronting the kahunas."

"Get off that horse," Zachary growled.

The tension between the two crackled. Rafe removed his foot from the stirrup on Eden's side of the horse. "Climb up. Can you manage?"

"Oh no, you don't!" Zachary latched hold of her arm and pulled her away from the horse's side. Holding her shoulders, he looked into her eyes. "Grandfather has promised to make me your guardian one day. Who does that say you should trust?"

She pulled away. "Stop it. I don't need a guardian. And I'll walk back to Kea Lani."

A glaring, quick smile flashed across Zachary's face. He came after her. He grabbed her and planted a quick but thorough kiss on her lips, then grinned, rubbing his cleft chin as he looked over his shoulder at Rafe. "Well, my brother?"

Eden might have slapped him, except that Rafe dismounted. Grabbing Zachary's shoulder, he spun him around and backhanded him across the face.

Zachary stumbled, dazed and blinking. Rafe caught her hand and calmly steered her toward the horse. "The sooner I get you out of here, the better."

Zachary looked at his palm, where a spot of blood from a cut lip showed. His eyes widened. Then, yanking off his riding jacket, he stormed after Rafe.

Rafe stopped and faced him. "You want more?" he inquired coolly.

"No, don't, Rafe," Eden cried, hating the conflict. "Please—"

"Too late," snarled Zachary. "It's you and me. I've been taking boxing lessons. This time I'm going to pound you into the sand."

Some of the Hawaiians started to gather around, attracted by the prospect of a fight. Eden ran to them, her eyes pleading. "Do something. Stop Rafe . . ."

They shook their heads no.

Eden glanced about wildly and saw the German overseer walking toward them from a recently planted pineapple grove across the road. She ran across the sand toward him. "Rupert, hurry, stop them, please! It's gone too far!"

Rupert ambled, as though in no hurry, his long arms swinging beside him. She had long suspected he didn't like Zachary. Few of those who had the misfortune of working under Zachary and Townsend held warm feelings for them.

"Ah, they are fighting over more than you, *Fräulein* Eden," Rupert said in a heavy European accent. "They have wanted this for months. Now, see, before they are both leaving Hawaii, like two stags, they wish to fight."

Lord, I don't know what to do, Eden thought helplessly as she looked about again. She started to run back with the intent of throwing herself between them when the sound of carriage wheels drew her glance down the road. Good, someone was coming.

But then her hopes were dashed. Townsend and Rafe's mother, Celestine, were coming from the direction of Kea Lani. This could not have turned out any worse!

The Hawaiians, seeing that it was Townsend, scattered at the threat of being blamed for rooting against his son. Rupert, too, suddenly found his energy and ran toward Zachary and Rafe as if he had come to stop the fight.

"All right, boys, enough, enough."

Townsend Derrington stopped the carriage on the road, his square jaw set like a bulldog. Celestine was urgently pleading with him, but he flung her arm aside, tossed the reins onto the seat, and jumped down. His strong proportions were noticeable beneath the white cotton jacket and frilled shirt.

Celestine, a frail picture of lovely dismay, was gripping the leather seat.

Townsend, in his early forties and handsomely golden like his son,

Zachary, took a few boundless steps, his boots sinking into the dry sand. He strode toward the two and came between them, turning on Rafe.

"Another brawl! Last month it was with Hollings' son."

"Hollings asked for it," Rafe said. "He damaged one of Ambrose's boats, then refused to pay. He's rich and spoiled. If his father didn't make excuses for him, he'd grow up. He should have paid up by now."

"So you beat the stuffing out of him."

"He jumped me when I turned to walk away. What was I supposed to do, surrender because he's Hollings' son?"

"Jumped you? That's not what Hollings says."

"And you take his word for it?"

"I don't know. And this time? Did your brother ask for it?"

"Yes, he asked for it."

"Lies," snarled Zachary. "He's bitter because you're running him out of Hawaii."

Townsend's eyes slitted as he confronted Rafe. "I suppose you think Zachary's rich and spoiled too?"

"I do think so, yes."

Townsend flushed with temper. "Your dark nature can't stand to see anyone happy, can it, Rafe?" He gestured toward the carriage. "That sight burns you too, doesn't it? Your mother—*my wife*—happily seated in a *Derrington* carriage."

Rafe pushed his dark hair from his sweating forehead. "You really expect me to answer that?"

Townsend whirled, gesturing angrily toward his son. "Zachary! Get over here!"

Zachary walked up, breathing hard.

"Who started this?" Townsend demanded.

Zachary gestured, touching his bruised chin. "Rafe, as always. He claimed the horse, then wanted to prance around with Eden, showing off."

Townsend shot a look at Eden. Inwardly she winced but called, "That isn't quite true, Uncle Townsend—"

Townsend waved her to silence. "Go on," he told Zachary.

"I tried to protect Eden. A couple of nights ago I saw her and Rafe sneaking off to the beach for a swim."

Eden's breath sucked in. How could he lie like that? She walked toward him indignantly. "How dare you—"

Again, Townsend waved her to silence. Eden looked over at the road toward Celestine, hoping she'd intervene, but she sat still and lifeless, her face partially shadowed beneath a fragile lace hat, as though there were no more will in her spirit.

"What is this?" Townsend was demanding of Rafe. "You were with Eden last night at the beach?"

Rafe wouldn't look at her. "No."

"He's lying," Zachary glowered. "I saw them together."

"That's not true," Eden cried. "It's Zachary who's lying—or he's confused me with someone else. . . ." She, likewise, refused to look at Rafe. Had he been swimming with another girl?

"Who were you with, Rafe?" Townsend demanded.

"I wasn't with Eden. She was helping Ambrose at the church. You should know the character of your niece by now. Don't compare her with the hapa-haoles at the waterfront haunts."

"Ambrose would lie to cover for both of you. So would Noelani."

"It's your reputation that everyone talks about, Townsend, not Eden's," Rafe said.

Eden winced. Too late now. She saw her uncle's lip curl and knew what was coming. She grabbed his right arm but couldn't stop him. He struck Rafe with his fist.

She threw herself between them, and Rafe, trying to shield her, took a second blow from his stepfather.

Townsend grabbed her arm and flung her aside into the soft sand like a rag doll. She landed in the warm grit, dazed but unhurt. The next few moments became a blur as she sat there, her brain refusing to respond. She blinked, watching as Uncle Townsend struck Rafe several times with Rafe simply taking it, apparently unwilling to lay a hand on his stepfather . . . until at last he fell to his knees.

Pain clawed at Eden's heart. She couldn't bear to watch anything so unfair. She crawled toward them.

"Uncle Townsend!"

Eden pushed herself to her feet and walked unsteadily toward Rafe, her shoes sinking into the sand. The wind had picked up speed and whipped at her skirts. She tugged at her uncle's arm and he turned to her, his face sweating and ruddy with temper.

She looked up at him wildly. "Can't you see he won't fight you back?"

Celestine had by now left the carriage and came up, also taking hold of her husband's arm. "Townsend! Do stop—for my sake. . . ."

He turned to Celestine. "He's getting out of Hawaii! Is that understood? He'll learn to respect the Derrington name or he'll never set foot in these islands again."

Eden stumbled over to Rafe and knelt beside him. "Rafe . . ."

"I'm all right," he murmured, struggling to get up.

"I'm sorry," she whispered as she tried to help him.

"Don't worry about it." He took the handkerchief she offered and pushed himself up slowly from the sand and looked over at his mother.

Eden, too, looked at Celestine and saw tears on her pale cheeks, her eyes full of pain.

Eden's fingers tightened on Rafe's arm, trying to keep him from reacting. She knew he blamed Townsend for his mother's grief.

"I'll be all right," he told Eden again. He walked down toward the water and stooped, rinsing his wounds. Eden felt sick and turned away.

She saw Celestine standing and watching her son, the knuckles of one hand pressed to her mouth. Eden noticed that the rings and bracelets on her hand glittered the colors of the rainbow in the sunlight. Eden felt pity. Celestine seemed the most miserable of women, despite her riches and handsome husband. She had everything Hawaii could offer, but she had lost her joy long ago.

Aware that Townsend strode toward her, Eden braced herself for a new onslaught. She met his stony gaze.

His breath came swiftly. "I'd make much of you meeting Rafe last night—"

"I didn't—it's not true! And I think you know it, Uncle Townsend."

"All right . . . because I know you're a decent girl. But Rafe is trouble. He always was. I want you to stay away from him."

"It's Zachary—"

"Never mind my son. I'll handle him. He's leaving Oahu for two years anyway. There's too much trouble in this family already. And you'll be leaving for San Francisco, so we'll say no more about it."

Eden's hands clenched to hold in her emotions. "After you struck Rafe unfairly? You'll say no more about it?" Her voice shook with angry emotion.

"Rafe had it coming. If it wasn't Zachary, it was the articles he's been writing in the *Gazette* just to stir up my father and the rest of the family. He doesn't care that he's making the old man ill. And Aunt Nora is in this with Rafe, and Liliuokalani. Rafe needed to have some sense slapped into him."

Eden closed her eyes with frustration and shook her head. "You don't understand at all, do you? He believes what he's writing. And he honored you just now when he wouldn't strike you back. He just stood there and took all your anger, you and—"

"There's no need to discuss it now. Enough is enough." Townsend snatched a cloth from his pocket and blotted his sweating face.

Eden steadied herself as Townsend went on. "Aunt Nora's been in correspondence with your mother's younger sister, who works at the nursing school in San Francisco. You've been wanting to go there, so your grandfather decided to let you go. You've got your chance."

His voice droned on, staccato-like. Yes, she had wanted to go, but now the traumatic conflict had taken away the joy she had felt earlier upon hearing this news.

"Your grandfather has already arranged for everything at Chadwick. Naturally we all wish you the best, Eden."

Eden's overloaded mind tried to take all this in. She stood there as her uncle walked back toward Celestine.

Townsend picked up Celestine's hat from the sand and shook it out before almost tenderly placing it upon her golden head. Taking her arm, he said something to her and led her back toward the carriage as though she were a frightened child. Celestine looked over her shoulder toward her son, but Rafe was still rinsing his face in the salty waves. Two Hawaiians had walked up the beach to join him.

Zachary followed after his father, refusing to look back at Eden. She did not feel angry. She felt momentarily empty as she watched him climb stiffly into the carriage.

A few moments later the horse-drawn vehicle moved on its way down the road as though nothing unpleasant had intruded into the tropical morning. The birds trilled in the branches and the roar of the sea filled the air. Everything appeared normal again, yet Eden knew it was not. She was convinced her entire life had changed. A new door stood open, allowing her entry into a nursing career. Her prayers were being answered, but she hardly knew how to respond.

Somewhat dazed, she thought, *I'm going to be a nurse.* This is what she had wanted, but not under these circumstances. The family was angry and divided. Rafe was being sent from the islands, and Zachary was leaving for Europe and Japan. Her heart ached, wounded.

She looked toward the heavens, then toward the sparkling water and Rafe. He was walking toward her, the trade wind tossing his torn shirt. He could have hurt Townsend, but he hadn't. She respected him for his restraint.

Eden swallowed the pain in her throat and waited for him, trying to portray a sense of dignity for them both.

FİVE

Eden watched Rafe walking toward her, leading the horse that Zachary had ridden. Except for a few bruises and a cut on his chin, he appeared unhurt. He stopped a few feet away and looked at her for a moment before speaking, as though nothing of consequence had occurred since he'd first offered her a ride.

"Where would you prefer to go? Kea Lani or back to Ambrose's place?"

"I . . . I think I'd better walk to Kea Lani," she said wearily. "You heard what your father said; we're not to be seen together before I sail for San Francisco."

"Townsend is not my father," he replied stiffly. "The only father I care about is buried on Hanalei—" he dropped his voice—"perhaps a victim."

Eden believed Rafe did not want her sympathy. Except for his Hawaiian friends, he was a loner and wished to keep emotional distance from the Derringtons. Still, she understood how difficult it had been for him to grow up on Kea Lani with a stepfather like Townsend. The Derringtons had never fully accepted him, any more than they had warmed toward her. His "real home," as Rafe had always made it clear to her, Rozlind, and Zachary while growing up, was Hanalei, the Easton coffee plantation located in the Kailua-Kona area of the Big Island.

Eden had heard many favorable things about Rafe's father, Matt Easton, from Ambrose, but she had no recollection of him. Rafe had been about ten when Matt was killed in an accident on the plantation.

"Since when was your father ever a victim of anything? Ambrose talks about his brother, Matt, as though he was always in control of events.''

Rafe made no further comment to either clarify or deny. He mounted the horse, edging it toward her.

"Since we've already been falsely accused of a midnight swim, I might at least see you home honorably in broad daylight.''

Eden was in no mood to protest. She felt exhausted from the emotional stress coming first from Zachary and then Townsend. It was a mile back to Ambrose and Noelani's house near the pearl beds and at least another mile to Kea Lani. The thought of meeting her uncle was unbearable, and she glanced down the dirt road, as if expecting to see the carriage again, then walked to the side of the horse.

"Thank you. Can you take me to Kea Lani?''

He reached down and pulled her up in front of the saddle. She was surprised when she felt his deft fingers pluck the orchid from her hair that Zachary had placed there, then toss it toward an oncoming wave. "Aloha," he commented wryly. "I don't think you'll need this to keep romantic memories of Zachary fresh in your mind while you're in San Francisco.''

She covered a smile and was careful to avoid close contact, holding to the pommel. "I didn't give you permission to throw the orchid away," she said casually, though she would have done so herself as soon as she got home.

"No, you didn't," he agreed lightly, smiling as he reached both arms around her waist.

She must not fall in love with Rafe, she warned herself. He was going away, and who knew when they would meet again? *Heart, beware*, she thought. She was not the presumptuous sort, nor reckless with her emotions. Pain had been too real in her life to risk feelings for a man preparing to catch a ship to Bora Bora.

Townsend had said Rafe was no longer welcome on Oahu. Rafe would never capitulate permanently if he wished badly enough to come back. But did he want to return?

They rode along in silence, and after a few minutes of soaking in the wealth of sunshine, her tattered emotions began to mend. Her spirits brightened as she drank in the view of the Pacific, like an endless sapphire stretching toward the opal horizon. The ocean's dainty waves were dancing in over the sugary white sand while on the landward side of the road, tall Hibiscus bushes with waxy green leaves grew in profusion with giant red flowers.

"Hawaii's like a healing balm," she murmured. "I shall miss it. I wonder if I'll adjust to the San Francisco fog."

Rafe's silence told her he agreed about missing the islands.

At last Eden turned her head and glanced over her shoulder, studying the bruise on his chin. "Does it hurt badly?"

He smiled. "Even if it did, I wouldn't want to admit it."

"To me? Or to anyone?"

A brow lifted. "Does it matter?"

She shrugged. "No. Curious is all. I am going to become a nurse, you know."

"Ah yes. Well, men don't enjoy admitting to women that they hurt."

"Masculine pride."

"If I get into any more trouble I'll show up at Chadwick and ask for you."

Eden turned her head away, her eyes narrowing slightly at his cavalier attitude. She said quietly, "I'm sorry it turned out so bad today. You showed great restraint when he kept hitting you like that, provoking you. I think he wanted you to hit him in front of Celestine."

Rafe was quiet for a moment. "I'm afraid my restraint is running thin. It's wise that I'm leaving. He had nothing to do with that decision. I made up my mind to leave Oahu before this morning. Looks like we're both saying good-bye to Hawaii."

She tried to speak calmly, holding her emotions under tight rein. "It's different with Zachary. Grandfather is sending him away to Europe and Japan. He hopes travel will make Zach more politically adept. His weak views on the monarchy, however, would affect any position he may hold in the future."

"Hypocrisy appears to trouble very few of the Derringtons."

Sometimes Rafe speaks about the Derrington family as if I'm not a member of it, Eden thought. She caught his gaze and asked, "What will Ambrose do when you leave? He counts on you to help him at the pearl fishery."

"Ambrose has Noelani. And Kelolo has offered to help out."

Kelolo was Noelani's brother, the father of Keno, Rafe's closest friend and ally. Eden had seen Rafe with Kelolo at the pearl fishery many times and had also heard that the older Hawaiian thought affectionately of Rafe.

She sighed over the turn of events. "I can't understand why Zachary behaved as he did today."

"Can't you? Zachary is spoiled enough to think he can take anything he wants. I warned you to avoid him."

Rafe *had* warned her—on several occasions—but he never explained why. Since he and Zachary didn't get along, she had thought Rafe might merely have personal reasons for not trusting his stepbrother, so she'd taken his warnings casually, even though she knew Zachary's intemperate ways.

"Zachary was on the way to Noelani's house to say good-bye to me," she explained, feeling a need to justify the situation of being trapped by him on the beach. "He wanted to be the first to tell me about my going to the nursing college in San Francisco."

"That was considerate of him."

"You needn't sound cynical, Rafe."

"About Zachary?" he laughed. "There's good reason. What did he tell you about your aunt Lana?"

She picked up the alert interest in his voice, though it seemed he was trying to mask it. "I don't think he even mentioned her. Why?"

"I'm just surprised that Ainsworth arranged to send you to that particular school."

"I've been asking him for over a year to let me go to Chadwick. My aunt Lana works there."

"Lana Stanhope. Yes, I know."

She looked at him, but his eyes were veiled. "It seems quite natural for me to attend the school where my aunt teaches tropical diseases. I understand she's one of the best."

He made no comment and looked toward the beach. "Chadwick will suit you well. It's a Christian college, isn't it?"

"Yes, and Lana also teaches church history. She takes a special interest in the history of missions in Hawaii."

"You're sure to get an A in that class. You know the missionary movement by heart."

So do you, she could have said but refrained. The Easton family in Hawaii dated back even before the Derringtons. Rafe had an ancestor among the original missionaries of the 1820s, though there was no official historical record of an Easton being among the first couples who arrived. There was some talk that the missionary Daniel Easton had come from England, and that was the reason he wasn't included on the official record of the New England missionaries. He'd also come from a failed missionary attempt on Tahiti, where sadly, the first single male missionaries had succumbed to the carnal temptations of the Tahitian women. Thereafter, the mission board made it a rule that only married couples could go out to Polynesia.

There was also a missionary church founded by Daniel Easton on

Hanalei when a friend, Hiram Bingham, preached and brought in the first widespread island revivals.

"The sooner you board the steamer for the Bay City, the better off you'll be," Rafe concluded.

Her enthusiasm grew. "Oh, Rafe, all this is such wonderful news. I know it must be of the Lord. Why else would I have an aunt who's a nurse?"

"I wish I could feel the same about my own departure. I was fired today from the *Gazette*. Ainsworth read my articles in favor of the monarchy and put the pressure on the editor in chief. I suspect Townsend also threatened to ruin the paper if he didn't let me go."

So he knew. "If I had any influence on my grandfather, I'd tell him he is wrong."

"He's always been bullheaded—if you don't mind my saying so about your grandfather."

In this instance Eden agreed.

"He speaks of democracy, then wants to shut down the opposition," Rafe said with a short laugh. "One of these days he'll meet his match."

She wondered if Rafe hoped that he would be the one to match him. "Do you plan to return and open a paper he can't shut down?"

"I don't know yet. . . . I like journalism, but I'm not sure it's what I want to do permanently. Keno and I are signing onto a merchant ship for the South Seas."

"What about Hanalei? I thought you intended to get your father's plantation back."

"I haven't changed my plans about Hanalei, but I'm not going to sit around and wait for Townsend to decide to restore what's mine. I'll make money enough to start a new place of my own in a few years, but I haven't made up my mind where. I'm not sure I want to grow cane. By the way, you said Zachary was on his way to Ambrose's to say good-bye to you when he met you on the road. Why did you come looking for him?"

She thought of the night when she had fallen down the stairs. She had mentioned that night to Rafe years ago, but he hadn't wanted to talk about it. *"Forget the past,"* he had told her. That was what the family always told her. Now that she'd received the note, however, the past could not be forgotten.

"I've been thinking about that night when we were children. When I fell. There's so much I don't recall about it. Zachary and I hid under the bed. He should remember. I don't know why he doesn't want to talk about it, but neither does anyone else."

She felt the tension in his body. "Maybe it's best that way," Rafe said.

"You and the others always say that, but you won't explain why you think so," Eden said with exasperation. "I think it's time I found out."

"You're going to San Francisco to study medicine. I doubt if you'll ever come back to Kea Lani. So why not forget it?"

"Oh, but I am coming back. This is my home. It's an ambition of mine to work in research with my father. I'll start off at Kalihi Hospital if I can."

"It would be a mistake to come back. The Lord has given you a new beginning. Use it to help you let go of the past."

She turned her head. It didn't sound like Rafe. His eyes were sober, but under her scrutiny he half smiled. "Can I give you another word of advice?"

"You will anyway, I'm sure. Go ahead. I've always respected your opinion."

He lifted a brow and smiled. "Why, thank you."

She turned her head away.

"Asking Zachary about that night is the wrong thing to do. He doesn't remember anything either. It's better if he doesn't . . . if neither of you do."

Eden had never fully considered the frightening effect of that night on her cousin Zachary. She had only thought of her own distress. Still, it was a strange thing to say.

"I can see that it might be better not to try to make him relive it," she admitted dryly. "It was . . . a dreadful night, a horrific storm. Unfortunately, I can't remember everything. There are gaps, important things missing. But I won't give up wanting to know the truth. I intend to find out everything."

"San Francisco will help you put it away. That is," he said quietly, "if Lana doesn't dig it up. I hope she's wiser than that. I think she is. Once you get involved in studying medicine at Chadwick, you'll forget."

"I wonder. Especially when someone else wants—" She stopped.

"Someone else?"

"Your warnings to go away and stay away only make me more curious."

Rafe laughed. "Then I'll need to change my approach."

"You're like Noelani and all the rest of them," she complained good-naturedly. "You never want to talk about it, especially about my mother. Do you realize I don't even know all the details of her death?"

"You're right," he said bluntly. "The family doesn't want to talk about it—any more than I want to talk about my father's death. I'd like to forget everything and begin a new life."

They rode in silence. Was she included in everything he wanted to forget? She had known all along that any feelings she might have for Rafe were risky.

Eden shut it from her mind. Was it possible Zachary did not remember any more than she did? Her brow wrinkled. Maybe so. There was a time after she had fallen when they'd told her that Cousin Zachary was ill. Months had slipped by before she saw him again. What had so upset him that he became ill? Could he have known something or seen something that disturbed him? Perhaps something she had not seen or didn't remember? It did seem strange that Zachary never spoke of that night.

"He must remember something," she repeated. "He was there, under the daybed with me. We must have been hiding from the thunder and lightning."

"Probably."

She turned her head to ponder his expression again and recognized that same arcane barrier that refused her scrutiny. She knew him well enough to understand he would offer no further insight unless he chose to. Her lips tightened.

"Then at least tell me how it is you know about my aunt Lana."

"I've been in the unfortunate position of living in the Derrington mansion, remember?"

"You've been living at the hotel for a year," she corrected.

"All right, then, before last year. I knew most everything going on at Kea Lani. And my mother's been unhappy recently and coming to the hotel to talk to me about things. She mentioned that both Ainsworth and your great-aunt Nora were considering your request to attend Chadwick where Lana works. So you see, there's no big secret. And it's clear that Mother should never have married Townsend. He's no good."

Eden agreed. On one of Rafe's late-night visits to Ambrose's house, when Eden had been there for the weekend preparing to teach, she'd been awakened to overhear Rafe saying that Townsend had married his mother because Ainsworth wanted the Easton land on the Big Island. Townsend's marriage to a grieving widow was the best way to gain control. Eden didn't want to believe this about her grandfather.

Eden often wondered why Celestine hadn't known about Townsend's reputation with women before she married him, but perhaps she was gullible. Or perhaps she had known but had mistakenly gone ahead and married him for reasons of her own. If that were the case, she had behaved unwisely, and it was a tragedy. She didn't seem as wise as her son. Though Rafe was of age now, there was the possibility that he wouldn't gain control of his father's inheritance. Townsend was trying to get Celestine to turn everything over to the Derringtons to manage and to change her will.

Eden wondered how much of Rafe's dislike for Townsend was the result of resentment over his mother's remarriage and how much of it was due to Townsend's lack of character. Rafe had been so close to his father, Matt, that no other man would have been good enough in his eyes to marry his mother.

Lord, the problems are so deep that only you can solve them.

Rafe left the road to ride the horse along the dry beach, where its hooves kicked up the sand. As they rode along in silence, Eden remembered something else disturbing and wanted Rafe's response.

"Zachary doesn't think I'm a Derrington. I wonder why he would ever think such a thing."

"He told you that?"

She noted his alert tone. She resisted the impulse to turn and search his eyes.

"He promised to learn the truth, to prove it to me."

"I suppose he also has some notion of who he thinks you are?" came his cynical voice.

She delayed, hoping her own voice would give no suggestion of the dismay she felt over the idea of being Rafe's blood cousin instead of Zachary's. "He says I'm your cousin—an Easton."

"So he hopes. There's no way you could be my cousin unless Ambrose is your father," he said flatly. "Ambrose was my father's older brother, his only brother, and there were no sisters. If Zachary told you you're an Easton, it's because he has an unrealistic hope of marrying you someday."

She should have been embarrassed by the blunt statement, but she wasn't. So Rafe understood this too. The thought was troubling.

"I'd never marry Zachary, even if he weren't my cousin."

"You'll have a hard time convincing him."

"I want the Lord to arrange my marriage."

Rafe grew silent again. She supposed that he had forgotten what she'd said about not being a Derrington, but after a few minutes he brought it up again. "If Zachary says he's going to snoop about, hoping to discover mysterious information on your birth, he's more worrisome than I thought."

That Rafe took it seriously gave her unease. "What would his 'snooping,' as you say, uncover? I am a Derrington."

"Yes, but you've heard the old adage about every family having skeletons in their closets. A family like the Derringtons may have one too many. In the end his snooping may produce something—not on you, but on someone else."

"That's a horrid thought," she said worriedly.

"In the end it may work against him."

————

Kea Lani Plantation had not changed in the nineteen years since Eden was born there. Her great-grandfather Ezra Derrington had first arrived from America in 1830 and settled in the Maunalua area near Koko Head. For reasons unknown to Eden, that first plantation house had been abandoned and he'd resettled in the Kalihi area, near Honolulu, hiring builders to ship magnificent materials from Europe to construct Kea Lani for Eden's great-grandmother Amabel.

The white-pillared structure with three stories was a replica of Amabel's ancestral home in Vicksburg, Mississippi. When their firstborn, Nora, inherited Kea Lani jointly with her brother, Ainsworth, she set about to transform Kea Lani from a Southern home to an island paradise. The magnolia trees so carefully shipped from Vicksburg to grace the long, shady lane leading up to the mansion were removed and replaced with two rows of coconut palms. Nora's private grove contained banana, mango, and cherimoya trees as well as pineapples and guavas. Many of the trees and plants were not native Hawaiian plants at all but were brought in from other tropical locations around the world by horticulturists.

Ainsworth hadn't concerned himself with what his maiden sister was doing with Kea Lani. Her interests were in Hawaiian history. As far as he was concerned, she could write all she wanted to about the old royal kings and queens and lecture at meetings about the perceived meddling of the first missionaries, with their stringent, puritanical ways. Ainsworth saw his sister's actions as inconsequential to his own interests. Hawaii's annexation to the United States meant the fulfillment of America's Manifest Destiny and was, therefore, inevitable. He intended to see the momentous occurrence take place in his lifetime. To that end he'd given his time, cultivating friendships in American politics and donating large sums of money to elect men to Congress who were in sympathy with annexation.

His other effort was focused on accumulating more and more plantation land for sugarcane and pineapple and in bringing thousands of Japanese and Chinese laborers to Hawaii to work the fields. These workers stayed, eventually outnumbering the native Hawaiians.

Ainsworth had achieved his goal of becoming one of the top five sugar-producing families in Hawaii. His success had opened the door for him to marry into the largest sugar-growing family in Hawaii with blood ties to California sugar growers, elevating the Derrington name to the top three producers.

His marriage had produced three male heirs: Douglas, Townsend, and Jerome. Although Douglas had died at an early age, he'd given to Ainsworth his first granddaughter, Rozlind, whom Ainsworth overcompensated because of his perpetual grief in having lost Douglas.

His second-born, Townsend, was another matter, one that embarrassed Ainsworth's Congregationalist standards inherited from the early missionaries. Townsend had been wild and irresponsible in his younger days, and he had hapa-haole children all over the islands. Townsend, threatened with disinheritance if he didn't settle down, had pleased Ainsworth by marrying Rafe's widowed mother, Celestine Easton. By marriage to Celestine, the Derringtons had accumulated the Easton plantation, Hanalei, on the Big Island of Hawaii, as well as the pearl bed on Oahu below the Kalihi area.

The marriage of Ainsworth's youngest son, Jerome, to the missionary schoolteacher Rebecca Stanhope had come as a disappointment to the family, but not as a shock. His humanitarian goals in medicine had made him a natural match for Rebecca, whom he'd met at the Royal School at a birthday celebration for one of the royal children.

Eden assumed that her lesser position among the Derringtons was due to the fact that her mother had come from an average family in New England, with neither land nor political power in Hawaii.

Now, as Rafe rode the horse into Kea Lani's carriageway, the distant blue-green waters shimmered in the sunlight. He stopped the horse in the dappled shade near the white mansion, and Eden wearily climbed down from the saddle.

"Since Zachary intends to do some research, I may do some of my own," Rafe told her. "I don't think Zachary will be pleased with what I'll turn up."

She was about to ask why he thought so, but he ended the conversation with a brief smile and a lift of his hand before riding the horse down the palm-lined road.

She looked after him, troubled. The trade wind stirred her blue cotton skirt about her ankles, and the sanguine trill of birds in the palms laced the morning heat with promise of a better tomorrow. As Rafe disappeared from view, she turned and walked up the wide front steps to the porch.

Maybe she should have shown Rafe the note after all.

SIX

In a gesture of subconscious determination, Rafe jerked his hat lower and strode along the edge of the lagoon. The full moon climbed above the blue-black water, causing it to shimmer with diamond sparkles. The fringed silhouette of coconut trees stood along the water's edge where he emerged from the beach. The mission church was ahead among the swaying palms near Ambrose's hut, where a familiar light glowed an evening welcome in the window. This time, however, Rafe was not looking forward to the meeting with his uncle. It would not be an easy good-bye.

A brittle smile touched his lips. His stepfather was congratulating himself, thinking he had forced Rafe off the island, but Townsend was ignorant of the plans Rafe had been making for months to embark on a journalistic expedition to track down a story on the Derrington family.

And what a story! If Rafe's plans went as expected, he wouldn't even need to deal with his stepfather when he returned to Oahu after the expedition. He could make terms between himself and Ainsworth Derrington, family patriarch.

Rafe wished no ill to Ainsworth. Actually, he respected the moral character of Eden's grandfather and his business savvy. There could be peace between them one day, even an alignment of purposes for Hawaii, if Rafe could quietly convince him to come to fair terms about yielding Hanalei. The information he intended to get from Jerome would give Rafe the strong bargaining tool he needed.

Rafe frowned as he continued his walk. The one proverbial fly in the ointment was Eden. He tossed his jacket over his shoulder. He hadn't counted on worrying about what she would think. He was rather surprised that he cared at all. He hadn't wanted to; he hadn't expected this prick at his conscience. He told himself he'd shrug it off. He'd figure out something. Some way to get around Eden—to shield her from knowing. Ainsworth was determined to keep the information buried, so there was little chance he would reveal what Rafe was doing. And Rafe had no intention of telling Eden himself. In the future he would simply inform her that her grandfather had made peace with him and rightly returned Hanalei and the pearl fishery. No one else need know the specific details about the terms he and Ainsworth would agree upon, not even Townsend.

He crossed the yard toward the hut. The only remaining difficulty was how to tell his uncle Ambrose aloha for the next two years.

A whistle sounded from farther down the beach, and Rafe stopped and waited. A moment later a virile young Hawaiian came trotting toward him, followed by two large dogs almost the size of ponies. The dogs came bounding up to Rafe, their tails wagging. They whined affectionately and pranced happily about their master as he played with them. Rafe threw a coconut and the two dogs went racing to retrieve it.

Keno, Noelani's nephew and Rafe's soon-to-be partner on a voyage to the South Seas and beyond, grinned. "We're in the money. The ship will soon be ours."

"You were able to sign up the captain?" Rafe asked doubtfully.

In the bright moonlight Keno produced a stack of American money from under his roomy shirt. "He is anxious. I showed him this." He ran his thumb over the edge of the bills as if shuffling a deck of cards. "Everyone has, as they say—'chipped in.' The captain and crew are anxious to sail. All that is needed is your black pearl for the ship's down payment. The owner waits in Honolulu."

Rafe frowned at Keno's optimistic grin and looked suspiciously at the money. "I like this less and less. The more your relatives are involved, the harder it is to make decisions—and I intend to call the shots. The ship will be in my name, I'm responsible for paying the debt, and I'll be giving orders to the captain. And what do you mean *everyone* chipped in?"

"Everyone," Keno repeated airily. "Every uncle, every cousin, every cousin's cousin."

Rafe's eyes narrowed. "I was afraid of that. And I suppose every 'cousin's cousin' also expects me to write an IOU stating who owns each plank of the ship."

Keno's eyes laughed. "Nothing so drastic, old pal. You only need to promise to double their investment on the return voyage."

Rafe stood, hands on hips. "Double," he repeated dryly. "Is that all? Relatives come cheap, don't they?"

"They think highly of you and your schemes. They know you are like all the other American haoles."

Rafe's eyes narrowed.

Keno laughed. "All my wise uncles have heard we will also voyage to the Caribbean. They have heard of how pirates capture chests of silver."

"Keno, that was in the 1600s!"

"They have great faith in you, Makua Rafe."

"Look, Keno, just take the money back to your family, will you? Tell them thanks for their confidence in my buccaneering abilities, but there are too many sharks in the Caribbean, and too many fingers in the pie ruin things."

"They will not know what pie you mean."

"Never mind. Just tell them I'll pay the captain and crew myself."

"With what? You were fired by old Thornley. Why turn down these good Yankee dollars?" He slapped the bills against his palm. "You want my family to be insulted by a haole?"

"Just take the money back," Rafe said through clenched teeth. "Tell them I've decided we're going first to Molokai."

"To the leper colony! They will think you are crazy for sure."

"Good." Rafe smiled coolly. "Fewer problems that way." He stooped and picked up the coconut that the dogs had laid expectantly at his feet. He handed it to Keno. "I'll meet you at Pearl on Sunday morning. I've got to see Ambrose and get this unpleasantness over with."

Keno sighed and shook his head, looking at the dollars. "Wasted."

The dogs trotted beside Rafe toward the hut.

"What are you going to do about the dogs?" Keno called. "Can't take 'em on the ship."

"We'll leave them for Zachary to care for."

Keno threw back his head and laughed.

Rafe's smile faded as he thought of Zachary's weird comment that morning on the beach about his "mad dogs." Zach had a phobia about them. Probably a holdover from that night when Eden had fallen down the stairs. The dogs had gotten loose from their kennel. . . .

Rafe's brown eyes flickered as he bounded up the steps.

He thought of Zachary again. In order to hide his present phobia, Zach had come up with the ridiculous tale about the dogs being sinister. In truth, they were simply a special type of mastiff that were first bred by his father, Matt, on Hanalei. When Matt died and his mother married

Townsend, Rafe had been permitted as a boy to bring two of the dogs with him to Kea Lani. From that time onward he'd been continuing the dog "family" with the idea of improving their strength to work with cattle. While he was away, Ambrose had offered to care for them.

"Gemini, Jasper, here! Stay!"

It was after eleven o'clock when he quietly tapped on the door. He often arrived at this late hour, coming straight from the *Gazette*. Rafe had grown emotionally close to his father's older brother after Matt had died on Hanalei. Ambrose had found Rafe when he was ten years old to explain that his father was dead. Rafe still remembered some of his uncle's words: *"You wouldn't be unhappy if you knew your father went to live in Jesus' home, would you? Not when you'll be going there too someday. We both will. Because we believe in the Lord Jesus."*

While growing up at Kea Lani, Rafe had arranged to slip away as often as he could to visit Ambrose. His stepfather had disapproved of those childhood visits to the hut and complained to Celestine that Ambrose was spoiling him. Townsend had even locked him in his room at night, but Rafe had usually managed to escape to visit Ambrose anyway. And Noelani always had island treats waiting for him. Rafe half smiled. She hadn't changed. And he supposed he hadn't either. The two of them were his family, his only family. The hut was a warm, comfortable place where the love of the Father had consoled his lonely heart. It still amazed Rafe that he could call Almighty God his *Father*.

He leaned his shoulder into the door a moment, troubled, considering his path into the future. He looked back down the steps toward the small mission church and felt a pull on his heart by the warm Hawaiian wind as the moonlight illuminated the cross.

I'm not really saying good-bye. Just aloha for a little while.

Ambrose must have heard Rafe's footsteps, for he opened the door. He was a hefty man, with a suntanned fatherly face and keen black eyes appearing doubly dark because of his shiny silver hair and rather long bristling brows. Those brows looked as though they were windblown. Rafe smiled. "Evening, Ambrose."

"Ah, come in, come in, my boy."

Despite the tropical weather, Rafe had rarely seen him in public without his knee-length black frock coat worn over a starched white shirt. An old gold watch persistently hung from his pocket. From childhood Rafe had been amused because the watch never kept accurate time. Ambrose was always ten minutes late behind the pulpit and kept the Hawaiians ten minutes past the service hour. The matter had become a tradition.

There was always what Rafe called a freshly bathed, minister-like appearance to his uncle that brought out the best in Rafe's behavior. Ambrose had had him memorize much of Psalm 119 when Rafe was twelve years old, quizzing him on occasion on certain verses—"*Wherewithal shall a young man cleanse his way?*"

"*By taking heed thereto according to thy word,*" Rafe had answered.

Ambrose had smiled, satisfied, and patted Rafe on the head. "*You'd better,*" he had warned.

Ambrose now stood in the doorway, an inch taller than Rafe, though Rafe was six feet, like his father Matt. He didn't look forward to the clash of wills that was sure to come now from his uncle, who had been raised a staunch Presbyterian.

Ambrose beckoned him inside, and Rafe entered, noting the familiar Bible open on the desk beside the glowing lantern. Ambrose always soaked up the Scriptures before he went to bed.

"I heard what happened today between you and Townsend," he said, shutting the door quietly.

Rafe turned toward him, sighing. "Look, Ambrose, I did everything to avoid it. I could have flattened Townsend and didn't."

Ambrose's mouth twitched. "Don't be so defensive. I was about to commend you for overcoming temptation. The Hawaiians are saying you showed respect for your stepfather. You've impressed them and me."

Rafe tilted his skeptical dark head. Did he mean it?

Ambrose continued calmly. "The Lord will bless you for honoring your father—no, don't say it. I know Townsend is not your father." He smiled. "You proved yourself more honorable than he. 'The discretion of a man deferreth his anger; and it is his glory to pass over a transgression.'"

Proverbs 19:11, Rafe thought.

"It's unfortunate the fellow is a brawler." Ambrose shook his head sadly. "What Celestine ever saw in him—"

"Let's not get into that," Rafe said quietly.

Ambrose sighed. "You're right. She's his wife now. She is to honor her husband." He squinted at Rafe's face. "A few bruises is all. You held up well; Townsend's a big man."

"If anyone could find anything good in this, I knew it would be you. I smell coffee. . . ."

"Yes, and Noelani wouldn't forget her haole pride and joy. She has saved some of her birthday chicken for you."

"I meant to come to the party, but after Townsend jarred my brains around, I was feeling a little dizzy,'' he said with a note of irony.

One of Ambrose's fluffy brows went up. He shook his head as if in disbelief over Townsend's behavior.

Rafe smiled and reached inside his jacket pocket. He pulled out a small package wrapped in red paper. "Give it to Noelani in the morning, will you? It's a birthday and good-bye gift all in one.''

"Good-bye?''

Rafe said nothing and walked toward the old black stove where the aroma of fresh Kona coffee lured him. Ambrose looked at the package, obviously pleased that Rafe had remembered her.

Rafe poured his usual cup. The coffee beans came from Hanalei Plantation. He vaguely recalled being a small boy of three or four with his father when he'd been out in the fields on his hands and knees among Japanese workers planting coffee plants. Remembering made the coffee taste especially good. His spirits brightened. Within a few short years he'd own Hanalei again.

Some warm chicken waited in a pan. He noticed that Noelani saved one of the best pieces for him. His favorite desserts—as only Noelani could make—also enticed him: *Haupia*, a creamy Hawaiian coconut pudding, and a piece of coconut cake with thick frosting and freshly shredded coconut.

Rafe felt his sore lip as he took a bite of the cake. "Zachary fared better than I, but he's nursing a sore jaw.''

"A darkly troubled young man. What did he do to upset you? You're usually so protective of Zachary.''

Rafe cast him a glance, hiding his surprise. Ambrose was the only one who recognized this. Everyone else assumed that he was out to humble and malign Zachary. Even Eden thought so. Rafe had been protecting his stepbrother since childhood . . . in more ways than one.

"Was he troubling Eden again?''

Rafe didn't like discussing Zachary. "Sending him off to England and Japan is the best thing Ainsworth could have done for him.''

"He's obsessed with Eden. It's unhealthy. The man needs medical care, in my opinion.''

Rafe remained silent. He took a second bite of the cake but hardly tasted it for the concerns weighing heavily on his mind. "Sending Eden to Chadwick was also a good decision. Did you have anything to do with that?''

"I sent a letter to Ainsworth after he returned from the States, requesting he act on her wishes. Are you telling me she's going?''

Rafe explained her upcoming trip. "Do all you can to keep her there, even after she graduates."

Ambrose scanned him. "I always thought you and she someday . . ." He didn't finish his thought.

Rafe shook his head. "I'm already committed. The next five years are going to be dedicated to my work. Even after I get Hanalei back, it will take years to bring the plantation up to where I want its production to be. I'm interested in a new strain of pineapple from South America."

"Eden feels the same about her life. She has convictions about working alongside Jerome one day."

Rafe set the plate down with the rest of the uneaten cake. The notion bothered him. "Chasing around the jungle is no place for a woman. Anyway, it won't happen. She's headed for disappointment. Someone ought to tell her."

"I'm sure you will," Ambrose said with a smile in his voice.

"Jerome won't allow it. Despite his letters to her, his mind is absorbed with his own driving passion. I don't think he knows anyone else exists."

"I'm not so sure, Rafe."

Rafe looked over at him. Did he know something more about Jerome that he didn't? He was almost certain Ambrose hadn't been in touch with Jerome.

"I'm inclined to agree with you about the jungle being no place for Eden," Ambrose continued, "but her dreams are her own. She's nurtured them for a long time. They're not something she'll abandon easily. If she doesn't work with Jerome in his research, she'll end up at Kalihi Hospital."

Rafe shook his head, his determined brown eyes glittering. "A mistake. She ought to stay in San Francisco. Can't Ainsworth pull some strings and get her a position at St. Francis Hospital?"

"I'm sure he could . . . if not he, then Nora. But Eden loves Hawaii, same as we do. She'll want to come back once she graduates."

Rafe reached for the chicken. It was time to tell Ambrose his plans— at least part of them. He began quietly, deliberately playing down the emotion.

"Jerome is at Molokai. A friend of mine saw him when he dropped supplies off on the beach for the lepers."

As though stunned, Ambrose lowered himself slowly into the chair behind the desk. "You're sure?"

Rafe watched him, noting the anguish. "I'm certain."

Ambrose rested his head in his hands, and the sight troubled Rafe.

His appetite disappeared as he stared at the chicken thigh with obvious distaste. "He won't be there long. I'll need to move at once to get my story."

Ambrose slowly raised his head. "Story? What do you intend?" He stood.

Rafe let out a breath. "You won't like what I'm going to tell you, Ambrose, but my mind is settled. I'm going there."

"To Molokai?" he repeated with a rush of disbelief.

The dreaded leper settlement was on Molokai, a detention camp where those with the disease were abandoned. A Belgian Catholic named Father Damien was assigned to the leper settlement at his own request in 1873 and later contracted the disease. It was said he was near death and that Jerome had gone to Molokai to meet with his old friend for a final time and to report what he had discovered in his worldwide travels about possible cures for leprosy. So far Jerome had found none, but his research continued.

"This is my opportunity to interview both men," Rafe said too calmly.

"And risk contracting the disease yourself?"

"I'll be careful. I'm after the truth. And I'm not stopping until I have it on paper and ready for publication in the newspaper. Then I'll pay a visit to Ainsworth. It will be up to him whether it's printed." Rafe folded his arms and met his gaze squarely. "I'm always willing to make a fair deal when it comes to Hanalei."

Ambrose didn't move. He stared at him while the lantern flickered. Outside, the wind was rising, shaking the vines and bushes. The cane shade on the open window rattled.

"How long have you known there was a story?"

Rafe shrugged. "Years. I've always been suspicious. Don't forget, I was there the night Eden tripped on the stairs."

Ambrose's tanned complexion looked a little paler in the light. "So was Zachary. He was hiding with her under the bed."

"But Zachary doesn't remember that night. I've quizzed him several times while growing up because I thought he might remember and was putting on an act. He's a good one for that. But I'm convinced that he's as blank as a coconut about that night. And because of Eden's bad fall, she doesn't remember either."

Ambrose shook his head in his palms. "Thank God."

"I want her memory lapse to remain," Rafe said solemnly.

Ambrose looked at him sharply. "So do I. But going to Jerome won't help that. It will only stir the dying embers of a raging fire."

Rafe's jaw tightened with resolve. "She won't know about this expedition."

"You deceive yourself, my boy. She's bound to learn what you're doing!"

"No, she won't. Why should she? This is between me and Ainsworth. No one else need know the story I dig up—he'll never let it go to print."

Ambrose paced. "This is close to extortion, Rafe."

"Oh come, Ambrose! Extortion? Hanalei belongs to me! If anyone's not played fair, it's the Derringtons." He walked toward him. "And it isn't over yet. Townsend's already using pressure on my mother to disinherit me altogether from Hanalei."

"I know for a fact Matt left Hanalei to you. One thing about Celestine—she won't go against Matt's wishes for the plantation. She loved him more than she loves Townsend."

"Townsend has been trying to convince her and Ainsworth to test me out on an unproductive section of property here on Oahu—poor soil with no water. 'First let's see if he can handle this,' he says. 'I know these Chinese. They won't work for him. Rafe's too easy on 'em, and they know it. He'll end up with half his workers in their bunks claiming sickness.' " Rafe banged his cup down.

"Townsend's plan won't fool anybody," Ambrose soothed.

"I'm not so certain. He's a very persuasive man, as I can attest. The argument this afternoon may have been just the beginning. I'm going over his head straight to Ainsworth. Laying out my story before him in a private meeting will convince him to cooperate. If I get Hanalei, it will be because Ainsworth forces Townsend to comply."

"And that's what you want, Rafe? Advantage over Ainsworth?"

Rafe took a bite of the spicy chicken, then set it back down on the plate and frowned as he wiped his hands on the napkin. He hated sticky hands.

"Only for a purpose. Yes, that's what I want, Ambrose," he said flatly. "More than anything."

"You're sure of that? Anything?" he repeated.

Rafe gritted his teeth as he rinsed his hands in the sink and dried them on a flowered yellow towel Noelani had made. He looked over at Ambrose through narrowed lashes and saw a slight smile as though he knew better.

"Are you sure you don't mean any*one*?"

"Yes," stated Rafe, affecting indifference. He wasn't going to let Ambrose corner him with a veiled reference to Eden. "I know exactly what

I want. I've had a good deal of time to think about it. And you and Noelani will be better off too."

"I'm content here. So is Noelani."

"You always dreamed of a ranch at Waimea," Rafe insisted. "I remember when I was a boy how you and Noelani would talk about it for hours, sitting on the steps."

Ambrose seemed to remember, and a slight reminiscent smile touched his lips. "Yes . . . that was years ago. It no longer matters when you're our age. All that begins to matter is that our lives end well, that we finish the race in serving our faithful Lord. He's been good to us. We don't have all the things that make others comfortable, but Noelani and I have had a pleasant life."

Rafe was moved. He admired and respected them. "You'll make it to the end of that race, Ambrose. If anyone can, you will. But you're not well. I want to do something good for you. I want you and Noelani to have your youthful dream." He walked over to him and took hold of his shoulders, his eyes softening. "I intend to see that you have that ranch. It's time Noelani did something else besides trudge to the mountains hauling taro roots. Your heart is bad. We both know it. I want her to be able to keep you around."

Ambrose's eyes filled with tears. He looked off toward the little door leading to the bedroom. The lines in his face deepened. "Yes," he said softly. "I'd like that for her too."

"You'll have it," Rafe urged quietly.

Ambrose's gaze swerved back to his and the old rigorous New England Puritanism rushed back. "If you want to do something for me, my son, set your ambitions on knowing God and His Word. That will do more to bring me happiness than any ranch in Waimea." He quoted from Third John: " 'I have no greater joy than to hear that my children walk in truth.' You've always been a son to me."

Rafe's heart wrenched. He didn't want to disappoint him. His hands dropped from his shoulders and his eyes flickered with frustration. "I won't let you down. I do want to know Christ. But I'd be less than honest if I didn't admit that I also want Hanalei."

"Of course you do! And there's nothing wrong with that desire, my son. But trust Him for it. He can do it without your taking matters into your own hands. I fear you're moving in the footsteps of Jacob, stealing the blessing God had already promised. Jacob could have rested in faith and waited on the Lord to bring it to pass."

Rafe threw up his hands and walked away. He flung open the back door and looked out. *Jacob!* "The Lord hasn't promised to give me Hanalei," he stated, "but it's still my inheritance."

"Sounds like you have it all worked out," Ambrose challenged. "What's more, you may very well get Ainsworth's cooperation. Hanalei will be yours by right. But unless these matters are handled wisely and according to the principles of God's Word, you won't have His blessing on your actions. In the end, nothing is gained by rushing ahead of God."

"I know these things, Ambrose," Rafe stated patiently. "But this situation is different."

"I've heard that before too. If I didn't know you better, I'd worry plenty. Things don't turn out as we first plan. Expectations are as fickle as the March winds."

"Well put. I hope I'm not a March hare," he said wryly. "I intend to handle all this wisely. I've no wish to injure Ainsworth or any of the Derringtons, including Townsend. But I have my ambitions in Hawaii too, and I'm bent on going after them. Sitting around and waiting for Ainsworth to decide to give me what's already mine is foolish. I'm going after it, and I don't feel as if I'm conniving like Jacob to get it."

Ambrose sank back into his chair. "Jerome won't cooperate. If he knew what you've planned to do with the story he'd leave Molokai before you could get there."

Rafe had expected Ambrose to respond this way. He walked to the desk, resting his palms, holding his uncle's gaze. "I prefer to be optimistic. I'm going to beat him at his game of running. Look, Ambrose, I'll have a better chance of getting to the truth if you come with me. Jerome always thought highly of you."

Ambrose shook his head firmly. "No, my son, the moment he finds out you're a journalist, he'll disappear again. I can't leave the church or Noelani. My advice is to leave Jerome alone."

Rafe straightened. He walked back to the table, lifted the mug, and drank the black coffee.

"Even if I were willing to throw my plans to the wind, I haven't any choice now except to leave Hawaii. Townsend worked Thornley over today and now he's scared half out of his wits. He fired me for my editorial piece in the *Gazette*—the very same piece he was so excited over when we went to press. Suddenly Thornley is for annexation. The paper's endorsing it tomorrow."

"Ah yes, the article in the *Gazette*. I read it and liked it."

"I don't have a chance of getting another job as a journalist in Oahu as long as Townsend continues to pay friendly visits to the newspaper offices."

He took his cup and walked over to the open door. He could see the steps leading down to the beach, the shimmering Pacific under the silvery moon. Eden's pure face came before him, the soft green eyes, the smile that could trouble him if he allowed it to. In exasperation he ran his fingers through his dark hair and leaned in the doorway, letting the refreshing wind blow against him. Still, a man had to do what drove his heart.

It was then he saw the ship sailing by with a dim golden light. He felt the tug of the sea, the call of his plans, and he knew that it was too late to change his mind.

Ambrose sighed as though he knew it too. "Do what you must, Rafe. I'll give you the benefit of the doubt. I'll stand by you. You've behaved wisely these years—and patiently. You deserve my trust and my prayers."

Rafe turned and looked over at him, satisfied. He needed Ambrose's understanding, his blessing. Even though Ambrose had his doubts, he was willing to trust him. That show of support encouraged Rafe.

"I promise you one thing, Uncle—whatever I come up with on this expedition, I'll keep it a family secret until I can first meet with Ainsworth."

"That's fair enough. It's likely the best I'll get from you. And what about Eden?"

"There's no need for her to be involved or to even know about it. She'll be in San Francisco."

Ambrose slowly nodded.

"I leave in three days," Rafe quietly told him.

Again, Ambrose nodded his agreement.

Rafe looked at his uncle. "There's something else. I'll need that black pearl as a down payment on the merchant ship Keno and I are buying. I'd like to have it tonight."

"Pearl?" Ambrose leaned back heavily into the chair.

Rafe gave him a careful glance. He didn't like the way he had responded, as though something was not right. Rafe walked toward the desk.

"Yes, the pearl. You know, the black one I brought up recently. I gave it to you to keep for me." His lashes squinted. "You *do* have it?"

Ambrose was silent.

"You didn't mail it off to the Sandwich Island Mission Board, did you? I wouldn't have minded, except now I'm in a real tight spot."

When Ambrose still didn't answer, Rafe brought the lantern closer to his uncle's unsmiling face. Rafe groaned when he read his expression. "You lost it. You dropped it through a crack in the floor." Rafe looked over at the green parrot on its wall perch. The bird took that moment to stretch a leg and a wing on one side, then on the other.

"Maybe Fishbait swallowed it," Rafe said dryly.

"Aarrwakk! Fishbait wants an oyster!" the bird jabbered.

Ambrose waved a hand and shook his head. "Unfortunately, my son, there's been some difficulty. . . ."

Rafe straightened, hands on hips. "Maybe I should have kept that fistful of Yankee dollars," he said of Keno's offer.

Ambrose pushed himself up from the chair and paced restlessly. "There's been a misunderstanding about that black pearl, my son."

"Ambrose—"

"Now, now." He stopped and pointed at him. "It was your mother."

Rafe watched him warily.

"There wasn't anything to be done about it, my boy. Word got out to Townsend of your find."

"Townsend!"

"He came for it two days ago. I flat out refused him at first. It rightfully belongs to you, I told him. The pearl fishery is yours through Matt after Celestine passes on."

"Ambrose, you didn't give him the pearl!"

"No. He seemed to understand. He was very polite and left. But then he returned the next day. What was I to do when he came with Celestine?"

It was like Townsend to put his mother into the center of things. Rafe's anger burned. "He brought her here?"

"Celestine didn't look well. That's what troubled me. She asked that I hand the pearl over to her. I felt that I couldn't refuse her, not when the fishery belongs to her."

Rafe shook his head in disbelief. The black pearl was gone!

"I'm sorry, lad, but what was I to do?"

In a few strides, Rafe was at the stove refilling his mug. He frowned, holding down his anger. Now he knew why Celestine had appeared distraught.

"She's torn between me and Townsend. In the long run it's better I'm leaving Oahu for a time. I don't want to put her through this conflict. If Townsend really loved her, he wouldn't expect her to make decisions that hurt her conscience. If I'm gone, she won't need to. I may dislike him, but I want the marriage to work for her sake. Right now I stand in the way. Did she say why she wanted the pearl?"

"Townsend's decided to use it for the sunken treasure in the diving contest tomorrow."

"The contest! You're sure?"

"Noelani found out from her nephew Primo."

So it is *his* pearl the Derringtons were risking. Not only risking it, but boasting that whoever brought it up could keep it. Every diver in Hawaii had heard. It was a grand publicity stunt for the Derringtons. The family had already hired photographers to send pictures to the newspapers in the States. Rafe was sure they planned to be center stage: Townsend, the big Sugar King, handing over the huge black pearl with a broad smile to some winsome young Hawaiian diver who had brought it up from the lagoon.

"It's just a stunt, all prearranged," Rafe explained. "Most likely they've hired Primo to bring it up. What Primo actually gets when he secretly gives it back is anyone's guess."

Rafe ceased his restless pacing. His mind was made up. "I'm getting that pearl back."

Ambrose looked startled. "You're not entering Townsend's contest!"

Rafe smiled evenly. "Why not? I wouldn't miss the excitement. And . . . I'm going to have a little talk with Primo. Where is he, do you know?"

"He was here at the birthday supper. He went home. But you can't risk retrieving the pearl. It could be dangerous, since Townsend wants it so badly. And Primo's bound to beat you. You know he's not only the best—"

"Yes, and he'll likely know exactly where to dive. The pearl came from my fishery. Too much depends on my getting it back."

"You're out of your mind, lad. Townsend doesn't intend for anyone to keep it."

"Naturally, but this time he'll be trapped by his own false publicity, as witnessed before an exhilarated crowd and the press."

"If you do get it, Townsend's not going to be happy about letting you keep it. That pearl's worth plenty all right." Ambrose shook his head. "I can't see him parting company with it for keeps, even if you do win it."

"He will—he'll have to if I bring it up. And maybe he'll learn something about the Eastons. If I win that pearl back, I'm saying something for my father, for you and me. We're just as proud as the Derringtons."

"You're as determined as Matt was. Always wanting to prove the Easton honor."

Rafe laughed. "Not always, Uncle. Anyway, I've got to go now. But I'll be at the contest tomorrow."

He walked out, calling to the dogs, who got up and trotted after him.

CHAPTER
SEVEN

The late night remained warm and muggy at Kea Lani as Eden sat at her bedroom desk with a beaded-glass lamp burning. If the weather held, hoolaulea would begin tomorrow with the well-publicized pearl-diving contest, followed by a luau that would last well into the night. And since it would be Saturday, she would be spending the night with Noelani and Ambrose before the church service and her women's Bible class.

The gilded clock downstairs chimed eleven.

Eden blinked several times trying to clear her tired mind. Her arms were cramped from hours of writing. She still had several pages more of research notes to arrange and catalog for Great-aunt Nora, who was beginning work on a book supporting the Hawaiian monarchy. Eden imagined the trouble it would cause between Nora and Ainsworth. The family had already divided into two ideological camps!

It won't bode well for me when Grandfather learns I've been helping Great-aunt with her research, she thought.

A large yellow-blue moth had been drawn indoors through the open lanai, and Eden, her mind dulled, watched it flutter hopelessly against the glowing lamp. Inevitably, as it had been all evening, her mind was drawn back to the note she had found waiting for her inside the church cubicle. The question repeated itself as it had several times that day. Who could have written it—and why now? Why not years ago?

She removed the piece of paper from her pocket and looked at the ominous words once more.

WHY DON'T THE DERRINGTONS WANT TO DISCUSS YOUR
MOTHER'S DEATH? WHAT ARE THEY CONCEALING FROM
YOU?

Eden quickly folded it and placed it inside her Bible, then stood from
the chair. She wouldn't think about it anymore until tomorrow when she
saw Ambrose.

She crossed the glossy oak floor and turquoise braided rugs and
stepped out onto the darkened broad lanai, where a breeze from the
mossy Koolau mountain range stirred in the century-old coconut palms
surrounding the plantation house.

The moist wind blew against her, twirling her wavy dark hair, bringing
unexpected reminders that Rafe was leaving Oahu. She gripped the lanai
rail and looked out toward the dark Pacific, where clouds partially flanked
the silvery moon. She, too, was going away, something she had wanted
for the last few years, yet an unfulfilled longing walked softly through her
heart, leaving her a little bewildered.

He knew she would be at Ambrose's tomorrow and Sunday. Would
Rafe come one last time to the mission church to say good-bye, or would
he leave from Pearl Harbor without a backward glance?

Eden drew in a breath of scented air from the roses below, then resolutely turned away, reentering her room with its warm honey gold furniture and sheer blue curtains.

Strange that the earlier years she had spent here at the plantation
house before living with Ambrose and Noelani were masked in such a
haze. Her fingers brushed the scar along her temple. If *only* some incident
could awaken her memory of the past.

Ambrose and Noelani must know more of the details about how her
mother had drowned in the boat accident. Ambrose might even have a
suggestion of who it was that had left her the note . . . and why. Was someone trying to frighten her or get even with the Derrington family? She
thought of Rafe. No . . . even though he wanted to get even, he would
never want to frighten her.

She sighed. She wouldn't think about it anymore.

Eden turned out the lamp and went to bed, exhausted and disturbed.
For a time she listened to the wind gusting, shaking the vines growing
along the lanai. The curtains billowed and the feel of rain was in the
warm, moist air. She could hardly keep her eyes open now. . . . Was the
hurricane returning?

Maybe there would be no luau after all. . . . Maybe Rafe wouldn't set
sail on the ship. . . . Maybe . . .

Eden drifted into a disturbed sleep.

An hour later the clock struck midnight, but she didn't hear it.

A twitch of fear furrowed her sweating brow and strands of dark hair stuck to the side of her face. She tossed restlessly in a nightmare. . . .

Eden was a child, alone, terrified, and running from something . . . but what? Her heart throbbed in her ears; her throat ached as though she had been crying for a long time. She ran up some steps. There was a large front door. The brass door knocker was a tiki head with painted fiery eyes. Its bizarre face frightened her.

Then she was lost in a large, strange house.

She stood in a room encircled with many tall windows. A sizzling flash of lightning lit up the sky and crackled. She could hear the wind. It banged on the windows and pounded the roof.

Suddenly her small, childish fingers were stained with red paint. She stood by an easel, with palettes of paint and artist brushes. A stringent odor clung to the cloistered room.

As if from nowhere Zachary appeared in her dream. He grabbed her arm. "Hide. Hurry."

They crawled beneath a cane daybed and hid, huddling together beneath the dust ruffle.

"Where's my mother?"

"Shh."

"Why?"

Zachary's hand went over her mouth, a childish hand, cold and sweating.

Eden saw a pale, glimmering candle flame.

A muffled whisper echoed in the sound of the howling wind.

The glimmer from the candle flickered, showing odd shapes like slithering serpents moving across the polished floor as though searching for her.

The dust ruffle lifted and a hand thrust under the daybed, reaching for her—

Eden awoke with terror constricting her throat and her body cloaked in dampness. She sat up, trembling, looking about her bedroom at Kea Lani until her familiar, safe surroundings began to calm her.

What a horrid nightmare!

No, this was not just a dream! She was remembering something that had happened in her childhood. At last she was beginning to remember!

Her heart thudded. She brought her hand to her temple and touched her scar. She felt it and shut her eyes hard, trying to remember more, but her mind refused to go on.

As the warm wind blew against the side of her room, she thought that perhaps it was best not to remember all that had occurred on that dreadful night. That candle, that hand, that muffled voice!

Eden covered her face with trembling hands and rested her forehead on her knees. She might wish the memory were just a strange nightmare, but she knew it wasn't. What had happened after that? She must have run away and fallen down the stairs. And Zachary? Why didn't he remember that night? Had something so unpleasant happened that his mind had blocked it?

Eden threw aside the coverlet and got out of bed. She stood barefoot on the hardwood floor, shivering with emotion. She went to the large dressing table and fumbled with the matches, lighting the lamp, anxious for a warm glow to chase away the shadows that still clung to her mind like a sticky web. She poured a glass of water and drank, cooling her dry throat. She looked up above the table to the shadowy reflection of a woman staring back from the mirror with mussed dark hair and frightened green eyes.

Outside the wind blew, reminding her of that night when she was a child. She shuddered and went to the lanai to shut the doors, but she heard the family peacocks screeching and stepped out into the deep tropical night. She peered below into the garden. The wind had not been able to blow out the lamps. She saw Hibiscus blossoms scattering along the flagstone walkway, their petals bruising. The peacocks were nowhere in sight, but she saw one of the pet monkeys swinging from a banana tree while the females chattered nervously under the leafy branches.

Eden went back inside and locked the lanai doors.

Seeking comfort and security, she picked up her mother's worn Bible from the table and turned out the lamp and returned to her bed. For a moment she listened in the darkness to the shaking vines. She began to quote the Twenty-third Psalm, and as the peaceful words filled her mind and soul, the fearsome phantoms from her mysterious past receded into the windswept tropical night.

———

Saturday morning dawned hot and overcast with the threat of rain in the Kalihi area of Oahu. Eden's heart remained tense from the night before. Even so, the guests were arriving for the hoolaulea.

Bowls of Hibiscus flowers and orchids were everywhere, giving a festive touch to the mansion, their beauty reminding Eden that the sunny days on the island would soon be exchanged for a foggy tenure in San Francisco.

Rozlind Derrington, three years older than Eden and wearing a slim, straight blue afternoon dress, came in from the front lanai. Except for her bright red hair worn up in a swirl, she could have passed as Zachary's sister rather than his cousin. She saw Eden coming down the stairs and called up, "The carriages are coming to pick us up. Hurry—or we'll miss the diving contest. Grandfather wants my photograph with the Hawaiian that brings up the black pearl."

"Oh, I won't be going, Rozlind. I have some work to do at the mission church."

Rozlind's head tilted with surprise. Then she looked at her worriedly.

Eden laughed. "Don't worry, I'm not ill. I'll be back for the luau for sure. I've been smelling that delicious roast pork all morning." She hesitated. "Maybe I'll attend the ball. I haven't decided."

Rozlind appeared curious. Eden considered telling her about the note and why she was anxious to see Ambrose but decided to remain silent for now.

"If you're wondering if Rafe will come tonight, I have it on good word that he will," Rozlind said. "Better make the most of the ball. I hear he's leaving in two more days. I thought you'd surely want to see the contest," Rozlind went on. "With Rafe diving."

Eden paused on the bottom stair, unable to hide her surprise. Did Townsend know that Rafe would enter the contest? She didn't think so. Nor would Grandfather be pleased. Except for Celestine and Rozlind, the family would surely try to thwart him. She decided to watch the contest after all.

Townsend's and Celestine's voices were heard in the outer hall, and as Rozlind went to join them in the waiting carriage, Eden heard Zachary. She wished to avoid a meeting with him and decided to walk instead of joining the family in the coach. She deliberately held back until she heard the horses pull away down the palm-lined carriageway. Then, once the carriage was out of sight, she left Kea Lani and began the walk in the direction of the pearl lagoon and the mission church.

As she walked along the road at a brisk pace, she wondered about Rozlind. She must have learned when Rafe was leaving from his close friend Keno. Rozlind had never been flighty when it came to men. She had done everything she could to avoid an early marriage. She was still trying to postpone an engagement to Tom Griswold, a relative of one of the larger sugar magnates from California. Eden knew why and it worried her. She had learned months ago that Rozlind was meeting Keno for strolls along the beach. They had to keep the meetings a secret. Both Eden and Rozlind understood what the Derringtons would do if they discovered that she was falling in love with a Hawaiian. Keno, too, appeared to understand better than even Rozlind that a romance between them was socially impossible.

Eden thought the situation was tragic.

At ten o'clock that morning the sun burst briefly through the clouds, then disappeared again. A large crowd had already gathered at the lagoon when Eden arrived alone.

The damp tropical wind began blowing, softly at first, moist and heady with the smells of sea and flowers, then gaining in strength. She watched the ruffled trail of yellow-tinged clouds deepen the sky. She had been right last night; a storm was slowly moving in.

Eden held her hat in place as the wind tugged at its brim and made her way toward some palm trees to view the main platform.

The contest was already in progress. She saw the large crowd and they appeared to be entranced by the divers. She saw everyone gathering around the platform where Ainsworth and Townsend stood in white jackets and trousers. Newspapermen and photographers were well placed. There were cheers and applause as the winning diver was escorted up from the beach to the platform, tanned, muscular, and still wet as a fish. Eden laughed to herself. It was Rafe. She also recognized Primo, who had come from the water just behind him looking out of breath and disgruntled.

Eden, still smiling, moved from the trees to catch a better view. Rafe was being announced as the winner. A quick look at Townsend showed his bewilderment. Rafe was then surrounded by journalists who knew him from the *Gazette*. Photographers gathered as well, readying the scene.

"Let's get a photo of the winner with his father, Townsend Derrington!"

"Well, Townsend, you must be proud of your stepson today."

"Oh . . . yes, yes of course!"

He looks stunned, Eden thought, amused.

"How about you, Mr. Derrington?" The photographer gestured to Ainsworth. "Want to step over and stand by your grandson?"

"This must have come as quite a surprise. Did either of you expect Rafe to find the pearl that you so generously donated?"

"No, no we didn't. We're both impressed and proud that we've such a great diver in the family."

As the cameras clicked and the journalists stepped beside them, Eden saw Rozlind come forward, all smiles as she posed beside Rafe. Then she did something that Eden thought was not part of the script—she drew Rafe's wet face down to hers and kissed him. There were more cheers and photographs. Eden couldn't see Rafe's expression, but when she looked away to Ainsworth, she saw his displeasure. Did the cameras catch it?

As the crowd pressed closer to the stand, applauding, Eden decided to continue on to Ambrose's house.

The walk seemed longer than usual. The wind was picking up and the clouds were blowing in. Rafe had won, but how had he managed it? He had an interest in hiking and other outdoor activities, including rough-water swimming at Hapuna, and he sometimes took his dogs with him to exercise them. Though he was a strong swimmer, there must have been more to finding the black pearl than employing his skills.

But now he would be leaving Hawaii. She doubted he would show up at the luau ball. She reminded herself that she, too, was sailing from Pearl Harbor next Wednesday for San Francisco and that good-byes were uncomfortable. After all, she thought with a frown, what was there to say?

With Rafe leaving, her own farewell to Hawaii would be easier.

EİGHT

Ambrose was standing near the fishing boats with his coat flapping in the wind when Eden arrived on the wooden wharf. He took her overnight bag and smiled warmly, looking up at the darkening sky.

"Looks like the Lord is sending our storm back." He peered at the dozen small fishing boats that provided the livelihood for Noelani's extended family.

"Kelolo should have arrived by now to tie them down."

"I'm sure he'll be here soon. No doubt he's at the lagoon." She tried to keep her voice casual. "Rafe won the dive and brought up Townsend's famous black pearl."

Ambrose did not look as pleased as she would have expected. Concern muted his black eyes as his silver hair whipped like a horse's mane in the wind.

"So," he said thoughtfully, looking off toward the sea, "Rafe beat out Primo, did he? Well, he got back his pearl after all. I was with him the day he found it, but you can be sure Townsend isn't happy about him winning the contest. No wonder Kelolo isn't here."

Eden remembered that Kelolo, Noelani's brother, was Primo's father.

"It won't be easy comforting Primo," she agreed, thinking of how disgruntled he had looked coming out of the water.

"Primo was certain he would win. Townsend was too."

She could understand Primo's confidence, but what reason would her uncle have for thinking so? He had opened the contest up to all the Hawaiian divers.

Ambrose looked down at her and his worried frown smoothed. "Come along, little one, we'd best get indoors. I'm sure Rafe will drop by later with the good news. Let's hope Primo doesn't decide to show up at the same time to gain sympathy from Noelani."

He looped her arm through his and turned her toward the hut, but Eden held back. "Ambrose, I want to talk to you alone first, if you don't mind."

"Ah yes, about Rafe, I suppose," he said with a trace of sympathy in his voice.

She reached into her pocket and took out the note, handing it to him. "No, about this," she stated quietly.

Ambrose read it and for a moment made no comment. She watched his face, noticing the lines tighten around his mouth.

"Where did you get this, Eden?"

"Someone left it for me inside the church cubicle. I found it after we came back from the meeting with the kahunas. What do you make of it?"

"You've no idea who left it for you?"

"None at all. I thought you might."

"Have you shown this to Rafe?"

"No. I suppose I should have, but when I met him yesterday, there was that dreadful business with Townsend."

"Yes, a sad moment. My dear, I don't know what to make of this—I don't like it. Someone is out for mischief."

She shivered in the wind, hearing the creaking hulls and dock lines. "I rather thought the same. Perhaps someone has a grudge against my grandfather and wishes to stir up trouble."

"If I were you, my child, I'd not let this worry you, though I can certainly understand why it would." He frowned, looking at the words again as she had done so many times. "The note suggests a dark purpose. That anyone would wish to upset you and make you suspicious of your father's family is disturbing indeed."

"Ambrose, just how did my mother die?"

He looked at the boats as though the topic made him uneasy. "Do you mean to tell me the Derringtons never told you?"

"They said she died in a—boating accident." She followed his glance as he looked away again from the boats with their chipped paint.

"That's what I've been told as well."

"Yes, but how did it happen, Ambrose? Surely you know."

A meditative look crossed his broad, sun-darkened face while he stared across the water at the wind whipping up the waves. "Jerome never fully explained."

She held on to her hat, studying his face. "You mean my father was with her when it happened?"

Ambrose looked pained and remained silent.

"She went out with my father?" Eden asked above the wind.

The breeze tossed his silver hair that had once been as dark as Rafe's.

"No, I don't believe they said Jerome was with Rebecca when the accident happened. He was away."

"They?" she inquired. "You mean my family?"

"Ainsworth and Nora."

"You're saying she went out in a boat alone?" she asked incredulously.

Ambrose looked at her, and sympathy reflected in his dark eyes. "No, my child, Rebecca wasn't alone."

The tension mounted in her heart. Her eyes searched his. "Who was she with, Ambrose? Do you know?"

"No, I don't know. No one ever told me, and I never wanted to ask. Jerome told me Rebecca went out with a friend. A storm came up. Before they could bring the boat back in, it overturned, and she couldn't swim the distance."

Eden had never heard this part of the story before, and the reality of her mother's drowning made her feel a little ill as the wind blew against her and the water rocked the boats.

"We'd better go inside," he said gently. "Noelani can make us some hot coffee."

The storm that took her mother's life—might it have been the one that she remembered on the night when she'd fallen? She laid a hand on his arm. "And her friend?"

He shook his head. "I've no idea about Rebecca's friend. I can't say if she made it back or not. I rather think neither of them did."

"She! Her friend was a woman."

His twittering white brows rushed upward. "Probably another teacher from the school or some friend from the church."

"I would think my mother and her friend would have seen the clouds and wind coming in—just the way we do now. Why would they risk going out in a boat? Or if they were already out on the water, they'd have time to come back in."

"Yes, it would seem likely. My memory of Rebecca was that she was a smart young lady. I can't speak for the other. Seeing as how neither of them were fishermen, though, it's possible they misjudged the situation.

Perhaps they didn't take the weather seriously enough, or they didn't understand it. Rebecca was from New England, you know."

Only later did Eden think more about what Ambrose had said. It didn't take a fisherman to read the weather, to see clouds rolling in with a rising wind. Something else Ambrose had said troubled her. It was possible that they hadn't understood the weather—*possible*, but not likely.

As the afternoon wore on and it began to rain, Hawaiians brought word that the luau and ball had been postponed indefinitely. Rafe had not come by, and Ambrose had gone off to try to get help from Kelolo and some of Noelani's other relatives.

By evening, rain slashed against the hut's small windows, and Noelani became worried about Ambrose.

"He's taking too long."

"Maybe he's waiting until the rain slows. He wouldn't want to walk here in this."

In order to distract Noelani from worrying about Ambrose, Eden questioned her about Rebecca's friend. Either Noelani didn't want to discuss the matter, or Rebecca's friend had not worked at the school with her.

"Best to leave the past alone, my *keiki*," Noelani told her gently. "Whoever left the note tries to stir up strife. Think of the future. Soon you will be studying medicine with Miss Lana in San Francisco. You have much to keep you happy, to look forward to."

"Then you've no idea who my mother's friend was?"

Noelani shrugged and filled Eden's cup with hot cocoa. "She had many friends. Everyone loved Rebecca."

When Ambrose did not return and the storm worsened, Eden again assured Noelani that he must have taken refuge somewhere and would return as soon as there was a convenient break in the storm. But as the night wore on, she, too, grew concerned. She wanted to go and search for him, but Noelani looked frightened and refused to let her leave the house.

"Noelani, sometimes the Lord delivers us out of the storm; other times He allows us to go through it so we learn that whatever happens, He is our confidence, our rock."

Noelani looked over at Ambrose's Bible sitting open on his desk. She nodded, then with an arm around Eden, insisted that she get some sleep.

Eden climbed the steps to the small loft above the kitchen. This space had been her bedroom until her fourteenth birthday, and she kept many of her personal things stored here. The cot was comfortable after a long, emotional day, but even though she was weary, she couldn't sleep. Eden lay there, fully dressed except for her shoes, listening to the rain while praying occasionally for Ambrose. At last she drifted off to sleep.

The howling winds awakened her. She blinked against a dazzling flash of lightning and sat up as the deep rumble of thunder shook the floor under her. The winds were so strong that she feared at the swaying of the little house. She got up from the narrow bed and went to the window, peering beyond the bamboo lattice. As she watched the strength of the waves, she heard a shout behind her from the bottom of the stairs.

"Eden, Noelani's hurt, and I need help with the boats!" he called up, cupping his hands to his mouth.

Her heart was smitten. While Eden had been resting, Noelani must have gone out searching for Ambrose.

"I'll be down, Ambrose!"

Quickly she grabbed her shoes. *Please, Lord, protect her. Don't take Noelani away from me. I need her—and Ambrose.*

A few minutes later Eden clambered down the ladder to Ambrose and they rushed out the kitchen door into the dark night, the wind shaking her with torrential wet gusts. The rain was pouring large drops that struck her face, instantly soaking her. The wind took her breath away and threatened to push her off her feet.

Ambrose's shirt was torn and blowing in the wind. He, too, looked as though he'd been injured, and her fear mounted as she remembered his heart condition.

"Where's Noelani?" Eden cried.

"I brought her in the house. It's her leg, but there's little time. Without the boats, we'll lose our sustenance. They're barely tied down; we've got to get extra ropes on them!"

A wilderness of sand, cliffs, and sea awaited her. The palm trees were bending toward the land, silhouettes with dark waving branches. The rain was beating heavily. Eden's dark hair whipped in her face.

She fought to keep her footing on the wooden planks. She worked frantically beside Ambrose to secure the boats, but in this weather she was sure it was a losing battle. It was dangerous to even be near them, much less attempt to tie on more lines. His desire to save them was now beyond realization.

"Ambrose—it's too late—"

But the wind sucked her words away and she doubted if he even heard her. He was trying to tie a rope to a boat that was rising and falling dangerously with the swells; the pilings groaned and the ropes and chains were snapping as large black waves began to splash over the wharf. They struggled against the force of the wind.

"Look out—Eden!"

She looked up to see a wave breaking over the boats and coming toward them. She had only a moment to glimpse a dark, turbulent wall before it crashed, engulfing her. The rope she held was snatched from her determined grip as she was swept along helplessly in a dark abyss.

"Eden—"

"Jesus help me," she called out in the midnight water. She tasted salty brine as it filled her nose and ears. As the swell dissipated, she tried desperately to swim in her bulky clothing in a direction that she thought was upward. She finally reached the surface exhausted and gasping for air. She was floating in the lagoon some distance from the wharf. "Ambrose!" she shouted, but her voice came as a weak, breathless gasp. She could see little but darkness. *Oh, God, where is Ambrose?* Then she heard a voice and answered, "Over here!"

A man was swimming toward her, the waves washing over his head. He emerged, close to where she floundered, and when he reached a hand under her arm, she realized it wasn't Ambrose, but Rafe.

"Don't struggle," he shouted.

Eden forced herself to relax her grip as he swam with her toward the beach. A few minutes later he helped her from the water and knelt beside her, turning her on her stomach. "Are you all right?"

"Y-yes—" she gasped, face down. Then he dove back into the water and disappeared.

She struggled to raise herself from the beach. Buffeted by the wind and spray, she crawled slowly forward across the sand, trying to peer into the swells. Most of the boats had been torn from their moorings and damaged, with sections of the hulls showing on the surface. Something within told her that Ambrose had gone down with the fishing boats. He wouldn't have been able to endure in these waves. Tears filled her eyes. *Ambrose! Oh, Ambrose!*

She sobbed into the wind and rain, now terrified that Rafe, too, would be pulled under.

It seemed that minutes had passed before a dark figure was crawling up onto the beach. Rafe had Ambrose and was struggling to haul him to shore.

Eden crawled toward them and watched as he worked to save him. *Please, Lord*, she kept praying. Once, she thought Ambrose moved, but it may have only been the strength of the wind about them.

Rafe worked desperately, pressing on Ambrose's back to clear his lungs as the frightening minutes encasing them grew longer. Eden felt cold and dazed. He was not breathing. Her eyes widened in fear and she clenched her cold hands into helpless fists, trying to hold back the sob that fought its way out of her heart.

She heard Rafe's voice shouting, "Ambrose!" He shook him hard. "Ambrose!"

The rain continued beating upon them. Eden covered her face with her bruised palms and wept. As she cried she heard a spasmodic cough; she lifted her face and saw that Rafe was encouraged.

"He's struggling to breathe!"

New hope and energy surged through her. She crawled toward them and looked down at Ambrose—he was moving!

Ambrose sputtered and coughed. Rafe waited until his breathing cleared and stabilized, then lifted Ambrose and carried him farther up the beach and laid him on the sand.

Eden managed to get to her feet and was making her way up the beach when Rafe came back to help her. "He's going to be all right."

"Oh, Rafe . . ."

Eden, shivering and exhausted, felt such great relief that she wept and laughed. Her teeth chattered as she sobbed, but both her cry and her tears were masked by the storm. She had tasted the sorrow of death and the joy of life restored in but a moment of time.

Rafe caught her hands and pulled her into his strong arms. He was smiling as she leaned against him. He swept her up and carried her back toward Ambrose. As the rain beat against her face, she blinked against the black sky thick with clouds. She knew the Lord had heard the cry of their hearts and had in His sovereignty spared him. She didn't need to see the stars tonight. The sky could be as black as it wanted to be. She knew that the promise of Scripture was true for her that night: "My times are in thy hand."

Eden made her way toward the house, still struggling against the wind and rain. The feeble light beckoned from the lower window, where Noelani waited. When Eden reached the door, she turned to look back into the torrential darkness. She could barely see Rafe coming, carrying his uncle.

She went inside, still dazed and shaken. Noelani was seated in the bamboo chair with her foot elevated. Her wise, dark eyes looked at Eden's face, searching. She must have read her emotions, for Noelani smiled. "It's all right, isn't it?" she said.

Eden smiled wearily. "Yes, it's all right, Noelani. Rafe is bringing Ambrose now. But we lost the boats."

They looked at each other, their eyes steady as the realization of deliverance grew.

"The boats," Noelani said and laughed. "The boats . . ."

Noelani lifted both her arms wide and held them open to receive her. Tears of joy ran down her face. Eden ran and threw herself into her arms.

———

It was dawn when, with Ambrose asleep in his bed and Noelani keeping vigil, Eden heard Rafe preparing to leave. Weary with emotional exhaustion, she entered the room and saw that he was already at the front door. Had he intended to leave without a personal good-bye? She paused.

Rafe looked at her from the doorway, but the room was still in shadows and she couldn't see his eyes, only the outline of his face. For a long moment neither of them spoke. Eden hesitated to walk up to him and stayed where she was. She was afraid to speak, afraid the lump in her throat would give her away. He must have taken her silence for resolve, for he slowly closed the door and leaned his shoulder against it, watching her.

"I don't know when I'll be back."

Moments of silence ticked by.

"No . . . I don't suppose you would," she agreed.

Another pause seemed to lengthen.

"I'm not one for writing letters either."

She held her hands behind her and her fingers interlocked tightly. Outwardly she gave nothing of her emotions away. Rafe was the kind of man who would retreat if she tried to corner him.

"I'm sure I'll be busy at nursing school. I wouldn't have much time to answer anyway."

A slight smile touched his mouth. "Yes."

Eden lifted her head. "Well, I wish you . . ." What did she wish for him? The facade of her heart crumbled and she turned away toward the kitchen. "I'd better get the coffee on for Ambrose when he wakes. I wish the best for you, Rafe."

"And you. Stay out of trouble in San Francisco. Good-bye, Eden."

"Good-bye, Rafe. . . ."

The door shut firmly. The sound brought such finality of separation that a catch came to her throat and she whirled to stare at it—only to find him still there.

Surprised, she stared at him. Why, he'd done that on purpose, just to see her response when she thought he'd gone!

He straightened from the door and walked toward her. He stopped, hands on hips. "You've armor a foot thick! 'Good-bye, Rafe,' " he repeated airily. "See you in ten years."

She stared at him, shocked. "And you!" she accused, pointing at the door. "You were just going to walk out, catch your ship with Keno, and vanish."

The room was lightening with the rising sun.

"Maybe I've reason to be cautious."

"What did you fear, that I wouldn't let you go? That I'd hang on to you and demand an affectionate good-bye . . . and make you promise to return?"

He lifted a brow and smiled. "Interesting. Would you?"

She flushed. "Absolutely not!"

"Forbid the thought!"

"You're a fine one to pretend hurt feelings—"

"What do you understand about my feelings? If you must know, I didn't trust myself to say good-bye to you. What do you think of that? I'm little better than Zachary. I, too, would like to kiss you good-bye, but unlike Zach, I respect you. If I did take advantage of the situation, it wouldn't be fair to you."

Her emotions came tumbling down, bruised and hurting. Unlike her feelings for Zachary, her heart yearned for Rafe. Her sense of disorientation was enhanced as she understood that he was being honest with her, that there was no certainty they would see each other again. This was not a time for commitment—perhaps there never would be.

"I'm not sure about a lot of things," he said, "especially myself. Even when I come back, what I do, I must do alone."

Eden managed to keep her dignity intact. "I understand. You needn't apologize."

"I'm not apologizing," he grumbled.

"It's not my intention to force you into caring."

"Look, you've got it wrong. It's not that I don't care—"

Eden rushed on. "But I'm not trying to wrangle some last-minute declaration from you about—about—"

He cocked his head. "About?"

"Oh, never mind."

"I just didn't want to hurt you," he said, composed.

"Oh, I see. Well, thank you, Rafe. That's very kind of you."

His eyes narrowed under his lashes.

"Let me return the kindness," she continued too calmly, her heart thudding. "I don't want to hurt you either. There are also a lot of things I'm not sure about. Even when I come back, what I intend to do, I will do alone."

He smiled wryly and folded his arms. "We have much in common. Therefore we should say our good-bye without regrets. I wouldn't want to get halfway out to sea and be troubled by a guilty conscience."

"And I would never want you to be so burdened. You may leave Hawaii as free as a bird."

"Why, thank you, Eden, for your maturity." He smiled, his rich brown eyes flickering with amusement.

She, too, managed a smile and held out her hand. "Good-bye, Rafe."

He searched her eyes intensely, then looked pointedly at her extended hand.

"Nothing like a good handshake among old friends," he said silkily. "Does this mean we part in peace?"

Her other hand, hidden behind her skirt, formed a fist. She smiled too pleasantly. "Why, of course . . . aloha." But the words almost caught in her throat, and her eyes wavered.

He hesitated, then reached for her hand, his fingers enclosing hers warmly. She stared at his hand, afraid to look up. Noelani had always told her that the eyes are the mirrors of the soul.

No words were spoken, but as Rafe continued to hold her hand, caressing it, his touch began to awaken other emotions. She tensed slightly. She sensed he felt it too—that inevitable smoldering of embers that could grow as vital and conquering as the storm.

She raised her eyes. The intensity of his gaze drew her, even as he pulled her toward him and she involuntarily swayed closer. His arms wrapped about her. His mouth tipped in a vague smile. "So much for brave words." He gently lifted her chin, and Eden felt their lips touching warmly as a sweet weakness turned her muscles to water.

His embrace tightened. His fingers caressed her face, moving through her still-damp hair. She sighed to herself as his kiss lengthened. They held to each other, trembling in the sultry wind that had blown open the front door.

"Not good-bye," he whispered a moment later. "But *aloha nui loa*."

Rafe released her and unlocked her arms from about his neck. He backed away until there was about ten feet between them, then looked at her for a long moment as if he wanted to remember her standing there. He turned and left.

Eden gasped and slowly sank to the divan. She felt weak, warm, and alive, yet the ache in her heart seemed far worse. "Aloha nui loa," she whispered, repeating the warmest greeting one could give in Hawaii. Not just good-bye, but also hello and welcome. He had welcomed her to his heart, but would she find a home there?

She laid her head on the arm of the divan and tried to hold back a torrent of emotions. It was still good-bye, no matter what else he had said. She knew him too well.

The warm wind blew against her, bringing uncertainty and loneliness. She understood as well as he that little had been solved. And now she knew the inevitability of a sweet memory that would haunt the distant miles between them, a memory to last for years, maybe forever. She loved him, yet what good did it do?

Perhaps I should have let him leave in silence as he had first planned, she thought. *Some gifts, however precious, are better when opened later.*

––––––––

The following week Ambrose was up and about, and the ministry at the mission church was going forward. Eden said good-bye to her relatives, and lastly to Ambrose and Noelani, then boarded the steamer at Pearl Harbor.

Fifteen minutes out to sea, Eden stood on deck watching Honolulu with its vibrant green and blue slide past her. With mixed feelings she watched the shimmering island slowly receding from view. The lush green foliage, bright red Hibiscus, and white sand waved good-bye. She imagined the sugar cane rustling in the wind at Kea Lani and gazed off into the distance to Diamond Head Volcano with its dark purple shadows. She envisioned haoles, the Japanese and Chinese workers, and the native Hawaiians. Her eyes misted as she reached to steady her hat with its trailing white ribbon. "One day I shall be back," she whispered.

PART
II

SEPTEMBER 1889 —
JANUARY 1891

nine

September 1889

The Island of Molokai

Hawaiian Islands

Rafe Easton, in a comfortable blue cotton shirt, sat with his typewriter at a makeshift desk of woven coconut husks and palm fiber. The breeze entered freely through the open door and windows of the grass hut that he and Keno had constructed on their first visit to Molokai.

Rafe had arrived a year ago on a previous trip to learn he was too late. Dr. Jerome Derrington had already left. Eventually Rafe tracked him down, but not until his shipping business had taken him to most of the South Pacific island groups between New Guinea and Bora Bora. At last, one night after Rafe had spent a couple of days on Tahiti, Jerome came walking into his camp, an ill, gaunt-looking man. "I hear you're looking for me," Jerome had said. "What do you want to know about leprosy?"

Rafe frowned as he remembered, the breeze ruffling his dark hair.

They had sat by a campfire that night as Jerome told him that he was working for King Kalakaua. Inquiries had been made to many tropical countries for advice and cures. Jerome had brought an Indian by the name of Mohabeer back to Kalihi Hospital, along with two Chinese, Sang Ki and Akana, and a Japanese named Goto. He had even included a Hawaiian kahuna named Kainokalani. To complete his research team, Jerome had sought out several Americans, men who mixed their own patented medicines, and a German bacteriologist, Eduard Arning.

"All to no avail," Jerome had said. "But I will never give up."

Jerome also told him that the German bacteriologist had gotten permission from Kalakaua's government to make the deadly experiment of implanting leprous tissue in the flesh of a condemned native murderer named Keanu.

Rafe, sitting in the quiet hut on Molokai, hearing the waves breaking on the beach, frowned at the page in the typewriter, seeing not his words nor thinking of Jerome, but of the few babies and small children he had seen while here. Did they contract leprosy at birth from their mother? Jerome had mentioned a Norwegian scientist, Armauer Hansen, who had identified the *bacillus leprae*, but very little was known about the way it was transmitted.

Rafe deliberately pushed the disturbing thought of children from his mind. The longer he stayed on Molokai the more pessimistic he was becoming. He'd already been here for three weeks, piecing together the last bits of information and research on what he had intended to be a newspaper article. But the research had grown and now the material could easily fit into a book-size manuscript, which was not his intention.

With a critical eye he reread the page. Satisfied that he'd at least gotten down a rough summary of the latest facts he'd accumulated, he shuffled the page into the rest of the stack, placed it in his satchel, and glanced at his watch—nearing four o'clock. He grabbed his hat from the water gourd and left the hut for his meeting with William Ragsdale.

The path among the swaying palms led along the sandy shore a mile up the coast. The settlement was located on an isolated peninsula on the north coast of the island, but Rafe would meet his contact halfway. Here was where the government schooner *Warwick* had first begun transporting lepers to Molokai in 1866. Wanting to stay as far away from the diseased as they could, the crew "dumped" the lepers into the water to make their own way to the beach and the settlement.

From what Rafe had learned, the settlement was in desperate condition, with the stronger preying on the weak and helpless and taking more than their share of the supplies. Some form of law was needed, but the authorities in Honolulu couldn't find men willing to even come near this northern shore of Molokai. It was mainly the missionary boats that brought in supplies.

He ducked under a low-hanging palm frond. He had another quarter mile to walk before meeting Ragsdale on the beach at some reddish lava rocks encircled with coconut palms.

In his recent travels Rafe had taken care to see which of the world's religions showed concern for the lives of their beggars, blind, lame, and the famine stricken. He had noticed that while most of humanity's downcast were left to passively endure their karma, or unquestioningly accept "whatever Allah wills," Christians, like the first Hawaiian missionaries, built schools, churches, medical clinics, and orphanages not only in their own countries, but in Africa, the Far East, and elsewhere, demonstrating that they did not consider God just a local or national deity. And Rafe had found that it was almost exclusively the followers of Christ who took an interest in the lepers.

The sun was now reaching toward the western horizon above a placid blue sea, where it would set amid a glorious splash of red. Rafe stopped, seeing William Ragsdale ahead, the wind blowing his shirt and wide-legged cotton trousers. He had a cloth tied across his face like a bandit. For the first time his right hand was wrapped in cloth.

Ragsdale had once been a parliamentary translator until contracting the disease. Now he was just one of the "unfortunates," facing a slow but certain death. His status meant nothing now.

A leper is a leper regardless of race, status, or wealth, Rafe mused. Ragsdale might have the good fortune to afford a *kokua*, a servant to help look after him as he grew more ill, but socially, he was just like the rest. He was an outcast, pronounced "unclean" by the governmental authorities. Like the proud Captain Naaman who had gone to the Jewish prophet Elisha seeking a cure for his leprosy, "he was also a mighty man in valour, but he was a leper."

Rafe loathed this moment. The sight of Ragsdale was revolting, but it wasn't the swollen patches of flesh that bothered him so much as the sudden reminder of what effect this whole story would inevitably have upon Eden. Ragsdale was trying to appeal to Rafe to intercede in Honolulu, or even in the States, for help. Some sort of system was needed for the distribution of supplies, yet no one wanted to come near the detention camp.

"Hello, Easton. I thought you might have caught ship by now."

"I'll leave tomorrow morning at dawn when the *Manoa* comes offshore."

"I envy you."

Rafe stood on the rock with the blue sea behind him, the sun inching toward the horizon off to the west. What could he say? What did anyone say in circumstances like this? Words of comfort might sound trite. Ragsdale had come to the settlement willingly, but many others had to be forced. When told he must live on Molokai in isolation from his family, a Hawaiian named Koolau, from the island of Kauai, had run away, taking his family and a group of other diseased Hawaiians with him. For months he kept the law at bay, killing several lawmen with his rifle.

"Have you spoken to Father Damien?" Rafe called. "Can he tell me anything about who the kokua is that worked for Jerome?"

Ragsdale's voice was muffled under the cloth. "Father Damien died in April. He told me to tell you he prayed for you. He asked that you not forget the dire needs on Molokai."

"I won't, but is that all he said? What about the information I need on Jerome?"

"He said nothing more. Even if he knows the truth, he'd never betray a trust by sharing the secret."

"Then let me speak to the kokua. Is the servant still alive?"

Ragsdale gestured his helplessness. "I can't find out. No one wants to talk."

Rafe put a damper on his frustration. There was nothing else he could do, since he couldn't enter the settlement.

"There's no more I can tell you," Ragsdale called. "Listen to me, Rafe, this settlement needs your help. Something must be done about the supplies. You saw what happened on the beach when the supplies were unloaded. Confusion! Tell King Kalakaua we need men from the police station to keep order! There is abuse of the women as well. Something must be done," he repeated.

"I'll report the matter to Kalihi Hospital and the missionaries in Honolulu," Rafe called.

"Good! I knew I could count on you. Get that information into a book—get it out to the people, not just in Hawaii but in America too. Tell them we need them!"

Rafe's jaw clenched. He stood on the lava rock buffeted by the wind.

"I can't promise anything, Ragsdale. Understand? Don't get your hopes up. I'd hate to think you were here waiting for something to happen that doesn't have a chance!"

Ragsdale said more, but it was lost on Rafe. Finally, Ragsdale lifted his bandaged hand in a wave, then turned his back to the ocean wind.

Rafe watched him walk away. At that moment he felt the weight of Molokai like a brick in his heart.

The words *"something must be done"* continued to echo in Rafe's mind even after Ragsdale disappeared.

Eventually he became aware of the silence, of the crisp palm fronds, of the sigh and sob of the Pacific waves, of the wind about the ancient lava rocks.

A few minutes later Rafe turned and walked back along the beach toward the hut. The waves were lapping in closer as the tide came in. The curling white foam licked at his feet. The sun, like a golden globe, began its approach toward the Pacific.

He had gone perhaps a quarter mile when a voice carried on the wind. Thinking it was Ragsdale who had come after him, Rafe stopped on the sand and looked behind him. His lashes narrowed as he skimmed the thick palm trees growing along the landward side. He didn't see anyone and walked on. The sound came again, this time unmistakable. A cry?

Rafe walked toward the sound where wild vines with purple flowers moved gently in the wind, reminding him that amid suffering and death there remained beauty, a promise of what had once been for the whole world and would one day be again. The wail of a small child tugged at his heart.

Someone called, "Please, Makua Easton, help us! Please!"

"All right, come out so I can see you," he called.

A moment later a figure he assumed to be a woman moved out from behind the palm trees. He could not tell if she was old or young, hapa-haole or full Hawaiian. As far as he knew, she might even be Chinese. The Hawaiians called the disease of leprosy *mai pake*, "Chinese disease," though no one knew how it had been brought to Hawaii. According to Jerome it had been observed in the Polynesian kingdom as early as 1830.

The person was covered from head to toe with a hooded garment with two eye holes. He could only imagine the heartbreak in those eyes—eyes that Rafe did not want to look into. Some manner of gloves were on her hands.

"Please, help me," she said again in a garbled voice.

Troubled by her plea, he couldn't bring himself to walk away as she hung back behind the palm tree.

"I wish I could help you," he said gently. "There is nothing I can do for your infirmity. There is hope and comfort in Christ."

"Yes, I know Him. He told me to come to you."

Rafe's eyes narrowed and he cocked his head, now cautious. "Jesus told you to come to me?"

"I have watched you for a long time. I know what you seek."

His eyes flickered as he watched the woman hidden behind the cloak, the palm fronds waving gently over her head.

"Do you know Dr. Derrington's kokua?" he asked her.

"You must not pursue that."

"Why not?"

"Why trouble the dead? No one can resurrect us but Christ."

Rafe stood still. He felt the warm seawater rush about his feet, pulling at the cuffs of his trousers.

"You know Dr. Jerome Derrington?" she said in a muffled voice. "You must take him something. It is over there in the basket. Do you remember Pharaoh's daughter?"

Rafe tensed. He started toward her, but she backed away. "Do not come near! Unclean! Unclean!"

Jolted emotionally by her words of Scripture, Rafe stopped. He heard the child begin to cry again.

"Wait!" Rafe shouted as she disappeared. "I can't take a child from the leper camp!"

Had she really gone, or was she hiding to see what he'd do?

"What you ask is impossible. I'd endanger everyone aboard the ship!"

"Please, you must take him, Makua Easton!"

So she hadn't run away.

"I'm sorry," he called.

"I am dying—there is no one to care for him. He doesn't have the disease!"

"You can't expect me to believe that. I understand your frustration, your helplessness, but I cannot take your child from this island!"

"He will die if you don't. You must, please! Dr. Derrington will know what to do with him!"

Rafe's eyes narrowed with frustration. "Then he'll just have to come back to Molokai and deal with it. Look, I don't want to sound hard-hearted, but if I took anyone from Molokai, child or adult, I could be arrested by the government of King Kalakaua. You know the laws of Hawaii—"

"He is not my child, but I can tell you he does not have the disease."

"I'll do this much. I'll promise to tell Jerome about the child."

"By the time Dr. Derrington comes, it may be too late. If the baby stays here, he will catch it and die a horrible death!"

She started to back away.

Rafe gestured. "Oh no, you don't. Come back here!"

She stopped.

"I'm not taking the child," he stated flatly, knowing he had to sound brutal in order to convince her. "There's nothing I can do, understand? Now, come back for him. I'm walking away and you wouldn't want to leave him unattended." Before she could protest, he turned his back and strode down the beach.

He half expected her to come wailing after him, thrusting the child toward him, but to his relief she did not.

He paused once and glanced back, but the beach was deserted. The glorious sunset added to his misery, for the awareness of beauty could make corruption all the more painful.

There is nothing to be done about it, he rebuked himself. *The child is bound to have leprosy. I can't risk the ship's crew. And who would care for him anyway? Who'd change him and give him milk?*

No, he'd done the right thing. The sensible thing. Sentiment was not always the answer. Sentiment got in the way of practicality!

Rafe strode on, anxious to get back to his hut and typewriter, to consider his plans. He noticed he could no longer look at the sunset nor find any satisfaction in thinking about his freedom from Molokai.

He was still trying to reject the cloud of depression that hovered over him when, finally nearing the grass hut, he saw Keno coming from the pineapple plants that were growing wild. Keno was whistling, and when he saw Rafe he called cheerfully, "Too bad you couldn't invite Ragsdale to join us for supper. My luau is the best Hawaiian cooking on the islands."

"Don't talk about any luau! Where's the coffee? That's all I want." He strode toward the hut, leaving Keno staring.

Keno ran ahead and stood in the doorway of the hut, blocking the entrance. He tossed Rafe the pineapple he was carrying. "Ho, pal, you stay there. How close did you come to the lepers? You have whatever it is all over your clothes!"

Rafe glowered. "I'm in no mood for fun and games, Keno. Step aside."

Keno must have seen Rafe's serious mood, for he sighed. "What happened?"

"There's nothing like meeting a woman dying of leprosy and having her beg you to take her child. You should try it sometime," he said briskly. "It makes you feel like a real heel to turn your back on her." Rafe tossed his hat onto the outside table with wobbly legs. He looked at the pineapple and thought of the seedlings he wanted to bring back from South America. "Not even the sight of a pineapple helps. Here. Take it." He threw it back to Keno, who caught it and ran with it over to the table, where he picked up his machete.

"How close did you come to her?"

"Close enough to hear a crying child in a basket. I wonder how Jerome ever stood this work. There's not much hope in it."

Keno gestured his head to where some clean clothing hung on a line.

"No hope for us—if you don't take precautions."

Rafe humored him as Keno snatched up the shirt and trousers he had previously boiled and then dried in the sun. A tub of steaming hot water for a bath also stood under a coconut palm. Keno carried a second bucket of boiling water from the cooking area and poured it into the tub. A cloud of steam fumed. "It's ready now."

Rafe smirked. "What's in there, lye?"

"Only a little." Keno went over to the pit he'd lined with hot coals. He checked the salmon cooking. "I worry because this flesh of mine must be kept handsome for the day I marry Miss Rozlind."

Rafe shed his shirt and his mouth tipped. "You dreamer."

"Go ahead and laugh. When I am rich and growing the best pineapples in Oahu—"

"When *we* grow the best."

"You will be amazed to see how suddenly the Derringtons mistake me for a blond and blue-eyed German."

Rafe took off one boot and tossed it, then the other. "There's no accounting for how far a man's optimism will go. You'd better buy a French powdered wig, just to help things along." He looked into the steaming tub. "Looks like a witch's brew."

"It is you who needs to worry. What will Miss Eden say when she learns you've dug up old bones Jerome wanted buried?"

He wouldn't discuss Eden. He tried not to even think of her. When he did, he remembered that steamy night in Ambrose's house when they'd said aloha. He could have written her by now, but somehow each time he began to type a letter he got no further than *Dear Eden* . . .

"Just bring some coffee, will you? Let me stew awhile in peace. That episode with the woman has made me feel like a villain."

Keno looked over at him, troubled. "Say, you are serious, pal. This really troubles you. Who was she? Did she say?"

"Just another leper."

"Interesting that she asked you to take the child to Jerome. She probably thought he could do something for him one day—a cure maybe."

"She said the child didn't have the disease."

"That is hard to believe. Naturally she would tell you so. You had no choice. You can't take a leper child aboard the *Manoa*. And all the way to South America?" He poured Rafe a tin cup of coffee from a pot on the open fire.

"No," Rafe agreed. "What would we do with him? He'd be crying for his mother all the way. What do we know about small children?"

"That's it, pal, absolutely nothing! And we have problems plenty big enough already."

"I'll agree to that." Rafe tried the rich black coffee.

Keno went back to his cooking, gesturing with his machete for emphasis. The metal shimmered like a small sword in the firelight.

"Feast your eyes on the sea. One last voyage! Then our plantation is no longer words, no longer dreams that dance in our heads. Ah no, but a living, growing success. Pineapples from South America! We will soon have famous names in the island and in America. Our new pineapples will make Parker Judson's seem too small and not sweet enough."

Keno used his machete on the pineapple he'd picked earlier. Several lightninglike chops caused the juicy fruit to dribble sweetly on the cutting board.

After Rafe had bathed and dressed, he joined Keno on the beach for their last feast on Molokai. He ate his share of the fruit with a knife and watched the deepening twilight turn into jewel-like shades of amethyst and jade. The colors seeped across the sky and cast a pinkish glow on the groves of palm trees until at last evening settled into night. The bed of coals glowed like red lava, and the salmon steaks sizzled as the aroma wafted on the breeze.

Rafe felt the warm, soft sand beneath his feet and the breeze blowing through his open shirt. Keno was right; when they rowed out to meet the *Manoa* at dawn, there would be just one more voyage—this one to Jerome's isolated jungle camp in South America. Rafe didn't look forward to a confrontation with Jerome over the past. It wouldn't be easy to tell him he knew the truth now, but when Rafe saw Ainsworth again, he would have the final piece of the puzzle to lay before him about Jerome and the drowning of Rebecca Stanhope.

Soon, he thought, he would leave here and forget all that he had seen.

Late that night, after the coals had died down in the cooking pit and all was quiet except for the waves rolling to shore, Rafe could see the stars through the open window in the hut. He couldn't sleep. He kept remembering the woman and the child; he seemed to hear Ragsdale's plea: *"Something must be done to help us."* An incident in the life of Christ came to mind. A leper stood afar off and cried out to Jesus, "Lord, if thou wilt, thou canst make me clean." Christ had looked upon him with compassion. He had done something unthinkable: He had reached out his hand and *touched* the leper. "I will; be thou clean."

Rafe thought that it must have been the first touch the leper had received in years.

The scene kept running through Rafe's mind. He finally got up and left the hut to walk down to the beach. The moonlight showed the ocean breaking upon the beach, washing the sandy shore clean.

Rafe was still there when dawn broke and the *Manoa* was waiting offshore. A longboat had been lowered and two crewmen were venturing toward the beach.

Keno gave a shout, and Rafe turned, expecting him to come running down to the beach to haul in the longboat. Instead he gestured wildly for Rafe to come.

Rafe had a premonition, like a lead ball dropping into his stomach. He walked, then ran toward Keno, who was backing away from something in the bushes.

"The woman?" Rafe breathed as he ran up.

"No, a child. She must have brought him here during the night. But why didn't we hear him cry? Is he dead?"

Rafe approached the woven basket. A baby, hardly more than eight or nine months old, was sound asleep on a blanket, sucking a tiny thumb. Rafe's heart sank. The child's fair skin and soft brown hair curled around its tiny pink ear. No signs of leprosy yet . . . but that proved nothing!

Rafe walked toward the clearing and looked around, though he knew she was not there. She would be too wise for that. She had brought the baby here in the thick of night and lulled him to sleep, then walked the long and lonely bitter path back to the settlement. Rafe's heart felt a pang—a pang he desperately resisted. He could see her walking like a ghost in a white-hooded cloth, alone, abandoned by all but God. Oh, how he tried to resist—but in his imagination he saw not a stranger but Eden. Eden with leprosy, Eden alone, Eden seeking his help and leaving her child for his kindness. . . .

Rafe came back and looked at Keno, who wore a stricken expression. "Don't go near the child," Keno said, alarm in his dark eyes. "What if—?"

Rafe hesitated and looked down. The breeze stirred the baby's light silken hair. He had to see, he had to know, and he knew Keno would never touch the boy. Nor could he ask him to. Rafe walked to the basket and without hesitation—for his mind was made up—stooped and drew aside the cloth. The child stirred and opened his eyes, then began to whimper when he saw Rafe.

"It's all right," Rafe soothed and proceeded to examine him. Minutes later he could find nothing, no bright spots or swelling, not so much as a blemish anywhere on his flesh.

"Do not keep him," Keno pleaded.

"He's clean."

"How do you know? What do we know about it? Next week, next month, who knows?"

"All right, then, *you* return him to the settlement!"

"Me! How can I do such a thing? Maybe the poor baby doesn't have it!"

"Exactly," Rafe said. "We might be saving his life. Then again—"

"He might be taking ours," Keno groaned. "Take him back."

"You take him."

"No, I cannot do it—"

The child began to cry and Rafe made up his mind. He picked him up from the basket, leaving all bedding and cloths, and carried him toward the longboat.

"You can't take him like that."

"Then find something to wrap him in," Rafe said flatly.

"Here." Keno took off his shirt, avoiding Rafe's eyes as he handed it to him. "You better have a fine tale for the crew. If not, we might find ourselves marooned for life."

The two crewmen were waiting to welcome them into the boat. When they saw the baby, one grinned and the other's mouth gaped open.

"Where'd you get him, mate?"

Keno grinned as though he'd thought of something extremely funny. "He got him from his *mate*, of course—why, that's Rafe's new boy!"

The crewmen looked at Rafe, then smiled broadly. "Your boy? Now ain't that something! An' you didn't even tell us all this time!"

"But where've you been keeping him? Not here on this forsaken island!" said the other.

Rafe looked at Keno with a wry look. "Go ahead and explain, Keno. You've done well enough so far." He walked toward the longboat holding the boy.

Keno shook his head. "Didn't you know?" he asked them.

"Know what?" asked one.

Keno lowered his voice in a sad whisper, but Rafe couldn't hear what was said.

As the crewmen rowed back out toward the *Manoa*, Rafe watched the island recede. It was too late to turn back now. It was done . . . for better or for worse.

TEΠ

December 1890

Chadwick Nursing School

San Francisco

The article in the *San Francisco Examiner* might well have come edged in black, judging by the ominous effect its arrival had upon Aunt Lana. Eden mused over this curious behavior as she walked the pine-scented carpet of brown needles toward Chadwick's rolling green lawn. A stone bench waited ahead beside a quiet pond where she often went for peaceful solitude to read her Bible and pray. During the two years she had attended Chadwick, the bench beside the pond's quiet waters had become Eden's daily refuge. She walked there carrying the newspaper with the article that had appeared to trouble Lana Stanhope.

The bench faced upward toward the white Victorian mansion that stood against a backdrop of green conifers, with cool sea air floating in from the Bay and whispering through the damp branches. The mansion, with dormer windows and brick chimneys, sheltered a private Christian nursing school specializing in tropical diseases. Eden had completed her course requirements at Chadwick in September, but had chosen to stay on at the college as a teaching assistant to help Lana with the freshman classes while waiting for the official June graduation ceremony. By then she hoped that Great-aunt Nora would have succeeded in convincing Dr. Clifford Bolton to find a position for her on the staff at Kalihi Hospital in Honolulu.

Dr. Bolton, a colleague of Eden's father, was a specialist in tropical diseases who worked for the Hawaiian monarch, King David Kalakaua. And Great-aunt Nora, always a philanthropist to her beloved Hawaii, was a friend of Bolton and had given generous financial support to the leprosy research. Few of the major health problems besetting the islands had receded as promised during the reign of Kalakaua.

In spite of efforts at segregation and banishment of lepers, the disease continued to make serious inroads among the Hawaiian natives. Recently, the increasing number of cases had frightened and panicked haole government officials. Even the former queen's cousin, a member of the legislative house of nobles, had been sent to the isolation settlement at Kalawao on the island of Molokai, along with many prominent haoles. Eden intended to return to Oahu to assist in this work, knowing that her father was also deeply involved, though her most recent letter from Jerome had come from Bora Bora. Now that Eden had completed her studies, she had written Nora two months ago and was waiting for a reply, but so far Nora had not responded.

Here, alone, with few sounds except the twitter of sparrows, Eden opened the *Examiner* to the section where Lana had been reading earlier that morning. What could have upset her? The words below a photograph of Eden's grandfather Ainsworth leaped up at her.

CHIEF MEMBER OF THE HAWAIIAN LEAGUE ARRIVES AMID RUMORS

Sugar magnate Ainsworth Derrington arrived in San Francisco yesterday from Honolulu aboard the U.S. steamer *Sacramento*. Speculation continues that Derrington is on his way to Washington, D.C., to hold secret meetings with members of Congress and the Secretary of State. Sources close to Derrington are suggesting the Hawaiian growers are nervous over recent decisions by the monarchy that penalize the plantation owners. The growers are seeking understanding and support from Washington for any move the Hawaiian League may take to encourage the Hawaiian Islands to become a territory of the United States. However, Derrington, representing some of the biggest sugar interests in Hawaii and California, denies that secrecy is involved in the talks. . . .

Eden, surprised by her grandfather's arrival, looked at the newspaper picture showing him standing in the midst of a handful of other Hawaiian planters, surrounded by journalists, outside the Palace Hotel.

Ainsworth was in San Francisco! Why had no one told her?

She studied his photograph. He looked healthy and strong, much the same as the last time she'd seen him at Kea Lani over two years ago. He was tall and slim, with straight shoulders and a dignified, unsmiling face sporting a well-groomed mustache. He was conservatively dressed in a business suit and vest, an expensive derby hat on his gray head. She had heard from him in September when he had congratulated her on concluding her nursing studies at Chadwick. A graduation gift would soon be arriving, he had told her. Yet it was December and she had not yet received it. Now that he was here in the Bay City, she anticipated a meeting with him before his train left for Washington, D.C.

Eden's smile faded and she continued skimming the article. Why did Ainsworth's arrival disturb Lana?

Ainsworth, when asked about his sister Nora's recent book, *The Spoils of Eden*, which was critical of Spreckles, Dole, and other haole growers, had stated that "he hadn't the time to read it yet." The question asked by reporters of why Miss Derrington had changed her mind about annexation, when like him she had once supported it, was greeted with his well-known acerbic tongue: "I'm told it's a woman's right to change her mind."

"You disagree with Miss Derrington that Big Sugar has stolen Hawaii from the Polynesians?"

"The sugar growers didn't steal Hawaii," the article reported him as saying. "Like the missionaries, we built Hawaii. We brought in the sugar cane, the Kona coffee. We built the schools, the churches, and hospitals. We paved the streets. Most of us are third-generation Hawaiians—offspring of the missionaries—and we were born there. We're not leaving now. Annexation makes sense, unless the United States government wishes to stand by and see the Japanese or British flag flying over Iolani Palace."

Eden frowned. The article went on to point out that his fiery remarks were typical of Ainsworth Derrington, and that past statements similar to these had evoked indignant responses from Honolulu, which suggested he and the Hawaiian League would find few "friends in Washington, D.C." Much to the alarm of King Kalakaua and his cabinet, the Derringtons boldly suggested that the hour would soon dawn when the Hawaiian monarchy, for the good of democracy, would inevitably step down and allow for free elections.

Eden gripped the paper and scanned the faces of those standing with her grandfather. One in particular was very familiar. She must be wrong, she thought. The last letter received from her grandfather had mentioned that Zachary was still traveling in the Orient as a "family-appointed" ambassador for the extensive Derrington pearl and sugar holdings. Then what was he doing in San Francisco?

Eden gave closer consideration to the newspaper photo. Although Zachary was not looking at the camera, how could she not recognize the blond and robust appearance of her cousin?

Eden was so absorbed in the newspaper that she hardly heard the horse hooves coming up the carriageway with the mail wagon. A few minutes later a lad jumped down from beside an older man, ran up the porch steps to the front door, and rang the bell.

Eden quickly folded the newspaper and stood from the bench. There was sure to be a letter from her grandfather suggesting she meet him for dinner at the Palace Hotel. With a light heart she quickened her steps up the sloping lawn toward the mansion. It had been over two years since that unfortunate incident with Zachary on the road to Kea Lani. He was older and wiser now, she told herself. They all were.

————

The horse's clopping hoofbeats were fading down the brick drive when Eden entered the wide front hall with its glossy hardwood floor.

Lana had already taken the mail into the front guest parlor and the door was open. Eden crossed the hall and entered expectantly.

The early afternoon had become foggy, and the large room was dim and remained chilly, though the Chinese servant, Jian Liu, had built a pleasant fire in the hearth. His wife, Hui, had baked some saltless almond cookies to go with the tea, and refreshments were already arranged on the long table for the dozen students and teachers at the school.

Lana was standing by the fireplace with her back toward the door when Eden entered, but she must have heard her footsteps, for she turned. Lana's hazel eyes, with the beginning of crinkle lines about them, showed alarm.

Eden paused at her reaction. "I didn't mean to startle you. I saw the mail wagon and thought—" She stopped.

Lana blinked hard several times, able to regain control of her emotions as Eden and the other nursing students were taught to do. Dignity— that was the thing that mattered! Dignity, a noble spirit, and self-control. A nurse must match the Florence Nightingale image that hung on the walls of the dormitory and the dining room.

Despite Lana's earnest face, Eden could sense the beginning of tears.

"Lana? Not unhappy news?" Eden started toward her across the braided oval rug, but didn't proceed when Lana's shoulders squared beneath the ankle-length gray dress she wore, overlaid with the traditional nurse's pinafore. She wore the head-nurse uniform well. One sensed a woman whose emotions churned much deeper than her attractive form would reveal. Her jawline was rather square, her long honey-colored hair was brushed smoothly back beneath her cap with a fringe of bangs across her forehead.

Lana had turned out to be a much younger woman than Eden had expected when first arriving from Kea Lani. Her figure was still youthful, and even now when they went out for dinner at Union Square there were many gentlemen who noticed her, though she never appeared to see them.

Eden glanced at her aunt's hand and saw a letter before she drew it behind her skirt. She must have realized that Eden noticed, for she brought it back out.

"From the Derringtons," Lana explained.

Eden's lively green eyes questioned her. "From my grandfather? I read the article in the *Examiner*."

Lana crumpled it, then leaned toward the fire. Stunned by her action, Eden guessed her intent and rushed to gain control of the wad of paper but could not reach her aunt in time. Eden gave a small cry as she watched the stationery ignite and burn into feathery gray ash. She turned to Lana, shocked.

"Lana! What's gotten into you! How could you?"

Lana's colorless lips formed a predictable line of steel, though her pale skin tinted pink at Eden's offended tone.

"It was sent to me. I had every right to burn it," Lana stated briskly.

Eden's taut fingers pressed the starched white pinafore covering her citron yellow cotton dress as she tried to make sense of her aunt's behavior. "He sent it to you?"

"It's better this way," Lana said, not explaining. She looked at her watch. "I've got a class to teach."

Confused, Eden shook her head. "Wait, *please*." She started after her. "I don't understand."

"I'd rather not discuss it." She headed out the door.

Eden caught her arm. "But why burn it?"

Lana tore her gaze away as though troubled by Eden's disappointment, hesitated, then let out a slight breath. She stepped back into the room and closed the door. For a moment they looked at each other, then Lana walked to the bay window, her voice drained of energy.

"Why?" Lana repeated dully. "Because he wants to stir up trouble that can only injure us. At thirty-five I don't care to alter the course of my life. And you've your entire life ahead of you. He'd ruin everything. I won't let him."

"Ainsworth?" She folded her arms. "I don't believe it. I've never been close to my grandfather. It was always Rozlind, but—" Her voice faltered slightly. "I'd like to be close to him. Anyway, I won't allow myself to think he'd make a decision to deliberately injure me or you."

Lana made no rush to explain and continued to look below onto the sloping lawn while the fog thickened, dripping moisture from the Monterey pine trees. Her silence ignited Eden's exasperation. Still, Lana continued to stare out the window as if expecting someone. Was she even listening? Eden wondered.

"What did the letter say? What did my grandfather want? Are you upset with him because of the article on annexation?"

Lana turned her head blankly. "Annexation? Oh—that. No." She waved a hand of dismissal.

Eden walked toward her now, thinking that perhaps she knew what Lana was upset about. Lana was well aware of her ambition to return to Hawaii to work with Dr. Clifford Bolton at Kalihi Hospital. Lana had said several times in recent months, "I wish you'd stay in San Francisco. A position can be arranged for you at St. Francis Hospital."

Had her grandfather's letter mentioned Eden's request to work at Kalihi?

"You know what working at Kalihi means to me," Eden told her quietly, joining her at the window. "There's an emotional connection there with my father. It's something I feel I *must* do. Did Ainsworth mention my letter to Great-aunt Nora? Is that why you're upset? I've asked for her assistance with Dr. Bolton to place me . . ."

Eden's voice stumbled into silence when Lana's eyes closed briefly, as though something she had said hurt her deeply. Eden bit her lip.

Lana dropped the sheer curtain of crocheted cream lace, which fell into place, and her head lowered for a moment. "The letter wasn't—from Ainsworth," she said, a catch in her throat.

Eden watched her, alert. "But you said it was from the Derringtons."

"It was from your cousin Zachary."

Eden noted the unpleasantness in her voice and considered the implications. Zachary . . .

But why should her aunt display such strong emotional reaction to Zachary?

At once the note she had discovered two years ago in the cubicle at the mission church crossed her mind.

Lana lowered herself into an overstuffed chair by the window and looked up at her with wet cheeks. Whatever was troubling her went deeper than a personal dislike for Eden's arrogant cousin.

Kneeling beside the chair, Eden took Lana's hands tightly into her own. "I didn't know you had met Zachary before. I can see you're very upset. Don't be. I can handle him," she assured her with confidence. "If the letter had anything in it about me—"

"No. I told you, the letter wasn't meant for you. Zachary wrote to *me*." She drew her hands away as if trapped and stood, walking toward the fire.

A grave mood descended on Eden's spirits. Zachary had always meant trouble. She had wanted to think he'd changed in the last years, but had he?

"What does he want from you?" Eden asked quietly.

"He's coming here on Saturday. He wants to talk to you. To both of us. I'd rather not see him. Maybe—I'll leave," she stated suddenly. "I've a few days off. I'll take the train to Seattle to visit friends." She turned expectantly. "You could come with me."

What was she running away from? She considered Lana to be a woman of courage, and it wasn't like her to avoid difficulties.

"I won't run," Eden said. "And neither should you. We've no reason to fear Zachary. He's here in San Francisco with my grandfather is all. No doubt he'll be going with him to Washington to meet some congressmen about the annexation of Hawaii."

Lana didn't look convinced. "I refuse to become mixed up in his plans. I won't have him meddling at this late date."

Late date? Late for what? And what made her suppose Zachary wished to meddle? What was there to meddle with? Again Eden thought of the strange note. She had already asked Lana about it when she first arrived. Lana had not seemed impressed or worried. She had doubted that anyone in the Derrington family was covering up the truth about Rebecca's death.

Now, however, the ominous feelings Eden had when she'd first discovered the note came inching back. Cautiously alert, she watched Lana, but it was clear her aunt intended to safeguard whatever troubled her.

"I'm late for class," Lana repeated. "We'll talk more about this later."

Eden looked after her, concerned, then walked to the fireplace where the letter had burned. *Perhaps my best recourse to learn what this is all about rests with Zachary*, she thought. *If he's coming here on Saturday, I'll be sure to meet him.*

When dinnertime arrived, Lana remained adamantly resistant to giving any clear explanations about the letter, despite her earlier promise to discuss more with Eden. That evening she became conveniently ill and withdrew to her room, taking her supper behind a closed door.

As for Eden, she slept little that night and lit her lamp several times to look again at a scorched piece of the letter she had retrieved from the hearth after her aunt left. Eden stared at the scrap, as though by doing so she might force the missing words to reappear.

A few were readable—*boat* and *discuss Kalihi work . . . Molokai*—but the rest was missing.

Eden tensed as she held the small piece of paper. Perhaps there was information in these few words, but at the moment they told her nothing she didn't already know.

Boat. The boat that Rebecca used when she drowned?

Eden got out of bed and paced. The doleful groan of the foghorns and the drip of moisture at her window told her the school was blanketed with gray mist.

In the glow of the golden lamp she turned to the presentation page of Rebecca's Bible. There, written in her even handwriting, were the names of her mother's parents and a sister, all deceased now except for Lana. There were also the dates of her mother's marriage to Jerome Derrington and the birth of their first and only child, a daughter, named Eden. Her name represented a spiritual link her mother had with Hawaii and the Garden of Eden ruined by the Fall of Adam and Eve. There also was a verse written—*"Declare his praise in the islands."* The date of her mother's arrival in Hawaii to serve as a missionary schoolteacher was written below the verse, as well as her name and Jerome's.

Eden held the Bible closely, as though she held her parents. Rebecca was gone—Eden had only faint memories of someone who must have loved her deeply. In her strange dream, which had recurred several times since that stormy night, Eden had been searching for her in an unfamiliar house but was unable to find her. The question remained—why?

She reached for a second item on the dressing table and looked at it, trying to remember. It was a miniature brass tiki head similar to the knocker she had seen on the door in her dream. Eden had picked up the trinket on the steamer before sailing for San Francisco from Pearl Harbor. She turned it over in her hand, rubbing it with her thumb, trying to remember the house where she had seen it before, but her mind remained in a mist.

Next she took the mother-of-pearl cameo she often wore and opened it. Inside were two small photographs, one of Rebecca, the other of Jerome, taken soon after they were married. Hers was not a beautiful face, but there was beauty beneath the quiet eyes, the light brown hair, and the serene expression. Jerome was a handsome man with a serious face, dark hair, and greenish eyes. Neither was smiling; neither looked especially in love, but a picture did not tell everything.

Coming to no conclusions, Eden sighed and put the items in her drawer.

———

The next morning Lana appeared more relaxed but still refused to discuss her reaction to Zachary's letter. From the day Eden had first arrived at Chadwick, her attempts to open doors of information about Rebecca had mostly ended in frustration. *"I wasn't in Hawaii when the accident took place,"* Lana had told her. *"So I can't tell you anything."*

As Eden sat across from her aunt at their private breakfast nook near Lana's room, Eden sipped her coffee, musing over the words on the scrap of letter—"discuss Kalihi work." Why did Zachary wish to discuss Jerome and Dr. Bolton's work with Lana? *No doubt to try to soothe her over my return to Kea Lani*, she thought sadly. Lana was taking her departure much harder than she had expected.

Eden spread Oregon blackberry jam on her toast. She came to the conclusion that Lana's behavior simply had to do with her disappointment over Ainsworth's arranging her voyage home, and that as far as Lana was concerned, Zachary was merely the bearer of bad news.

"I was told Great-aunt Nora didn't approve of Jerome's marriage," Eden commented. "I know we discussed this before, but did my mother mention this to you as well?"

Lana shook her head and refilled her chinaware blue cup. "It wasn't just your great-aunt who disapproved. Your uncle was against it too. Townsend carried on worse than Nora."

Eden stopped between bites of her toast. "Townsend?" she asked, surprised. "I must say I'm shocked to hear it. He isn't the sort of man to hold convictions where women are concerned."

Lana hesitated, as though wary. "I suppose it was jealousy."

Eden lowered her toast to her plate. "Jealousy! Townsend? Townsend was jealous over *my* mother?" She thought of Rafe's mother, Celestine. "That cad!"

Lana smiled ruefully. "And more. Oh, don't get me wrong. He didn't *really* care for Rebecca. He liked all the women," she said with a tinge of scorn.

Did he like you too? she wanted to ask but caught herself. Lana would have been even younger than Rebecca, and there was no denying that Lana was more attractive.

"But dear Rebecca wasn't his sort," Lana said victoriously. "She was too wise for his traps. He tried though. He came to call on her when Jerome was away."

Eden's eyes narrowed. She could have boxed his ears for such audacity. *Her* mother!

"For his visit, Rebecca held a Bible study." Lana smiled reminiscently. "He never came back. He didn't like that sort of thing. Sin and all that, you know. He didn't want to be reminded. As for his jealousy, I suppose his pride smarted because she didn't succumb to him the way the other women did. So he was rather cool toward his younger brother Jerome."

Eden laughed. "A Bible study. Good for Mama."

"And Jerome was everyone's favorite, as well as being your great-aunt Nora's preferred nephew—almost like a son. She thought Rebecca was out of place socially in marrying a Derrington." Lana's hazel eyes appeared to darken a shade. "It's rather unfair of Nora, though, to even think such a thing. The Derringtons themselves came from old missionary stock. They walked away from the pulpit to raise sugar cane and got rich doing it, but the early Derringtons started out just like Rebecca. She was special." Her face softened. "She was always a more committed Christian than I. She was very dear to me and kind."

Kind seemed an odd way for Lana to speak of her older sister. In the lull that followed, Eden frowned. "Doesn't it appear odd to you that Rebecca went out in a boat with a storm coming in?"

Lana's mood became subdued again. "Ambrose wrote me after I came to San Francisco that she died in a storm. The boat capsized and—my sister drowned. I don't know any more about it than you do."

Wasn't Lana ever curious? Hadn't she ever bothered to write the family and ask questions?

"I'd rather not think about her death," Lana was saying. "I'm inclined to think whoever left that note for you must have carried some grudge or jealousy against the Derrington family. Maybe to use you for gain. Perhaps to intimidate your grandfather." Her eyes pleaded across the table. "If you let the past alone, Eden, you'll be happier. We know Rebecca is safe with the Lord. That's all that matters."

That was the same advice Ambrose had given her: Leave the past buried. Eden didn't want to leave it buried until she was fully satisfied that she had the facts concerning the tragedy that cut short her mother's life.

"There was someone else with my mother in the boat when she

drowned. Ambrose thought it might be another schoolteacher, though no one seems to know anything about her or what may have happened to her."

"He must have been mistaken." Lana looked at her watch, then murmured something about getting to her class and left the table.

Eden sat at the table a minute longer, thinking. If Ambrose was right and someone else had been with Rebecca, there seemed no way to find out who it could have been. She had already written to the New England mission board about her mother shortly after arriving in San Francisco. She had been told by the board a few weeks later that Rebecca Stanhope had been a model missionary teacher. Her love for the Hawaiians, for her students, and for God had been exemplary. However, they had no information to give her about a colleague from the board who may have worked with her at the school.

Her father might be the only one able to answer her questions, but it wasn't likely he was coming home anytime soon. Often she would look at the small photograph of her parents and wonder, *Who are you, really?*

ELEVEN

With Lana's heavy schedule, she had asked Eden to take her afternoon freshman class of church history on missions. Since the San Francisco newspapers were all writing about the arrival of the Hawaiian King David Kalakaua, who was staying at the Palace Hotel with his entourage, Eden was teaching a subject dear to her heart, dealing with the pioneer missionary movement to the Hawaiian Islands. She had assigned reading homework for all her first-year students and used the hour-long class each afternoon to discuss what they had read. As the week ended, she led a final discussion, asking the girls simple questions.

Eden folded her arms as she leaned against Lana's desk and faced the small class of eight girls.

"With Hawaii so much in the newspapers and King Kalakaua visiting our city, we've studied about the early Polynesians and the primitive history of the islands, as well as the arrival of the first New England missionaries in the 1820s. Now we'll review some of what we've studied. Margaret? Let's start with you. What can you tell us about the earliest history?"

Margaret, a redhead with sharp hazel eyes behind small spectacles, stood beside her desk. At sixteen she was the youngest of the freshman girls enrolled at Chadwick. "We think the islands became inhabited around A.D. 900. Like the other islands of the South Seas, there was cannibalism and infanticide."

"What was their main religion?"

"Mainly spirit worship and pantheism—earth, sea, and sky. The Englishman Captain James Cook had already discovered the island of Tahiti in the South Pacific and was sailing from there to the west coast of North America when he discovered the cluster of what we call the Hawaiian Islands. During his first visit in 1778, the Hawaiians thought he was a god, but on his second visit the following year there was a quarrel with one of the Hawaiian chiefs, and Captain Cook was killed on the beach before he could get back to his ship."

"Even so," Eden said, "contact continued and trade was established with the Western world. The islands became a stopover for the ships trading in the Far East, and some of the Hawaiian boys began to sail with them. Some youths even found their way to America. What happened to cause an interest in Hawaiian missions?"

Margaret continued. "Hiram Bingham and a group of missionaries sailed from New England for the Sandwich Islands in October 1819."

"Yes, but what prompted them to go to Hawaii?"

"Oh . . . one of the Yale students—"

"Edwin Dwight," Eden said with a smile.

"—found a Polynesian, a Hawaiian, sitting on the front steps of Yale University, crying."

"His name was Obookiah. Why was he crying?"

"He was frustrated because he and the Hawaiians couldn't read or write. Edwin Dwight tutored him and also explained the Gospel of Christ."

"Obookiah professed faith in Jesus," Eden said, "and Edwin had hoped that the Hawaiian would return to his people and teach them Christianity, but God permitted something else to happen. What?"

There was a moment of silence, then Margaret spoke up again. "Obookiah became ill and died during the winter of 1818, and his tragic death reached the hearts of the Yale students more than his life. Scores of New Englanders felt called of God to take the knowledge of Christ to the Hawaiian Islands."

Eden nodded.

"It was the American Board that decided to send the first missionaries," Margaret went on. "Within a year of Obookiah's death, the board had Christians ready to sail to establish schools and Christian churches."

"How many brave young couples went?"

"Seven—six of them were married just a few weeks before sailing."

"Then what happened?" Eden asked, walking about the room. She glanced out the window onto the green. The fog was drifting in.

"Hiram Bingham was a graduate of Andover Seminary and he became the leader of the group. He married Sybil two weeks after he met her, and two weeks later they sailed for Hawaii."

Eden walked to the large map showing the coastline of California, Oregon, and Washington. "Captain James Cook had called the chain of islands the 'Sandwich Islands' because the Earl of Sandwich had financed Cook's voyage when he discovered them." She pointed to the map. "It's not that far at all. The voyage can be made in less than two weeks, but what of the first missionaries?"

"They sailed from New England, so it took them five months," Margaret said. "They landed and were met by friendly natives—*too* friendly, if you ask me. Weren't they mostly naked?"

Eden did not answer but walked back to the window facing the front lawn of the Chadwick mansion. Margaret continued, growing more meticulous as she proceeded.

"There was opposition from merchant traders and sailors aboard the whaling boats from other countries. Members of the *Dolphin*, a Boston ship, became angry that the prudish New England missionaries were teaching the Hawaiian girls not to swim out to the boats and—"

"Prudish?" Eden interrupted with an arched brow.

Margaret shrugged. "Well, you know what I mean. The first missionaries were rather prudish."

Eden had heard this before and it vexed her. It seemed so unfair to judge servants of God that were far more dedicated than she.

"I don't think they were prudish," Eden stated. "I think they were dedicated to the Great Commission and to the Hawaiians."

"Well, they've been criticized."

"Yes, and consider the source," Eden protested. "The criticism they've received usually comes from individuals who have no interest in world missions. The missionaries accomplished a great work for God in the islands. They established schools and churches, and created a Hawaiian alphabet! The kings and queens of Hawaii were educated by the missionaries, and they're able to read and write their language because of them. We can't blame the missionaries for being shocked by what they first saw, can we?"

Several others applauded and Eden flushed. She wouldn't make a good teacher, she thought. Teachers were to lead calmly and not to argue emotionally. She was too involved in the missionary past of Hawaii to remain detached. *I'd better stay with a nursing career*, she thought.

Margaret shrugged. "I suppose you're right . . . we must allow for their attitude since they came from stuffy New England."

"Despite their 'stuffiness,' as you call it—were they faithful enough to stay and serve Jesus Christ amid great temptation and hardship?" Eden asked quietly.

There was a moment of respectful silence. Margaret's blush receded and her eyes grew grave. "Yes. The Hawaiian girls put on muumuus. Before, they used to go aboard the whaling ships to entertain the drunken sailors. When the missionaries taught them the Bible, they stopped going because they knew God's Holy Spirit lived in their hearts. Their bodies belonged to God."

"As do ours. I suppose the whalers became angry when they were denied their debauchery?"

"Some of the whalers became so angry with the missionaries that they came ashore and attacked their houses, including Hiram Bingham's. They tried to burn down the Christian churches and schools. But Mr. Bingham and the others pressed on valiantly and hundreds more of the Hawaiians became Christians. Eventually schools and churches were overflowing, and even more were built across the islands."

"Thank you, Margaret. You may be seated." Eden turned to a dark-haired girl. "Kathleen, when was the king's mother baptized?"

"1823," Kathleen said briskly, standing by her desk.

"Yes, that's right. Can you tell us about Queen Kapiolani? We studied about her last week."

"Yes," Kathleen answered. "The Hawaiians lived in fear of the goddess Pele, who supposedly lived in the volcano crater."

"Kilauea crater," Eden added. "And also in Mauna Loa."

"After Kapiolani became a Christian, she climbed the crater, something no one ever dared to do because they were afraid of Pele. But she climbed there and declared to all her people that Jehovah is the one true God. Because no hurt came to her and Pele couldn't harm her, many more turned to Jesus."

Kathleen sat down again, and Eden glanced out the window at the foggy bay, but in her mind she saw the tropics, the palm trees, white beaches, and blue water. She went on to review the history. "By 1830, after only ten years, a second group of missionaries arrived from America, and they spread out to the other islands. Some were faithful to their divine calling, while others . . ." She hesitated, for her great-grandfather Ezra Derrington, who had married Amabel from Vicksburg, Mississippi, marched across her mind. ". . . others became wholeheartedly involved in business enterprises."

"Like the Derrington sugar plantations?" one of the girls asked innocently.

"Yes, and the Hollings and Easton plantations," Eden said, showing no embarrassment.

The girls grew silent, and Eden went on with her lecture, walking slowly about the room. "The A.B.C.F.M.—" She stopped. "Who can tell me what that stands for?"

"American Board of Christian Foreign Missions" came the dull echo from the class.

She stopped before the bay window, noticing the dark silhouette of a coach in the cobbled drive below. Thinking a parent was coming to collect a daughter for the weekend, Eden quickly turned from the window to summarize her Friday lesson.

"Some of those sent out wanted to be free of the board, and when the 1837 economic panic hit America, it appeared as though God was giving them their heart's desire. There were sixty missionaries on the islands by that year and the mission board could no longer support them all. The financial 'panic,' as it was called, allowed many to go into planting. Even so, all was not lost. By 1840 the missionaries could look back upon the great success of establishing the Christian church in Hawaii. And now it's left for us to carry on that work. Our obligation is no less. Perhaps it is even greater, since our blessings from God overflow."

The young ladies looked at her gravely. "That will be all for today," Eden said. "Next year Miss Stanhope will discuss the great revival that broke out on the islands, led by Titus Cohen." *But will I still be here?* she wondered.

She smiled. "Have a blessed weekend. Merry Christmas!"

"Merry Christmas!"

The students closed their notebooks and turned happily to each other. The college was closing down until after the New Year of 1891.

Next year in Kea Lani, Eden thought, and considering Lana's disappointment in seeing her leave San Francisco, she encouraged herself with thoughts of the Lord's sovereignty. Who was in control of their circumstances and future? A sense of peace filled her heart as the answer became clear.

The classroom door opened and Lana entered. Eden could see she wished to speak with her.

Lana walked up to Eden and glanced out the window. "It's Zachary," she announced in a low, taut voice. "He's come early. He's sent up a message asking to speak with you. He wasn't supposed to come until tomorrow."

Margaret and Kathleen walked to the window and peered below into the front court. "Look at his coach."

"I'd rather look at *him*," Kathleen said in a low voice.

"Kathleen, your mother is waiting downstairs," Lana said, trying to urge the remaining girls to leave the classroom.

Eden gathered her teaching materials from the desk. She locked the top drawer and handed Lana the key. "Don't worry about Zachary," Eden said quietly.

Lana's expression was tense, but she made no further comment.

A few minutes later Eden made her way to her room, where she freshened herself, changed into an appropriate dress, then went downstairs and out the front door to meet Zachary.

TWELVE

Eden's light mood sobered once she entered the chilly afternoon air. Hesitantly she walked toward the waiting coach parked beside a tall hedge. The bare branches of a maple stretched like thin, dark fingers into gray fog, and the wintry cold stung her cheeks. She paused, straightening her fur hat with jade green satin trim, her narrowing gaze locked on the coach door.

Zachary must have wearied of standing and had climbed back inside to wait for her. His attention remained focused on a newspaper.

The coachman noticed her first and climbed down from the driver's seat to assist her, while Zachary stirred, turning his fair head toward her. He swung the door open and stepped to the pavement.

Zachary had taken on a striking resemblance to Townsend with a cleft in his chin and burnished blond hair that waved across his tan forehead. He smiled and took her hand between his, his polished manners the pinnacle of gentlemanly graces. There was, however, no mistaking his restrained presumptuousness, and she remembered quite well that he was capable of extreme emotional change—from icy grimness to outbursts of laughter or temper. She found that she was no less wary of Zachary than she had been two years ago.

"Well, Eden! Congratulations on meeting your goals. You're an astounding woman. The family is proud of you. I see my concerns for you were all in vain."

Eden covered a wry smile. "Hello, Cousin Zachary," she greeted, withdrawing her hand when he continued to hold it. "You wondered whether I was surviving my nursing classes? So your correspondence convinced me," she said with a laugh.

"Ah, but I wrote you," he insisted. "No point telling you how disappointed I was when you refused to answer."

She arched a brow. "Refused?"

"Even in my travels for Grandfather, I thought about you and wondered how you were faring here at Chadwick. Naturally by now I had hoped that you'd pardon my youthful indiscretion on the road that day."

That he claimed to have written to her came as a curiosity to Eden. "I didn't receive your correspondences. Are you sure you mailed them?"

"My dear, you underestimate me."

"I'd never do that."

"*She* must have destroyed my letters."

She. Meaning Lana, of course.

"I wrote you an apology confessing I lied to my father that day. I'm ashamed to admit it. Very immature of me. I later retracted that tale, so your reputation with my father remains untarnished. Rafe was actually keeping company with some island girl." He smiled, and there was a slight bitterness to it. Was it toward Rafe or the girl? Eden refused to entertain thoughts about Rafe. *Two years. Not one letter.*

"So then, you didn't get my correspondence?" Zachary was saying. "Well that accounts for your silence. I feel a trifle consoled."

She watched him, surprised he would even admit he had been untruthful. She hoped the change in him was deep and genuine.

"I'm sorry you didn't get the letter telling you I'd made amends." He shoved his hands into the pockets of his tweed jacket and looked up thoughtfully toward the mansion.

Eden followed his gaze to an upper window where a curtain moved. Would Lana have disposed of those letters? Eden didn't care to antagonize Zachary by telling him her aunt had burned his most recent letter. There was already enough tension between them. If Lana didn't trust Zachary, his feelings toward her were also apparent.

"I'm sorry Miss Stanhope refuses to see me." He sounded perturbed. "What's it about? Do you know?"

It was difficult to judge whether or not his portrayal of hurt was genuine. Eden glanced toward the mansion again. "I don't know what she is troubled about. I was counting on you to tell me. There seems some reason why she wishes to avoid seeing you."

Eden cast him a glance, but getting beyond his murky facade was indeed a challenge.

"Strange," Zachary agreed. "I've never met her. Oh, I should take that back. I did meet her when I was a boy. I used to see her now and then at the school where Rebecca taught. She gave no reason for avoiding me?"

This was the first Eden had heard about Lana visiting the Royal School. She must ask her about it. Eden was under the impression Lana had never visited Oahu or Kea Lani.

"No, except that she felt she didn't want you meddling at this late date."

His blond brows twitched. "Meddling, you say? A bit like a cat with ruffled fur, isn't she?"

"Lana wouldn't explain, but she did mention my mother's death." She watched his response, noting that his pale blue eyes dusted with golden lashes became distant.

"Did she? Odd . . . I wonder why."

"I've no idea. I thought you'd be able to clarify things for me."

"Me?" he scoffed. "Why should I understand her paranoia?"

"It was your letter that upset her. Did you mention my mother? Aunt Lana seems to avoid discussing her sister's death."

"What reason would I have to bring up your mother now?"

"That's what I'd like to know."

He shrugged his heavy shoulders and looked bored. He took out a pipe and bit on the end but didn't light it. "Odd woman, it seems."

"I don't think my aunt is odd at all. She doesn't like to talk about my mother's death because they were close. Now that her sister's gone, Lana has no family."

"She has you. And I suspect she doesn't want to see me because she feels I'm taking you away."

"Her behavior is understandable, and I wish she'd return to Hawaii with me."

"She'll never do that unless she's forced to."

Eden thought his remark strange. She scanned him, but he frowned thoughtfully. "She wishes to hold on to you as long as she can. Is Miss Stanhope possessive of you?"

"Possessive? Aunt Lana? Hardly. She's more like a sister really."

"My letter explaining that Great-aunt Nora wants you back at Kea Lani must have upset her. She feels intimidated by Nora's wealth perhaps."

"Lana isn't the sort to be intimated by Derrington wealth," Eden said, unconvinced.

"Maybe not intimidated—but afraid of losing you, just the same."

His thoughtful tone caused her to look at him. He appeared interested in the mansion and gestured toward the pond as they strolled toward it. Zachary continued.

"As I suggested, Miss Stanhope may be afraid of losing you to the Derringtons. She wishes to keep you in San Francisco."

"Even so, she expects me to return to the islands one day. She knows about Kalihi Hospital and Jerome's work there and why I wish to be involved."

"I should say."

"What do you mean by that?"

Tendrils of fog drifted in from the bay, and she drew her elbow-length capelet about her, tightly holding her silk umbrella with its stylish long handle.

Zachary was gazing up toward the dormer windows. "Nothing really." He paused, tapping the pipe stem on his teeth. "Come to think of it, I may have mentioned Rebecca in my letter. I told Miss Stanhope that Nora has come to terms with her conscience about opposing Jerome's marriage to Rebecca. So much so, she's considering you as her main heir instead of Rozlind."

Eden hardly heard him. She had turned her head in time to see Lana looking down at them from the window before letting the curtain drop into place. The look on her face had not been one of fear but of anger.

"Nora credits your research on Hawaii with enabling her to complete her manuscript on time," he said. "She's here for lectures and an author tour, supporting the monarchy."

"Yes, I read about it in the *Examiner*."

"There's more today. Have a look." He took the paper from under his arm and opened to where he'd been reading.

Nora Derrington to lecture from her current book, *The Spoils of Eden*, in the Crown Room at the Palace Hotel, Monday at 7:30 P.M.

The announcement of Nora's author tour in the United States, beginning in San Francisco and culminating in Washington, D.C., was underlined in black ink. Other paragraphs of the article reporting that the elder Miss Derrington was in direct opposition to her brother, Ainsworth Derrington, the sugar magnate, were also circled.

"I'm pleased her work is finally out. Her illness set her back," Eden said, satisfied to think Great-aunt Nora had considered her support important.

"Nora just might leave you her share of Kea Lani," he said with a gleam of speculation in his voice. "If she does, you'll be a very rich woman one day soon. You won't need to act like Florence Nightingale."

Eden's mood dampened quickly. Is that all he thought of her rigorous studies to gain her nursing degree?

"Look, Zachary, I hope you're not implying my loyalty to Aunt Nora these recent years was conditioned by a scheme to become her heir."

He smiled, the cleft in his chin deepening. "Come, Eden, of course not. If I were to suggest such a thing, I'd be pointing a finger at myself, wouldn't I? I'm an avid annexationist because pleasing Grandfather means he'll turn the reins of the Derrington enterprise over to me when he retires."

She didn't like the sound of it. "I hope there's more genuine conviction in our lives than deciding what we believe based upon how it affects our inheritance. I happen to feel strongly about my medical pursuits— and the Hawaiian monarchy."

"How strongly do you want me to believe in annexation? Enough to fight in a revolution? Well, it may come to that."

"I pray it won't," she said, remembering how he had been willing to store up rifles and ammunition. "Speaking of revolution seems rather too glib, considering that people will lose their lives, some for all eternity."

His smile faded. "They all want a revolution, Eden, and Grandfather is in the forefront. There's no stopping it. We might as well get used to the fact that it will come. Kalakaua is an ill man, and his sister is bound to reign after him. Once that happens—it's only a matter of time." He smiled suddenly, boldly. "I'm sorry. Let's not get into that. Whatever happens needn't come between family. Though Great-aunt Nora is threatening to move out of Kea Lani if it does." His gaze became earnest. "The sooner you come back to Kea Lani, the happier we'll all be."

All? she wondered. She tried not to read anything personal into his words.

They had walked across the wide lawn and were standing by the pond. The white-and-red goldfish moved about the water.

Zachary struck a match and lit his pipe. "Nora's been telling everyone she couldn't have written that book without you."

"She could have, had she not gotten ill this past year. I enjoyed doing the historical research."

"Unfortunately, it's come out at the wrong time as far as Grandfather's concerned. He won't be pleased you assisted her. The content has him riled."

"That's not what he told the reporters. He said he hadn't even read it."

"Naturally he'd say that. He's mad at Nora for coming up with reasons to continue the monarchy."

Some of those ideas had come from Eden's research while here in San Francisco.

"I haven't read the completed book yet," she admitted.

"Don't worry, you will. Nora will see you have a copy when you meet her. She wants to see you at dinner tomorrow night after her lecture at the Palace Hotel. She also invited Miss Stanhope."

"Then Nora asked you to write to Lana?"

"As well as arrange for your return to Kea Lani. And Grandfather wants to see you too. He'll be in touch."

"Are you traveling with Nora on her lecture tour?" Eden asked curiously.

"Heavens no. She considers me a 'roustabout in town.' She wouldn't have sent me to arrange your meeting here tomorrow night if there'd been anyone else. No, I'm with Grandfather. He's on his way to meet with friends in Congress about annexation. I suppose you read about it in the paper." He looked at her. "It's Rafe who is Nora's man."

Although Eden was curious about Rafe's whereabouts, she knew better than to be the one to bring him up to Zachary. From the way he watched her she could see that time had not mended the distrust between the two stepbrothers.

"I see you haven't heard," he admitted. "I'm amazed he hasn't kept in touch with you."

"I haven't heard from Rafe since I left Oahu," Eden said, her voice expressionless.

"Neither has anyone else until recently. I hear he's been coming and going on the island for the last year. Ambrose is the only one who sees him. Keno and Rafe have some sort of a merchant shipping business. Wouldn't surprise me if they were involved in opium with that notorious Captain Whaley down on the wharf."

Eden didn't know who Whaley was, but she didn't like Zachary's scornful tone. She was trying to catch any news about Rafe. Ambrose wrote to her every few months about the mission church and of his concerns for keeping it open and accessible to the Hawaiians. It seemed that the Derringtons wanted to sell that section of land, and the church and its flourishing Hawaiian congregation stood in their way. Any reference to Rafe had been absent from his letters. Eden had thought it was because

Ambrose didn't know where Rafe was.

So Keno and Rafe were in a shipping business! As for the opium, she dismissed Zachary's charge at once. When it came to Keno and Rafe Easton, she knew them too well to believe they would stoop to such dark means.

"Except for Celestine and Ambrose, I know for a fact the family would like to see Rafe stay away," Zachary said. "Unfortunately, Celestine is very ill and has been asking for him. The last I heard before leaving Honolulu, Ambrose was trying to contact Rafe."

Celestine seriously ill? Eden was burdened thinking about it. What could be wrong with Rafe's mother? Eden's worries were averted when Zachary suddenly shifted the topic. He reached into his tweed jacket and removed a small package, then put it into her hand.

"For you, Eden. An early welcome-home-to-Hawaii present. I'm sure that's what Nora is planning to discuss with you tomorrow night. That, and the position you want at Kalihi Hospital. And now"—he removed his pocket watch and glanced at the time—"I've got to hurry. I'm to meet Grandfather for a press conference." His eyes flickered with subdued excitement. "Like Celestine, Kalakaua's health is on the decline. Princess Liliuokalani may soon become queen."

Eden wondered that Zachary didn't appear saddened by the prospect until she understood it wasn't the king's life he was concerned about but what would happen when the king's sister took over the Hawaiian throne. Nor did Zachary seem especially concerned for his own stepmother, Celestine.

Eden, however, was more anxious than ever to see Great-aunt Nora. If anyone in the family understood what was happening in Hawaii, it was her great-aunt.

A restive spirit settled over Eden's heart as she watched Zachary walk back to the coach and climb inside. A moment later the horses trotted down the carriageway into the foggy afternoon. Eden realized she would likely meet Rafe again when she returned to Kea Lani, now that Celestine had requested to see him. She was not certain how she felt about that idea. She tenaciously refused to let her heart dwell on Rafe Easton.

CHAPTER

THIRTEEN

"I wish you wouldn't go, but if you must, you should go in style," Aunt Lana told Eden. "Miss Nora will expect you to conduct yourself as a Derrington in public, even if she hasn't sanctioned you as her niece before the San Francisco elite." And to Eden's pleasant surprise, Lana left her room and returned carrying a stylish short fur capelet.

Lana stopped in the doorway as Eden turned toward her wearing a Nile green satin sheath with a sheer overlay of black lace. The green of her gown flattered her unique eye color. She wore her dark hair in fashion, high on her head, and around her neck hung a string of rare black pearls— the gift Zachary had brought to her.

Eden arranged the pearls and turned her head, gauging their effect. Strangely, though the pearls captured her attention at once, they also brought Rafe to mind. . . .

For a moment, her eyes swerved to the scar on her temple. Would Zachary notice it tonight and mention that mysterious night at Kea Lani?

A slight intake of breath from Lana caused Eden to turn with a smile, thinking her response would be much as her own. "Aren't they beautiful, Lana?"

But the ashen tone of Lana's skin caused Eden to rush to ease her into the small chair by the door.

"What is it? Are you ill?"

Lana closed her eyes and tried to steady herself by breathing in deeply. "That strand of pearls," she choked, tears spilling down her cheeks.

Eden touched the smooth, cool spheres. She suspected Zachary of some cruel device, but why would he give her something to hurt Lana like this? She hurried down the hall for a glass of water, and when she returned, Lana had walked over to the vanity table to the package that had contained the necklace. She had the package in hand and was turning it over as if looking for an address or a written message. Eden stood quietly watching her, holding the glass of water.

"Aunt Lana?"

Lana's back stiffened. "I'm all right." Her voice was strong as she turned, her tearful eyes rushing to the pearls, a flush of hot pink warming her face. "Where did Zachary find them?"

Feeling as though she'd been used for a heartless trick, Eden sank to the edge of the bed, the joy of wearing them to the Palace Hotel ebbing. "I don't know," she admitted dully. "There was no message inside. He gave me the package before he left yesterday. He said they were an early welcome-home gift. I thought them exquisite," she confessed. "They obviously aren't to you. I'm sorry. I wouldn't have worn them if I'd known. Would you mind telling me what they mean?"

The paleness around Lana's mouth slowly faded. "Naturally you didn't know; you mustn't blame yourself. There's nothing wrong with the strand itself . . . they're lovely."

Eden made up her mind quickly. What good were the precious black pearls if they had a sickening effect on Lana? She walked briskly to her vanity and began to unclasp them.

Lana looked sheepish. "Oh no, Eden dear, there's no need to remove them."

Eden sighed and turned to her. "Lana, why are you behaving like this? It's not like you. What's wrong with them? They must have belonged to the Derrington family. It's not like I'm accepting a personal gift from Zachary, and it doesn't obligate me to him in any way."

Lana closed her eyes again and shook her head. "It's not that. They were Rebecca's." She covered her face with both palms as if to get ahold of her feelings. It was the first time Eden had ever seen her aunt break down, and her own heart felt squeezed with pain. Eden's trembling fingers removed the strand. This time she looked at them with her heart instead of her senses. At last—something precious that belonged to her mother.

"She wore them the last night I saw her alive. She . . . she gave them to me. She asked me to return them to Jerome with . . . with all her love. 'Tell him I'll never stop loving him. Tell him I'll hold him in my heart forever.' Those were her last words to me."

Deeply moved, Eden considered the pearls.

"She wore them at the wedding luau on Kea Lani," Lana continued. "She was so proud of them. They were the first beautiful piece of jewelry she'd owned. They first belonged to Jerome's grandmother Amabel."

"Oh, then how precious!" Eden whispered, pained and delighted at the same moment. It didn't matter what Zachary's motives may have been. The black pearls were her mother's, given to her father—

She looked at Lana quickly, searchingly. "If she gave them to you to return to my father, how is it Zachary had them?"

Lana swallowed and shook her head. "I don't know. Jerome must have left them in his room at Kea Lani, with wedding photographs, letters, things like that." She took out a handkerchief from her pocket and wiped her eyes.

Eden caressed the pearls. To own something so personal and beautiful that once belonged to her mother was endearing. But after a moment of silence, Eden became more aware of the tension emanating from Lana. A glance in her direction when Lana didn't think she was being watched chilled Eden's heart. There was animosity in her eyes, but whether it was directed toward Zachary or the pearls, she couldn't tell.

"There's something you're not telling me," Eden insisted gravely.

"It was seeing the pearls again after all these years and . . . remembering. It all came back—the loss, the disappointment."

"Disappointment?" Her gaze followed Lana across the room to the white wicker chair with a blue satin cushion. Lana picked up the fur capelet and sat down with it as though she were exhausted. Her fingers mechanically stroked it like some kitten on her lap. "Seeing the necklace on you was a shock." She smiled stiffly. "You look lovely, Eden. Enjoy yourself tonight. Rebecca would want you to. She would be pleased if she knew you had the pearls."

Eden wasn't satisfied. There was something more. "Was it a wedding present?"

Lana blinked. "She wouldn't have worn it at her wedding otherwise. I may be wrong—but I think there's a portrait of Rebecca wearing the pearls."

Eden grew excited. "You mean an actual painting?"

"There are several novice artists in the Derrington family. Your great-aunt is one of them. She used to love to paint Hawaiian sunsets. And she did Princess Liliuokalani when she was a girl at the Hawaiian Royal School. Rebecca arranged the sitting. I think she said Nora had a small studio above her room. I don't know if she's kept her paintings all these years or not. You might ask her about it tonight if you get the chance. She may have turned the studio into an office since she's now writing about Hawaii."

Eden watched her. "How is it you know all this, Aunt Lana? I thought you said you never actually visited Kea Lani."

Lana's fingers ran along the fur. "I haven't shared everything with you about my past. I suppose I can't keep it from you any longer." She looked up, her hazel eyes meeting Eden's with a level gaze. "If I don't tell you, Zachary probably will."

Why would Zachary want to tell her something about Lana's past? Eden's heart beat faster. She walked slowly toward her. "You don't need to tell me unless you really want to."

Lana blinked hard and lowered her eyes. "I did live on Oahu. I joined Rebecca as a missionary nurse" came her quiet confession. "I arrived six months after she began teaching at the Chief's Children School. Jerome arranged for me to serve at Kalihi Hospital in Honolulu. He was good friends with . . ." She hesitated and said quietly, "Dr. Clifford Bolton. I didn't tell the truth when I told you I worked on Tahiti."

"Aunt Lana . . ."

"I went with Cliff—Dr. Bolton—to the leper colony on Molokai, doing research for the king. The outbreak was raging at the time and something had to be done for the lepers."

Eden went to her, a tender smile on her lips, and knelt beside the wicker chair, taking Lana's cold hand into her own. "But why hide it? I'm so proud of you!" Her eyes searched her aunt's. "I don't understand. You know I feel God's calling to do the same. Why—you could introduce me to Dr. Bolton—"

Lana pulled her hand away and stood, walking quickly to the mirror. Taking her handkerchief out, she blew her nose. "No, no, I can't do that. I can't ever see him again. I let him down—I ran away from the work." She pulled at a strand of honey hair, nervously poking it into her chignon. "I couldn't take looking at the disease anymore—it's horrible, Eden. What I did wasn't wonderful, even if I did show mercy in God's name. I began to dream about faces without ears and noses—" Her voice grew stiff. "And neither was I loyal to God or the medical mission staff. I . . . wasn't dedicated like Rebecca. I began to hate the lepers. I was the younger sister, and she was stronger . . . and she loved. I stopped loving. I stopped caring. I couldn't take the horrors I saw there. And then the worst happened—I broke, I cowardly turned and ran away!" She straightened her shoulders and smoothed her hair again, then looked at Eden with forced dignity. "I'm ashamed to tell you. But that's what happened. I came here to San Francisco and got a job at Chadwick."

Eden was very still, her heart aching for Lana. She wanted to comfort her, but she didn't think her aunt would accept it. "I don't see any shame in coming back to San Francisco," Eden said firmly and stood. "What happened is between you and the Lord. No one else has a right to question your decision to come home. I don't see that it should matter to Zachary."

"He'll use anything to get what he wants."

"What does he want?"

"You . . . to return to Kea Lani."

Eden decided not to tell her that she did in fact want to return; Lana was too upset. She changed the subject. "Look, you've done wonders teaching here at Chadwick. And the class you're starting on church history honors what God has done throughout the centuries. I know it's going to have a lasting effect on the students. They're especially interested in the first missionaries who went to Hawaii. You mustn't be so hard on yourself, Lana. You need to look in the mirror and forgive yourself for being human."

Lana smiled wryly. "Thank you, but I really don't care to take a long look. I think I shall always be hard on myself." She sighed. "I wish I had been harder on myself when I was in Hawaii. Dr. Bolton tried to help me. He was patient and understanding, but . . . well . . ." She sighed and threw up a hand. "That wasn't what I wanted from him."

Eden's eyes rushed to Lana's. "Oh."

Lana smiled, then flushed. "Yes . . . I fell for him. He was so dedicated—and handsome too. I think most of the girls were infatuated. I never told him why I ran away. Any number of times I sat down to write and explain, but I couldn't. And now . . . well, it's too late; it's all over."

Eden walked toward her hopefully. "Maybe not."

They looked at each other. Eden smiled. "We're all prodigals, each in our own way. And each of us can have our own particular homecoming. And I'm hopeful enough to believe the Lord wants us to try. I want to work at Kalihi Hospital, Aunt Lana. Great-aunt Nora could arrange it if she wished. And if you wanted, I know you could go back too. We both could."

Lana shook her head. "I don't know. I'll need to think and pray about it. I feel almost embarrassed going to God now and telling Him I'd like to go back. It's been so long since I quit the work. Nothing is ever the same. The tide of history washes away everything."

"Not everything. Faith, hope, and love endure. The greatest of these is love. And God's love lasts forever."

Lana smiled tenderly. "Yes, but one can't always go back to begin the race over again."

"No, but you can begin again right where you are now. And isn't it true that all any of us have is today? You're a nurse, whether teaching at Chadwick or serving at Kalihi. So you might as well serve wherever God places you. If you went back, Lana, you could get past that hurdle in your life that you've marked with bold, black letters of failure."

Lana mused, almost wistfully, then drew in a breath. She looked at her gold pendant watch. "You've little over an hour to join Nora's lecture at the Palace Hotel. Do take the cape; it looks like rain tonight." She smiled. "There's so much of Rebecca in you—and Jerome. We'll talk about it again."

Eden's troubled gaze followed her aunt out the door. Eden wanted to continue discussing Hawaii, but she could see Lana didn't. So this was the secret she had wanted to keep from her, that she feared Zachary would tell. It didn't seem so dreadful to Eden. Lana ought to feel pleased that she had cared enough about the Polynesians to voyage to Hawaii at all. And her work on the leper colony at Molokai was indeed something that was praiseworthy, even if she hadn't stayed through the years.

It wasn't until after Lana had left the bedroom and Eden picked up the capelet and put it around her shoulders that she looked in the mirror and carefully clasped the black pearls back into place. She must find out from Zachary how he'd gotten them. For Lana, the pearls rekindled sad memories. Eden saw them differently. They shone with the hope of reconciliation. Now, perhaps, reconciliation for more than just herself—for Lana too.

FOURTEEN

It came as a pleasant surprise when Eden received a message at five o'clock from her grandfather informing her that he would come by Chadwick to pick her up and take her to the Palace Hotel. Eden was to first have dinner with Great-aunt Nora, who wished to talk with her alone, and then the two of them would attend a reception for King Kalakaua given by his American supporters. Her grandfather was expected to be there, as were many other international officials and ambassadors who held posts in San Francisco. All in all, Eden was looking forward to an exciting evening.

She had learned soon after arriving at Chadwick that her grandfather, previously a charter member of the Hawaiian League and the short-lived "Hawaiian Rifles," was now a member in good standing with the new Reform Party, made up of conservative haole planters and business owners, many of them with ties to the early missionaries.

The Reformers blamed the '87 "Bloodless Revolution," as it was now called, on King Kalakaua's stubbornness in dealing with the grievances of the haole planters and other conservatives on the islands. David Kalakaua, described by his critics as a flamboyant monarch who wished to imitate the world powers of Europe, had been accused of putting Hawaii into great debt. His grand schemes and sometimes unwise policies were attributed by Ainsworth Derrington and other Reformers to his "Premier of Everything"—Walter Murray Gibson.

Gibson was a Mormon who had made himself strong by supporting the causes of the Hawaiian natives and winning their allegiance. After the

Mormon Church in Utah had called home their elders from Hawaii during the Civil War, Gibson had deceived the natives and taken complete possession of their land on the island of Lanai. From there he had moved up into politics, becoming a friend of Kalakaua, who trusted him despite Gibson's many critics. Gibson's son had been the only other haole in the king's legislature before the '87 Revolution.

The Reformers, mostly descendants of the early missionaries, had disliked Gibson and his hold on the king, who Ainsworth said was "open to flattery and easily deceived."

Men like Eden's grandfather had long demanded a new constitution limiting the rights of the monarchy, and it had been Gibson's and Kalakaua's scandals that had given them the opportunity. When Gibson was accused of leasing out rights to sell opium and taking bribes, the haole reformers in the Hawaiian League had found their trigger to spark the revolution, and "Old Gibby," as Walter Murray Gibson was called, had been the first member of the cabinet they insisted Kalakaua dismiss.

Ainsworth had been elected to the new legislature in a special September election in 1888, as had the respected conservative haoles like Lorrin Thurston and Judge Sanford Dole, both of missionary ancestry.

Eden was waiting for her grandfather when he arrived five minutes late. The tall, slender man with silver hair and mustache was the essence of dignity in his black broadcloth suit and derby hat as he stepped down from the coach. Conservative in all he did, he greeted her likewise, taking her hand into his. He planted a grandfatherly kiss on her forehead and his clear blue-gray eyes radiated his approval.

"Well, Eden, my dear, I must say you've turned into a quality young woman. I'm told your conduct here at Chadwick has been a true credit to the Derrington name."

His approval was all she needed to relax and smile the affection that was in her heart. "That you think so, Grandfather, pleases me so much. I've looked forward to your arrival from the moment I saw the article in the *Examiner*."

"Well, I'm glad someone has," he said humorously. "I can't say my presence in the Bay City is being received with much gladness elsewhere."

"King Kalakaua?" she asked with a smile.

His white brows raised. "No, the British."

"The British!" She wondered what bit of humor he alluded to, but his expression told her it wasn't intended as such. Still, Eden smiled as he helped her inside the coach. "I think you can hold your own, Grandfather, even against the British."

He laughed and climbed in beside her. Eden was surprised to find another distinguished older gentleman sitting across from her on the leather seat. She had expected the ride to the Palace Hotel to give her some precious time alone with her busy grandfather, but the other man's presence spoiled that. Nevertheless, Eden concealed her disappointment and smiled a greeting at the gentleman her grandfather introduced as Parker Judson.

"We met at Kea Lani," Judson told her. "If I recall, you and I were the only ones siding with Nora in a debate on annexation."

Eden remembered Judson's name from among her grandfather's associates but could not recall the particular night he mentioned. She did know that Judson was considered one of the most influential planters in Oahu. His presence here tonight indicated he was now in favor of annexation. What had changed his mind?

"Sugar controversy, young lady," he told her gravely, as if having read her mind. He took out a Cuban cigar to chomp on without lighting it. "You know the price lately of a ton of pure Hawaiian sugar?"

"No," she said. "I don't."

"It's dropped from a hundred dollars a ton to sixty—a debacle brought on by Kalakaua's refusal to sign the sugar treaty Minister Carter negotiated with Blaine, the United States secretary of state. Ainsworth's been right about annexation all along. We should have removed Kalakaua in '87 and saved ourselves a bunch of trouble. Until we become a territory of the United States, we'll always be left to the whims of an immature and sullen royalty."

Eden, uncomfortable with his words, said nothing and looked from Parker Judson to her grandfather. He, too, appeared distressed, but also satisfied in thinking he'd been right about annexation all along. Most planters had previously sided against it.

"The plantations will go out of existence by the end of the next harvest, young lady," Judson continued, "and I'll be one of them. Unless a radical change takes place soon, more plantations will collapse during the next year with a loss of many millions of dollars. Continuation under existing conditions is impossible. Any change in the Hawaiian government is preferable to what we've endured under Kalakaua."

Eden wasn't sure she agreed, but now did not seem the time to make her views on Hawaiian independence known. Her grandfather went on to say that Parker Judson had voyaged with him from Honolulu to help convince Congress of the need for action on Hawaiian sugar. The meeting between him and Judson tonight was hastily arranged, which explained his presence in the coach. Judson had gotten in touch with Ainsworth only minutes before he left the hotel to escort her to Kalakaua's reception, informing him that they needed to discuss the "sugar matter" again before meeting with Kalakaua that evening.

Hawaii's previous treaty with the U.S. had allowed Hawaiian raw sugar the privilege of entering the United States duty free, but ominous changes had occurred on the American political scene. Benjamin Harrison had just been elected President, and in April of that year he had signed into law the McKinley Act, allowing *all* foreign sugar to enter the American markets tariff free.

"Hawaii's privileged place is now meaningless, and the planters are plunged into a depression," Ainsworth explained.

"Why wouldn't the king sign the sugar treaty?" Eden asked. "The success of the sugar planters means a successful Hawaii."

Ainsworth smiled. "Now you're talking like an annexationist, Eden. Does this mean your grandfather has won you to his side at last?"

"It all has to do with Pearl Harbor," interjected Judson.

Eden tried to recall what she'd read in the papers about Pearl Harbor.

"The sugar treaty also grants the U.S. Navy exclusive rights to use the Harbor," Ainsworth told her. "Kalakaua refused to sign the treaty, even after President Harrison promised to continue American favored status toward Hawaiian sugar. He guaranteed the kingdom's independence, promising to land troops if necessary.

"It was the landing of foreign troops that Kalakaua found offensive," Ainsworth went on. "He told his cabinet it sounded too much like Hawaii becoming a protectorate of the United States government. I wish that it was."

"Foreign troops!" Parker Judson scoffed, leaning forward on the seat. "American soldiers? Did you and your friends in the legislature explain that American troops won't come ashore without requesting the king's permission?"

"Oh, we explained all right, and he understood perfectly. Thurston told him if he didn't sign the new sugar treaty it would ruin the economy of Hawaii."

Eden knew her grandfather and Parker Judson expected the Hawaiians to feel the same about American troops as they did. She spoke up. "Hawaii is a sovereign nation, don't forget."

"Yes, yes, I understand, young lady, but you and Kalakaua must also understand our dilemma. Unless America buys our sugar, the plantations—including Kea Lani—will go bust. Isn't that right, Ainsworth?

You're in this economic malaise too. There's no question in my mind that without the American market, we won't survive. And if it means an American Navy at Pearl Harbor, so be it. I'd sleep better at night anyway—especially after Wilcox riled the natives and Chinese into marching on Iolani Palace. Demanding their right to vote! I'd welcome the U.S. Marines as well!"

"This isn't the first time Kalakaua has refused to comply with the advice of his ministers," Ainsworth complained. "As a member of the cabinet, my experience has been one of constant frustration and struggle to get him to do his duty."

"Bah! He'll be warned tonight of the history of other past sovereigns who brought disaster upon throne and country. He'd best pay heed."

"He's been warned already," Ainsworth said, lowering his voice. "Thurston warned him at Iolani Palace."

"What was his response?"

"He said simply, 'I am willing. Let it come.'"

"Kalakaua can be stubborn, but the future looks little brighter with Princess Liliuokalani in the wings."

Ainsworth tapped his fingers against his vest. "I've reason to think she'll be even more resistant."

Eden remained silent. She wondered what Great-aunt Nora would have to say about all this. Derrington sugar from Kea Lani must now compete with foreign sugar dumped free on American markets. But at the same time, American growers in Louisiana and elsewhere would be compensated by the government, paying the planters an extra two cents a pound. She could understand her grandfather's dour mood and Parker Judson's sudden willingness to become involved in the politics of Hawaii's future. The new law spelled financial disaster for the haole planters on all the islands. King Kalakaua may have unintentionally forced most of the planters to side with annexation—something that surely would not have happened had he understood what his refusal to sign the new treaty was going to mean for the planters.

"One or two plantations may still be able to survive," Judson was saying. "But most will soon fold up if Hawaiian growers are held to the fire much longer."

"That's why we're meeting with Kalakaua tonight," Ainsworth said. "When the sugar industry of Hawaii is in trouble, the entire kingdom can feel the rumble of Kilauea." He spoke metaphorically of the volcano crater where the Hawaiian idol-god Pele supposedly lived.

More than sugar was about to bust. It had been two years since the start of the Reform legislature in 1888. There were deep rumblings of trouble from the native population, who naturally favored their ruling alii, King Kalakaua.

"They rallied under Wilcox," Ainsworth told her. "He led an armed band of Hawaiians, hapa-haoles, and some Chinese against Iolani Palace, hoping to undo the Revolution of '87. They expected to arrest me, Lorrin Thurston, and Sanford Dole."

"What happened?" Eden asked anxiously. "You weren't actually detained?"

"I would have been. Wilcox was arrested but later released. Now he's formed an opposition party to run against us in the legislature. It's called the *National* Reform Party. Unfortunately, matters don't look good for us at present."

"You mean you think you and the reformers will be voted out of the legislature?" Eden asked incredulously.

"Wilcox is firing up the Hawaiians and other Asiatics, inflaming them with the race issue. He's telling the Chinese and Japanese they have the right to vote along with the Hawaiians. It plays well."

"They're not citizens of Hawaii," grumbled Parker Judson. "They were brought in for one purpose—to work on the plantations. We can't possibly survive in office or in running Hawaii if they band together. We're already outnumbered."

"Wilcox is a hothead," Ainsworth said. "Kalakaua denies it, but some are saying he's giving him gifts to hand out to the natives to vote National."

"Gifts of money and whiskey," Judson murmured. "Maybe opium too."

"Opium," Eden groaned. "He wouldn't."

"Bah," Parker Judson said over his cigar.

"There's no proof of opium peddling," Ainsworth said with a frown. "We need to be careful about heating up the charges. However this matter turns out, we've got to be fair. Look, Parker, ultimately it comes down to annexation. Without it, Hawaii will be lost. We might as well come to grips with it."

"I have, and the others in my corner eventually will too. This sugar situation is wising them up."

"You know what Kalakaua would say," Eden said quietly. "The native Hawaiians want their monarchy. They don't want annexation to the United States."

"I don't believe that's true," Ainsworth said. "A good many of them would vote against it if it were put to them today, especially with Wilcox haranguing them as he does. But fortunately, we don't have to face that vote now. There's time to show them it's the best thing. I'm confident the Hawaiians will eventually be persuaded and vote to be aligned with America. There's a bond between us, Eden. It was instilled in their hearts by the coming of the first-missionaries. Down deep, it's always been aloha."

"If we survive the sugar price depression," Judson complained.

"Kea Lani will never close." Ainsworth's eyes flickered with passion. "If sugar busts, we'll make money in something else. I'm in Hawaii to stay." He looked at Eden and laid a hand on her arm. "I've a hunch you feel the same way, Eden."

An affection she had never felt before drew them together, grandfather and granddaughter.

"I'm anxious to go home, Grandfather," she said, but she couldn't bring herself to admit that her plans at Kalihi Hospital and the mission church near the pearl fishery might not earn his coveted blessing. After tonight in the coach, listening and perhaps understanding a little more for the first time what he and men like Parker Judson felt and believed, she did not have the heart to make a stand against her grandfather's dream of Hawaii's annexation to the United States.

She thought once more of her meeting tonight with Great-aunt Nora. It was Nora who held the key to getting her placed on Dr. Bolton's leprosy research staff at Kalihi Hospital. Even now Nora would be preparing for her lecture at the Palace Hotel on her book *The Spoils of Eden*. Nora, too, would fully expect Eden to side with her against annexation.

It was with growing perplexity that Eden stepped from the coach before the entrance to the Palace Hotel. Above her rose the famous structure, its many bay windows aglow with light from chandeliers.

The doorman ushered Eden and Ainsworth inside with a bow. She felt approving glances stealing her way but pretended she didn't notice as she walked arm in arm with her grandfather into the great court filled with tables, flowers, and potted palms. Tall columned galleries ran through several stories and encircled the building, rising to meet a vaulted, glass roof. Near a doorway there was a sign announcing Miss Nora Derrington's lecture on *The Spoils of Eden*, but to Eden's dismay, the time had been changed from 7:30 to 6:00 P.M.

"Oh no, we've missed Nora's lecture in the Crown Room," Eden told him.

From behind her shoulder Parker Judson chuckled.

"I don't understand," she said to her grandfather. "Why would the hotel management change the time after it was advertised in the *Examiner*?"

Her grandfather's face remained philosophical, but she saw a brief exchange of glances between him and Judson.

Guests were filing out, women in jewel-tone gowns and men in dark jackets. Eden glanced into the room looking for Nora but saw Zachary instead. He spied her and Ainsworth and appeared surprised to see them together, then recovered and made his way toward them.

"Grandfather—hullo, thought you'd be upstairs at Kalakaua's reception by now." He nodded toward the Crown Room. "Everything's gone awry. The hotel manager changed the hour of Nora's lecture at the last moment. Nora's fuming. She's blaming you," he told Ainsworth.

Eden wondered about the crowd that was leaving, wondering where they had come from. Apparently, so did her grandfather.

"The group seems large enough. Where did they all come from?"

"Last-minute manipulations by Rafe," Zachary stated in a clipped voice.

"Rafe?" Ainsworth asked, surprised. "He's here?"

"He was." Zachary looked troubled. "I don't know where he went. Doesn't much matter. I'll admit he did a ringing job rounding up the king's supporters, though. He located them somehow—even made a call on the manager at the St. Francis. They used every cabby they could find to ferry them over here in time."

"One would think he worked for the fire station," Ainsworth grumbled.

"Rafe is here, you say?" Parker Judson came awake. "He's just the fella I want to see. Where'd he go?"

"I think he left," Zachary said.

Eden felt as though the blood had drained from her head. Rafe . . . in San Francisco?

Parker looked at Ainsworth. "You didn't invite him to Kalakaua's reception, did you?" The hope that Ainsworth had done so came with a strain in his voice.

Ainsworth turned sharp eyes on Zachary as he answered Parker's question. "Why would I? Don't we have enough problems without Rafe stirring up more?"

"You can bet Nora is dripping honeyed compliments all over him," Zachary said. "He saved her lecture and book signing from total defeat."

"Wonder what he's really doing here," Zachary said, directing his comment toward Eden. "Doesn't it seem strange he'd choose to show up in San Francisco now?"

"Maybe it's Kalakaua he's interested in seeing," Ainsworth interjected, saving her from having to answer her cousin. He turned to Eden, who stood in silence, trying to keep her thoughts from reflecting in her face. "We separate here, my dear. I believe Nora is expecting you to dine with her. Afterward you'll both come up to the reception. Zachary, would you escort your cousin to Nora? Then join me upstairs. Come along, Parker," he said turning to the sugar grower. "You and I have some convincing to do with Kalakaua. I hope he's sober!"

Eden watched them depart and walk toward a grand staircase where a shimmering chandelier cast down its light on the spotless red carpet.

She heard Zachary's voice in her ear. "Come along, Eden, you look beautiful."

"What reason would Parker Judson have to see Rafe Easton?" Eden asked abruptly.

Zachary shrugged. "Who knows? Parker's always got some new scheme brewing. I noticed he seemed to light up when he learned it was Rafe who had come to Nora's rescue. It certainly couldn't be because of his political views. Most likely he just likes a man who can tackle a tough job. Maybe Rafe's got something on his mind about sugar. Whatever it is, it won't go over with the family. He's been gone for two years and we want to keep it that way."

He took her arm, but Eden drew away. "You don't own Hawaii, Zachary. If Rafe wants to come home, he won't let you or your father stop him."

Zachary, plainly annoyed that she would defend Rafe, smirked. "With you on his side, you're probably right."

She looked away and walked with him through a wide doorway into another huge dining room gleaming with mirrors, sparkling crystal, and polished silver. Eden was hardly aware of the elegant surroundings, however. Her mind was on Rafe, wondering about his presence in San Francisco and what Parker Judson wanted to see him about.

"I wonder what Grandfather will tell Kalakaua tonight," Zachary mused. "I hear there's some British spy prowling about trying to discover what the king's up to about Pearl Harbor. All in all, it should be a chummy evening."

"You're not serious—a spy? Here?" So that was what her grandfather had meant about the British when he'd greeted her.

"Of course. And toasting the Stars and Stripes with Kalakaua's best gin while they're at it. The disagreement over Hawaii's destiny has always been fought in the most dignified and respectful of ways—at least until the shooting starts."

Eden nearly glared at his glib tongue. "There's not going to be any shooting."

They passed elegant waiters in black and white carrying large trays loaded with steak and lobster, wine and champagne.

The headwaiter addressed Zachary as "Mr. Derrington, sir," and included Eden with a gracious bow. Much ceremony was made while escorting them to the reserved table. Eden felt conspicuous as once again eyes turned in her direction. Zachary seated her, then whispered, "At least with dear old Nora, there's little doubt where I stand in her estimation. Wait here, my dove—I shall be but a moment."

A few minutes later, seated at the table with white linen cloth and shining silver, Eden mused over the evening thus far as the tapered candles flickered like burning rubies tinged with amber. She realized she had forgotten to ask her grandfather about Celestine's illness.

The deterioration in Celestine's health was not the only situation that had worsened since Eden's departure two years ago. Judging from her grandfather's frown when he'd learned Rafe was here in the city, Rafe's welcome at Kea Lani had also weakened.

Should anything happen to Celestine, Rafe would be sole inheritor of Matt Easton's land. Unless . . .

Eden was troubled to even think of the possibility. *Unless* Uncle Townsend had convinced Celestine to leave everything to him, including Hanalei Plantation.

Eden sat a little straighter. No, she wouldn't do that. Celestine would never be so unfair. As Matt's firstborn son it was right and just that Rafe have what belonged to him.

Eden loosened her grip on the side of her velvet-cushioned chair when she heard Zachary say, "Eden, here's Great-aunt Nora."

CHAPTER
FIFTEEN

Eden stood to greet the aristocratic Nora Derrington as she walked to the head of the table. Nora had never accepted the notion that older women should dress only in black. She wore a smartly tailored burgundy gown of a silky texture, the color flattering her fragile skin and platinum hair worn in the style of Queen Victoria. She couldn't have weighed much more than a hundred pounds, but she was a storm of energy and Eden liked her vinegary facade. Underneath there was a tender heart.

Cousin Zachary drew back a chair for Nora. "This is Eden, your niece."

Nora looked up at him impatiently. "I know who she is," she scolded. "Am I senile?"

"You'd have a hard time convincing your audience tonight of that. You did a splendid job, Auntie dear."

"Thanks to Rafe, who collected the crowd," she countered.

Eden glanced at Zachary and saw his mouth twist.

Nora's silvery green eyes turned on Eden and warmed, a smile breaking on her petite lips. "Hello, my dear. You're looking wonderful as usual. Such a charming gown. You favor your father—so much like Jerome and nothing like Rebecca."

She held out her fragile hand, obviously expecting Eden to take it and plant an affectionate kiss on her upturned cheek.

Eden smiled at her audacity—nothing like Rebecca, indeed!—and obliged her, kissing her cheek. As she drew away she felt her great-aunt's acute appraisal.

"Now run along, Zachary," Nora urged. "Your constant buzzing about is becoming tedious."

Zachary gave a brittle smile, turning to Eden. "Nothing like being told I'm intruding. All right, Nora dear, I'll run along." He smiled. "See you later, Eden."

Nora watched Zachary as he walked away. "I almost feel sorry for Ainsworth."

Eden looked at her quickly. "For Grandfather . . . why?"

"His plans for Zachary, like Townsend before him, have met with bitter disappointment."

The only plans Eden could think of were the ones in which her grandfather intended to turn the family enterprise over to Zachary when he retired. Yesterday at the pond at Chadwick, Zachary implied that matters were progressing in that direction.

"It's not Ainsworth's disappointment that worries me, though," Nora said. "It's Zachary's when he finds out."

Eden wondered what she meant. What was there for Zachary to find out? She, too, watched him until he left the dining room and walked to the grand staircase.

Nora continued thoughtfully as though Eden understood. "Zachary hasn't the temperament to accept disappointment. He's not *resilient*."

Eden was now clearly absorbed. "What disappointment do you speak of?"

"It hasn't happened yet. Ainsworth is still wrestling with the decision, trying to make up his mind. It's been very difficult for him. He spoke about it to your cousin Rozlind before coming to San Francisco. That's why he brought Zachary with him on this excursion to Washington. Personally, I don't see Ainsworth has much choice. He could still decide to make Rozlind his primary heir, but so far she refuses to cooperate."

"Is something wrong, Great-aunt Nora?"

"Yes. Several *things*, as you put it, are quite wrong. First of all, Rozlind—the poor confused child—has been seeing a Hawaiian! When caught by Zachary, she insisted he was an alii, because he's six feet tall. Ainsworth and I called her on it at once. He's related to Kamehameha the Great, she told us. Pure nonsense, of course, but we couldn't reason with her."

Eden hoped her face didn't give her away. She had known when she was still in Hawaii that Rozlind was seeing Rafe's friend Keno. However, Eden hadn't given much thought to it these last two years, because Keno had sailed with Rafe when he left Oahu. In the letters Rozlind had written her there'd been no mention of her marriageable future, and certainly no mention of Keno.

Nora went on. "Matters changed for the better for a time, and Rozlind began to show a willingness to come to her romantic senses."

Did Nora mean to suggest that Rozlind had since strayed from that decision?

The term *alii* was a familiar one to Eden, whose years with Noelani had taught her much about the native culture. The Hawaiian alii claimed to go all the way back to the beginning of the self-proclaimed royalty of the Polynesians under Kamehameha the Great, the first conqueror-ruler of the islands. According to the animistic religion and traditions of the early Polynesians, the Hawaiian Islands and the Hawaiian people were one. Hawaii was a god; Maui was a god; Kauai and the other islands were all gods, as well as the first parents of the favored Hawaiian gene-alogy, known as the alii, the royal ruling class who became the Hawaiian monarchy. To keep the royal bloodline pure and the alii six feet tall, they intermarried. Only an alii could marry an alii. So uncles married nieces. Aunts married nephews. For any ordinary Hawaiian to look into the face of an alii had meant a cruel and certain death.

"Then Rozlind is seeing Keno?" Eden asked quietly.

"She was until—" Nora stopped, a fleeting shadow of pain crossing her face.

"Until what?" Eden asked, growing tense with uncertainty.

"I shouldn't have brought it up," Nora murmured with self-incrimi-nation. "I can't go into everything now, not tonight. Some things must wait for Kea Lani. The Derringtons always kept some things behind closed doors. Tragedy is one of those family skeletons we've kept carefully hidden away."

Tragedy! Then Rozlind was not taking the loss of love as courageously as Eden had expected she would. Rozlind had always been a young woman of calm resolve. Poor Rozlind!

"But what has all this to do with Zachary?"

"For years Ainsworth hasn't been able to decide whether to make his beloved Rozlind his primary heir or his one grandson, Zachary. He finally decided on Rozlind, but then . . ."

Eden thought she knew. "Rozlind insists on seeing Keno?"

"That's part of it. So Ainsworth chose Zachary. Now he may be forced to choose Rozlind after all. When Zachary learns this, it will devastate him."

"Then Rozlind has given up thoughts of Keno?"

Nora looked distressed. "You might say the decision was mutual. I suppose you wonder why I'm telling you this tonight. It's because I intend to do what's best for Kea Lani's future." She bristled. "After all, Ainsworth isn't the sole voice in the plantation's destiny. I own half of everything. And I shall leave it to whomever I choose."

Eden remembered what Zachary had said about Nora favoring her. Eden felt unprepared for anything so dramatic. "Great-aunt Nora, I—"

Nora raised a frail hand. "We won't get into details tonight," Nora stated, as though reading her thoughts, "but I do want you to come home to Kea Lani. And the sooner you do, the more at peace I will be. If anyone will add a stabilizing effect to the family, it will be you, Jerome's daughter. Naturally Ainsworth won't be pleased about your political affiliations with Princess Liliuokalani, but he'll have to accept them. Even as he's had to accept mine through the years."

Eden thought of the emotional closeness she had sensed with her grandfather tonight in the coach and felt a tug at her heart. She didn't want to disappoint him.

"I suppose Zachary told you what happened about my lecture?" Nora asked, changing the subject. "If it hadn't been for Rafe's unexpected arrival, my evening would have turned into utter catastrophe." Her eyes sparked. "I blame Ainsworth for the attempted derailment. Either him or Parker Judson. Wait until I see them at the reception."

"I'm surprised the king is able to attend a reception. I was told he isn't well."

Nora looked bothered. "Zachary told you? One would think he was a supporter of Princess Liliuokalani the way he carries on about Kalakaua's health."

Then Nora did understand Zachary's hope for a revolution should Liliuokalani ascend to the Hawaiian throne, Eden thought.

"As far as I'm concerned, the king's ill health can be blamed on his relentless enemies with their constant badgering. It's shameful the way they've maligned his reputation. The things they say about him can't possibly be true. He's a devout Christian; I'm sure of it."

Eden wasn't so certain, but she kept silent as Nora went on to tell her about Kalakaua's travels in California and how she had been invited to join his entourage. "Kalakaua, bless his heart, arrived on December fourth aboard the USS *Charleston*. The United States arranged for it. Very generous of them, and a very commodious voyage, by the way. Admiral George Brown was a most generous host. The ocean voyage proved beneficial to the king's health and to mine—though I think he's overtaxing himself. We in the king's entourage have been tremendously busy, though graciously entertained by His Majesty's friends and acquaintances throughout California. We made stops in San Diego, Los Angeles, and Santa Barbara before arriving here. He's worn to the bone, and after tonight, so am I. So, my dear, you can well understand why I haven't had a free moment until tonight to meet with you. I sent Zachary to Chadwick yesterday."

Eden felt relief. "Then—it was *you* who arranged tonight through my aunt Lana."

Nora's frank gaze studied her face. "Rebecca's sister? No, what has she to do with this? Our meeting is strictly a Derrington family matter. Do I need her permission?"

"No, naturally not, Auntie, only . . ."

So. Zachary had *not* told the whole truth. The letter to Lana had not come at Great-aunt's request. The deception disturbed Eden. He hadn't changed that much after all, she decided sadly. More disturbing, what was Zachary's motive in unsettling Lana?

Nora watched her, her silver brows crocheted together in a little frown. "Is that what Zachary told you? That I sent Nurse Stanhope a letter?"

"Well, yes . . . but perhaps I misunderstood him," she said, trying to ease the matter. She would rather find out from Zachary himself what motivated him.

Nora turned solemn. "No, you didn't misunderstand. And you're too smart to believe you did. I asked him to arrange this dinner, but I sent no letter to Nurse Stanhope; I had no reason to. I don't like it when Zachary goes poking about, even searching rooms."

Searching rooms?

"One never knows what's on the boy's mind. What did he tell you about the letter?"

Eden explained but left out the darker details of Lana's emotional duress over his perceived meddling.

Nora's frown deepened. "I shall speak to him about it. Enough for now, my dear. I feel myself growing weary. Let's order our dinner and talk more afterward." She turned to the dignified waiter who had stood waiting unobtrusively in the background. He came forward and placed two menus in front of them that were mostly in French. Nora ordered for them both.

"I'll be in the city until after Christmas," Nora said a few minutes later. "I must attend the king's banquet on the thirteenth, and the festivities at the Mystic Shrine on the fourteenth. I worry about Kalakaua. He's much worse than anyone knows," she whispered. "If anything should happen to him . . ."

Eden watched her.

"It's my opinion Liliuokalani will soon become Queen of Hawaii," Nora said in a low voice. "When she does, she will need every friend she can garner. Ainsworth and the Hawaiian League fear she'll call for a new constitution. With that wild-eyed Wilcox rousing the natives and demanding a constitutional convention, anything could happen."

Eden remembered what her grandfather and Parker Judson had said about Wilcox leading the opposition to take over the legislature in the next election.

"Liliuokalani is a staunch admirer of Queen Victoria," Nora said. "As such, she will be a determined ruler doing what she believes best for her own people. And that might mean a move to repeal the Constitution of 1887."

"Is that what worries you, that she might?" Eden asked.

"I'm not sure what she'll do. I'll admit I hope she doesn't make the move."

Was she afraid of a revolution, one that would far exceed the changes forced upon Kalakaua in 1887?

"But you believe in so many of her goals for her people," Eden protested. "You've listed them in your book."

Nora's face took on a look of weariness, and her age was revealed as her shoulders stooped a little under the rich burgundy. "Yes, but I believe a trap is being laid. The League is just waiting for her to try to repeal the constitution. When she does—there will be another revolution."

Eden looked at her, uncertain of her own beliefs. Annexation was one thing, if it were done peacefully and with the support of a majority of the Hawaiian natives, but to think her grandfather would be part of a deliberate plan to force Liliuokalani's hand was disturbing indeed. Was Nora overreacting?

Eden was sure there were those in the League quite willing to goad the new queen into making a move that would give them an excuse, but not all.

"Our cause needs friends," Nora said. "I've spoken to Rafe Easton tonight. He hasn't come to any conclusions yet about where he stands in all this. He's always supported the monarchy, but people change through the years. He seems to have changed. How he would react to an actual revolution is another matter. Rafe appears to be holding back from a decision."

Rafe was not the sort to hold back from making a commitment to a cause he believed in, Eden thought. If he were waiting, there was something else on his mind, some other reason why he hadn't shown his hand tonight to Nora.

"Rafe was fired from the Honolulu *Gazette* for supporting Kalakaua," she reminded Nora. "And that story in the paper was the main reason Townsend wanted him out of Oahu. Isn't it a little unfair to say he's standing back now, uninvolved? After all, he's been gone from Hawaii for over two years, and you said he rescued your lecture tonight."

"Don't misunderstand me. I think rather highly of him, though he does appear to have something on his mind that makes me uneasy. There was always a bit of rogue in him, I thought. But now that Celestine is so ill and asking for him to come to Kea Lani, I think this may be the hour Rafe's presence can be of benefit to us and the monarchy. But he and Townsend don't get on at all, and I don't see any reason why that should change in the near future." She lifted the gold and ruby watch she wore around her neck. "Oh dear, it grows late. We best get straight to the point. I received your letter about wishing to serve at Kalihi Hospital with Dr. Bolton. I haven't decided yet. There are other matters we'll need to discuss first and we're running out of time if we're to meet Ainsworth and Kalakaua." She turned her bright gaze upon Eden. "First, how important is it to you?"

Eden's heart beat faster. "To work on the same project as my father? Oh, Nora, I want this more than anything!"

"Is it important enough to do whatever it takes to accomplish it?"

Eden wondered what she might be hinting at but smiled. "Well, almost anything, as long as it pleases the Lord."

Nora looked satisfied. "No weakling like Rebecca, are you?"

A second jibe at her mother. "From what I've heard Ambrose say about her, my mother was far from being weak-willed—not when she left New Bedford alone to come to Hawaii and teach."

"Don't get upset. Rebecca did have her strong points to be sure, but you take after Jerome. No doubt about it. You've changed since you were that frightened child." Nora's gaze reflected her keen interest. "That brings me to my next question. Just how much do you recall of your early childhood at Kea Lani? Especially the night of the storm."

This is not what Eden had been expecting. She wanted to get the matter settled about Kalihi. Why was Nora asking this now?

Eden picked up her water glass and turned the stem in her hand. "I don't recall much, but there are a few things."

"For instance?"

Eden looked at her across the candle flames. "Well—until I saw you just now, I'd forgotten being taken to your room that night. You told me stories until I stopped crying."

An uncomfortable silence settled between them.

"What has Zachary told you about that night?"

So Nora knew about her hiding with him under the daybed. Naturally, she would.

"Actually, I've never talked to him about it, nor has he mentioned it to me," Eden confessed. She thought of Rafe. "I've been cautioned not to."

Nora's silvery green eyes were searching. "Cautioned by whom? Rafe?"

She was surprised Nora would guess so easily. "Yes."

"I doubt if Zachary remembers anyway."

"Strange you should say that. So did Rafe, before I left Kea Lani."

"Did he?" She looked curious and bold.

"Yes, and it's odd," Eden continued. "Why shouldn't Zachary remember?"

"Not so curious. You don't remember either."

"But I fell . . ."

"Yes. And Zachary didn't. Then Rafe hasn't explained about Zachary?"

Eden had often suspected that Rafe knew more than he'd been willing to tell her. "What could Rafe explain about Zachary?"

Nora looked weary, as though the subject burdened her. "Well, you'll have to know sometime. It was easier to keep it from you when you were young, but you're a wise young woman now and you'll be coming home to Kea Lani to stay. Zachary underwent a state of severe depression, dear. It lasted several years while you were away living with Ambrose and Noelani. What happened to him was as wicked as your fall down the stairs, though it left him no physical scar. The doctor thinks something must have frightened him or shocked him into that condition. He wasted away to skin and bones, poor boy. Somehow it's affected his early memory— in some ways similar to the effect of your fall."

Eden stared at her across the table. "How awful for him."

Tears filled Nora's eyes. "Yes. That's why I'm concerned about Ainsworth's decision. Zachary hasn't been happy lately, and his grandfather, hating to disappoint him, is hesitant to discuss it."

"Is that the reason Grandfather is reluctant to leave him heir of the Derrington enterprise?"

Nora glanced away. "Partly, yes. I suppose he could have another relapse."

Eden reasoned there had to be something more to her grandfather's decision, but she could see that Great-aunt Nora wasn't going to delve into it tonight.

"What do you think could have frightened him so?"

Nora contemplated for a long, sober minute before answering. She picked up her fragile water glass, her rings sparkling in the light. "The storm. He's always been afraid of tropical storms. And that night was close to becoming a hurricane."

"Yes, I realize now that it must have been a hurricane. I was terrified too, but you gave me confidence through the night."

Nora smiled sadly as if remembering. "I did tell you stories, and you did fall asleep at last." Her smile faded. "Then something came up, and I left my room. When I returned, you were gone. Perhaps a flash of lightning awoke you. You ran away. We looked all over but couldn't find you."

Eden stirred uneasily, a sense of brooding hovering over her soul. Somewhere, just out of reach of her consciousness, memories were stirring. She gave up trying to remember and shook her head. "We?"

Nora sipped from her glass, her thin fingers sparkling with jewels. "Celestine was with me."

Eden didn't remember leaving Nora's bedroom. Unless . . . after Nora left, Eden had gone searching for her mother? That could account for running into a frightened Zachary and the two of them hiding from the thunderstorm under a daybed.

She remembered the staggering zigzags of light flashing angrily across the Hawaiian sky. Still, that room had appeared different from any place she'd ever been at Kea Lani. It hadn't seemed to be a bedroom at all. She remembered being very high up, with lots of window glass.

Nora watched, evidently alert to any change in Eden's face. "So then . . . you do remember."

Eden's hands perspired in her lap. She fought back an unreasonable sense of terror. She could never live with herself if she foolishly surrendered to fear now in front of Nora. After all, it wasn't as if they'd never discussed her fall before.

"Eden?" Nora prodded gently.

Eden stirred at the sound of her voice and looked at the frail elderly lady sitting across from her. In spite of the tone of her voice, Nora's eyes revealed misgiving.

Eden smiled ruefully. "Yes, I'm all right. I'm sorry. Some of it is coming back, and it's a little frightening."

"That's understandable; it was a dreadful night. We were upset when we couldn't find you."

"Recently I remembered having hid with Zachary during the storm. I remember painting easels, and canvas—" She stopped, recalling what Lana had said about Great-aunt Nora being an artist. "Then it *was* your bed I hid under with Zachary that night."

Nora's expression became veiled. "I don't know for sure; it may have been. We were looking for you and didn't find you until that dreadful moment when you fell. It had rained that day from noon onward. Since I was unable to take my long walk, I was as nervous as a caged parrot. In those days I often painted when restless." Her eyes appeared to brighten. "I finished quite a charming painting of you that same day. Do you remember?"

"No . . ."

"I still have the painting somewhere. When you come to Oahu I'll show it to you. Anyway, you had come to me out of fear of the storm. Later Celestine and I looked for the other children to inquire about you. I found Rozlind in her room asleep looking like a little red-haired angel. Nothing, so it seems, ever appeared to bother her." Nora smiled reminiscently. "And Celestine searched for Zachary and Rafe. She said she couldn't find either of them. We were downstairs by then. Celestine heard you in the upper hall crying. Do you recall this?"

Eden tried to remember. She shook her head, her welling emotions making it difficult to speak as she visualized a hand reaching under the daybed—

Eden set her cup down so quickly the delicate gold-rimmed saucer rattled.

Nora leaned toward her. "Do you remember how you fell?"

"No . . . only of someone reaching under the bed to bring me out."

"We were all looking everywhere for you, under divans, chairs, beds."

"But no one found me until I fell, and yet the hand . . ."

"There's obviously a dark and painful gap in your memory, Eden. We did find you, but by then you were on the lower stairs, unconscious." Nora shook her head, wincing, as if the memory disturbed her as much as it did Eden. "Most distasteful." She took a quick swallow of water, and her frail hand trembled. "Well, this is most unpleasant . . . perhaps we should let the matter go. Oh good. Here's the waiter with our dinner. I do hope we both still have an appetite."

So that was all there was to it, Eden thought as dinner was served. Nora made it sound so simple. Perhaps it was. But what about the note someone had left her about her mother? Could her mother's death have anything to do with that night? She could ask Nora about the note, but one look at her pale, aging face and Eden's spirits fell. How could she? The note hinted that the Derringtons had done something wrong. How could she confront either Nora or her grandfather without making it appear as if she didn't trust them?

As for the night of that long-ago hurricane, the fear she had experienced must have come from her bewildered young imagination, enhanced by wind, thunder, lightning, and rain.

SiXTEEN

Eden walked beside Great-aunt Nora while a man in a red-and-gold uniform escorted them past a ballroom where ambassadors from around the world had waltzed and dined through the years. Venetian cut-glass glittered from the French chandeliers like clusters of suspended crystals. Silvery mirrors reflected scarlet drapery and cream-colored lace. The sweeping staircase ahead offered a panoramic view of the scene, and high above that hung a vaulted, glass roof.

As Eden and Nora were led up the stairs to the Gold Room for King Kalakaua's reception, a second uniformed man intercepted them, carrying a silver plate with a white envelope.

"Excuse me, Miss Derrington," he said to Nora. "A message for you."

The older woman's brows lifted with interest as she read the message and glanced back down the stairs. Eden followed her gaze to see a stout man towering in a double doorway. His evening clothes of black broadcloth and pristine white contrasted with a ruddy face, rather flabby jowls, and a gray walrus mustache below a pointed nose. He bowed quickly and walked toward the stairs in black patent-leather shoes. In a few steps he was below them, bending over Nora's veined hand as though she were a member of the royal family.

"Ah, Lord Blount, I didn't realize you were in the Bay City."

"It was a rather hasty departure," he confessed. "Commissioner Wodehouse sent me on a bit of business. I left Mauai Plantation a few days after King Kalakaua departed on the USS *Charleston*. I didn't know you voyaged with his party until Wodehouse informed me."

Wodehouse, as Eden knew, was the British commissioner tirelessly serving the cause of England in the Hawaiian Islands. She had heard her grandfather berate him on many occasions for his political intrusion into the state of affairs between Hawaii and Washington.

As for Lord Blount, if she remembered his story correctly, he was in some way related to the British legal guardian of Hawaii's Princess Kaiulani, who was being schooled in England.

"This is my great-niece, Miss Eden Derrington," Nora was saying. "Eden, you've met Lord Erwin Blount?"

When the introductions were complete, the three of them slowly mounted the stairs. Nora turned to Lord Blount. "What brings you to San Francisco, Erwin? Or need I ask?"

He looked at Eden in such a way that she suspected he would prefer to speak to Nora alone. Was Blount the spy for England's interests in Hawaii? she wondered.

"You needn't worry about Eden," Nora said with a wave of dismissal. "She wholeheartedly supports our cause. Always has. If I have my way, she'll be of immense benefit to us in the future."

Blount looked pleased. "Splendid."

His voice turned low and indistinguishable except to Nora and Eden, yet his outward behavior was gregarious and affable. Eden noted that anyone who happened to glance their way would think Lord Blount to be discussing Nora's earlier book lecture, or perhaps showing exuberance over Kalakaua's reception.

"Commissioner Wodehouse is expressing anxiety over Kalakaua's visit here to the West Coast. Rumors abound over concerns that talk of annexation will occupy a considerable part of his visit. He may even journey to Washington to negotiate a cession of Pearl Harbor to the United States Navy in exchange for a favorable sugar treaty. I'm to take immediate steps to protest on behalf of the British government."

"Rumors, Lord Blount," Nora said airily, "grow like dandelions. I know for a fact Kalakaua has no plans to journey across the country to Washington, D.C. in winter weather."

"You're a brilliant woman, my dear Miss Nora, but Commissioner Wodehouse was pacing the floor in Honolulu when I was whisked away on the first steamer for California. What assurances can you give me, if any?"

Nora lifted her trailing burgundy gabardine and ascended the stairs like a princess, seemingly in no hurry to waylay his anxiety. She looked calm and in control, and Eden was proud of her as well as faintly amused that the elder lady knew more of the state of affairs than did Lord Blount.

"I have it on the highest word that he won't be going," she said. "His doctor, no less. Poor Kalakaua's health is too poor for such a long, wintry trip by train. I'm desperately worried about him, Erwin," she said, frowning. "I'm not supposed to know, but the doctor suspects Bright's disease—and his heart is ailing."

Lord Blount pulled at his walrus mustache. "Dreadful, indeed. Good grief! Then Liliuokalani may soon be queen of Hawaii."

"That should please England."

"Precisely! She's dignified and sensible, endowed with more ability and principle than her brother, who is deficient in both, if you want my opinion. British interests would be much safer under her rule than they have been with either of the last two kings. Liliuokalani has always shown leanings for England. It's because she trusts our loyalty to the independence of Hawaii."

Eden could imagine her grandfather's ire if he could overhear Lord Blount's boast. She was beginning to believe what Zachary had told her about the inevitability of a revolution.

But if England was worried about America's influence on Kalakaua during his visit to San Francisco and the cession of Pearl Harbor, America too had its concerns. Not about Liliuokalani, but about her niece, the lovely young Princess Victoria Kaiulani, daughter of Likelike and Archibald Cleghorn. After Liliuokalani, Princess Kaiulani was in line for the throne. She had long been under British influence and was even now attending Harrowden Hall in London for her schooling in "all things British." If Kaiulani ever became queen, Ainsworth and the other annexationists feared she would give the ultra-English in Hawaii excessive influence in Iolani Palace. Her guardian was the Englishman Theo Davies, a staunch Tory who was known to be resolutely opposed to American predominance in the islands. Recently he had denounced the negotiations that Kalakaua's minister to Washington, Henry Carter, were trying to bring about for a sugar treaty—asking for exclusive rights to the use of Pearl Harbor in exchange for a sugar deal. After all, as her grandfather liked to point out, it had been U.S. taxpayers' money and know-how that had turned the Pearl River into the great harbor that it was during Kalakaua's reign.

Eden struggled with the news of England being brought into the negotiations, her emotions pulling in two directions. Her heart felt no particular loyalties to London, her ancestral roots being centered in the United States. Rebecca Stanhope had come from New Bedford, and the

Derringtons had first arrived from the Old South. The early pioneer missionaries had also come from America.

As they were nearing the staircase landing, Eden could see journalists gathered and what looked to be important foreign dignitaries milling about with beverage glasses.

"What I can tell you is that Minister Carter is here from Washington," Nora told Blount. "He'll meet with Kalakaua several times, but you can tell Commissioner Wodehouse the minister is advising Kalakaua to hold out on further negotiations until after the first of the year."

"It was the matter of Pearl Harbor and the landing of troops, if needed, that caused the king not to sign the first sugar treaty Minister Carter negotiated," Eden said. "Why would he change his mind and sign now?"

"Kalakaua is like a drowning man with the weights of illness and financial debt hanging about his neck," Lord Blount said. "And with the severe drop in sugar prices, Hawaiian growers are casting revolutionary glances his way." He looked at Nora. "You're certain Carter advised him not to sign?"

"That's what I'm told," she insisted. "It will be better for Hawaii to wait until after the new year."

"England isn't convinced," Lord Blount said. "I've an urgent message to the king from Wodehouse."

"There should be no difficulty in passing it to him," Nora told him. "Come along, Erwin. We're just in time for his gala entrance."

Outside the Gold Room, Eden saw newspaper journalists in a roped-off section scribbling notes. Cameras were set up for photographs of King Kalakaua with various ambassadors and American businessmen after the reception. As she started to look away, her eyes swerved back. *Impossible!* Eden's mind shouted, but she was wrong. How could she forget the face of Rafe Easton? It had been over two years, but his dark, earthy appearance was unmistakable. Was he working as a journalist again? But surely not for the San Francisco *Examiner* or *Chronicle*. Just then King Kalakaua made his appearance in the doorway of the Gold Room to greet his guests, but Rafe was not watching Kalakaua. His eyes were on Eden. She turned her head away, remembering that he had not been in touch with her once during her years at Chadwick.

Rafe watched Eden and felt an unexplainable tweak of irritation when she did not appear to recognize him. A muscle twitched at the corner of his mouth. He was not surprised by her beauty or her grace. Two years had only enhanced them. He had always found her Christian dedication appealing, and he was pleased to know that she had graduated from Chadwick Nursing School with honors. He had bought a gift on one of his voyages in advance of her graduation, intending to send it to her. But the jade comb that matched her eyes was still in his desk aboard the *Manoa*. He had decided against giving it to her.

Rafe hadn't expected her to be here. He had arrived earlier that evening to attend uninvited. That she was at the very reception he intended to use to confront Ainsworth compounded his dilemma. The leather satchel at his feet, with supposedly journalistic essentials, actually contained a typewritten journal of information he had gathered over the last two years.

Since leaving the leper colony at Molokai the previous year, he had voyaged on the *Manoa* to South America for pineapple seedlings. He had also located Dr. Jerome Derrington as planned and spent two weeks with him in his camp in Brazil among the Indians where leprosy was widespread. Rafe also had, in his satchel, a letter from Jerome to give to Ainsworth.

Yes, he thought with a note of cynicism, he had what he wanted. His mission was accomplished. But matters had not turned out well for Jerome; nor would they for Eden if she learned the truth.

The *Manoa* had docked at San Diego and Santa Barbara before returning to Pearl Harbor, and at both ports Keno had brought newspaper articles reporting on Kalakaua's visit to California. The king would remain in San Francisco until well after the holidays, the articles had said. They went on to report that Ainsworth Derrington was also in San Francisco, with a trip to Washington, D.C. scheduled for after Christmas. Matters had fallen into place for Rafe to confront Ainsworth during the week the *Manoa* would stay in San Francisco Bay, and then things had gone sour. He had come to the Palace Hotel after learning of the reception, only to have Nora inform him that Ainsworth would be late because he had, in a rare display of grandfatherly pride, gone to pick up Eden at Chadwick to escort his granddaughter to the royal reception.

He debated with his heart, which thudded steadily in his chest. He had wrestled through the consequences of the decision he had made that night in Ambrose's kitchen. He had worked and planned to get to this moment. The opportunity was here, the hour was now. He should seize it.

Rafe watched her approach the Gold Room with Nora and a round-bellied Englishman.

Lord Erwin Blount lived on Kauai, where he managed a large plantation owned by wealthy English investors in London. Rafe was aware that the British were seeking even larger tracts of land, especially on Kauai and the Big Island. He had learned, too, that an English company had owned an exclusive right for some years to build and operate a steel railway throughout Honolulu and its suburbs. In opposition, American interests were advising Washington to lay a telegraph cable from the West Coast to Hawaii to bring the Hawaiian people into daily contact with America. Land ownership and the Honolulu railroad were similar to other projects planned by the British government in hopes of influencing the Hawaiians to bond with British interests instead of American ones.

Rafe watched Lord Blount speak to Nora. He knew that Blount worked for the British commissioner in Honolulu, James Wodehouse, and Rafe easily guessed why Blount was here in San Francisco. England was worried about Pearl Harbor going to the United States Navy in return for a sugar deal. He probably brought a message to Kalakaua from Wodehouse urging him not to sign any treaty with Washington while here in California.

Rafe's grim mood was heightened by seeing Eden. She was a lovely image in green satin with an overlay of black lace, her dark hair swept up in fashionable waves and curls. Around her throat she wore a strand of pearls. It made him think again of the gift he had bought her while in Java. His lashes came together as he took a second look; his thoughts stopped abruptly, jarred by what he thought he saw.

Black pearls! No, they couldn't be the same ones that belonged to Rebecca.

A flash of anger burned in his chest. *Who* in the Derrington family would have given them to her? Ainsworth? No, never him. He would be alarmed if he saw them on her.

But wait—wouldn't Ainsworth have noticed the pearls in the coach when he brought her to the hotel?

Rafe tried to make sense of the jumbled bits of information. The one thing he could think of was that something must have kept Ainsworth from noticing them. Had Eden worn a wrap? His gaze dropped to her arm. She carried a fur capelet. That might account for it. And the coach may have been in shadows. Or Nora Derrington may have given them to her after she arrived at the hotel.

Nora. How much did she know? Jerome hadn't mentioned his aunt, but that meant nothing.

He looked toward the Gold Room where the light from the chandelier glimmered and twinkled brightly. Ainsworth would see those black pearls when she entered the room. Rafe guessed that someone had planned it that way, but why? He snatched his satchel and shouldered his way through the milling journalists, straight for Eden.

"Ho there, Easton!" a voice called boldly from behind him. "Wait up. You're just the fella I want to see. I've been looking for you!"

Just then Rafe saw Eden, Nora, and Lord Blount come to the open door of the Gold Room. He heard the proprietor read off their names distinctly to King Kalakaua, and then they passed through the double doorway into the brightly lit room.

Parker Judson walked up to Rafe. Rafe recognized the sugar grower. Except for giants like the Californian Claus Spreckels, who had practically turned the island of Lanai into one large plantation, Parker Judson was one of the biggest. And like Spreckles, Judson also had a name for power-brokering that caused smaller planters and businessmen to rally around him as a trend setter and innovator. Parker was a friendly sort, likable, and yet as relentless as a shark when it came to business.

Parker walked up, a hefty man in a casual white tropical-weather jacket and trousers. The jacket was unbuttoned over his rounded stomach, and he wore a western bolo tie with tips of heavy gold knobs formed into Hawaiian pineapples.

"Hullo, Easton, I was told you were back. You're just the fella I want to talk to."

Rafe was curious. He'd never had much interaction with Judson, though his father, Matt, had known him on the Big Island when the two were younger. Judson had landed in the Mauna Loa area a few miles from Hanalei. Judson had plantations throughout the islands, as well as other businesses like the J&P Sugar Company and the Pacific Steamship Line. Many of his newer plantations were smaller, known as "upstart" plantations, experimenting with unique strains of tropical fruits and nuts or improvements of established ones. Judson's main holdings were on the Big Island and dated back to the late 1840s and 1850s.

"Hello, Mr. Judson." Rafe switched his satchel and shook Parker's extended hand. "Traveling with Kalakaua?"

"Not if my neck depended on it. I'm with Ainsworth. We're on our way to Washington by train in the morning. Why don't you come along? We could use a fresh young mind."

Rafe smiled. "I doubt if Ainsworth would appreciate my company."

"Ainsworth is a bright fella, but he needs to break loose and take more risks."

"Annexation isn't risk enough?"

Parker chuckled and glanced toward the Gold Room. "I'll give him that." He lowered his voice. "Where do you stand on this nowadays? You got fired from the *Gazette* a year or so back, didn't you? For some editorial defending the monarchy?"

Rafe rubbed his chin with a half smile. "I guess I did get fired."

Parker Judson's eyes were bright and wily. "Change your mind on Kalakaua?"

Rafe let out a breath. "I don't know. Maybe. Nora asked me that too."

"Ah, Nora, the silver-haired darling of the monarchy. She and I used to have dinner with Kalakaua and old Gibby before he died. Spreckles used to be there too. He and the king used to play cards and drink gin. The British fella was there too. One day Spreckels says something like, 'I got the best hand. I got four kings to play.' And the British fella asks him, 'Kalakaua is the king. Who's the fourth?' And Spreckles says, 'I am.' The king got so mad he got up and walked out of the room in Iolani Palace. It was soon afterward that Kalakaua decided to borrow money from London to pay off the huge debt he owed Spreckles. By that time Spreckles almost owned Hawaii. That was in the good ol' days when he was developing Sprecklesville on Lanai. . . ." He looked at Rafe again, speculatively.

"Truth is, I've been too busy to think about Hawaiian politics," Rafe said.

"So I heard. Voyaging all over the place. Heard you're going back to Oahu to stay this time, though."

Rafe wondered how Judson knew.

"That means you'll need to think about where you are in all this. We'll all need to come flat out and make a stand soon. I've made my choice. Hawaii's either a republic, or it's annexation."

Rafe was somewhat surprised at the change that had come over Judson. He knew that many of the planters, Judson included, were against Hawaii becoming a territory of the United States simply because they differed with American policy, which was against bringing in Chinese coolies to work the plantations. The Hawaiian planters insisted they needed thousands of them since the native Hawaiians were considered unhealthy and undisciplined in their work habits. The Chinese, however, were so anxious to escape miserable conditions on the mainland that they worked cheaply for long hours. The native Hawaiians and hapa-haoles complained that the haole planters were changing the balance of race in the islands.

"Cheap sugar prices are breaking us," Parker Judson said. "It was the monarchy who refused to sign that treaty when the U.S. offered it a year ago. Things are going to get worse in Hawaii for sugar before they get better. Got a few minutes? Let's talk somewhere in private, son. I'm real interested in those South American pineapples you've got aboard the *Manoa*. I'd like to take a look at them."

Rafe was irked but kept his restraint. "Would you mind telling me how you found out, Mr. Judson?"

"Hard to keep good information like that quiet, especially when Keno's bragging all over Fisherman's Wharf about how you're going to turn my pineapples into sour apples."

Rafe winced. "That sounds like Keno. I'm sorry, Mr. Judson, but we nursed those seedlings for the entire seven-thousand-mile Pacific voyage. I've brought them back for my own place when I get it."

"Of course you did. Smart idea. Always did think you were a bright young lad. You have a lot of potential, Rafe. You take after your father. What do you say we talk? Talk's cheap, they say, but a good new strain of pineapple isn't . . . especially with the depressed market. Land isn't cheap to come by either. But land is something I have plenty of at the moment. Maybe we have something in common."

They exchanged looks for a long moment, sizing each other up.

Rafe glanced toward the Gold Room. He heard laughter and voices. "All right, Mr. Judson. I've got ten minutes."

Parker smiled, satisfied. "Why don't we go downstairs where it's quiet? Don't worry, Kalakaua's known to keep late hours. I'll see you get back here in time for your story. But if you're going to grow pineapples in Oahu, you won't have time to work on a newspaper."

Rafe smiled and switched his satchel to the other arm. "I've already gotten my story."

They walked down the corridor toward the grand staircase. Parker took out a gold cigar case and flipped it open, offering him one. Rafe declined, and Parker struck a match to the tip of the long, slender cigar. "There's something else on my mind, Easton. Been thinking about it even before the *Manoa* arrived from South America. It concerns that pearl fishery out by Ambrose's place . . . the one Matt started a generation ago. You own that? Or does Townsend?"

"Eventually I will," Rafe said flatly. "Townsend doesn't own anything that has the Easton name on it."

"You're wrong there."

Rafe stopped on the stairs and looked at him for an explanation.

Parker lifted both brows. "Townsend's got Miss Celestine, doesn't he?"

Rafe's mouth hardened. "My father, Matt, had legal papers drawn up before he died. When my mother dies, it all reverts back to me."

"Does Townsend know that?"

"He should," Rafe said. "I told him that often enough when I was a boy and got cuffed for it. I suppose I was a little touchy. I've outgrown that."

"Have you?"

Rafe looked at him, but Parker didn't seem to mean anything by it; he was looking at his cigar thoughtfully.

"What are you getting at, Mr. Judson?"

Parker started back down the stairs again. "Maybe I don't know myself. Just talking off the top of my head, I suppose. But it could be Townsend didn't take you seriously. He may not believe Matt arranged those papers. You sure of it?"

"Yes." Rafe frowned, shoving his free hand in his trousers pocket. "Why?"

Parker didn't explain immediately. He began to talk again about the pearl fishery near Ambrose and Noelani's hut.

"That land reaching from the lagoon and all the way up toward the Koolau Mountain Range—now, in my opinion, that's good pineapple country."

"Maybe."

"Maybe!" Parker laughed.

"I admit I was thinking of the Big Island and Hanalei. There was always a nice-size virgin section Matt never used for coffee."

Parker thought about it. "You're right. That would work too. But I was thinking of Oahu. That land by the fishery."

They stood in the salon below the stairway where chandeliers glowed and waiters moved about. Parker Judson gestured off to a smaller salon where there were marble gold-veined tables and white and crimson satin divans and settees. He gestured for a waiter to bring refreshments. "What'll you have?"

"Just coffee," Rafe said and sat down on the chair, carefully keeping his satchel beside him.

Parker laughed. "Coffee. Say, I like you, Easton!"

"Thank you," Rafe said with a slight smile. "And now, what about my pearl fishery?"

"Ah yes, that . . . I'm afraid there must have been some mistake about Matt drawing up legal papers. Celestine has given it to Townsend. And

Townsend just sold it to me before I left Oahu with Ainsworth. I've got all the legal papers. And I paid handsomely for it."

Rafe was perfectly still. He watched Parker, who watched him in return with an anxious look.

The waiter brought a tray of refreshments and set it between them. Parker waved him aside when he offered to pour. When the waiter had left, Rafe said quietly, evenly, "I want that fishery back, Mr. Judson."

"I thought you might, Easton. But I'm not interested in doing that."

"I want it back. Not just because of what it's worth or because I've been cheated out of it. There's more to it than getting my due. Matt established that bed before Hanalei grew into a success. Some of my first recollections as a boy were of hearing him talk to Ambrose about those oysters from the black pearl beds of Marutea. I want it back because of my uncle as well."

"Ah yes, Ambrose." And then Judson leaned back into the white divan and went on. "That land all around there is pineapple land. I'd stake my fortune on it. Now, who's to say you and I can't get together on this? You've got the drive, the energy, and I've got the rheumatism." He smiled. "But I've got the land too. I've started other plantations. You've heard of them. Smaller ones. I have one going now on the Big Island. A fella I met a few years ago named John Macadam had a new nut tree." He poured himself champagne. "Macadamia, he called it. Those trees are beauties now. Flourishing as if Hawaii were their native soil." He sighed and leaned back again. "In some years we'll begin harvesting. Same thing could be done with a new strain of South American pineapple.

"My father was once clear thinking enough to have bought into Hellyer's mine out in Virginia City in the boom days. The mine's stripped now. I'm not so interested in silver mines or pearls. As for the fishery itself," Parker continued, "hate to think of your uncle Ambrose losing his house and boats out there. 'Course, if you and I were in this new venture together . . ."

SEVENTEEN

Eden entered the Gold Room with Nora and Lord Blount, her mind on Rafe. What was he doing in San Francisco as a newspaper journalist? At that moment she saw David Kalakaua, king of Hawaii, dark, wavy haired, courtly, and elegantly attired in a rich royal blue jacket with gold braid and ribbon. He was tall, proof to his people that he was an alii, his forebearers being the fighting chiefs of Kona. Eden noticed he had lost weight since the last time she'd seen him in Honolulu at a kingly function. Her nurse's eyes scrutinized him. Great-aunt Nora was right. He did appear tired and emotionally strained, as though bordering on severe illness. Eden greeted him warmly, and after Nora offered a few words, they moved on in the receiving line, leaving him with Lord Blount and his message from Commissioner Wodehouse.

Hawaiian guards in Kalakaua's entourage stood in gaudy uniforms, the gold thread glimmering in the light pouring down from the chandeliers. The guests, too, shimmered in high fashion and their best Nob Hill jewels. Eden touched her mother's black pearls around her neck, thinking they were perfect for the occasion since they'd come from the islands. She glanced about for her grandfather but didn't see him in the throng. Maybe he had stepped out into the adjoining salon where refreshments were being served.

Although the surroundings bespoke the pomp and wealth and dazzled her senses with much satin and polished brass, Eden felt strangely uneasy and she didn't know why. Was it her imagination that the atmosphere seemed far from secure and tranquil? Certainly not all of those present were in support of Kalakaua. She perceived some shadowy intrigue that lingered, despite the Christmas decorations that adorned one side of the large room near an eight-foot decorated spruce tree.

Eden's gaze scanned the ambassadors of many nationalities wearing ornate garb and the officials from the embassies in unfamiliar uniform. They stood in official aloofness from one another, waiting for Kalakaua to join them.

Besides a host of various international figures, the best of the social strata of San Francisco were there as well, though Eden could not have identified them by name. She did recognize some railroad magnates and sugar growers, including the giant and stellar entrepreneur Claus Spreckles, the millionaire known as the Sugar King.

"One thing about him," Nora whispered, "he gave America the first sugar cubes for our tea *and* the first granules. Any man who could do that deserves our gratitude."

Eden smiled and looked about again for her grandfather. "I wonder where Grandfather and Zachary went to?"

"I don't know, dear, but my age is telling. I'm dreadfully tired. Would you mind if I went up to my room?"

"No, Aunt Nora," she hastened, "of course not. Would you like me to go with you?"

"I wouldn't hear of it. You stay and enjoy yourself. Wasn't that Rafe in the roped-off section for journalists?" she asked with a crafty gleam.

So Nora had noticed him too. "Yes, and I'm surprised to find him here. Did he tell you earlier that he was working on one of the San Francisco papers now?"

"No, and I'm sure he isn't," Nora said with confidence. "He says he arrived on the *Manoa* from some hard-to-pronounce place in South America. I rather think his station among the journalists was a masquerade, but I've no notion why. If he wanted to see either of us, he could have arranged it earlier."

"Yes," Eden said too casually, "I'm sure he would have." *Yet he didn't*, she thought to herself.

"Ainsworth and Zachary must be about somewhere," Nora went on, "unless something important came up. I can't imagine what. Oh bother! Here comes Lord Blount again. I've had enough of his surmising for one night. I may not agree with annexation, but I certainly don't want Hawaii in the grasp of Queen Victoria either."

Nora slipped away unnoticed, and Eden, growing uncomfortable when some foreign ambassador lifted his monocle and fit it into his eye to stare at her, also moved away into the milling guests.

What was Rafe up to? Why was he pretending to be a journalist? It appeared she might soon have the answer to her questions when Parker Judson came through the door with Rafe. The proprietor said something, perusing a list of invited guests, but Parker waved it aside. "Nonsense, he's with me," came his assertive voice. "Where's Kalakaua? I want to see him. Come along, Easton!"

Heads turned at the interruption. Some brows were raised over Parker's effrontery, and others looked noticeably curious when they saw Claus Spreckles walking toward them, hand stretched out for a warm, friendly shake. Any newcomer who was a friend of the mighty Spreckles deserved second notice.

"Well, Parker! Welcome to San Francisco!" Spreckles enjoined.

Eden remembered what Mr. Judson had said earlier that evening. When Zachary mentioned that Rafe was in San Francisco, her grandfather had looked disturbed, but Parker Judson had suddenly lighted up and said, "He's just the man I want to see." When someone as powerful as Judson wanted to see you, it was considered noteworthy.

The camaraderie of Spreckles and Judson no longer held her interest, and her gaze strayed to Rafe. He stood a short distance away from the two sugar kings. His eyes met hers and he appeared to start toward her when her grandfather and cousin Zachary appeared from some side chamber with Kalakaua's ambassador to the United States, Henry Carter.

At that moment several things seemed to occur at once. Parker Judson said, "Well, Ainsworth, congratulate us. Easton and I have made a deal to monopolize the pineapple business of Hawaii," and he laughed. Ainsworth and Rafe looked at each other, and Eden's heart felt the stiff silence. Then her grandfather saw her and eyed the black pearls at her throat. Her heart froze when he turned ashen. Zachary took hold of his grandfather's arm, as did Judson and Spreckles, and the three men led Ainsworth off into a chamber. Eden heard someone call for a doctor, and the private physician of King Kalakaua came rushing across the salon into the chamber. A buzz of voices filled Eden's ears; then she, too, realized that she was hurrying toward the chamber to her grandfather. A chill fear gripped her heart. She didn't look at Rafe, but she sensed he was watching her. Before she realized what had happened, his hand caught her arm tightly, stopping her in her tracks.

"Don't go in there," he ordered in a low voice.

Her eyes swerved to his and her feelings stumbled into confusion. She could see his seriousness, but also his anger. She could only think it was because he didn't like her grandfather.

She tried to pull away without making a scene, but Rafe simply drew her closer, as if to comfort her, and propelled her away to a somewhat private corner of the salon, where there was a chair and table with fresh gardenias on it.

"What are you doing?" she demanded quietly.

"Sit down and take those pearls off," he murmured in a low voice.

"What?" she gasped. Then glancing toward the guests, she whispered, "Are you out of your mind?"

The guests were watching them and making sympathetic comments among themselves as though she were beside herself with concern.

"Stand aside," she said. "My grandfather may be having a heart attack and you're keeping me here!"

"If he is, seeing you walk in with those pearls may do more harm than good."

"You're not making one whit of sense," she argued, but her shaking fingers reached behind her dark hair to find the clasp.

"Maybe not, but we won't take chances," Rafe insisted.

She opened her small beaded handbag, carried fashionably over her shoulder on a long, thin gold chain, to drop the pearls inside.

"Better give them to me for now."

"Give them to—" Eden raised her eyes to his, her lips parting slightly at his audacity. "To *you*!"

For the first time a faint smile played on his lips. "I'll return them later."

She trusted him but wondered why he was doing this. Confused, upset, even afraid over what was happening, she stared up at him. He looked down at her with apparent calmness, yet she sensed intense emotion just beneath his reserve.

"Would you mind explaining what's going on?"

"Not yet," Rafe repeated.

A new surge of energy flowed through her. She stood quickly. "My grandfather may be very ill. I've got to go to him. I've got to see how he's doing."

"There's nothing you can right now that Kalakaua's doctor isn't already attending to." He held out his hand for the strand of pearls. "Do you trust me with them or not? Do you expect me to dash out the door with them and escape on the *Manoa*?"

They looked at each other for a long silent moment. Despite the seriousness of the situation and Ainsworth's condition, her lips turned into a rueful smile. "I trust you."

"Thank you, Miss Derrington," he said, bowing his dark head.

Eden couldn't understand his reasons, but she released the pearls into his hand.

Unobtrusively, he slipped them into his pocket, then glanced toward the throng. Zachary had come out and was making an announcement with King Kalakaua at his side.

"Thank you for your concern for my grandfather," he was saying. "His Majesty's physician and Mr. Derrington both wish to assure everyone here that he's feeling much better. He has requested that you go on with your pleasant evening, and he offers a special apology to His Majesty for interrupting the gathering. Thank you."

A buzz broke out, and Zachary turned away, said something to the king, then paused when he saw Eden. His eyes shifted abruptly to Rafe and his expression noticeably stiffened. He walked across the salon toward them.

"Are you sure Grandfather's all right?" Eden asked.

"Just a slight dizzy spell. The rich food, he says."

"I want to speak to him," Eden said.

"He's asked for you." Zachary glanced to where the pearls had been, noticed they were gone, and looked at her. She avoided his gaze and turned to Rafe.

Rafe looked toward the chamber. "I came to speak with Ainsworth tonight, but since I'm not the company he'd likely appreciate, the meeting can wait until he's up to it."

Eden was curious as to why Rafe wanted to speak to him.

Rafe looked at Zachary. "One shock tonight is enough."

Zachary's mouth tightened. "Shock?"

"The black pearls Eden was wearing," Rafe admitted. "They appeared to upset him. Didn't you notice?"

"Strange you'd think that. No, I didn't."

"Didn't you? My mistake—I thought you had."

Eden tensed. Zachary's fair skin flushed. "No," he stated again with sharpness. "Why should I notice something like that? Why should the pearls upset him?"

"They were Rebecca's, weren't they?"

"So what?" he almost snapped. "Why shouldn't Eden have her mother's pearls after graduation from Chadwick?" He looked at her, his blue eyes animated. "You did a splendid job, Eden."

Eden looked at Rafe. *Well?* she wanted to say. *You've prodded him about the pearls, but for what reason? And it didn't work! He doesn't appear to even know what you're getting at. And neither do I.*

"It should be interesting to learn what Ainsworth says later on about having seen Rebecca's pearls on Eden," Rafe told Zachary. "I wonder if he agrees with you that they should have been given to her tonight."

"Are you saying Cousin Eden shouldn't have gotten them?" Zachary asked with a scoff, scanning him.

What is he getting at? she wondered.

Rafe looked at her steadily. "Nora gave them to you tonight?"

"What does it matter who returned them to Eden?" Zachary interrupted impatiently. "They belonged to Rebecca. They should go to her daughter. Everything she owned should go to Eden."

"Does that mean everything my father owned should be returned to me?"

Zachary, caught in his own words, looked angry. "Come along, Eden. Grandfather is waiting."

"It matters who gave the pearls to Eden," Rafe continued smoothly, "because someone apparently wanted to startle Ainsworth tonight by having Eden wear them. Someone who thought it would be to their advantage. I'm rather curious as to who that might have been."

Zachary's eyes turned icy blue. "More than one person might wish to take advantage of my grandfather."

Rafe fell into an astute silence.

Noticing, Eden was taken by the change.

Zachary turned. "Coming, Eden?"

"Yes." Eden, troubled over more than her grandfather, glanced at Rafe again. She wanted to say something that would bridge the emotional distance that was expanding between them, but words failed her.

Rafe hesitated, then reached inside his jacket and pulled out what appeared to be a soiled, sealed envelope. "This letter is from Rio de Janeiro. I promised someone to deliver it to Ainsworth. See that he has it, will you?"

Eden accepted the envelope, but did not recognize the South American name.

"Eden?" Zachary repeated. "Coming?"

She turned away, her heart weighing heavy in her chest, and walked toward the chamber where her grandfather was resting. Zachary opened the door for her to step inside, and she glanced back at Rafe. He was leaving, passing through the double doorway into the hotel corridor.

Ainsworth was sitting in a chair when Eden entered the room where several others were gathered, including Parker Judson. Eden went to her grandfather and sat near him on a settee. She was pleased when he took the initiative to reach for her hand, giving it a gentle squeeze that told her not to worry.

"This would have to happen now," Parker said over his cigar, pacing. "Maybe there was something put in your food, Ainsworth."

"Don't be a firebrand, Parker," Ainsworth said quietly. "There was nothing wrong with my dinner except I overate. A sin of the affluent. Indulgence claims the lives of thousands."

Parker, with a hefty build and rounded stomach, looked at him askance.

"Grandfather, is there anything I can do?"

"No, Eden, it will pass. It was simply coincidental. There's nothing seriously ailing with my health, as the physician will tell you, but it appears I must cancel that trip to Washington." He looked over at Parker. "We'd better send a wire to Blaine's secretary explaining the cancellation."

Eden waited to see what her grandfather would do when he noticed the pearls were gone. Oddly, he didn't appear to notice at all. Had Rafe been mistaken? She earnestly wanted to believe that he was wrong. After all, why shouldn't her grandfather, a man in his sixties, grow a little light-headed after such a demanding day?

Down deep in her heart, if she took the time to analyze those thoughts, she knew she didn't believe them, but here in this pleasant, warm room, where a smaller Christmas tree and ornaments shined brightly, it was easier to tell herself she did. The mood had lightened. There were smiles on those present as everyone realized that a tragedy had not materialized. Even Parker Judson had mellowed and was discussing his new projects in Hawaii. He would begin a new plantation, he said, and he had just the right man he could trust to pull it off.

Only Zachary was subdued. He had walked to a window by the Christmas tree and was looking out in silence as the others talked, both hands shoved restlessly into his trouser pockets.

Eden was alone with her grandfather when he inquired in a low, stiff voice, "Did Rafe leave?"

"Yes." She kept her voice as casual as she could. "He said something about coming to speak with you, but that it could wait."

"I want you to stay away from him, Eden. He's a bitter young man and he poisons the atmosphere wherever he goes. I'd like to keep him off of Kea Lani too, but I can't very well do that when his mother is married to Townsend."

"I thought you had *wanted* Townsend to marry her," she ventured boldly.

"I did, but I've lived to regret it. I'm sorry for Celestine. She's a sensitive woman—not the right one to put up with Townsend's foolishness."

"Doesn't that make you more sympathetic toward Rafe?"

"No," he said flatly, his white brows bristling. "I have no sympathy for him whatsoever. He resented Celestine making a new life for herself after Matt died. Even as a child he did what he could to ruin their marriage."

"Oh, Grandfather, I don't want to upset you, especially now, but I can't believe that about Rafe."

"Well, you best believe it, young lady, because it's so." He squeezed her hand firmly. "When you come back to Kea Lani, Eden, I want you to stay clear of him, just as Rozlind must keep away from that Hawaiian cohort of his. You're a Derrington, Eden. I'm growing more proud of you by the hour, but you must begin behaving as a member of the family. If it weren't that Celestine were gravely ill and not expected to live much longer, I wouldn't allow Rafe at Kea Lani. But considering she's his mother, I can't bring myself to order him to stay away."

Eden's hopes were dwindling. She wanted to protest her grandfather's conclusions about Rafe, even defend Rafe's right to Matt's inheritance, but she was likely to alienate Ainsworth if she argued. If she was ever to have any good influence in the future, she must win his respect as well as his affection.

She felt she had more reason now to believe in his acceptance than at any time in her youth. She had grown up to become a woman he appeared to be proud of, even as he had always taken special pride in Rozlind. Her heart cried against doing anything that risked breaking that fragile new relationship. It must grow strong, sinking its roots deep into rich soil.

"Do you know why Rafe came tonight to speak to you?" she asked quietly.

"No, and at the moment it doesn't matter. I haven't the time or the inclination to hear him out. I suspect it has to do with Hanalei. But he'll need to deal with Townsend about that. I've no say in the matter."

She wondered if that were true. She thought he might have more to say than he would admit. He had a great deal of influence over Townsend.

Zachary went to answer a knock on the door and returned a moment later with a note.

"It's for you, Eden. Nora's been told about Grandfather and wants you to come up to her room. The number's written on the paper." He handed her the note.

"Assure her I'm all right," Ainsworth told Eden. "I'd go up myself, but I've some final business to attend to with Kalakaua." He stood and Eden rose from the settee. He took her hands and planted a kiss on her forehead. "You'll be going back with Nora and Zachary, I suppose?"

Eden's heart warmed. "Yes, Grandfather."

He smiled wanly and looked at her for a long, thoughtful moment. "Good. I'm glad. Maybe at long last we'll actually get to know one another."

He released her hands. "Good night, my dear."

Eden hesitated. She had no reason to suspect the letter Rafe had given her would upset her grandfather, but she had a premonition it might. Still, she had no right to keep it back after Rafe had entrusted it to her.

"Rafe asked that I give this to you before he left."

His expression altered as he looked at the envelope.

"A colleague of yours?" She asked curiously, after a moment of strained silence.

Grandfather didn't appear to hear her, and murmuring that she excuse him, he walked to the other side of the room to read it.

As she walked to the chamber door, Zachary came up beside her. "I'll take you to Nora if you like."

She didn't want Zachary with her. She wanted to see Nora alone.

"I'd rather you didn't," she admitted. "Nora's tired and I don't think she wants more company."

Zachary's displeasure was muted. "Of course," he said. He tried to smile pleasantly. "I'll be in touch with you at Chadwick about the voyage home. I don't know how long Nora expects to stay in San Francisco."

Eden didn't think she would stay long. She would be leaving, too, by train, on her author tour promoting her book. Eden said nothing to Zachary about it and, bidding him good night, left the salon to find Great-aunt Nora's room on the third floor.

Strange . . . so much had been made of the pearls, yet Grandfather hadn't even mentioned them! Rafe was wrong.

Then she remembered Lana's strong reaction when she had seen them. Lana had admitted her own reasons for being distraught, but Eden's grandfather had completely avoided the subject. Had it been deliberate?

E·I·G H T E E N

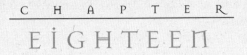

Great-aunt Nora was waiting when Eden arrived. The older woman was daintily dressed in a gray fluffy robe over a gray flannel nightgown. She sat propped up in a bed with satin coverings and blue beaded lamps burning on the end tables. Her book, *The Spoils of Eden*, sat open on her lap. Her gray hair appeared to have been hastily woven into one braid, which hung across her small, slightly stooped shoulder. The silvery green eyes looked at Eden anxiously.

"How is Ainsworth?"

Eden smiled encouragingly and sat down beside Nora on the satin cover.

"The king's physician assures us he'll be all right," Eden said brightly. "Just a minor dizzy spell brought on by the stress of a long day."

"Ainsworth thrives on stress," Nora said, dismissing the doctor's diagnosis. "There must have been something else that upset him so."

Eden saw nothing in her great-aunt's face to indicate she understood. Rafe had asked if Nora sent the pearls. Unlike Ainsworth, Nora hadn't appeared to even notice them.

"I'm sure we can trust Kalakaua's doctor," Eden soothed.

"Well, yes, you're right about that. If Ainsworth says he's feeling all right, I'll need to take his word for it."

Nora looked exhausted and Eden prepared to leave. "You'd better get some sleep."

"There was something else I wanted to talk to you about, Eden." She laid the book aside and fixed her with a clear and candid gaze. "I've been thinking about our discussion at dinner. I suppose the fright I received over Ainsworth got me to thinking. I am getting quite old—"

"Oh no, you—"

"Now, now, none of that, my dear. I'm very practical about these matters. The mirror never lies. I told you tonight I needed you, and I want to reiterate that. I don't want to be selfish about these things, but I'll need someone to support me as I back Liliuokalani. I have high hopes for you. I suspect Ainsworth does as well."

Eden remembered her grandfather's warning and also his revealed affection. The bond between them was growing.

"Then I'm right about Ainsworth," Nora said dully, looking at her. "Well, it doesn't surprise me. Rozlind has been such a disappointment to him recently, and Zachary—well, no use going into that again. You know what I told you about him."

"Nora, I want my heart to be loyal to both you and Grandfather. It's painful to think I'm being asked to choose. I love you both."

"But you're not so naive, my girl, as to think you can be a fence-sitter. One day soon you'll need to decide which political side you're on."

"Yes," Eden admitted wearily. She had always assumed she was on the side of the monarchy. But recently, there'd been new tugs at her heart. Did they come from a reassessment of the facts about the destiny of the islands or from her growing love for her grandfather?

"I needn't remind you of the wide differences between what I believe is best for Hawaii's future and what Ainsworth believes," Nora went on.

"We all agree we don't want Hawaii to become a territory of Great Britain or Japan," Eden said.

"Yes . . . but it's Liliuokalani we must agree on," Nora said. "If I'm upset tonight about Ainsworth's dizzy spell, it's also because I've learned something else about Kalakaua. He worsens, dear, despite his brave front tonight. He is a very ill man. Anything might happen."

Eden was silent. Liliuokalani was waiting behind the royal curtain to be crowned queen of Hawaii.

"The moment she assumes the throne," Nora said, "I fear the Hawaiian League will begin to put plans into operation to remove her. You know how this sort of thing will divide us, don't you?"

Eden knew, and her mind drifted to not just her family, but to Noelani and Ambrose, to Rafe and Keno, and to thousands like them.

What of me? Where do I stand? She had been so certain only days ago.

Nora watched her alertly. "I fear Ainsworth may be considering you his heir in place of either Rozlind or Zachary."

"Oh no, he wouldn't—"

"One never knows what Ainsworth will do. He will consider what he believes is best for Hawaii, and for the Derrington enterprise. And if he could make a good match for you—well, you've turned into a bright and charming young woman, Eden. I think he's surprised by this. We all are, though I always felt you had potential."

Eden couldn't even imagine being placed in such a difficult situation. Nor did she want to supplant Rozlind or Zachary—not to mention deal with their disappointment and resentment.

"Then I would refuse it," she said firmly.

"You say that now, but as you get older, you'll see things differently."

Eden considered Nora's words but was confident she wouldn't change.

"So it looks as if you can have your choice, doesn't it? It puts you in a very precarious position."

"I don't understand."

"You will inherit a great deal one day, Eden, from either Ainsworth or me. Naturally, whichever side you choose to align yourself with will determine your inheritance, as well as the portion of Kea Lani that will then fall to Rozlind or Zachary. In order to protect the Derrington fortune, it would seem unwise for us both to make you the primary heir. And besides, inheriting all that wealth so suddenly might ruin you."

Eden smiled wryly. She seemed to have come a long way since sleeping in the loft above Ambrose's kitchen.

"You don't know me, Great-aunt Nora. Yes, it would be wonderful to be rich and important, I suppose, but my heart and ambitions belong to our Savior. I want to serve Him as I carry on my parents' work. I think that in the end this may get me into some trouble with both you and Grandfather."

"You can carry on your parents' work, but remember that they were both loyal supporters of the monarchy. Naturally, then, you would follow in their footsteps," she urged. "Especially after all the support you've given me in writing the book."

"I was told my father wasn't as involved in politics as either Grandfather or Uncle Townsend. Father worked at Kalihi Hospital and the leper detention camp. That's my ambition as well."

Nora frowned as if the mention of the dread disease upset her, but Eden pressed on. "Nora, why didn't you ever tell me that my mother's sister worked with my father?"

Nora's face went blank. "I thought I mentioned it to you years ago."

"No, and neither did anyone else."

"It must have slipped our minds. Yes, I guess Lana did work there for a time. Why do you ask?"

"Because I've learned that she also worked for Dr. Bolton. I want to join his staff and eventually serve alongside Father in his research."

Nora sighed, obviously disappointed. "Traipsing about the jungle from one isolated camp to another sounds dreadfully tiring and dangerous. Ainsworth would be very upset if you did."

"Surely you wouldn't refuse my request out of fear for what Grandfather would say?" Eden pressed.

"You're right, I wouldn't. But I will need you with me at Kea Lani."

"I would still be at Kea Lani for at least a year if I worked with Dr. Bolton at the hospital. And the extra training would prepare me to serve with my father," she insisted.

Nora looked at her craftily and smiled. "If I agree to this request of yours and speak to Dr. Bolton, will you cooperate with me in support of Liliuokalani?"

Eden hesitated. "Great-aunt, you're using mild extortion."

Nora's smile deepened. "And you're doing the same with me, dear."

Eden smiled. "I don't see why I wouldn't support Liliuokalani," she said carefully.

Nora appeared satisfied. "Then we'll proceed slowly concerning Kalihi once you've gone home."

"Does that mean you'll talk to Dr. Bolton about me?"

"Yes. I suppose you want Lana to go with you to Kalihi?" Nora frowned.

"I confess I've thought about it."

"She won't go," Nora said firmly. "She'll never go back."

Eden chose not to pursue the issue for the present. It appeared as though the Lord was answering her prayer! She might be working with Dr. Clifford Bolton in the future; then if the Lord opened the door, she would eventually join her father. Her thoughts turned to the leper settlement on Molokai, where her father had done his early research.

"Did my father ever talk much to you about the work on Molokai?"

There was a guarded moment before Nora spoke. "Yes, he discussed it. Before he left Oahu he came to me and told me he was expanding his research on the disease by visiting other countries. He had a camp in Tahiti, and one in Samoa, I think—or was it Tonga?" She shook her head. "I can't recall. He was always going somewhere, even South America. I tried to dissuade him. We needed him at Kalihi and Molokai. But Rebecca—her death, the drowning—it depressed him so much that he seemed driven with a passion for being involved in medical work, especially to find a cure for leprosy." Nora looked at her and took a deep breath as if the discussion had drained her. "You're wrong about his disinterest in Hawaiian politics. He was a friend of Kalakaua and Liliuokalani. Kalakaua, in return, was very supportive of Jerome's work on Molokai, as were Dr. Bolton and the Kalihi Hospital staff. They still are. I think Dr. Bolton still goes there now and then."

"To Molokai?"

"Yes."

Perhaps she could go too, Eden thought, if Nora arranged for her placement on Bolton's staff. Her excitement grew.

"I'm pleased about tonight," Nora said suddenly. "Somehow, I knew I would be able to depend upon you."

Eden, too, was satisfied. "I'll do my best, Aunt Nora."

"Nothing must be allowed to interfere with your return. Hawaii needs her best daughters. Especially now." She handed her the book. "I meant to give this to you at dinner tonight. I'm indebted to your historical research. I know you'll do what's right about the fate of the islands and people we both love."

Eden held it, feeling its smooth jacket. She knew that her grandfather felt the same as Nora about doing what was best for the Hawaiian people—and with equal passion. But there would be no pleasing everyone. Whatever decision was finally made about annexation, many in this generation would experience disappointment.

What do I believe, really? she thought. Hiram Bingham and the first American missionaries had not gone to the islands to colonize but to teach Christianity. King Liholiho at that time opened up the Hawaiian Islands to them in order to dispel darkness with knowledge, and the missionaries brought a great light by teaching God-given truths. Then they built the churches and schools and created the Hawaiian alphabet and their written language. In the generations that followed, their offspring were born true "Hawaiians." They went on to build businesses and plantations and were called in by the Hawaiian kings to provide counsel and hold positions in the government. As "new Hawaiians" they had wanted the best possible form of government and law for their country—but what was best? A republic or a monarchy? Since these new Hawaiians had such close ties to the United States, it mattered what Americans felt on this subject. America, of course, had little tolerance for kings and queens, believing that monarchs too often became dictators and ruled for their own benefit.

Aware that Great-aunt Nora had been watching her struggle, Eden smiled and planted a kiss on her wrinkled cheek.

"I enjoyed our late-night talk. And thank you for the book." She stood and smiled at her great-aunt. "Good night."

Eden headed toward the door. Her heart was full but vaguely troubled as well. There were no easy answers or simple choices.

She walked down the hotel corridor toward the stairway, intending to return to Chadwick. She had learned a few things tonight, but most of her questions remained behind locked doors. She wondered if Rafe Easton held some of the keys.

NINETEEN

Eden assumed that Zachary was still with Ainsworth as she descended the hotel stairway and went into an outer salon with a wall of mirrors, where lights reflected like dangling diamonds. The glossy floor was adorned with palatial crimson carpet and leafy palms in brass urns. She stopped. Zachary appeared to be waiting for her as he paced, hands in trouser pockets. *I can't take any more of him tonight*, she thought desperately. Could she retreat without being seen? Slowly she began backing away until she came to a tall palm. She stepped behind it just as Rafe casually walked up. He glanced toward Zachary, then swiftly led her back toward the stairway.

"I've got to speak with you alone," he said in a low voice.

Eden glanced back over her shoulder. Zachary had seen her and started in their direction.

"He's coming," she said.

"This way."

They ran through an archway into another salon and past two huge marble pillars to avoid being seen. He propelled her behind an alabaster screen where potted palms grew thick and green.

Eden glanced through the lattice to see if Zachary was following, only to see that he had rushed up to the archway and stood glancing in both directions. He did not enter the salon but turned away hurriedly. He must have decided they'd gone back upstairs to Kalakaua's reception, she thought.

The area was nearly empty now, except for passing strangers walking to the stairway. Eden turned toward Rafe and saw his suave amusement. She screened her emotions from the dynamic incursion of his presence. After his long absence she would not permit her heart to be taken captive again, not when her plans were at last moving on the right path.

In spite of the lack of direct lighting, his chiseled features retained the sharp contrasts that were etched upon her mind. The contour of his chin, the rich brown eyes below a slash of brow as dark as his hair, returned a rush of memories she had resisted in his absence. She wanted to be safe, to avoid confronting emotions that could stand as obstacles in her path. At the same time, she knew it was unfair to consider him as threatening, even though he'd always been a force to reckon with as they grew up on Oahu. It was Zachary she was trying to avoid now.

"Now that we've escaped, maybe I can convince you to avoid another trap, that of returning to Kea Lani."

Trap? She lifted both brows. "Now, why would you even wish to try to convince me of something so utterly inconceivable?"

His mouth turned downward. "I'm up to the challenge, especially where you're concerned. Why? Because I'd hate to see you get into more trouble."

"That's exceedingly thoughtful of you, but I've no plans to wade into any trouble I can't handle."

"Rebecca's black pearls are another reason." He lifted the strand from his inside jacket pocket and held them up. They glimmered. His brow lifted. "You do want them back, don't you?"

A brief smile tugged at her mouth. She held out her palm. "Yes. How clever of you to run off with them."

Rafe slipped them back inside his pocket. "I'll turn them over to you in the coach." He looked at his watch. "Nearly ten-thirty. I'm leaving soon for Honolulu and I need to get an early start tomorrow. Keno and I still have much to get ready. And you and I have a good deal to talk about."

"More about this trouble you're hoping to warn me against?"

"Yes, I've been attempting to keep up with what Zachary has been hatching to further his aims."

She started to protest, then decided she did want to talk to him. She was curious, but not so much about Zachary as about what Rafe had been doing for the last two years.

"I'd be very disappointed if you didn't trust me enough to give me a chance to talk to you before I leave," he said.

"Very well," she responded simply.

He stepped aside and Eden walked past. *I need a ride home anyway*, she told herself.

Outside the Palace Hotel a driver brought a coach around the stone half-circle. Rafe led her through some loiterers to where the vehicle stood in line with several others, all jamming the great court so that foot traffic was obstructed.

The fog had lifted, but clouds blowing in from the Bay were sprinkling chilling drops onto Eden's face. Rafe opened the coach door and handed her in. They moved down the wintry city street through the misty rain. The interior flickered with two small gas lamps beside each window.

Rafe leaned over and handed her the strand of pearls. Eden didn't put them back on, but held them, musing over the trouble that had erupted at their recent appearance. Did Rafe think they had come from his father's pearl bed?

She hardly noticed the direction the coachman was taking them until they passed Market Street. They reached Union Square and drove past the St. Francis Hotel, which displayed expensive goods in small shops named after the White House and the city of Paris.

"Did Nora mention the pearls when you went up to her room?" Rafe inquired.

So he knew about her visit with Nora after the reception.

"No. She was worried about Ainsworth and we—"

"Yes?"

"We discussed my future in Hawaii," she said, reluctant to bring up the subject. She knew he would not be as optimistic about her homecoming as Nora—or her grandfather and Zachary. "We discussed the fate of the Hawaiian monarchy."

"A profound topic," he said laconically. "About the pearls . . . if Nora had sent them as a gift through Zachary, she would have noticed you were wearing them at dinner."

Eden wanted him to be wrong. She didn't want trouble. If by any slim chance they *had* been sent by Nora, then Rafe was making more out of the situation than was warranted.

"She didn't wear her pince-nez to dinner," she said rather jubilantly.

"Good try, Eden, but she doesn't use them. The dear has unusually good eyesight for her age. She'll be the first to tell you so."

She thought of the book on Nora's bed when she'd gone to her room. It had been open, the reading lamps burning, but she hadn't been wearing eyeglasses.

"Rather unusual for her not to mention them," he said. "That particular strand is quite valuable."

In the lantern light, she met his speculative gaze. "All right, then, it's likely she didn't have anything to do with sending Rebecca's pearls. I'm wondering what you're getting at."

"I'm convinced she did recognize them, but for reasons of her own she didn't want to discuss them with you. We also know from Ainsworth's reaction he didn't send them. He was shocked when he saw them on you."

Eden winced. Would she ever forget that stricken look on his face?

The pearls were cool to her fingertips. She rehearsed in her mind Lana's behavior when she had seen them earlier that evening. What would Rafe do if he knew?

"Lana also reacted strongly tonight when she saw the pearls," she told him.

She expected his interest to grow and wondered when he didn't appear to pay particular attention.

"Lana said her emotional response came from seeing them again after all these years, especially on me; it was such a shock. She said something else interesting—that there may be a portrait of Rebecca wearing them. She said there were several artists in the family, including Nora."

"Did she?" he said nonchalantly. "Interesting. About Zachary . . . did he tell you the pearls belonged to Rebecca when he gave them to you?"

She thought back to their meeting by the pond. "No, he never mentioned what was inside the gift box. Lana recognized them at once and asked where Zachary got them. She said Rebecca wore them at the wedding luau on Kea Lani and again before she died. She gave them to Lana to return to my father. Rather odd, don't you think?"

As Rafe watched her, she had the notion he was trying to learn her exact thoughts. "Why do you think so?"

She turned the strand over between her fingers several times. "Return them to my father . . . Usually when a woman returns a ring or jewelry, doesn't that mean a broken relationship?"

Rafe tapped his chin, and Eden wondered why he suddenly seemed so alert.

"Yet from all I've heard about either of my parents they were very much in love," Eden went on.

She was facing questions her mind had refused to bring out in the open until now. "Yes, it's strange she gave them back, and to Lana. Almost as if—"

Their eyes held. "Yes?" he said quietly.

"As if she wouldn't see him again," Eden concluded. "And then she went away with a friend in a boat—in a storm—" She shook her head. "It makes no sense." She lifted her head to look at him and wondered why he seemed relieved.

"Ambrose said she went out with a teacher friend from the Royal School," Rafe said. "Why don't we leave it there, Eden?"

Eden didn't want to leave it shrouded in mystery. "But Rebecca couldn't have run away with a friend, Rafe."

"No one ever said she tried to run away. Why do you think that?" He was watching her again.

"I don't know. . . ." she mused. "Somehow the feeling that she might have keeps stirring in my mind. Anyway, Lana said my mother had precious words for my father to go with the pearls. She spoke of loving him always, of holding him in her heart forever."

He looked at her, absorbed with his thoughts. "Lana told you that?" He seemed displeased.

"Those aren't the words of a woman breaking a vow," she said firmly. "My response to Lana was that the pearls were even more precious to me, but when I looked at Lana I was startled by the animosity in her eyes."

"Probably toward Zachary for sending them and stirring up trouble."

"And then there was the letter. . . ."

Now he was fully alert. "A letter? To you?"

"No, to Lana, from Zachary." She explained about Lana's strange behavior.

"That confirms my opinions about Zachary's motives," he scowled thoughtfully as he played with the window sash. "The letter, too, was meant to intimidate. This time Lana."

"But why intimidate her?"

Rafe flicked the silken cord aside. "Why not? She wants to keep you here in San Francisco with her. And Zachary wants you in Hawaii to further his aims. He probably told her Nora wanted to bring you home and not to do anything to stop you."

Despite Rafe's casual manner, Eden noted that he was watching her, as if wondering if she would accept his explanation. Her hand tightened on the pearls. She looked down at them again—shiny, smooth, and black.

"And what would Zachary's motives be concerning the pearls?"

"I think you already know. That unfortunate incident tonight with your grandfather was staged by him."

"Why do you say that? Zachary would have no reason to distress him.

He's always been close to his grandfather."

"Yes, but not so devoted that he won't battle to keep what means most to him. Ambrose tells me your grandfather's threatening to leave control of Kea Lani to you instead of either Zachary or Rozlind."

Eden felt embarrassed. "Nora mentioned that tonight. But I don't believe Grandfather would go through with it. I don't want him to. I told Nora that tonight. She knows I want to follow my father in his work."

"Ainsworth will always do what he believes is the right thing for the Derrington heritage and for his beloved Hawaii. He's that kind of man. And he'll do what he must to protect the venerable Derrington name."

She sighed. "I just don't see that Zachary gains all that much by having me home at Kea Lani."

"I think you're wrong. He believes either Ainsworth or Nora may leave you a large inheritance in the Derrington enterprises."

"He did mention that Nora might have something like that on her mind when he came to Chadwick yesterday, but I thought he was trying to flatter me. Nora said tonight that Grandfather hasn't told Zachary about his decision yet. A lot still depends on what Rozlind does. So Zachary wouldn't be scheming to regain control."

"He may suspect it, though, which accounts for the pearls, and his coming to see you at Chadwick. He's obsessed about inheriting Kea Lani."

Obsessed. A strange way for Rafe to put it, but she had to admit he was probably right.

"I can understand in a way," she said. "From childhood he's been trained to accomplish one thing—to follow in Grandfather's footsteps."

"And now those footsteps appear to be leading him far afield."

Eden felt chilled and leaned into the plush seat. The wheels churned over the bumpy, wet cobblestones behind clattering horse hooves.

"You've left someone out who may have asked Zachary to bring the pearls to me."

Rafe watched her pensively. "Who could that be?" he asked smoothly.

"My father. He gave them to Rebecca as a wedding gift. Perhaps he wanted me to have them for graduation. He knows I've been majoring in tropical diseases and he's pleased about it. I got a letter from him some months ago, mailed from Rio."

A gust of December wind buffeted the side of the coach, and the raindrops pelted the small windows. Eden awaited Rafe's response and wondered at his silence.

"Did he mention the pearls in that last letter?"

"Well, no, but—"

"Jerome didn't send them to you. Zachary hasn't seen him in years. Look, Eden, there isn't any mystery as to who brought you the pearls or why. It was Zachary. How he got them and where is a matter for Ainsworth to tackle—as I'm sure he will when he gets back to Hawaii from Washington. If you want my opinion, Zachary snooped about Jerome's old room at Kea Lani and found them. Unfortunately, who knows what else he may have discovered?"

"What would give him the liberty to think he could search my father's things?" Eden said indignantly.

"Ainsworth will also want the answer to that question. Let your grandfather handle Zachary. But I think you'd better be prepared to be courted by Zach should Kea Lani be left to you."

"Courted!" She was embarrassed. Her thoughts rushed back to that unpleasant incident on the beach two years ago. "He's a blood cousin."

"He likes to pretend otherwise to make you think he's not."

Zachary had said she was an Easton, and that he'd prove it. Had that been the reason for searching Jerome's room? Perhaps he had come across the pearls and decided to use them. Rafe, too, had told her he would do some investigating, but to prove Zachary wrong. Had he? If he had done any searching during these last few years, Rafe said nothing about uncovering any new information. Whatever he was thinking was kept behind his suave facade.

Her eyes turned toward the rain blurring the coach window. She had hoped Zachary had outgrown those foolish ideas. From his behavior tonight it appeared that he hadn't, though when he first arrived at Chadwick yesterday he seemed to have changed. Sadly, he was still just as spoiled and headstrong about having his own way as when he was a boy.

Eden had no intention of allowing herself to fit into any of her cousin's plans.

"But—even if you're right, and he unwisely thinks he can manipulate me, what about the pearls? What made him think my wearing them tonight would intimidate my grandfather?"

Rafe was silent a moment too long. "Because Rebecca wore them the last time she was seen at Kea Lani. It's purely psychological, but they're connected with something the Derringtons find wholly unpleasant—Rebecca's tragedy."

Eden's throat felt tight. Yes, she thought, her fingers feeling the pearls. She could understand their feelings now. Her grandfather had been stricken, and Nora had preferred not to see them in order to forget about Rebecca.

And yet the pearls are precious to me, she thought, *because I have no memory of the tragic incident. They're simply something that belonged to my mother.*

"Her drowning," Eden agreed quietly. "Very unpleasant for all of them."

Rafe didn't answer. He played with the silken sash cord on the window shade.

She looked up at him.

"What concerns me the most is that Zachary may think he knows something more. The pearls were an immature way for him to show his grandfather that he has some leverage."

"Leverage? For what? To make Grandfather leave him heir?"

"Exactly."

"That's dreadful," she murmured. She grew more upset as she remembered the pained look on her grandfather's face that evening. And Zachary had used *her* to accomplish it. He hadn't cared about the emotional attachment she would feel toward her mother's wedding pearls.

"Are you sure, Rafe?"

"As sure as I can be. I've done a little research myself recently."

She wondered what kind he was referring to, but her mind reverted to what he was now saying.

"If Ainsworth decides to disinherit Zachary in favor of you or Rozlind, then he'll cause the kind of trouble he dislikes."

Eden's heart thumped. She squeezed the pearls in her palm.

"They should have been given to me by my father, because they belonged to Rebecca," she said quietly. "Not by Zachary, trying to use me to accomplish his plans. He was selfish. He doesn't care whom he hurts sometimes—" She stopped, emotion welling up in her heart. She swallowed hard, not wanting to display her feelings in front of Rafe.

"I'm sorry," he said softly. He leaned over and laid a hand on hers. "Regardless of everything unpleasant, they were still your mother's pearls. She'd want you to have them. They're better off with you, who loves her memory, than hidden away in some dusty, forgotten place. Now that you know why Zachary sent them, you can avoid his schemes. And that is my only motivation for telling you all this."

His eyes were as warm and dark as the pearls, and she became too aware of him and the tenderness of his comforting touch as he held her hand. She now knew that the real reason he had wanted to warn her was to keep her from further hurt. She also felt that if she hadn't displayed her disappointment, he wouldn't have unveiled the tender side of his emotions. He would have maintained the psychological wall between them. A wall that had been there for years. He was at times beyond her comprehension. Did he really care about her or did he have some other hidden motivation? Was there something more he wasn't telling her?

"Yes, you're right, Rafe. I should simply appreciate the pearls because they were my mother's and forget everything else, especially Zachary's troublesome tactics."

"To say the least," he said wryly and leaned back in the seat again. "And now, let's get back to your future. If you don't mind my saying this, I'd be cautious about receiving anything more from Zachary. Also, what's wrong with staying on at Chadwick for another six months or so? Lana tells me the college can place you at St. Francis Hospital."

Her eyes swerved to his. "Lana *told* you? When did you speak with her?"

"Ah, that. Yes, I meant to tell you she corresponded with me once or twice these last couple of years. She happened to mention St. Francis."

She couldn't let that slip by! "Lana wrote you? She never told me."

"She must have forgotten." He offered a charming smile.

"How did she know where you were?"

"Oh, I wrote to her—occasionally," Rafe said coolly.

"Occasionally."

Yet he didn't write to me, Eden thought.

"Yes, occasionally," he repeated airily. "I passed through San Francisco once. Unfortunately, I was very busy and you were in class. I didn't want to disturb you. You might have been dissecting a white rat or something of that nature."

So he had been in San Francisco. . . .

Eden found she was seldom satisfied with his explanations. He wasn't the sort to be in town for long, unless it was true that he had a shipping business and perhaps had arrived with a cargo. If so, then that might explain his interaction with Lana. But he wasn't telling her everything.

"Did you write to Lana about what you were doing in your travels?" she asked in a nonchalant tone.

"I didn't have much to tell. I was fighting the hurricane season in the Gulf of Mexico aboard the *Manoa.* You wouldn't have found it interesting."

At least she had learned that he'd been sailing in the Gulf of Mexico. She leaned back into the seat, watching him.

No, she thought again, *he's not telling me everything.*

When the coach arrived at Chadwick, Rafe opened the door and got out, then assisted her down to the stone carriage block. The rain was worsening as a storm was blowing in. So much remained unsaid, unexplained. She turned and looked up toward Chadwick mansion, where a lamp glowed in the lower hall. The pine trees sighed in the wind.

He escorted her up the steps and onto the wide front porch.

"Do you have a key or must you waken Lana?"

"She said she'd leave it open for me."

He tried the latch and the heavy oak door slid open.

Eden stepped inside. "Lana, you stayed up," she greeted her aunt, smiling. "You've met Rafe Easton, of course?"

CHAPTER

TWENTY

Lana came down the stairs, hand extended, showing no concern that Rafe's presence might make known their previous correspondence.

"Of course Rafe and I have met. How are you, Rafe? I was hoping you'd be the one to bring Eden home" came her subtle aspersion to his stepbrother. "Will you be staying long in San Francisco?"

"A few days. I'm on my way to Oahu."

Lana suggested that Rafe stay and enjoy the fire in the parlor while she retired for the night. There were drinks and some Christmas cakes on the parlor table, she told them, as though she may have expected him. Then she bid them good-night and went up to her room.

Eden watched her go, curious about her behavior, then a moment later looked toward Rafe. He had walked over to a hall table where a large portrait hung above on the wall.

Eden smiled wistfully. "That's my mother . . . and Lana when they were in their teens. The nursing college honors Rebecca as a pioneer missionary in Hawaii." Now, for the first time, Eden understood why Lana was also included in the portrait the school had decided to display. She wondered if Rafe knew that Lana's early medical service had also been on Molokai as a missionary among the lepers. Thus far, Rafe had surprised her by understanding far more than she had thought possible.

Rafe looked at the painting for a long moment. "So that's Rebecca."

Eden joined him by the table, mildly surprised. "You don't remember her?"

199

"Vaguely. If you take after any of the Derringtons, it would be Miss Amabel Bancroft."

If? Eden's spine stiffened. Why did he say that? As though she didn't take after her mother.

"I think I look like my mother," she said a little stubbornly.

Rafe turned his head and studied her until she flushed.

Eden turned away. "Oh well . . ." she said, as if it didn't matter.

So he thought she looked like Amabel. Well, Amabel's blood certainly mingled with that of the Derringtons. Eden made a mental note to seek out the painting when she returned to Kea Lani. She did know that Miss Amabel had come as a bride to Judge Melvin, first of the Derringtons to arrive in Hawaii, and that she was said to have been a southern belle before the Civil War.

Eden turned her daughterly devotion on the rendering of Rebecca's demure face.

"She was practically a saint. So self-sacrificing. I'd be satisfied if I could match my mother's love for God and the Hawaiians."

Rafe looked from Rebecca to Lana. "They make a fine pair of sisters, and don't forget all that Lana has accomplished here in San Francisco."

"Yes, of course," Eden said, but continued to look at the elder Stanhope sister. "Sometimes I've wondered what she'd think of me if she knew I was following in my father's footsteps into medicine instead of becoming a teacher. I'll even be working at Kalihi like my father."

"Kalihi Hospital?" Rafe asked abruptly.

"Yes, didn't I tell you? Oh, I must have forgotten with all that we discussed. Great-aunt Nora is arranging it for me." She folded her arms, tilting her head to the side thoughtfully as she gazed at Rebecca. "Would she be proud of me, do you think, Rafe? Or would she be disappointed because I didn't choose to work at the school as she did?"

She hadn't intended to say this much, especially to Rafe, and was startled when he took hold of her shoulders, turning her to face him. She stared up at him under the hall light, seeing his eyes narrow and his jaw flex.

"Kalihi Hospital?"

"Why . . . yes, with Dr. Clifford Bolton. My father practiced there with him and did notable work in tropical disease." *And Lana too*, she almost said, but caught herself. Rafe may not know, and Lana had wanted to conceal the information.

"In the leprosy work?"

"Yes. I'll be getting further training. Someday I'm going to join my father's research team. Maybe even go to Molokai and see his work. There's so much kindness that can be done there—"

"You're not going to Molokai. Not if I live to stop it."

Stunned by his unexpected response, she stared at him, catching a glimmer of something that puzzled her, then made her smile.

"Why, Rafe! You're upset."

His lashes narrowed as he scanned her face, and she could see he read her secret pleasure and understood it. Immediately his hands dropped from her shoulders and the familiar nonchalant attitude was back in place.

"I don't think women should be traipsing about jungles or leper camps taking extraordinary risks."

Eden folded her arms and tapped her foot. "Well, well. I don't think we'd better get into *that*."

"I suppose not." He smiled easily. "It won't do you any good anyway. The Derrington men won't allow it."

"So now you suddenly align yourself with the Derrington men? Men whom at other times you dismiss with a certain—what shall we say, contempt?"

"Face it, my dear, on a few obvious things we would agree—such as the inadvisability of permitting you to canoe down a croc-infested river with a medical bag under one arm somewhere in the wilds of Hoonie-Noonie land."

"Rafe, don't exasperate me. You know that's what I'm training for."

"I don't know anything of the sort. You were training to be a nurse. You can be a nurse anywhere."

"Jerome's work is different. Hawaii's different—especially Molokai; you know that."

She could see by the molten flash in his dark eyes that he did know, that his love for the islands might even surpass her own.

He was deliberately silent as he looked at her and appeared to make a sudden decision to close the door on the subject. He looked back at the painting.

"I wish you wouldn't return to Kea Lani yet. Why can't you wait another year? Work at St. Francis?"

"Oh, Rafe, don't ask. Be fair. I've got to go home. I promised Nora."

"Promised what?" There was a low note in his voice that made her tense.

"Nora asked me tonight if I would support Princess Liliuokalani."

Rafe watched her. "And you agreed?"

"I told her I didn't see why I wouldn't support her. In return, Nora promised to speak to Dr. Bolton about me. I'm sorry if that displeases you. It's not that I don't appreciate your concerns or your advice, it's just, well, I think you already know I'll do whatever I must."

Rafe turned to scrutinize her, looking troubled by his thoughts. "Nora's old and in ill health, though she hides it. I'm sure she'll seek allies as her options become fewer."

Eden believed he wasn't sharing everything. A rumble of thunder reverberated over the bay. The rain slashed against the windowpane.

She hesitated, as if to placate him. "Don't be angry with my decision. I wish you understood. I want to thank you for trying to help me tonight."

He smiled with grim amusement and took a step toward her. "Thanking me is a way to convince me to back off, isn't it?"

"That's not why I thanked you," Eden said quietly, stepping back. "I meant it. I'm grateful for your . . . friendly interest. And for our discussion. You've given me a great deal to think about."

He smiled. "Have I?" he said flatly.

"Oh yes."

"I've given myself too much to think about as well. And I don't like the possibilities."

"About Zachary?" she asked.

"Oh, about a lot of things." He came up to her.

Eden felt the edge of the table as she moved backward, trying to appear nonchalant. Rafe tilted his head, giving her a searching look.

"There's nothing I can do to stop you. I wish I could. There's so much in the past that needs unraveling, Eden. I have the impression that once the unraveling begins, more than one person may get hurt." He lifted his hand to the side of her face, softly running a finger up her cheek until reaching the scar on her temple. "I just don't want it to be you." He looked down at her for a long moment.

Eden returned his gaze, listening to the rain until the sound filled her heart as well as her mind. Another stormy night on the warm beach of Oahu descended into her memory . . . countless moonlit nights in Oahu when the trade wind swayed the palm fronds and the air was emollient with warm sweetness.

She tore her gaze away and straightened from the table, brushing past him to the open doorway of the parlor.

"What would you like? Hot chocolate or coffee?"

Rafe didn't answer. She breezed into the parlor, calling more steadily than she felt, "You can have both. Lana made too much."

Rafe entered as the fire crackled and rain tinkled on the glass panes. He leaned in the doorway, watching her.

The red embers sizzled in the fireplace. The pear-shaped damask lamp shades with champagne fringes glowed agreeably, the light falling on the Queen Anne–style dark wood furniture. Cream and burgundy rugs offset the heavy damask drapes. She went to the divan and sat down, pouring the refreshments.

"You seem very close to her," he stated.

"My mother?" she asked, anxious to change the subject from Kalihi.

"No, I was speaking of Lana. I could see it in your eyes tonight when you saw she'd waited up for you. You were pleased."

Eden considered, mildly surprised that he noticed what she had not. "Yes, I think you're right. We have our ups and downs, but we get along well. Lana's been like a sister to me."

Perhaps now was an opportunity to learn more about him and what he'd been doing all this time. Perhaps she could delve a little deeper.

"What about you and Keno? What did you do when you left Hawaii two years ago? I wondered how you both had fared," she said with just the right amount of concern.

"We fared miserably for the first few months, if you want to know. We ended up in an exotic little spot—just the kind of place you'd like to set up a medical tent—called Bora Bora."

Holding the coffee urn, she glanced at him across the room.

He smiled and walked up, taking the cup. "I remember waking up on the beach with a loincloth-clad warrior standing over me with a machete. My presence here now is due to the fact that the old fellow was more hospitable than I thought at first glance."

Eden laughed.

"Amused, are you? It wasn't so funny at the time. I gained little from that adventure except a concussion and the loss of some pearls I intended to use to finish paying off the owner of the *Manoa*."

"Oh no," Eden breathed in genuine dismay. "Not the black pearl?"

"So you know about it? No, not that one. These were some other pearls. You should feel sorry for me, Eden. At a young age I was defeated, discouraged, and humbled—and ready to come back to Mama."

"I doubt it," Eden scoffed good-naturedly. "One thing about you, Rafe, you'll never give up on your goals. I always wondered about that contest," she mused. "I arrived in time to see you coming out of the water and being brought to the grandstand, where you produced the pearl. I wondered how you did it. Primo looked as though he'd just swallowed a squid."

"Yes," he said dourly, "and with good reason—he'd failed to keep his end of an agreement with Townsend."

Eden laughed again. Rafe sounded as she remembered him from their childhood.

"Ainsworth still wonders how I did it."

"What do you tell him?" she asked.

Rafe arched a brow. "That I'm half fish. And as much Hawaiian as my loyal Polynesian friends—one of whom just happened to clue me in on what he'd learned."

"And so your Hawaiian friends—those men on the beach that day— told you where to dive for the pearl?"

"Something like that." He sat down beside her on the divan and stretched his legs toward the fireplace. "What he'd learned was that Townsend gave Primo the black pearl before the contest had begun. Townsend only pretended to throw the real pearl into the water in sight of all the reporters and divers."

Her brow wrinkled. "But how did *you* bring it up?"

"I took a starting position close to Primo. After the pistol was fired and we dove underwater, I simply took it from him."

She covered a smile. She didn't dare ask how he simply took it. "I see. It was very smoothly done. From where I watched the contest, nobody suspected anything." She looked at him leaning his dark head back against the divan. "And roughing up poor Primo underwater doesn't trouble your conscience at all?"

"My dear girl, should it?"

"Well . . . ." She pursed her lips thoughtfully.

"The pearl belonged to my father, from whom the Derringtons—" he paused and inclined his head toward her—"stole it."

Eden grimaced.

"That pearl bed was left to me by my father, Matt. Townsend knew it. But it didn't stop him from somehow controlling Celestine emotionally. Now she's selling it, and I've no idea if I can get it back or not, though I'll try."

"The pearl fishery is being sold?" she cried. "But how can Townsend get away with it?"

"Townsend's a lawyer," he said wryly. "And Judge Spalding is his friend."

She recognized the underlying cynicism in Rafe's voice.

"But if Matt left it to you . . ."

"I'll know more once I talk to Celestine. Parker Judson insists the deal is finished, that he made it with Townsend on the up and up. He may be right, but I won't give up until I see the documents."

"Parker Judson?" She recalled the sugar king entering Kalakaua's reception with Rafe and how many heads had turned with curiosity. "You were with him tonight. What's Mr. Judson got to do with the fishery?"

"He claims he's bought it," Rafe stated. "He wants to back me on some adjacent land to grow pineapples. I have to admit the idea is tempting. I had plans of my own, but not in that area. And he's offering to start on much more acreage than I'd be able to do."

"How much?"

"Oh, about a thousand acres."

Her breath paused. Astounded, Eden met his flickering warm brown eyes. For a moment the silence turned awkward. *A thousand . . .* thought Eden.

"I . . . guess I shouldn't be surprised," she said. "Not when Parker Judson's involved."

Rafe refilled his coffee cup and stood, going to the fireplace. He leaned against the mantel, watching the dancing sparks as a gust of wind swirled through the chimney.

Thoroughly bewildered, Eden retreated behind her cup of hot chocolate, musing. If Rafe and Parker Judson did go into some partnership, it could mean that Rafe might become an important voice in Hawaiian politics in the coming years. She scanned him meditatively, wondering if she preferred him in a breezy cotton shirt, struggling with Ambrose to eke out a living with the boats.

The rain was falling harder now against the windowpanes. "Well, congratulations, Rafe. Anything Mr. Judson's involved in is usually a tremendous success."

"Once I talk to Ambrose and my mother, I'll understand better what I can do. Even if she insists on selling, Ainsworth may still be the key to it all."

Grandfather? Eden wondered. "Grandfather mentioned Celestine tonight—I'm dreadfully sorry she isn't well, Rafe. I hope there's something to be done. But Grandfather didn't say anything about your stepfather wanting to sell the pearl fishery."

"Ainsworth wouldn't say anything. He's a better man than Townsend."

"Did you know he's going to Washington with Parker Judson?"

"Yes, that's why I need to speak to Ainsworth soon. He's the main reason I'm here."

She was anxious to know what he wanted from her grandfather and remembered the letter. Eden suspected it had to do with Hanalei. She could imagine her grandfather's reaction when he learned from Parker that he was backing Rafe on a thousand acres! He would certainly try to dissuade him.

"You mentioned the pearl fishery. Where's the new Oahu plantation going to be located?"

He looked at her over the rim of the cup. "Not far from Kea Lani."

Again she was totally surprised. The silence grew.

"I see," she said uneasily. "More competition for the Derringtons."

"That wasn't my first intention," Rafe said tonelessly. "All I ever wanted was Hanalei."

"Then that's what you want to discuss with my grandfather—Hanalei?"

"Yes, among a few other matters. Look, Eden, I know what you want to ask me. I'm not out to punish your grandfather. I've no interest in making things uncomfortable for him—or Townsend, for that matter. But the past has to be dealt with. I'm sorry you're in the middle of this. If there was anything I could do to change that, I would. Unfortunately, there isn't."

She stood, smiling uncomfortably. "Yes, I know. I'm really very happy for you." But was she, down deep in her heart? She realized they were both uncomfortable with what the other was planning to do with their lives.

"Does my grandfather know yet? About your deal with Mr. Judson?"

"No. He started to tell him when your grandfather had his attack."

"Oh yes, I do remember Mr. Judson mentioning something about your monopolizing the pineapple business together. He never had a chance to explain further." She remembered her grandfather's stern look at Mr. Judson's comment.

"I would have made it in Hawaii without Judson's backing anyway. Now it means I'll be able to start shipping on a larger scale a few years sooner."

She liked his confidence, but his manner worried her too. There was something more to all this than just what was on the surface, but she couldn't tell what. Rafe didn't look especially pleased about partnership with Parker Judson. Any man about to get such an opportunity with a thousand acres of Oahu land would normally be shouting it through the roof, but Rafe was almost moody about it.

Naturally, it was because the one piece of land he cared deeply about was Hanalei on the Big Island. He expected to get the plantation back, but how? Through Parker Judson's influence perhaps?

"Are you going to grow coffee on Oahu, like Matt did at Hanalei?"

"No, only pineapples, though I brought back some excellent coffee beans from Brazil."

"Where did you get the pineapples?"

"South America. While we were in Rio."

She thought of her father's medical research in South America. She would have mentioned it, but after their discussion in the hall she thought it best to avoid the matter.

"They come from French Guiana. They're one of the best varieties I've found anywhere, and they should thrive in Hawaii. Well, at least we think so. What we're doing now is just a beginning, an experiment really. Parker's just as excited as I am."

She was drawn by his enthusiasm. "So is that what you've been doing all this time, looking for new kinds of plants in South America? That is, after leaving Bora Bora?"

"Yes and no. We've been other places too. Mostly the tropics. The Blue Mountains of Jamaica—some of the best coffee-growing land in the world is in those mountains. I've got some fresh pineapple aboard ship in addition to the plants. Come on board the *Manoa* and I'll give you some to taste. It's as sweet and juicy as candy. It puts to shame those presently growing in Hawaii."

"The *Manoa* is *your* ship?"

"Mostly mine, though Keno, his father, brothers, and half a dozen cousins would disagree. They own a share—a plank apiece," Rafe said with a smile. "It makes for a very interesting business strategy—not always peaceable, I assure you, especially when they're all arguing about their 'take' in the latest haul of whatever we take home to Pearl Harbor. They're worse than all the Derringtons and Eastons combined."

Eden laughed in spite of herself.

"We'll be selling the ship soon after returning to Hawaii—if it doesn't sit here in the Bay so long that it sinks first. It's served us well these years, though we had our doubts about it holding together when we caught hurricane winds in the Gulf of Mexico on our last voyage. I've had one too many years in sea spray and ocean wind. I'm ready for pineapples."

She walked over to the fire and warmed her hands. Rafe, too, was going home to Hawaii. He would be there when she arrived to work at

Kalihi Hospital. He would begin a plantation not far from Kea Lani. No, the family wasn't going to be pleased, but her heart felt unexpectedly light.

"You can save that bite of pineapple for when I visit your new plantation. What will you call it?"

"I don't know yet. At present there is little there but a bungalow. Nevertheless, for you, dear Miss Derrington, I'll roll out the coconut carpet. If I can survive on bananas for the next few years, I may just make it. Townsend doesn't have much chance of running me out of Hawaii this time, not with Judson's backing." His brown eyes shimmered. "Townsend would have his hands full trying, even if I weren't with Judson. I'm determined to stay this time."

She eyed him cautiously. "I've little doubt that you can make it succeed. I hope you do."

She had thought she sounded cheerful, at least amiable, until he gave her a searching glance that disagreed.

"That's congenial of you, Eden. Why do you 'hope' I'll make it?"

She turned away, busying herself by replacing the cover to the crystal serving plate. "After losing Hanalei Estate? I hope things work out. I've always been in favor of your getting it back from the Derringtons. You know that."

"I'll remember your kind words of support when I'm broiling under the sun with a pick and shovel."

She smiled. "I'll come to cheer you on."

His gaze held hers. "I'll remind you of that when I need it most. Not that I'm likely to get the new plantation going soon at this rate." He stood, hands on hips. "I need to leave and get back to Honolulu. I should have been there two weeks ago—Keno is nursing our cargo of young plants and grumbling about each day we stay holed up in this foggy San Francisco Bay. And now," he said, "there's one last matter. I've been thinking about that letter Zachary sent to Lana. You said she was very upset. What does Lana think of Zachary?"

Lana's earlier fears came pouring back into Eden's mind. She couldn't very well tell Rafe about the secret Lana feared would be disclosed to public scrutiny.

"What did she tell you?" he persisted.

She faltered. "About the letter?"

"Yes, Zachary's letter. The one you mentioned briefly in the coach."

"Well, she didn't want Zachary even coming here," she admitted, glancing toward the parlor door. It stood open and the mansion was silent. "In order to avoid him, she mentioned taking a train to Seattle."

"Sounds rather drastic for a courageous woman like Lana."

"That's what I thought at the time."

His avid brown eyes gave her his unswerving attention. "Did she explain her concerns?"

Eden had the feeling Rafe already knew and was trying to discover what she knew. She had felt that way about some of his questioning before.

Eden stood and walked about the room. "Lana has some, well, rather complicated and embarrassing secrets she doesn't want unveiled."

"Does Zachary know of them?"

"No, that's just it, Rafe, I don't think he does. Remember what you said in the coach about his knowing some information but misconstruing it? I think it may be that way with Lana."

"Lana didn't tell you Zachary had unearthed some deep, dark secret?"

"No, not at all. I rather thought she was afraid he might have. But as far as I'm concerned there is no deep, dark secret. She told me what it was."

He walked up to her, searching her face. He must not have found what he was looking for. His expression became bland. "What did she tell you?"

Should she explain? "Just that she had served as a medical missionary with Dr. Bolton and couldn't take it anymore. She ran away to San Francisco."

Rafe watched her. He seemed satisfied with that answer.

Eden looked over to the fireplace at the sizzling coals. In her mind, she could envision the letter curling and turning gray.

"And her words to me were that she didn't want him meddling. That she wouldn't become 'mixed up in his plans at this late date' is the way she put it."

"You're sure she never told you what those plans were?"

"No. She said to let the past stay buried, that the future belonged to me, and she asked me to forget Hawaii."

Eden heard the wind tugging like fingers at the dormer windows. The rain needled the glass panes in the room like spraying sand.

Eden left the window and walked toward him.

"She didn't explain anything in the letter?"

"No . . ."

"Nothing?" he persisted quietly. "A word, a suggestion?"

Under his smoldering gaze she returned to the window, drawing back the curtain and looking out. She watched the falling rain to cool her emotions. He walked up, took her arms, and turned her around to face him. "You're not telling me everything, are you?"

"After she left, I saved what I could of the letter. There were a few legible words on a scrap. Nothing that made sense to me."

His gaze grew alert. "Yes?" he urged.

"There were the words *boat, discuss Kalihi work,* and *Molokai.*"

Rafe considered in silence, but she couldn't ascertain if the words meant anything to him. He released her and looked out the window, absorbed in his own thoughts. He was deliberately silent, then appeared to close the door on their discussion. He walked over to the Queen Anne chair and picked up his coat.

His sudden and calm change disconcerted her and she followed him to the door.

"What? You're leaving?"

"Yes, I must. I'm sailing in a few days for Oahu. There is much to get ready." He smiled and opened the front door, letting in the cold wind. "When you get to Kea Lani, should you need anything, you'll know where to find me."

Eden watched as he darted out into the rain and climbed into the coach. The driver came from his enclosure under the roofed porch and scrambled up into the seat. A flick of his whip and the two horses trotted away, their hooves clacking on the dark wet bricks.

Eden came aware as a flash of lightning blinded her. A rumble of thunder reverberated in the night, followed by heavy rain.

She would go to Hawaii. She would pursue her work, her dream. There was a good reason why she must return—an enduring reason that would constantly beat in her heart. Any stirrings in her heart for Rafe Easton must be held in place with bit and bridle.

Eden shut the front door and slid the heavy bolt into place, then walked across the dim hallway. She climbed the stairs to her room. "I'm going home," she told the walls, "and this time, if God wills, no one will stop me."

TWENTY-ONE

Outside of Eden's bedroom window at Chadwick Mansion, a gust of wind sent the tinkling chime of shells whirling. The string snapped and the chime she had placed there nearly a year ago fell mutely to the flower bed below.

Inside, Eden tossed in a fitful slumber. Subconscious memories from a mist-shrouded past mingled with the brooding storm. A twitch of fear furrowed her sweating brow, and strands of dark hair stuck to the side of her face. She dreamed she was a young child again at a strange house. . . .

Eden sat on the seat of a carriage in front of a big house. The fringe on the carriage top jiggled cheerfully in a warm, sweet wind. Her own childish laughter sounded in her ears, then suddenly—shouting voices! Her mother was running into some trees. Someone was chasing her! Fear filled Eden's heart. "Mommy, Mommy," she screamed. "Come back, Mommy—"

Eden's own cry awakened her from the nightmare. She sat upright in her bed, damp with perspiration, just as a brilliant streak of lightning lit up her room at Chadwick. Her breathing rasped in her dry throat. "O Lord," she whispered reverently.

She was trembling, her sweaty hands clutching the covers. She *remembered*! Yes! She had been with her mother in a carriage somewhere at a mansion—but where? *Think! Think!* she told herself. But did she really want to know?

She buried her face in her palms. *Oh, Rafe . . .* Her heart longed for him now. If only he were here, he would help her.

I have the Lord, she told herself. *Even if I never have another, I have Him.*

I can be strong. I have everything I need in Jesus. As the moments slipped by the speed of her heart slowed and she grew calmer, more confident.

She looked up toward the window where she had left the drapes drawn. The storm in San Francisco had finally blown over, and from the bay came the sound of the harbor bell. She breathed deeply, continuing to calm herself.

Her bedroom was dark, but through the window she could see the moon trying to peep through the mist. A pale shimmer of light reached like fingers between the limbs of the trees and cast a swaying shadow across the wall. Reliving the terrifying moment made her realize there was something more just beyond her childhood memory.

No, it wasn't just a nightmare. Had she been afraid of more that night than the hurricane, when she'd hidden beneath the daybed with Zachary? What was it Nora had told her tonight at dinner? That something had taken her away, and when she came back they couldn't locate her. Celestine had heard Eden in the hall, screaming. Afterward they had questioned the other children. Rozlind was in her room asleep, but they looked for Zachary and Rafe.

Eden's perspiring skin felt chilled in the December night. Zachary had been with her hiding under a daybed, but where had Rafe been?

Eden threw aside the covers and stood. She should have mentioned all this to Rafe again, but there'd been so much to discuss when they'd met, and she wasn't sure she wanted him to know that she continued to have nightmarish fears. It would only give him more reason to suggest she stay away from Kea Lani.

She slipped into her dressing gown and went barefoot to the window. She must get her mind on something else. Anything else.

Darkness covered the front sloping lawn, but there was just enough light shining from the front porch to make the rain glisten on the carriageway. The pine trees were dark outlines against the sky, and a faint glimmer of moonlight moved upon the face of the pond.

What do I know? she wondered. *I know I was searching for Rebecca. I know I hid under the bed with Zachary. And tonight I remembered something else. I remember being with my mother in a carriage outside of a mansion—a mansion I'm sure wasn't Kea Lani.*

Eden touched the scar along her temple. The feeling, however, remained that there was more waiting in the dim recesses of her mind—if only something would jar her memory and unlock the door.

The note that had been left for her at the mission church took on a new foreboding shadow. Whom had her mother been running away from? Why had terror filled Eden's heart?

Rafe . . . I've got to talk to him before he sails. I must ask him about the note and who he thinks left it.

She paced. Did she dare go to the *Manoa* and ask him that? What would he think if she did anything so bold? But hadn't he invited her to sample his South American pineapples?

She stood still, her fingers grasping her gown. Yes, she'd go to his ship first thing in the morning. She hurried to her bureau and opened the top drawer where she kept a special box of Hawaiian mementos. She uncovered the note of two years ago and carefully opened the paper. Yes, she would show this to Rafe tomorrow.

––––––––

As morning dawned gray but dry, Eden was already awake and dressed for her secret venture out to the harbor. She glanced at her blue-gray woolen dress with black ribbon trim and decided it was practical and modest for a venture aboard the *Manoa*. She smoothed her hair into a French chignon and was about to add a charming hat with a small lace netting when a tap sounded on her door.

"Eden?"

It was Lana carrying a tray with an urn of coffee and two cups. Eden managed a cheerful smile. "Good morning. My, you're up early."

"I've been awake for hours," Lana confessed. "Oh—" she said, glancing her over. "Are you going to the station to see your grandfather off?"

"Well—no, actually I was going to do several things this morning," she said truthfully. "I thought I'd do some Christmas shopping at Ghirardelli Square and maybe have lunch there."

"I wish I were more in a holiday mood," Lana groaned.

Eden looked at her affectionately. "What is it, Lana? What's wrong?"

"Oh, just the fact that you'll be leaving soon. I always knew the day would come, and now it's finally here." She set the tray down and poured.

"You can still go back to Kalihi," Eden told her. "What a surprise for everyone that would be."

"Ah yes," Lana said with a wry little laugh. "Quite a surprise. How did your meeting with Rafe go last night?"

Eden wanted to ask her about their correspondence, but Lana wasn't ready for that. Unless that was the reason she had come to her room this morning.

"Lana? Why were you so afraid of Cousin Zachary?" she asked pointedly, accepting the cup of coffee.

Lana took the abrupt change in topic casually enough. "Oh, you misunderstood me. I wasn't afraid of him. I simply didn't want him to arrange a meeting between you and your great-aunt. I suspected she had changed her mind about you and asked you to return to Hawaii. As I confessed moments ago I've grown rather selfish about having you with me." She shrugged defensively. "I didn't want you to leave San Francisco. It's as simple as that. But let's not allow your decision to ruin our Christmas. Will Nora be having you over at the Palace Hotel on Christmas Day?"

"I don't know. Her schedule is full. She's with King Kalakaua and his entourage. They've been attending dozens of ritzy parties and fabulous dinners."

Lana laughed. "Ah, the rich—what they get by with."

"I suppose, but it could be that this life is all they've got, in which case I don't begrudge them. Lana—" Eden turned grave. "Are you sure that's all there was to Zachary's letter? You weren't afraid of him?"

"No, I'm not afraid. Please don't worry. I thought the meeting would stir up old questions about the past better left forgotten."

"What questions would he stir up?" Eden persisted. "You mean about the way my mother died? I dreamt about her last night. . . . I dreamt that I was in a carriage with her. She was running away from someone and I was terrified."

"A nightmare is all."

"I don't think so. There is a mystery surrounding it, isn't there? Do you realize I know almost nothing about how it happened? You were there, Lana. You must know what really took place. Why won't you tell me?"

Her aunt flushed. "No, I wasn't there." She walked away to Eden's vanity table and checked her honey-colored braid. "You're making too much out of my silly response to Zachary's letter. I told you it arrived unexpectedly. I wasn't prepared emotionally. And then those pearls. I overreacted because I wanted to avoid trouble." She turned. "I've always been the one to run—run away from the very kind of trouble we're discussing this moment. Not Rebecca."

A tense silence followed in which they stood looking at each other. "I have nothing more to tell you, Eden." With that, Lana turned to leave the room, but Eden stopped her.

"No, Lana. There's more to it than what I'm told. She's my mother. I have a right to know!"

Lana was pale and stiff. "Who put you up to this badgering? Zachary? I wasn't there when the accident was reported to have happened."

"Only *reported* to have happened? Ambrose once told me Rebecca drowned in a storm when the small boat she and a friend had taken out was overturned. Were you the friend that was with her, Lana?"

"Me!" She looked hurt and sank into a chair. "I just told you I was in Honolulu with Clifford. If you don't believe me, you may ask him when you see him at Kalihi Hospital."

Eden sighed, feeling guilty. "I'm sorry. Of course I believe you. It's just that all these questions are getting to me, making me more suspicious than I need to be." She walked away. "That dream last night upset me. So much is happening all at once." Eden turned and looked at her. Lana's face was drawn. "You don't suppose there was no friend with Rebecca, do you? That they were mistaken?"

Lana rested her head in her hand as though it ached. "I don't know, Eden. I wish I could tell you, but I can't."

Eden walked up to the chair where she sat. "What do you mean, you 'can't'?"

"My sister went away that day. It was the last I ever saw of her. I don't know what happened."

"Went away?" Eden frowned. "To where?"

Lana shrugged. "I'm not sure. A gathering of some sort. A prayer vigil, I think. You'd better ask your grandfather. I suppose Rebecca may have taken a boat—but I just don't know. I was in Honolulu. I was only told the next day that Rebecca had drowned."

Eden felt cold. "Where was my father? Do you know?"

"Jerome?" Lana stood and walked about restlessly. "He must have returned on the inter-island steamer the day after her death."

"Then my father wasn't there when Rebecca drowned?"

"No, if what they say is true. I wasn't there when it happened, so I can't say for sure. I've no way of knowing. They say he'd gone to one of the other islands—Kauai, Maui—I don't recall exactly. Maybe even Molokai. He may have been there working."

Eden frowned, trying to remember more details. "Somehow I was under the impression he was there, somewhere—and I think I was with him. If only I could remember. That house that I saw in my dream last night. It was real, Lana. And I'm sure it wasn't Kea Lani."

Eden was half speaking to herself, trying to remember more, but Lana looked at her nervously.

"Maybe you shouldn't try so hard, Eden. Maybe you should let it go."

"Now that I'm at last beginning to remember things? I can't let it go now. I've got to know the truth. I've got to find that house. If I do, I'll remember everything—I know I will."

Lana watched her warily. "The truth isn't always what we want to hear. Sometimes it's better not to know everything. I don't know if Jerome was there that night or not. I haven't seen him since before Rebecca's death; he took the loss very badly, I'm told. He went away. He buried himself in his research."

The words still echoed in Eden's ears even after Lana left her room. Her father hadn't been there when her mother drowned. Why did this disturb her? Perhaps something in her own memory contradicted this? Had *he* been with her and Rebecca that day in the carriage? At that unknown house—where?

Eden was suddenly startled as she remembered something. She went to her desk and took out a tiki-head door knocker, looking at it thoughtfully. That's where she had seen it before—or rather, one like it—on the door of the house she hadn't been able to remember. A house with just such a door knocker, with a glassed-in room high above ground, with the daybed where she'd hidden with Zachary.

Yes, she was beginning to remember bits of what had happened, and as she did, she knew she would soon have all the pieces together.

TWENTY-TWO

The foggy air was damp and gray when Eden arrived at the San Francisco wharf. A boy of about twelve with his cap askew and a hole in his pants at the knee straddled the rail along the quay.

"Hello," she called cheerily. "How would you like to earn a dime?"

He looked skeptical. "Doin' what?"

"Deliver a message to a Mr. Rafe Easton aboard the *Manoa*. Tell him Miss Eden Derrington wishes to come aboard."

"Sure, lady. Can you write all that stuff down, names and all?"

She handed him an envelope. "It's all written. When you return I'll pay you."

He hopped down, tucked the envelope inside his torn shirt, and sauntered away with an air of boldness.

Eden waited on the quay, ignoring the looks cast in her direction by workers and fishermen. She walked over to the rail carrying her red umbrella, the one bright spot in the gray morning. She squinted into the swirling mist, making out the ghostly hulls of many ships. They all looked the same to her: big gray hulls with dispirited sea gulls sitting on their ratlines and prows. The water lapped sleepily against their sides. Chains creaked and groaned in rhythm with the swells. Birds twittered and screeched as they flapped their wings through the salt-laden mist on their way out to sea. The water lapped against the pilings as she peered over the railing, and some sea lions with long whiskers slapped their front flippers on the water to frighten the gulls from their catch.

Eden heard voices and footsteps and turned to see a handsome dark-haired man wearing his white shirt open as though the Hawaiian trade winds were blowing. Keno walked toward her with the boy beside him.

"Hello, Miss Derrington," Keno called with a friendly smile. "Rafe sent me to bring you aboard."

"Thank you," she called, smiling, and walked toward him, pausing to pay the boy who had done his job well.

Eden walked beside Keno down the quay, her concerned thoughts briefly turning to Rozlind.

"The *Manoa* is farther down the dock," he said, and after a few minutes he pointed out a merchant vessel bearing the Hawaiian flag.

Rafe appeared out of the swirling mist, coming to the side of the ship. Eden mounted some steps that led up the side, where he steadied her a moment as her feet landed softly on deck.

Rafe bowed. "To what gallant deed do I owe this honored visit!"

Eden looked at the rugged figure in a casual blue cotton shirt and trousers. "Did you get my message?"

He reached into his pocket.

" 'Must see you,' " he read aloud. " 'Eden.' "

Rafe briefly scanned her, taking in the stylish hat with black netting that reached just below her eyes. "I'm intrigued to learn what this is all about." He lifted a brow. "If you've come asking for a voyage home, I would have to break my heart and refuse such a charming visitor."

Eden twirled her red umbrella. "Rest assured, that's not on my mind."

Rafe briefly took her in.

Eden glanced at Keno, who was standing to one side with a grin, watching Rafe.

Rafe smirked at him and gestured with his thumb. "Don't you need to water the pineapples?"

Keno offered a fake Oriental bow. "Already too soggy. But your wish is my command." He walked away.

Eden's amused gaze followed him across the deck to where dozens of small pineapple plants were set out.

"They hope in vain for sunshine," Rafe told her wryly. He looked up into the fog. "Miserable stuff. It just sits there wrapping its wispy tentacles about us like an octopus."

Eden laughed. "When are you leaving for sunny Hawaii?"

"Believe me, just as soon as possible—I'm hoping tomorrow." He motioned her toward some steps that went up, and she walked with him.

"If we don't head out of here soon, there won't be any pineapple plants to offer Judson. Ah! That's it, you must have come to taste the pineapple. Hey, Kapu!" he called up to an old man whom Eden thought to be Chinese. "Get one of those fresh pineapples ready for Miss Derrington! We have a royal guest."

"You called him *kapu*. That's Hawaiian for 'taboo.' "

"That's what his friends call him. He's Chinese. He doesn't know what it means." Rafe smiled.

A couple of crewmen brought out a table, and Kapu held a sharp blade in one hand and a mammoth-sized pineapple in the other. He bowed at the waist to her, then plopped the pineapple on the table.

"Oh my, it's huge, Rafe! Nothing like Mr. Judson's little pineapples."

"Those were from Malaya. Wait till you taste this one. It's called a Cayenne."

"What's Kapu waiting for?" she whispered when the man stood looking at her.

"He wants you to inhale its fragrance."

Eden walked up to the table and made an elaborate display of smelling the pineapple, as though she'd never smelled one before. "Wonderful, wonderful," she told Kapu.

"Now, are you ready for the sweetest pineapple you ever tasted?" Rafe asked her.

"I'm waiting!"

She winced as Kapu, his hands moving with the skilled speed of a sword-fighting fire dancer, slashed, hacked, cut, and rolled, producing round sections of juicy gold flesh.

Eden applauded as Kapu laid a section on a plate and brought it to her, bowing again.

Eden took a bite, preparing for a tangy, acid tartness but was surprised by the mellow sweet taste.

"Oooh . . . it's superb!" Eden said, taking a second bite, then a third.

Rafe handed her a napkin. "I think we've done it, Kapu. She's addicted."

"These will grow from the plants Keno is nursing?" she asked with delight.

"If we can get them out of San Francisco alive," Rafe said as the fog drizzled down upon them like dew.

"No wonder Parker Judson is turning over a thousand acres to you."

"They'll flourish in Hawaiian soil," Rafe said.

When the pineapple was gone, Rafe took her from the chill December fog into his cabin, where Kapu brought in a pot of freshly brewed Brazilian coffee and two mugs.

"The flavor is rich and strong," she said. "Do you intend to plant some of these beans at Hanalei?"

"I've some new varieties to try, but I don't think I can improve on what's already there. Kona coffee is simply the best. And now," he said, pulling out a chair for her, "suppose you tell me what's on your mind."

Eden looked up at him through the netting on her hat, wondering how to begin. He watched her, then with a wry smile, reached over and turned up the netting.

"It's coming between us," he said dryly.

Eden took in a breath and stood. "All right. This will explain itself." She handed him the note.

Rafe opened it and read. Eden watched his expression change into speculative anger. He turned the piece of paper over, looking at it. "This isn't part of Zachary's letter to Lana?"

"No. I've had this since Oahu."

"When did you get it?"

"Two years ago in Ambrose's cubicle at the mission church, just before I left."

"Two years—" He stopped and looked at her with a narrowed gaze. "And just now you tell me?"

Eden walked over to a desk. "I thought it might have been a strange prank someone was playing on me. I asked Ambrose about it, and he thought I should ignore it, since I was leaving Kea Lani."

Wearily, Eden sat down, placing her cup on the desk.

"Ambrose never told me about this," he said, restrained irritation in his voice. He walked up, caught both her hands, and looked at her.

"It's nothing for you to concern yourself with. There was no crime committed against your mother, I assure you."

How could he be so sure? Or was he just saying this to ease her worst fears?

"This note hints of good old Cousin Zachary again—just like the letter to Lana and the pearls. I think he wanted you to run with this note to Ainsworth and carry on about your mother's death. When you behaved calmly instead, he resorted to the pearls. Remember, even two years ago Ainsworth was upset with him, threatening to leave everything to Rozlind. Keno tells me it was Zachary who went to Ainsworth and your great-aunt about his relationship with Rozlind."

"Oh, Rafe, do you think that's all there is to it?" Her eyes searched his.

Rafe looked bothered by her question. He frowned a little. "I'm saying I don't think the Derringtons are covering up a murder."

Murder. At last the horrid, unthinkable word was spoken, and she shuddered, feeling cold from more than the damp breeze blowing in from the open doorway.

"That's what you were afraid of, wasn't it?" he asked gently.

Her eyes lowered, and she nodded.

"And that's exactly what Zachary wanted you to think when he wrote this. He was hoping it would inflame you enough to barge into your grandfather's office at Kea Lani with outrageous suspicions, accusing him of hiding your mother's death. What bothers me is that Zachary's been digging into things all this time. He must have gotten those pearls from Jerome's room. There's no telling what he knows. But I aim to find out. I'm going to see him before I leave. Is he at the Palace Hotel?"

"Yes," she said dully, "but he is supposed to leave soon with Grandfather for Washington."

"I'd forgotten. . . . Well, we have a few months' reprieve, then. Look, Eden, I don't want you worrying about this. You did well by coming to me now. I wish you had done so in Hawaii when you first found this. I'll take care of it, all right?" He didn't wait for an answer, and folding the paper, he slipped it into his shirt pocket.

"But . . . what is there to cover up about my mother's death?"

He paused as though her question came as a surprise. Then, letting it slide, he walked over to the table and picked up his cup. "What makes you think there is?"

"Oh, I don't know. . . . For one thing, why was I hiding with Zachary under the daybed that night? I always thought I was fearful of the storm, but now I'm beginning to wonder."

"Why not? Zach is still terrified by them. It's a phobia. That and dogs." He frowned to himself.

"Nora explained about Zachary's memory lapse. She told me he'd been ill as a boy, during the years I was with Ambrose and Noelani."

Rafe looked mildly surprised. "I didn't think she'd tell you about that. The Derringtons are good at hushing things up."

She looked at him with interest. That was a strange way to put it.

"Did you know about it?" She could see he didn't like the direction the conversation was going.

"Sure, I knew about it."

"You never told me."

He looked at her with a lazy stare. "There are a good many things I haven't told you. I think you can understand why I would not want to

talk about Zachary's moods. There are more pleasant things to discuss."
He set his cup down. "Yet I would suggest that you avoid him."

"You've told me that many times already," she said wearily.

"Maybe I haven't told you often enough. You're responding like Ainsworth and Nora," he said shortly. "They're ignoring it, but I think they're making a mistake. They're proud, and they feel shame over mental maladies or physical impairments. First Zach left this note at the mission church, next was the letter to Lana, then the pearls. They're all symptoms of his problem. When he gets obsessed by something, he doesn't let go. I've been willing to gloss over his avid dislike of me, but I don't like his troubling you like this."

She walked over to him. "Last night I remembered more of my childhood incident with my mother. Bits and pieces sometimes come back through my dreams."

She had his full attention.

"There's a house somewhere—maybe a mansion. And there's a tiki-head door knocker and a room high up, all glassed in. I'm sure that's the house and the room where I hid with Zachary the night I fell down the stairs. That was the night he was so terrified. And I think it's where I last saw my mother."

He grew perfectly still, watching her. The ship creaked and a foghorn sounded.

"I sat in a carriage with her in front of that house. She was afraid of something—and ran away toward some trees. I remember crying after her, but she didn't come back."

Rafe hesitated. "Anything else?"

She shook her head.

"I'll talk to Zachary when I see him again," he said. "In the meantime, I wouldn't let any nightmare trouble you."

Eden opened her handbag and removed the small brass tiki head. She showed it to him. "Have you ever seen a door knocker like this?"

His expression revealed nothing. "This style is common in Hawaii. You could find dozens of houses with door knockers like this."

"But there are none at Kea Lani," she said.

"No," he said simply.

Eden eyed him suspiciously. "Why is it I think you know more than you're willing to tell me?"

His gaze held hers. "If that were so, Eden, would you be able to simply trust me, knowing I'd do nothing to hurt you?"

His question took her off guard and helped to free her burdened spirit.

Suddenly she felt like smiling again. After all, perhaps she was paying too much attention to her dream. It gave her nothing but disturbing feelings and recollections about things that happened long ago.

"Yes, but I admit that I'd be trusting a very elusive and disturbing man, Rafe Easton." She went to the desk to pick up her cloak. Her eyes drifted across the desk to a typewriter and a thick stack of typed papers sitting in an open leather case. "Oh, you're writing a book, Rafe?" She reached and picked up the first page.

Molokai Leper Settlement, 1870s.

In a flash he plucked the sheet from her hand. She looked at him, surprised, as he put it back on the stack, closed the case, opened a drawer, and placed the papers inside.

"So that's why you could speak with such understanding last night about Molokai. How interesting! Is it a book?"

"No."

"A research document?"

"Not exactly."

"Let me read it," she pleaded. "It must be packed with information. Why, I'll wager you know more about my father's work on Molokai than even Dr. Bolton."

Rafe caught her gaze until she wondered at his expression. He was upset that she had seen it, but why?

"I'll take you back to the quay," he said briefly.

Eden stood there watching him as he grabbed his coat from the back of a chair and slipped into it, avoiding her eyes.

Just then she tensed. "What's that sound?"

They looked at each other. "Do you hear it?" she asked, her brows coming together. "Why, it sounds like a small child crying."

Rafe scowled and jammed on his hat. "Let's go, Eden."

"But—"

He walked over, took her hand, and firmly marched her toward the door.

"But, Rafe, I'm sure I heard—"

"First a dream about a tiki-head door knocker, now a baby crying," he teased. "What next?"

"Yes," she murmured, her steps slowing to a stop on the deck. "What next?"

Rafe followed her stare, then winced. Kapu, grinning, carried a tow-headed toddler in his arms. He said something to Eden in his pleasant singsong tone and pointed first to Rafe, then to the child.

Rafe muttered under his breath.

Keno, whistling noisily, walked up to Kapu, took the little boy, handed him to another crewman, and gestured down below. The crewman walked hurriedly away and down the steps.

Eden turned and looked up at Rafe. "Whose baby?"

"Ah . . . Keno's."

"Keno's!"

Keno walked up, looking from Rafe to Eden, then frowned. "Oh no, pal, not me. If that word gets back to Oahu and drifts on the trade wind to Rozlind . . ."

Eden watched them and saw Rafe's jaw flex. Her heart sank like a rock. "The baby looks completely haole to me. What's it doing aboard the *Manoa*? I thought you didn't take passengers."

"We're delivering the child to someone on Oahu," Keno said cheerfully. "And the baby will be glad to get there too; I can tell you that."

"Oh . . . I see. There really are a good many things you haven't told me," Eden said, slipping her cloak on.

Rafe took her arm to escort her off the boat.

"I can find my own way back," she stated.

His eyes narrowed, and he stood hands on hips. "Sawtooth!" he shouted.

A big burly haole came up, his red hair showing in the thickening fog. "See Miss Derrington to her coach."

Rafe turned on his boots and walked away.

Eden looked after him, her cheeks burning.

Minutes later, as Sawtooth led her down the wharf to her waiting coach, he murmured, "Sure be glad to set sail tomorrow. Never seen so much fog. Makes me feel as if I'm losing my sight."

Eden said nothing.

They reached the coach, showing black in the gray mist. The driver started to climb down to open the door when he saw the crewman and stayed put, tipping his top hat. Sawtooth opened the door and helped her inside. As he started to close the door, Eden couldn't restrain her thudding heart.

"Sir, that child—whose is he?"

He smiled, revealing a gold eyetooth. "His name is Kipp, miss."

"Kipp?"

"That's right. Kipp Easton. Rafe's boy. Born to him by a missionary gal on Molokai who died there. Sad story . . . learned it from Keno. But at least he's got the boy."

He closed the door. "Good mornin' to you, miss."

The driver flicked his whip and the coach surged forward. Eden grasped the sides of the seat to keep from falling.

Rafe strode back up the stairs into the cabin, threw his hat onto the table, and flung open the drawer. He removed the journal. He looked up with a scowl when Keno stood in the doorway.

"Why didn't you tell her?" Keno demanded.

Rafe ignored the question. "Tell the captain we're leaving in the morning for sure."

"You should have told her."

Rafe dropped the journal onto the desk and glared at Keno. "She wouldn't have believed it anyway. She's looking for reasons to doubt me. It would suit her well for me to have fathered the boy. And Kipp's age fits. Even his eyes are brown." He slammed the desk drawer shut and the cups rattled.

"You're going to have to tell her the truth sometime. Not only about Kipp, but about that journal and your meeting with Jerome."

"No, she doesn't need to know about Jerome. Ainsworth will hush it up, just as he has all these years. The only thing that worries me is how much my stepbrother has dug up these last few years. He was on to something even before Eden left for Chadwick. If he does know, he'll use Eden to get what he wants from Ainsworth."

Keno shoved his hands into his pockets. "Like someone else I know?"

Rafe straightened, his eyes flashing with anger.

"This has nothing to do with Eden. I'm trying to keep her out of it. All I want is my father's plantation."

"Sure, I know. Don't get riled. Say—you have my sympathy, pal. You're in the same canoe as I am."

"What do you mean by that?" Rafe was in no mood to be placated.

"You're in love with that girl, same as I am with Rozlind. And neither of us has much chance of it working out in the end."

Rafe walked out from behind the desk. "That's where you're wrong." He looked Keno straight in the eye. "I'm not in love with Eden."

Keno laughed. "Are you trying to fool yourself or me?"

"Neither, old buddy. You didn't let me finish. I'm not in love with her enough to marry her. Just enough to be miserable when she floats in and out of my life."

"Oh, I see. There's a difference. This time you're going to let her float out of your life for good."

"That's right."

"That's why you've been so involved in trying to protect her lately? Trying to keep her from ol' Zachary and from Molokai and all that?"

"Not wanting her to get hurt doesn't mean I intend to get down on bended knee and propose marriage."

Keno pursed his lips and walked toward the door. "Good thing you don't want to. She'd turn you down anyway."

Rafe looked after him with a smirk. He sank into a chair and put his feet on a scuffed table. He tapped his chin and stared out the open window. *That look in her eyes when she saw Kipp*, he thought. *It was written all over her face that she suspected he was mine*. Hurt and angry, he nursed his injured pride. Let her think so. Only when she swallowed her own pride and asked him if Kipp belonged to him would he tell her the truth. This time *she* was going to be the one to admit she cared enough to be hurt.

He frowned. But he didn't think she'd ever ask.

Miserable, Rafe drummed his fingers. Well, he wasn't going after her. And he wasn't going to send her an explanatory message to Chadwick before the *Manoa* set sail. He'd done all he could these last years to guard her, even denying himself the moment with Ainsworth at the Palace Hotel that he'd planned and worked for these years. Now he'd need to wait until he was back on Oahu. He had done so many things for her. Worrying about her finding out the truth, trying to keep her from going to Molokai, warning her about Zachary—that clod! And what did he get in return? The first moment Eden had a chance to doubt his reputation, she bought it—hook, line, and sinker!

He pushed the table away with his boot and stood. No, he wasn't going to her this time. If she wanted to know about Kipp, she could just find him in Hawaii and ask if there'd been another woman.

There wasn't another woman, was there, Rafe? You wouldn't do that to me, would you? You know there's always been something between us, even though we haven't said so. Remember all those times when we were growing up and we looked at each other and pretended we didn't notice each other? Yet I thought of you every time the Hawaiian moon came up big and white over the sea, and every time it set in glory. Remember that night in Ambrose's hut when you held me and kissed me good-bye?

"Yes," he murmured, "and I wish I didn't."

But how well did she remember?

She doesn't, he reasoned. *And neither should I*. This time he was finished with Eden Derrington.

Calmly, he made his decision, and as he walked out the cabin door he was sure he meant it.

TWENTY-THREE

After leaving the harbor, Eden garrisoned her emotions and refused to even think about the small child she had seen aboard the *Manoa*. For all practical purposes the incident had never taken place. Each time it came to mind, bringing a sickening sensation in her heart, she would refuse to consider it. More than ever she was anxious to return to Oahu to pursue her goals.

Each day she read the *Examiner* to keep up with news on the Hawaiian king, who was still in the city at the Palace Hotel. As long as he remained, it was likely Nora would stay also. The society page reported that Kalakaua was receiving invitations from all over the state of California for festive entertainment but that he could only accept a few, due to his health.

The new year of 1891 was barely three weeks old on a foggy night at Chadwick as the clock struck eight. Eden was in her room reading Greataunt Nora's book when word was brought to her that Zachary was waiting in the parlor.

As she went downstairs Zachary was pacing in the hall in a long, dark winter coat, his hands shoved in his coat pockets. He stopped when he saw her, his hair glowing golden under the lamplight, then went up to the stairs. He projected a new vigor from the last time she'd seen him at Kalakaua's reception.

"I've news. Not all pleasant."

On guard at once, Eden waited, bracing herself for the worst.

"Kalakaua's dead."

"The king," she breathed. "When?"

"This afternoon around two o'clock at the Palace Hotel. Spreckles was with him; so was his physician and the captain of the USS *Charleston*. They think he had a stroke, but the doctor also revealed he had Bright's disease."

"I'm sorry to hear it," she said gravely, pondering the difficulties sure to lie ahead for Hawaii.

"You know what this means, don't you?" Zachary asked, his eyes alert with his own musings. "Liliuokalani will take over the Hawaiian throne. One move on her part to rescind the Constitution of '87 and the revolution will be under way. The islands may be a U.S. territory before summer!"

Eden ignored his optimism. Like Rafe, she believed a long, dark road lay between the day of Kalakaua's death and the raising of the U.S. flag over Iolani Palace.

Zachary, however, was pacing the hall, talking excitedly. It seemed the king's body would be brought back to Honolulu aboard the *Charleston*, and they would be returning with his entourage and some dignitaries from America, who would attend the royal funeral and pay their grieving respects to the king's sister, Princess Liliuokalani. Since there was no wire service between the West Coast of the U.S. and Hawaii, the uninformed Hawaiians at Honolulu would be preparing to welcome their king home with festivity as he was about to be carried ashore in a casket.

"How's Nora taking it?" Eden asked.

Zachary threw up his hands. "You know Nora. She had this strange sentimentality for Kalakaua. One would think she was Hawaiian herself," he scoffed.

His indifferent attitude irked her. "He was our king too."

"Speak for yourself, dear heart. Oh come, Eden, don't look at me like that. Look, if you and Nora and other royalty lovers want to cry into your hankies, go ahead. I'm just not willing to join you. Neither is Grandfather, or a whole lot of other haoles. Of course, Grandfather is too respectful to show anything but sadness right now. Parker Judson too. But my guess is that it's not due to Kalakaua's passing, but to Liliuokalani's accession to the throne."

Zachary told her they would leave within a few days for Honolulu and that Grandfather asked that she have all of her business at Chadwick concluded in time for the voyage.

"Then he's not going to Washington?" she asked, surprised.

"No, Grandfather felt it wouldn't look good for the future election in the legislature if he went off to discuss annexation while Kalakaua's body is being escorted ashore to Iolani Palace. He should be at the funeral looking somber for the newspaper photos."

Eden didn't think her grandfather was as heartless as Zachary made him sound. She could see why it was important for him and members of the opposing Hawaiian League to be lined on the street with hats at heart when the king's funeral procession passed by.

Zachary continued to be animated over the recent events, even after they sat down in the Chadwick parlor and the housekeeper, Hui, brought them tea. He had hardly given Eden time to consider the dark news about Kalakaua when he handed her a letter. "From Nora. I have a happy surprise for you." He smiled as Eden opened the envelope and read.

> By now you've probably heard the news about King Kalakaua. We both know what his death will mean for our beloved Hawaii and what lies ahead after the coronation of Princess Liliuokalani. We must be prepared to support her upon our arrival at Kea Lani. Any plans you have to start your work at Kalihi Hospital must wait until political matters settle down and she is safely on the throne.

Eden frowned as she read the words,

> I know you will agree to wait patiently.

Wait for what? And how long did Nora expect her to wait before meeting with Dr. Bolton?

Nora's next words took her completely by surprise.

> Zachary has told me of your affection for your mother's sister, Lana Stanhope, so I am writing her separately concerning her return to Kalihi Hospital. If possible, she should arrange to voyage with us to Honolulu on the USS Charleston. Whatever Miss Stanhope's decision, I know that you will be prepared to return home. . . .

There was more in the same vein, but Eden stopped reading and looked at Zachary. He smiled as though he had accomplished some feat that would delight her.

"I knew you wanted Lana to come back to Hawaii, so I've taken certain steps to see that it's going to be accomplished," he said confidently.

"What do you mean, you've 'taken certain steps'?" Eden asked warily.

"You'll see," he said secretively, his eyes glinting as he smiled.

"Zachary, I don't think it's wise to interfere with Lana's plans. It's one thing to ask her to consider, but trying to arrange the circumstances—"

"Now, now, don't rush to conclusions. Naturally she'll make up her own mind. I just helped things along a little."

Eden stood abruptly, Nora's letter still held tightly in her hand. "You'll need to explain first. How did you help things along?"

"By speaking to Grandfather and Nora both," he said innocently. "And a few weeks ago, I just happened to run into someone at one of the holiday parties who might help."

Eden watched him, growing more concerned by the moment.

"Old Mrs. Bolton, Dr. Clifford Bolton's mother. She was here making the social rounds over the holidays because she knew Kalakaua would be here. He hadn't invited her along in his entourage, but she didn't let that stop her. She came anyway and arranged to attend many of the same functions. She wants to go back with us on the *Charleston*, but Grandfather put a stop to that. He's sent word to the ship's captain to refuse her. She's quite an old gossip, you know. Fun to talk to and loaded with usable information."

He looked at her and laughed. "Guess who was with her? Clifford!"

Eden tensed with a surge of anger. "You didn't bring up Lana, did you?"

"But naturally."

"Zachary, you shouldn't have."

His golden brows shot up. "Bolton himself asked about her. I've learned she used to work at Kalihi. Did you know that?"

Eden didn't like the suggestion in his smile, but there was no use pretending now. "Yes, she told me. And I feel quite certain you knew, too, *long* before you came here or 'just happened' to meet Dr. Bolton at a holiday party. Lana likes working at Chadwick. I'm doubtful she'll take the step to change things and return to Hawaii."

"Do you want her at Kalihi Hospital?"

His question was strange, as though his benevolence assured her he had control over the outcome. "I've already made my wishes known to her," she said carefully. "I would prefer Lana make up her own mind."

"Without undue pressure from me? Is that what you mean to say?"

"Yes, that's what I mean. That you seem to have discussed her with him is disturbing."

"Nonsense, Eden. What influence could I possibly have over Dr. Bolton?"

Could Lana's past have been raised in his letter? Or had there been some other topic?

"What did you tell her in that letter you wrote?"

His mouth twitched. "You ask in a tone that conveys your suspicions. What could I have put into the letter that would upset her?"

"Then you know your letter disturbed her?"

"Naturally!" His eyes darkened with temper. "I told you so when I first arrived. The woman sent a scathing note to the Palace Hotel, threatening me if I didn't stay away."

Lana's personality had never seemed threatening, though she had been upset on the afternoon she'd burned his letter. Eden didn't blame her now, knowing what she did about Zachary.

"I ignored Lana's threat because Nora wanted me to see you," he went on. "I was right, wasn't I? Aren't you glad I didn't retreat like a frightened puppy?"

She scanned him doubtfully. "What did you tell her in the letter—that you wanted to arrange a meeting between me and Great-aunt Nora?"

"What did she suggest I'd written?" he asked warily.

"She didn't suggest anything, but she was clearly upset."

"Oh, that—" He gestured impatiently. "She knew matters would end as they have, with your returning to Kea Lani. She'd prefer to keep you with her, as a daughter."

She looked at him thoughtfully. "What did you tell her about my mother, the boat, and Molokai?"

Startled, he didn't speak.

"I just happened to find a remnant of your letter after she tried to destroy it," Eden explained.

He watched her guardedly.

"There's no use denying it, Zachary. I still have the scrap. Would you like to see your handwriting?"

"So I mentioned her sister."

"What reason did you have?"

"Do you really want to know?" He smiled strangely.

Eden's heart thumped and her hands turned sweaty. "Yes. If you have anything to say."

Zachary's smile faded. He paced, hands in pockets, looking at his black patent leather shoes.

"Very well. I was going to tell you anyway after we got back to Kea Lani." He stopped and looked at her. "I asked her about the day Rebecca was supposed to have accidentally drowned in the boat while your father was working on Molokai."

Eden felt the blood drain from her head.

Zachary watched her like a nervous wolf.

Eden sat down slowly in the chair. Her voice was so quiet that Zachary walked closer toward her. "Why ask Lana?" she said.

He shot a glance toward the door. "I felt she was a safe person to ask. Now I don't know. She's trying to cover for someone too."

Eden stared up at him, her hands gripping the arms of the chair. She hadn't expected this turn of events from Zachary. "Did you write that note to me and leave it in the mission church?"

He scowled and looked defensive, beginning to pace again. "Yes."

Eden was strangely relieved. He was confessing, and Rafe had been right.

"Why did you do it? Were you hoping I'd run to Grandfather or Aunt Nora and demand answers?"

He looked at her, startled. "Who told you that? Rafe?"

She said nothing and he smirked.

"Rafe thinks he knows all about Rebecca's death. He doesn't know anything. I left the note for you all right because I . . . as I grew up, I was beginning to remember things about that night."

Eden tried not to shake, but emotion gripped her. He had her spellbound as he paced back and forth like a caged tiger.

"I didn't want you to leave Kea Lani and come here. I hoped the questions I raised in the note would be enough to change your mind. I wanted you to stay and keep trying to find out about Rebecca. I didn't tell you directly because I didn't want Rafe to find out. He'd have been furious with me for upsetting you."

"What did you mean a moment ago when you said Rafe didn't know about my mother?"

"That he's been poking and prying about recently, the same as I have. But he's wrong. I know something he doesn't."

Her heart slammed in her chest at the secretive gleam in his eyes.

"What is it, Zachary? Tell me," she urged.

But he shook his head. "It must wait until we reach Honolulu. I can show you something then. It's supposed to be a secret."

Eden walked up to him and took hold of his arms. "Tell me what?"

His mouth tightened. "It will have to wait, Eden."

She could see he meant it, and she swallowed her frustration. "Are you saying you think there was—something more?"

"You know about the boating accident in that storm," he stated shortly. "I've heard you ask the same question that bothers me. Why would she take a boat out with a friend when a storm was blowing in? We know what we've been told. Rebecca couldn't make it back to shore in the rising waves, and when the boat overturned, she drowned."

Eden shuddered. "Yes, that's what we've been told."

"I've reason to think otherwise."

Do I really want to pursue this now, with Zachary? she wondered but said nothing as Zachary went on.

"What if she didn't take that boat out? What if she didn't drown? What if she died some other way? As a result of someone's violence maybe."

Hearing him suggest her dreaded fear made Eden recoil. "Surely not *that*, yet perhaps, well . . . perhaps some accident other than drowning." She could feel his alert stare.

"But why would the family want to hide an accident?" he asked. "It's as though they're trying to protect someone."

"Protect?" she repeated, her mind spinning. She was thinking of her dream, of her mother running, of *someone* seemingly chasing her. She thought of the storm, of hiding with Zachary under the daybed, both of them frightened. Yes, they both knew.

"Zachary, that night we hid under the bed—you *do* remember, don't you?"

He paled, grew rigid, and walked away, reaching into his pocket for his pipe.

"Zachary, why were we so afraid? What were we hiding from? Did we see something? Were we hiding from someone who knew we had seen something happen?"

She sank to the chair, feeling weak with apprehension. "I don't remember everything. If only I could—"

"Don't try," he ordered, casting her a glance.

"Do you remember?" she whispered. "They say you don't."

He lit his pipe. "No, I don't remember."

He was behaving oddly. First trying to convince her of wrongdoing toward Rebecca, then turning cold and distant when she brought up that night in the storm. Yes, why couldn't something have happened to her mother? she thought. Dreadful things happened in the most respected families. The thought left her sickened.

"I'll admit their furtive actions have overshadowed the actual events," she said.

He resumed his pacing. "Even if she didn't have a boating accident, she met her demise in some way. Who in the family would wish to hide the cause of her death? Unless they're trying to protect Jerome."

Jerome! His almost matter-of-fact tone set her back and she looked at him. "My father?"

Zachary shrugged. "He's the most likely one. He left Kea Lani too. Almost immediately after her death. For all practical purposes he disappeared. Except for Grandfather, who ever heard from him?"

"I have," Eden protested, suddenly discovering that she was unwilling to bring her father into the unpleasant scenario.

"A letter a year doesn't prove much, does it?"

Rafe had said much the same thing. She had to admit that her father was lax in his correspondence, but his possible involvement in a crime against her mother was too disturbing to think about for long. She stood.

"I can't believe it of him. I won't."

Zachary was quiet, meditative. He sighed. "Maybe you're right after all, but there is something—something I can show you once we're home. Look, Eden, I've said things tonight I wouldn't admit to anyone else. I've kept them bottled up for years, but I'm not the only one who knows something is wrong. So does Rafe. And so do you."

"Yes, but not *murder*. I'll never believe that of my father," she said indignantly.

"Then maybe it wasn't Jerome. Maybe it was someone else. And maybe Jerome knew who it was and left because he couldn't bear it."

"I'll ask Rafe. I'll go to him when we get back to Oahu," she stated.

"If I were you, I wouldn't. He wouldn't tell you anyway. He's trying to keep you in the dark. Don't say anything to anybody," he warned, walking up to her, his eyes holding hers.

"What about the pearls, Zachary? Where did you get them, and why did you give them to me now? Were you trying to intimidate Grandfather?" she challenged quietly.

He looked pale and drawn under the flickering light. "Did Rafe suggest that?"

"Is it true?" she persisted.

His shoulders sagged a little. "Yes." He sank down in the chair and stared at his pipe. "I wanted to let him know I knew something, and that he and Nora weren't going to cut me off from the Derrington enterprises so easily. He owes me the right to carry on the sugar business after him, and I . . . I rather lost my better judgment. I found the pearls in Jerome's bedroom, along with the wedding photos. For some reason that I haven't been able to understand yet, those pearls upset them both."

"And you caused Grandfather to become severely shocked at the reception."

"That wasn't my first intention. I only wanted to let him know I would assert my rights. I admit it didn't work out."

She looked at him wearily. Zachary's schemes were never wise, she thought. All the more reason to be cautious of him as Rafe had suggested.

Zachary appeared to guess what she was thinking. He stood and approached her, his eyes unexpectedly pleading. For a moment he looked almost boyish and vulnerable.

"I don't like to be used to intimidate Grandfather—or anyone else," she said, troubled.

"I'm sorry about the pearls," he admitted.

She wondered if he meant that.

"Nora says she needs you," he went on. "We both do."

Personalizing the request added an awkwardness to the moment.

"I want to learn about my mother's death. As a child, my questions about it were shunned by the family," she said. "Now that I know we both feel the same way, we're bound to come to the truth. Can you remember what happened that night? We'll help each other," she said. "Think, Zachary! Do you remember a big house with a high room? A room surrounded with windows?"

He walked away slowly toward the door. She followed, watching him intently.

"A room surrounded with windows," he repeated. He opened the front door and stood against the backdrop of misty darkness, looking out. "No," he said after a moment. "But once we return to Kea Lani we can help each other remember. I'll see you in a few days aboard ship."

Eden's heart felt cold and desolate as she climbed the stairs to her room in the quiet mansion. Was Zachary right about her father and mother? It couldn't be true. The tick of the big hall clock emphasized her isolation. For years she had suspected something was wrong, but hearing Zachary discuss it made it seem more real. Perhaps her dark suspicions were true, but she just hadn't allowed them to come to the surface.

Reaching her bedroom, she closed and locked her door, leaning there in the silence. It couldn't be true, she thought again. She went to her vanity table and took the cameo locket from her jewelry box. With stiff, cold fingers she opened it. She stared at the small photo of her parents. Her father, darkly handsome yet profoundly serious, stared back at her.

"No," she whispered, and soon tears blurred her vision and his face was gone. She snapped the locket shut and grasped it in her hand, holding it to her heart.

"I won't believe it," she said.

The next morning Lana was waiting for her in the hallway as Eden left her room to go down for breakfast. Her lips tightened as she gestured Eden into her bedroom. She closed the door.

"I've received a letter from Dr. Bolton. A boy brought it early this morning. Clifford is in San Francisco."

Eden managed a blank expression. She didn't dare share Zachary's theories about her mother's death, though presumably Lana must already know from reading his letter. No wonder Lana had been so upset. Zachary's suspicions must have come as a total shock to her. Her accusations about "his meddling after all these years" now made sense.

"Nora also said she was writing to you. I suppose she's offered you some incentive to return to Honolulu?" Lana continued, her hazel eyes bright with emotion. She brushed her fingers through her mussed hair, now loosened from her professional chignon and hanging down her back. She looked younger, and once again Eden noticed how attractive Lana could be.

"Zachary! He had the audacity to contact Dr. Bolton about me. To—to tell him to make me a job offer or he'd have his great-aunt Nora withhold financial assistance from the leper program!" Lana paced in her stockinged feet, one hand on her hip, the other in her hair. "I've been humiliated." She whirled, her face tinged with emotion. "I'm convinced Clifford thinks I'm behind this. That I urged Zachary to do this. That I'm trying to wrangle my way back. As if I would! As if I'd ever push myself on him or anyone else!"

Eden walked softly to the cherrywood chair and sat down on its tapestry cushion. She was still distraught herself over Zachary's charge about the death of her mother. Eden hadn't seen Lana in such a temper since Zachary's letter had arrived. She tried to soothe her aunt. "I'm sure Dr. Bolton is professional enough to realize you had nothing to do with all this conniving."

"Oh, don't count on it. He's misjudged me in the past. Why not now? He'll think I've tried to arrange all this. He's rather conceited that way. Unfeeling, so precise—and judgmental."

"Maybe not. And don't forget he knows Zachary and the rest of the

Derringtons better than you do. It's likely he's had to put up with some of Great-aunt Nora's demands in the past to get funds for special research projects."

Lana dropped to the bed, sinking her head against the pillows, looking across the room at Eden. "It's like you to give us all more credit for reasonableness than we deserve. If anything, he'll suspect me of approaching Nora Derrington on the subject of my return. Especially when she gets back to Kea Lani and sends him a letter asking to arrange for your internship under his supervision."

Eden didn't see why Lana thought that but could understand her concerns. She didn't want to make light of them by waving them aside. "As department head of tropical diseases, he's bound to be wise enough to see what Nora's doing." She stood from the chair and approached Lana. "Perhaps if I returned and worked at Kalihi for a few months first. Then I could talk to Dr. Bolton about you, since I know you far better than anyone else—your work here at Chadwick, your nursing awards, the charitable work with the Chinese immigrants here in the city."

Lana looked alarmed and stood quickly, almost as if the idea flustered her because it would set her in an admirable position with Dr. Bolton.

"No, I'd rather you didn't," Lana said. "And anyway—he wants to see me."

Eden brightened. "Does he? Then why don't you see him? Wouldn't it be good to get all of this behind you? Whatever you decide about Kalihi, you would at least be at peace with Dr. Bolton."

Lana walked to the other side of the room as though she didn't want to have her feelings boxed. "I don't want to see him. What would I say after all these years?" She looked at Eden almost helplessly. "It's been so *long*, Eden. I've . . . I've got gray in my hair."

Eden could see her anguish. "I suspect he has a few of his own. He doesn't expect you to still look twenty-one."

"But all of this interruption in my life. I didn't want it to happen. I've already made up my mind that I will retire here in San Francisco," she lamented.

"Well, the Lord surprises us sometimes, doesn't He?" Eden smiled. "Just when we think we have everything figured out, He shows us we still have some growing to do."

Lana turned and looked at Eden apologetically. "I'm sorry to unload on you like this. I've disappointed you."

"No, you haven't. I always knew you were human," Eden said with a half smile.

Lana laughed. "I know I told you I'd give it serious thought, about going back and facing spiritual failure and all that—but I didn't think it would come to me. Clifford is coming *here*. I keep telling myself it's just too late for me to want to deal with the burden of it. I'm happy here," she insisted. "I simply wish to leave the past where it is."

Eden knew it was wise not to argue with her. It must be Lana's decision. "If Dr. Bolton is the kind of man I think he is, now that he knows you're here, I rather suspect he won't take no for an answer. He'll want to see you. Anyway, Lana, the invitation is extended to join us if you want it. We're all going back with the king. . . . Sadly, to his funeral."

Lana's weariness showed. "Yes, I've heard. It's the death of an era and the beginning of something new for Hawaii. Who knows where it will lead?"

As Eden watched her, she decided that Lana must have been deeply in love with Clifford Bolton at one time. Did she still care? Perhaps it was the fear of seeing him again after so long that made her insist she would not return. Eden found herself wondering what he was like, and what he may have thought of her aunt in the past.

Yes, both death and life mingled together on the stage of history. Kalakaua was dead, and Liliuokalani would soon sit on the throne. Yet God ruled over all. The Lord sits supreme forever. His plans and purposes march on toward the final conflict of the ages and the establishment of His throne: *Thy will be done on earth as it is in heaven.*

That afternoon as Eden packed her trunk for the voyage home to Hawaii, her heart was perplexed over all she had recently learned. Her raw emotions seesawed back and forth between what Zachary suspected and her refusal to believe it. The dark head of doubt and fear raised her suspicions. *What if it's true? Could my mother have been murdered?*

Finally she surrendered her torn and ragged emotions to her heavenly Father. *I know I can trust you with all my tomorrows, with every door you open or shut to me. With all things you allow in my life, both dark and light. And may your truth set us all free to follow your paths.*

The USS *Charleston*, carrying the deceased Hawaiian monarch and his entourage home to his islands, was ready to sail from San Francisco Bay. Nora, Ainsworth, Zachary, Parker Judson, and Eden were on board. Just before the ship departed, Eden received a hasty message from Lana.

Decided to meet with Dr. Bolton for lunch today after all. Things are falling into place in my life. Clifford will be returning to Honolulu in a few more weeks with his mother, who is down with a winter cold. I'll be returning to Kalihi Hospital this spring or early summer, just as soon as the Lord provides a replacement for me here at Chadwick. Aloha, Eden dear. See you in Hawaii.

Lana

Eden laughed and went to the ship's rail to look back at the San Francisco Bay. Though she couldn't see Lana out in the throng that waved and shouted as they pulled away from the dock, Eden waved anyway as the first happiness she had felt in weeks flooded through her heart.

Aloha, Lana, she thought. *God be with you till we meet again. This time at Kalihi Hospital!*

P A R T

III

TWENTY-FOUR

Honolulu

Iolani Palace

January 29, 1891

Honolulu was in a festive mood to welcome home the "Merry Monarch," King Kalakaua. The triumphal arches were draped in colorful bunting, and garlands of orchids and Hibiscus flowers were everywhere. As the news that the USS *Charleston* had been seen rounding Diamond Head moved among the throng of Hawaiians on the streets of Honolulu, their excitement mounted.

Rafe had ridden into town, not to see Kalakaua, but to meet with several haoles in the legislature whose families dated back to the pioneer missionaries. He and Ambrose had drawn up plans to improve the delivery of goods to the leper settlement on Molokai, and he needed the legislature's support to enact new laws.

Rafe wasn't under any illusions. Getting protection laws passed would be difficult. Even among the conservative Missionary Reform Party, where he expected a stronger interest in deeds of grace, there existed a secret belief that leprosy was contracted by immoral living and was just recompense in the flesh for sin. While they agreed that mercy should be shown, the moral stigma remained strong, and active involvement in meeting the needs of those afflicted was low. Except for the dedicated Protestant missionaries, who had a zeal for reaching out to the lost for Christ, and the pioneer Roman Catholic priest Father Damien, who was now dead, everyone in the islands considered it taboo to have contact with lepers.

Rafe thought of Kipp. The child was as healthy and strong as any he'd seen in Honolulu. So far, the rearing of the baby, who was now around two years old, had been shared by him and Keno. At times, Rafe couldn't believe that he had taken on the responsibility of the young child—until he remembered the tragic woman on Molokai. He could still envision her following after him, persistently pleading with him until he could no longer walk away and forget.

He frowned as he thought of Eden. "That boy had better appreciate his good fortune when he grows up," he thought wryly. Down deep in his soul Rafe knew the child's destiny had not depended on fortune. He was convinced the Lord had wanted him to take the child, not only that he should live, but for some unknown purpose in the future. Perhaps when Kipp became a man, this divine purpose might become known. So far Rafe hadn't even told Ambrose where he'd gotten him. The guarded secret remained between Keno and him. If word got out that he'd taken Kipp from a leper woman on Molokai, there would be an outcry and perhaps even the insistence that the child be returned. Fear did strange things to people. While it was obvious that Kipp did not have the disease, it would be years before anyone would accept him as "clean."

Rafe maneuvered his horse through the gathering crowd on Merchants Street and rode past the Spreckles Bank, the Bishop Bank, the W. O. Smith Law Offices, and onto King Street. He noticed the crowd gathering at Kawaiahao Church across from Iolani Palace, and another crowd at Aliiolani Hale facing Punch Bowl Street and Queen Kapiolani's house. Kawaiahao Church had first been pastored by pioneer missionary Hiram Bingham, who, along with the other missionaries, had created the written Hawaiian alphabet, which was used to translate the Bible. Bingham had been popular with the Hawaiian leaders but very unpopular with the whaling captains.

Rafe noted the mood of the Hawaiians and hapa-haoles was more perplexed than festive, and he paused on King Street across from the palace. "What have you heard?" he questioned a young Hawaiian lad who ran up beside his horse.

"Don't know, Makua Easton. The *Charleston* was seen coming round Diamond Head. But the flags are at half-staff."

Rafe turned in his saddle and pushed his hat back, glancing toward the shimmering blue Pacific. This would give Parker Judson something to get worked up about, he thought. Without the desperately needed trans-Pacific cable, it took weeks to get news from the States. They were in the middle of the Pacific relying upon ships for communications.

The *Charleston* had voyaged with Kalakaua to America over two months ago and was now returning with the flags at half-staff. It commonly meant the vessel carried bad news. It could mean an important personage on board had died. Rafe thought it might be either the captain or King Kalakaua. Turning his horse and settling his hat, he rode toward Iolani Palace.

Ambrose wasn't at the legislature when Rafe arrived. Though speculation of dark news was rife, everyone at the palace seemed determined not to talk about it until they had a response from Liliuokalani, who was still at her house.

Rafe used the opportunity to gain support for his plans and gave what he thought was a worthy argument to the three haole legislators, all friends of Ainsworth Derrington, Lorrin Thurston, and Sanford Dole.

"You realize, Rafe, this will need the support of Dr. Bolton and his staff at Kalihi Hospital, as well as the king," Jedediah Bishop told him as they met off to one side in the legislative chamber with Asa Whitney and Caleb Emerson.

"Bolton's in San Francisco," Rafe said. "When he gets back to Honolulu, Ambrose will arrange to meet with him and others on his staff."

"Where is your uncle?" Asa Whitney asked of Ambrose.

"I met with him last night. He should have been here. He must have gotten caught in the crowds."

Asa had stood up from the table and walked over to the window. "That looks like Ambrose now, hurrying from Kawaiahao Church. A crowd's following."

Rafe and Bishop joined Emerson at the window. The crowd grew larger, and a second group of Hawaiians came running up King Street, shouting and pointing toward the harbor.

"The *Charleston* must have docked," Rafe said.

Jedediah Bishop exchanged glances with him and they seemed to read each other's minds. They were walking across the chamber toward the door when Ambrose came in. He was out of breath from hurrying, and his silvery brows appeared to bristle.

"Kalakaua's dead," he exclaimed. In stark contrast with the noise outside, a silence descended over the haole legislators.

––––––

No one in the islands had realized the critical state of King Kalakaua's health when he'd departed from Honolulu in November. News of his death did not reach Honolulu until the morning of January 29, when the USS *Charleston* appeared, its yards aslant and flags at half-mast, bearing the royal remains. As soon as the ship docked in the harbor, official word of the king's death was sent to Princess Liliuokalani and members of the cabinet and legislature. Not long afterward an official group from Iolani Palace was formed to walk over to Washington Place, the house of Princess Liliuokalani on Beretania Street, to officially offer condolences and, to the secret alarm of many of the haole officials, prepare the strong-willed princess to become Queen of Hawaii.

Would Liliuokalani take the prescribed oath to support the Constitution of 1887? they wondered. Refusal to do so, or an attempt to circumvent the requirement, would be construed as a revolutionary step. As regent during Kalakaua's absence, she had already worked closely with the cabinet and legislature, mostly run by the Hawaiian League, which favored a republic.

"She's a natural-born politician," Jedediah Bishop said.

"She's a sovereign to be watched with a keen eye," Asa Whitney warned.

Crowds soon gathered in front of her house and at the Central Union Church across the street. Not far away on Palace Walk at the barracks, and farther down Beretania Street at the armory, authorities were arranging for action. At once the Hawaiians draped the festive decorations with somber funeral crepe.

At the harbor, American sailors and marines led and followed the casket up the streets of Honolulu into Iolani Palace, while a brassy, somber dirge from the band filled the air.

Rafe heard the Hawaiians weeping in the street. *"Nalohia ka Makua,"* they cried, which meant, "Gone is the father!"

Eden donned customary Victorian black and accompanied the Derrington family and other important haoles in government and business to Iolani Palace. She walked in the somber file of guests through the glittering throne room where Kalakaua lay. As they filed past, Eden was remembering the many past gala spectacles that the king had given in this same room. How quickly things changed. How soon life on earth was over! How important to abide in God's priorities, she told herself.

Eden saw the royal rosewood casket surrounded by the notably tall *kahilis*, handsome, muscular, full-blooded Hawaiians who testified to Kalakaua's lineage in the alii families. Island chiefs formed his honor guard with their sons and the finest of Kalakaua's private troops. There were foreign diplomats from England and France, and the most influential haoles who, like Eden's grandfather, had unequivocal interest in the future of Hawaii. They were all there, as though they had always supported him and grieved his passing. Ironically, Eden thought many of them had somber faces because they would now be dealing with Queen Liliuokalani.

As Eden glanced about the throne room, she covered her surprise at seeing Rafe. He stood on the other side of the room appropriately garbed in black, standing beside the hefty Parker Judson. As Rafe's gaze met hers, she remembered the young child she had seen on the *Manoa*. She remained unresponsive and stood with a straight spine. He had disappointed her with his shameful life-style and she could *not* pardon him. No, not even though her heart ached at seeing him again. The very thought that he'd been with a woman turned her icy cold. She ripped her gaze away when she saw his faint smirk. *He knows what I'm thinking*, she thought. Well, let him!

Eden felt miserably guilty as she filed past Kalakaua's casket. Her heart should be tender and pliable, forgiving, understanding, leaving all things in God's hands, but she found herself swallowing what felt like a barb in her throat.

She glimpsed Kalakaua for the last time. He was in uniform; at his side lay his sword and scepter. Across the tunic of his rich blue livery was gold braid and an assortment of precious medals and decorations that world leaders had bestowed on him during his travels. Tears came to Eden's eyes. But was she crying for the king, for Rafe, or for herself? She didn't know.

Then the magnificent feather cape that Kamehameha the Great had worn before his people was placed over the casket as a Hawaiian symbol of the everlasting right to reign.

————

When the day of the funeral arrived, Eden walked with Nora. The mourning process of ancient times called for loud shrieks and wailing. Before the missionaries had brought hope in Christ, the ancient chiefs would knock out their teeth and mutilate their flesh like the prophets of Baal in the Old Testament Scriptures whenever a king died. "*We sorrow not as others who have no hope*," she thought.

Kalakaua's wake was decorous, but in the funeral procession out to Nuuana Valley for burial in the royal mausoleum, Eden recognized members of the *Hale Naua*. They marched as Kalakaua had wanted them to, in the ancient ways. The arrival of the high priest of Hale Naua caused a mild stir, since the group was considered a secret heathen society. The high priest was dressed in ancient fashion and carried the esteemed feathered helmet, the kapu stick, and a sacred gourd.

All this while the Royal Hawaiian Band played, followed by Kalakaua's troops from the Iolani barracks. More than two hundred of Honolulu's citizens, haole and native, formed the double line to take the catafalque from the palace to the royal mausoleum. Between these twin-roped lines walked the mourners of the royal family, the government ministers, and those on Liliuokalani's guest list.

As Kalakaua was laid to rest, Eden was thinking not just of the deceased king but of those who had invested their hearts and minds in Hawaii and its people. Her heart gave tribute to the pioneer missionary Hiram Bingham and his wife, Sybil. No longer did the Hawaiians have to prostrate themselves on the ground and grovel at the sight of an alii death march. Eden saw thousands of Hawaiians lining the streets and sidewalks respectfully bidding him good-bye. There were Hawaiian troops, American sailors, missionaries, haole planters, and businessmen, while the very last of the alii walked David Kalakaua to his resting place.

Perhaps Hawaii is already American, she thought. The Jewel of the Pacific lacked but one thing: the Stars and Stripes above Iolani Palace. She glanced at all those present with hats in hands, her grandfather among them, and saw the new Queen of Hawaii, Liliuokalani, which meant, "Lily of the Stars."

TWENTY-FIVE

That morning as Eden entered the Kea Lani dining salon, the doors leading onto the lanai stood open, granting a stunning view of white sand and aquamarine sea. Despite the tranquil beauty, emotional tension crackled between her grandfather and her uncle Townsend. Her grandfather, looking stately, dressed all in white, his small, neat beard glinting, sat imperiously at the table taking breakfast on the lanai.

"They left three weeks ago and you only now tell me?"

"As ill as she is, I didn't have the heart to stop her," Townsend said.

"Celestine has every right to visit Hanalei, but with that Hawaiian back, we can't let Rozlind out of our sight."

The Hawaiian, Eden knew, was Keno. Rafe had arrived back in Hawaii before the Derrington family accompanied the king's body on the *Charleston*. He had come to Kea Lani to visit his mother, and Eden wondered if Rafe might not have had something to do with Celestine's decision to go to Hanalei.

"The boy's with Rafe," her uncle said. "Don't worry about him."

To men like her grandfather and uncle, all the Hawaiians were called "boys," despite age or size, unless they had land, money, or power.

"He doesn't dare show his face around Rozlind," Townsend added.

"What's to stop him from learning where she is and going to her?" Ainsworth asked shortly.

"I'll stop him if he tries."

"How are you going to stop him?"

Townsend, muscled and tanned, his golden hair tinged with gray at the temples, reached for the coffee urn, refilled his cup, and took it to the lanai rail, where he sat on the ledge, his booted leg drawn up.

"He knows what I'll do to him if he goes near her."

"No. There will be none of that. Maybe I can reason with the boy. If not, I'll buy him off. I've a plan for Rozlind. These last few weeks I've made up my mind about Zachary. I'm sorry, Townsend, but he just doesn't suit me to control the Derrington estates."

Townsend looked glum but resigned. "I know. He'll have to accept it. Father—I'm thinking of bringing home Troy from California, of giving him my legal name. He'd make a strong son. What do you think? Would you accept him on Kea Lani?"

"Have you discussed it with Celestine?"

"No. She's too ill."

"Then the matter will need to wait. I want to discuss Rozlind. You know the fears we have over her behavior. I want you to go after her, Townsend. I want her back on Kea Lani."

"All right, Father." His rugged face with its cleft chin showed impatience. "I'll bring Rozlind back to Kea Lani."

"When?" Ainsworth asked in his quiet but overriding manner.

Townsend scowled at his cup. "Soon as the next inter-island steamer heads for the Big Island."

Eden quietly went to the side bar in the salon and poured herself a cup of Kona coffee, thinking she would slip out unnoticed. She'd skip breakfast and ride out to see Ambrose and Noelani. She mused to herself as she filled her cup. Although the family had been careful not to mention Troy publicly, Eden remembered hearing his name on occasion. She suspected he might be one of Townsend's sons away at college in the States. Did Zachary know he had another stepbrother? What would he do if Troy were brought home to Kea Lani as a member of the family?

Her uncle's voice again penetrated her thoughts.

"Look here, Father, you'd better do more worrying about Rafe than Rozlind. He's out on that thousand acres he's boondoggled with Parker. In a few years he'll be a rival for Kea Lani."

"I know that."

"Rozlind can be easily handled. Send her on a voyage to England. Arrange a suitable marriage. She's avoided Griswold for too long. He has good business ties, lots of land."

"I intend to arrange a marriage," Ainsworth stated.

"Good. But what about Rafe? He's got over a hundred new coolies out on that stretch of land. That's just the beginning."

"Parker beat us out this time, and he's too big to stop."

"If it was just Rafe, we might try to do something to thwart him," Townsend said.

"Messing with Parker is a mistake. I need him on the next trip to Washington. He's for annexation, and that counts with me."

"Yes, but we've got to harness Rafe—stop him somehow."

"I intend to" came her grandfather's calm, confident voice. "I've decided to ride out there to see what he's up to with Parker. To thwart a threat in the future, I'll have to find a way to join forces."

"Join forces! With Rafe?"

"Just the way I did with the Hollingses. The days of war are over, Townsend. The easiest way to divide and conquer is through marriage ties. Family joined to family. I've no choice now but to accept Easton."

"Father, you're out of your mind!" Townsend bellowed.

"Sit down, Townsend," Ainsworth said tonelessly. "You've never managed to master your appetites or your temper. Yes, I've decided to bring Rafe into the Derrington enterprise. You're partly to blame for this."

"Me! I want to keep him out."

"Exactly—a mistake. You ran him off Oahu. You underestimated him. Now he's back with something to prove to us. And I've no doubt that he'll prove it. I'm not waiting until the votes are in to build bridges to him. I've been doing a good deal of thinking since leaving San Francisco. I'm going to make him a deal. It's time the Derringtons and Eastons were united in marriage again."

"Father, you can't mean this—"

"I do," Ainsworth said icily. "I'm going to arrange a marriage between Rafe and Rozlind. It will be a far better match than yours was with Celestine. It will end this matter between Rozlind and the Hawaiian boy and will consolidate our holdings. Through Rafe, we may be able to connect with Judson, maybe even buy him out."

Rozlind! Eden stood at the side bar as if molded to the spot.

"You're making the biggest mistake of your life," Townsend cried.

"No," Ainsworth said flatly. "My biggest mistake these years was in listening to you about Rafe. I should have seen years ago that he's just the man I need in the family. Instead, I've wasted years propping up Zachary. Rozlind has family blood and good sense."

Someone entered the salon, his footsteps faltering as he heard Ainsworth. Eden turned, her face unable to conceal her dismay.

Zachary stood there, and from his expression, he, too, had overheard.

He walked up and looked at her. He must have read her feelings. "Well, well, looks like Grandfather has pulled the rug out from under both of us. From the look on your face, maybe I should say *jerked*."

He walked onto the lanai.

Eden mused, and a moment later her grandfather came out, saw her, and stopped.

"Ah, good morning, Eden my dear. Have you had anything to eat yet?"

"Um . . . no, Grandfather."

"After breakfast I'd like to have your company this morning."

She blinked quickly, trying to align her face into a demure expression so he wouldn't guess she had overheard.

"My company?"

"I'm riding out to see Rafe, and I'd like you to come with me. There's something I want to talk to you about on the way."

Somewhat numbed, Eden managed an appropriate response and hoped she didn't look ill. He scrutinized her for a moment, then left the salon for his office at the back of the house.

She heard Townsend and Zachary talking in low, urgent tones, but she had no wish to join them. Her appetite had fled, and she turned and left them, going upstairs to her room to change. She longed for the company of Ambrose and Noelani and the sight of the little white mission church. Everything was crowding in at once, and her emotions felt frayed at the edges.

I won't think about it now.

An hour later, donned in a lime green frock of cool cotton with a matching lace-trimmed sun hat, Eden sat beside her grandfather in the open carriage as the driver brought the team of horses up the coastal road toward the Kalihi area of Oahu. The sunlight was warm, and fleecy white clouds tumbled across the azure sky.

Thick ferns grew in abundance under the familiar palm trees along the red-earth volcanic road, and the Hibiscus bushes and wild orchids were all in bloom. A few monkeys brought in years ago by her great-grand-father chattered, while birds squawked and flew about in their private paradise. The banana trees, along with the mango and guavas, which were also brought into Hawaii from elsewhere, were as productive as ever. The nostalgia of coming back home swept over her with a pang, compounded by the news of her grandfather's plans with Rafe and Rozlind. She knew he was watching her as if a little bewildered by her mood, for she could not hide all of her concerns. She dare not tell him the secret of her soul.

She wouldn't tell anyone. She wanted to deny it to herself.

"You're unusually quiet this morning, Eden."

"Am I, Grandfather? I don't mean to be. I suppose I'm wondering why you wished my company."

"Well, we have several things to discuss. I shall begin with Jerome. I've some good news. A letter arrived in San Francisco that I've meant to share with you, but with Kalakaua's death and all that has demanded my attention, I'm afraid I've neglected to do so. Jerome wrote that he will be coming home either this spring or summer. He's coming to stay."

Eden turned to him, smiling with happiness for the first time that morning. "Coming home?" she cried excitedly. "My father?"

He smiled, equally pleased. "Yes, indeed, to join his research partner, Dr. Bolton, at the hospital. I must say it's about time." His wan smile tightened. "He's been away far too long. He's become nearly a stranger. We'll need to get to know him again. That, of course, includes you. You've not had the family life you deserved, Eden, my dear, and I'm as much to blame as Jerome. Unfortunately, it's not possible to make up for past mistakes as easily as one would like. I hope to try harder while I still have a few good years left. I can never make up for my failures; nor do I expect you to shrug them off and deny your hurts. I confess I've favored Rozlind since her birth. . . . She was the child of my firstborn son. I unwisely favored her at your expense."

Eden tried to concentrate on his words, but thoughts of her father vied for attention.

"I can't explain all the reasons for what happened when you were growing up. I can only tell you we made mistakes, and while I can't make up emotional losses, I can do something financially for you that is fair and just." He patted her hand awkwardly. "Nora also tells me you want to work with Dr. Bolton at Kalihi Hospital."

She looked at him, restraining her emotions from running away with her. She didn't think he would approve of too much display.

"She assures me it can be arranged, and I've agreed that if this is what you want—a career in medicine—you certainly can have it. Jerome told me to be sure to tell you he's looking forward to having his daughter working with him as a nurse. You may find yourself a husband at the hospital—who knows?"

Tears oozed from the corners of her eyes. Her heart knew both thankfulness and disappointment at the same time. God had not given her everything she desired, but how could she deny that in His loving grace He had given her more than she deserved? Her cup was full, and if it wasn't exactly running over, there was enough to satisfy her thirst.

Her father was coming home to Hawaii—*permanently*. Whatever mysteries remained would be answered. How wrong Zachary had been in suggesting those evil things about her father! That he was coming home to stay seemed to prove Zachary wrong. Thank God that he was.

Yes, and Jerome even wanted his daughter working closely at his side. It looked as though her desire to join him in his research would be fulfilled after all. A bright future lay ahead—an exciting, adventurous future. And even her grandfather was building understanding between them. She could never be as close to him as Rozlind was, but he wanted to be her grandfather just the same. And her aunt Lana would be coming to Hawaii too.

She looked at her grandfather and saw that he was watching her alertly. She smiled. "Having a grandfather for even a few years is better than never having one at all." She reached a hand toward him and he took it, looping her arm under his.

"What an arrogant old man I've been," he said with regret. "I fear I haven't yet learned all my lessons. That's the unfortunate part, Eden."

Eden felt a cool shadow cross her heart, but it was quickly gone when he smiled and patted her hand.

———

It was nearing noon when they arrived at the pearl fishery, less than a half mile from the road. A new road had been cut and cleared to reach inland toward the mountains. Sitting on the edge of her seat, holding her hat in place as they bumped along the yet ungraded road, Eden's eyes scanned the land on both sides of her. The mission church stood alone in the empty field, but Ambrose and Noelani's thatched-roof house built on stilts was gone! On the way, she had imagined herself running up the pathway, rushing up the wooden steps, throwing open the front door, and smiling at Noelani. "I'm back again, Noelani! Just as I promised," she would say, embracing her.

The driver continued to maneuver the horse-drawn carriage up the road. *The house has got to be standing*, she told herself, refusing to believe in defeat. She remembered lying awake in the loft, pretending to be asleep while Rafe talked with Ambrose at the kitchen table. Townsend had thought he was locked in his room at Kea Lani, but Rafe had always managed to get away. Now the little Hawaiian house was gone, forever. Her hands clenched. Rafe had done this. He had betrayed them for success and money. Anger and pain vied for control. She swallowed. At least the mission church was still there—but for how long?

On either side of the road the land was being cleared for planting—land that stretched to an invisible bright blue horizon. The earth was a rich brownish red, perfect for growing. The direct sunlight was hot, the trade wind refreshing, and she knew she was looking at success, but in her mind she saw loss. Disappointment now seized her.

Ainsworth caught her attention by gesturing ahead with his white Panama hat. Eden looked and saw two wooden poles holding a makeshift sign that was nailed in place, stretching across the road.

Hawaiiana Plantation.

The foliage was being cleared, the palm trees toppled and hauled away. Coolies—the unflattering name commonly used for workers brought in from China—were bent over, working the miles of acres. They looked like white ants with cone-shaped cane hats scrambling along the reddish earth. Trees were being cut as far as she could see.

The carriage moved forward perhaps for another mile before they came to some thatched-roof huts surrounded by a ring of palms and rambling vines. One of the houses was larger than the others, and she saw a number of people moving about outdoors.

"Stop here," Ainsworth told the driver. "Go find out where we can find Makua Easton."

"Yessir, Makua Derrington."

Eden shaded her eyes, staring toward the houses. Was Noelani there—and Ambrose?

The wind ruffled her hat and dark hair, and her heart thumped. She heard people shouting orders and the sound of saws, shovels, picks, and spades. Hammers echoed from someplace still farther in the distance.

She looked at her grandfather to see his reaction.

"It's horrible," she breathed. "Everything will soon be gone."

"Progress, my dear. You're looking at what will one day exceed everything except Sprecklesville," he contradicted. "Wish I had thought of those South American pineapples. Cayenne, he calls them. One thing about Rafe, he's ambitious. And the more we discount Rafe, the more bullheaded Parker becomes, wanting to prove he was right in backing him."

Eden had no choice except to agree. She had sampled that prized new pineapple, and she knew the depth of Rafe's determination to succeed. Still . . .

"It's hard to be impressed when Ambrose's house is gone," she said somberly. "Maybe the mission church will be next." She looked off toward the huts and house being built but couldn't see any sign of either Rafe or Ambrose. "I don't understand about Uncle Townsend," she said, turning back to her grandfather. "None of this would be happening if he hadn't sold the pearl fishery."

"That's not quite true. Parker arranged to get this land long before he bought the fishery from Celestine through Townsend. It was Townsend's mistake. It angered both Rafe and Ambrose. If I'd been consulted first, I'd never have allowed Townsend to sell it."

"I've wondered why he did," Eden said, looking at him curiously.

The mood changed at once to uneasiness. "Townsend was having trouble with a few dozen natives who attended the mission church. He claims he warned Ambrose to keep them in line and he didn't do it. He backed them in their complaints until the problems they caused far out-weighed any benefit of keeping the church open."

Eden tensed, fearing the worst. Then the church was in jeopardy!

"Celestine said 'sell!' So that's what Townsend did. She got a fair price for it from Parker."

"Trouble? I've never known the Hawaiian Christians to cause trouble before."

"Ambrose had them riled."

Eden shook her head in disbelief. "Grandfather, Ambrose isn't that sort of man, and I think you know it as well as I. He's calm and dignified and keeps all his emotions locked up inside."

Ainsworth's lip twitched with grim humor. "Sounds like an infirmity that I've struggled with."

"Did Uncle Townsend say what kind of trouble?"

Her grandfather didn't answer at first. "He had some disagreement with Ambrose, and he'd decided it was time to sell the fishery." He cleared his throat, adding quietly, "Including the church property."

"Oh no! Then it *will* be torn down like Ambrose's house!"

"I didn't say that. Truth is, I don't know. It seemed easier to sell than be villainized by Ambrose for shutting it down. He considers the place a sacred remnant of the past—the pioneer missionaries and all of that sort of sentimentality."

"Sentimentality, Grandfather? It's more than that," she pleaded. "Rafe and Mr. Judson can't shut the mission church down. Jerome and Rebecca built it, established it. You can't allow it."

"I'm afraid I've nothing to do with it."

"You could use your respected influence."

"On Rafe Easton? I have very little. That's why I'm here. I hope to begin changing past mistakes. As for the church, Eden, it meant little to Jerome, though it was Rebecca's pride and joy. Jerome hadn't been out there in years, even when he did come to Oahu."

This was not what Eden had been told while growing up at Ambrose and Noelani's house. Her father had had the church built because he believed in the idea her mother had espoused.

"That's Easton coming now."

Eden turned her head and saw Rafe walking in their direction across the cleared section of land. "If you'll excuse me, Grandfather," she said tonelessly, "I'd rather go say hello to Noelani and Ambrose if they're here."

"As you like. What I have to say to Rafe may be better received alone."

She thought she knew what that was from what she'd overheard at breakfast, and she didn't care to listen in! She fought to keep down the frustration from growing in her heart as she climbed down from the carriage and started briskly toward the buildings under construction. As Rafe approached her head on, Eden lifted her chin as though she didn't see him and marched ahead, her slippers sinking without mercy into the soft, churned soil.

Rafe stopped, looking at her, hands on hips, while she glanced at him from the corner of her eye and struggled past.

"Going somewhere, Miss Derrington?" came the faintly challenging tone.

"That's right," she called airily. "Do you have any objections, Makua Easton?"

"Yes. You're walking straight into about two feet of loose dirt. And you're trespassing," he goaded smoothly.

Eden stopped, her lashes narrowing, and looked over at him. He wore a rakish smile as he walked up and stopped a few feet in front of her. He lowered his hat and scanned her.

"Did you come to see me?"

Eden laughed shortly. "Should I? I can't conceive of any reason why I should trouble myself. You've already knocked Ambrose's house down, and from what I hear the mission church is next. It's obvious that you and I no longer have anything in common. It's my grandfather who wishes to see you."

"Your reasonableness affords me great delight. I always told myself, now there's a woman who doesn't rush to judgment, but patiently waits with a sweet temperament for all the facts. I see my estimation of you was perfectly correct."

She looked at him, unsmiling.

"The mission church is still standing, isn't it?" he asked flatly. "And you can thank me that it is. I had to talk myself blue in the face to keep Judson from tearing it down. Even that is no promise for the future, but for the present it's safe."

Her eyes rushed to his, relief flooding her heart, but before she could apologize, he looked toward the carriage. "What does Ainsworth want?"

She saw the speculation in his face. Her own mood altered. "I'd better let him explain. But it appears the old adage is true: 'Power and money talks.' You're suddenly the man of the hour."

Rafe pulled his hat lower against the sun, still looking off toward the carriage. "So the mighty Derringtons want to make peace, do they? Well, this is a windfall. What's he willing to give me to join forces on the great adventure of life?"

Eden's eyes scanned him, and her half smile was sardonic. "His grand-daughter."

Rafe's gaze shot to hers, taking her in from head to toe.

Eden added, masking the pang that nipped at her heart like teeth, "Rozlind, of course. You'll likely get half of Kea Lani with her—quite a windfall indeed. And maybe even Hanalei. Congratulations, Rafe. You've finally won."

He stared at her, but his expression was swiftly concealed, his eyes unreadable.

Eden looked away before her feelings could manifest themselves in her face. "Where are Ambrose and Noelani?"

"Ambrose isn't here. Noelani's in that hut to your right" was all he said.

Eden walked ahead, telling herself she was doing just fine emotionally and refusing to analyze the painful sense of loss filling her soul. *It had to end like this*, she thought. *I have my calling and Rafe has his. Soon my father will be home. Soon I'll be involved in what I've always wanted. And Rafe—*

Her emotions tumbled. Tears stung her eyes. Rafe would have everything he wanted. Who could ask for more?

As Eden drew near the palm-thatched cabana built up on stilts, she smiled and climbed the wooden steps. "Noelani! I'm back," she called, but somehow her words did not sound as joyful as she had imagined they would.

Eden sniffed the enticing aroma of cooking. Noelani was fixing lunch, and Eden unexpectedly began to relax. She threw off her hat and looked about, turning full circle.

Noelani heard her and came through the kitchen door. A warm smile softened her face, and her arms were outstretched. "Eden, child, aloha, aloha!"

They embraced, and Eden kissed the cheek of the woman who had filled the role of both mother and friend.

I belong here, she thought. *And I'm not ever leaving again.*

TWENTY-SIX

While Eden sat on rattan furniture in the open cabana with the tropical breeze blowing freely through the open spaces, Noelani served Eden's favorite recipe of fried bananas sprinkled with coconut and sugar. Over hot coffee, Noelani explained all that had been happening. It was true that the old thatched-roof house near the mission church was gone, but Rafe was arranging for a new house with more rooms and comforts and a special large cooking room that Noelani had always wanted. Ambrose would have his own upstairs study with built-in library shelves for all of his biblical reference books.

"Things are going well, child, but we still worry about the church. Makua Judson told the workers to tear it down. Rafe stopped them. Bless him. But things are still unsettled. Ambrose is there now. The structure sits in the middle of land all cleared for miles around."

"Yes, I saw it. . . ."

"It stands like a lonely beacon amid an ocean of red earth."

Eden got up from the chair and walked about the cabana, looking out and below at the men hard at work on another small hut.

"They can't tear the church down," Eden protested. She looked at Noelani in her bright red-and-yellow muumuu, her hair worn in a European knot at the back of her head. "There's something I don't understand about my uncle selling the pearl fishery. Townsend claims he was weary of the trouble the Hawaiian Christians were causing him at the church. He said Ambrose was stirring them up. Do you know what Townsend was talking about?"

Noelani's black eyes heated. "Yes, if you think it wise to know. It may be better if you did not."

Eden grew uneasy. "I want to know the truth."

"Townsend did not do honorably with the niece of one of our church elders. Akela came from Maui to visit her uncle. She was pretty and Townsend saw her. Unfortunately, she was flattered by the attentions of a wealthy and powerful haole. He gave her things she never had in Maui. It all turned out bad, child. She is expecting. Her father was shamed and angry. He went to Ambrose, who was also angry. Ambrose went to your uncle and demanded what he was going to do about his sin, but Makua Townsend denied any involvement with the elder's niece. He called her a liar and a bad woman. He said to send her back to Maui to work on the plantation where she had come from. The Christian Hawaiians at the church banded together under Ambrose and insisted honor be done. One thing led to another and there was a fight between Makua Townsend and one of the Hawaiian men. Then Townsend sold the pearl fishery to Parker Judson, who had long wanted it, and threatened to close down the church."

Eden was indignant. So that's what it was about. Knowing her uncle's reputation, she wasn't surprised.

"And he got by with it," she murmured.

"No, child, he didn't get by with it. Everyone knows what he did. And he knows too. The Lord knows. Someday in God's own time and way He will bring all to light and do justice. But we want His mercy as well. Akela sinned too, and she claims to be a Christian. Makua Townsend does not."

Eden walked to the edge of the open cabana and looked out across the red-brown land to the distant dirt road. She could see the carriage parked beneath the blue sky and glittering warm sun. Her grandfather had gotten out, and he and Rafe had walked farther off into the distance and stood alone talking.

"The child Akela carries is related to me," Eden said. "I have a Christian responsibility toward her and the baby when it's born. Where is she?"

Noelani nodded her understanding. "Back on Maui," she said sadly. "With her parents. They work at Wailea Plantation."

"I'll see what I can do," Eden said.

"Ambrose will be pleased. He intends to go there to see the family. Her uncle, one of our elders, will also feel comforted knowing you care."

"It's the least I can do," Eden said quietly. She was thinking of another child. Rafe's boy. She swallowed back the sudden passion to ask

Noelani what she knew. Where was the child now? Who had the mother been? The crewman from the *Manoa* had told her the mother had been a missionary on Molokai—could such a story actually be true? She checked herself. It wasn't any of her business, she thought again firmly. And since there would not be anything between herself and Rafe—ever—she needn't satisfy her feminine curiosity. She turned away from looking across the wide landscape.

"Noelani, there's something I want to ask you and Ambrose about my mother. Since he's not here, maybe you can give me an answer."

Noelani suddenly looked guarded. "If I can."

Eden told her again, as she had in the past, about hiding under the daybed with Zachary, about the hand that had reached beneath to find her. "I never remembered anything more about it until recently."

Noelani's sharp eyes watched her with new alertness. "You remember how you fell down those stairs when you were a little girl?"

"No," Eden said with a sigh. "If *only* I could. But I had a dream when I was in San Francisco at Chadwick. When I awoke I knew I had been dreaming about things that actually happened." She walked toward her and knelt beside Noelani's chair, intensely searching the older woman's concerned face.

"I was seated in a carriage outside a mansion—but I don't think it was Kea Lani. I remember that everything was pleasant, until suddenly my mother was running away and someone was chasing her. I remember a sense of fear, of loss, and I think I tried to run after her, crying for her to come back—" She stopped, feeling the same tight emotion well up in her chest.

Noelani's dark eyes filled with something like anxiety and pain. She shook her head. "You must not think about such things, Eden. You must let it go."

"But why, Noelani? You know something, don't you? Something you won't tell me." She took the woman's wrinkled hand and squeezed it, her eyes pleading. "I want to know. I have a right to know."

Noelani's gaze dropped to her lap. "I do not know. I was not there. But I think you ran into the house that you remember, looking for Rebecca. I don't know how, but you must have fallen while searching for her."

"Where did she go?"

Noelani was silent.

"Did she run away? Was it then she got on a boat with a friend and got caught in that storm?"

Noelani shook her head. "I know nothing of that. Only what the Derrington family said happened. They told Ambrose she went out with a friend and the boat was overturned in the waves."

"Maybe there wasn't any 'friend' . . . but an enemy."

Noelani looked bewildered. "Enemy?"

Eden told her briefly of Zachary's suspicions, avoiding mention of her father.

Noelani frowned. "Makua Zachary told you this? It is wicked! How could he say such a thing? Did you tell him about that note you found?"

"Zachary left it," she said wearily.

Noelani looked relieved. "You see, child? It is only your confused cousin so full of guilt and fear himself that he troubles you with dark thoughts."

Eden could see she wasn't going to learn much from Noelani. Even if she knew something, the old woman didn't want to talk about it. Probably because Ambrose had told her not to. But Noelani startled her with her next words.

"That house you remember was not Kea Lani. You are right. There is another big house that belonged to your great-grandmother Amabel."

Amabel's house! Why had she never been told there was another house on the island? Eden gripped her hand. "Where is it located?"

Noelani hesitated. "On Koko Head."

By the time Eden left the cabana and went down the steps, she had made up her mind. She would say nothing to anyone in the family. She would go to Koko Head and see Great-grandmother Amabel's house for herself. The truth, she now believed, waited for her there.

She shaded her eyes and looked off toward the carriage. Her grandfather and Rafe walked into the field and stood together as though Rafe was explaining his plans for the plantation.

Eden decided to walk back to the carriage. As she passed a smaller thatched-roof hut, the door was open and she saw a young Hawaiian woman sitting on a woven palm rug. The child that Eden had seen aboard the *Manoa* was in her arms, apparently asleep, and the woman was crooning something in Hawaiian. Eden was sure Noelani had deliberately taken Kipp to the servant to care for while she visited with Eden. So Noelani, too, had wished to keep the boy a secret.

Rafe listened to everything Ainsworth Derrington offered, then was quiet for a long moment, considering. Circumstances were falling into his lap like rich, sweet coconuts. He felt the sun beating down on his back, the breeze ruffling the loose-fitting cotton shirt while he gazed off toward the Koolau Mountains, reflecting shades of purple, emerald, and charcoal.

"Let me get this straight, Mr. Derrington. You want to make a deal with Mr. Judson to pay off my debt in this operation. And in return I owe the Derrington family *nothing*."

Ainsworth's eyes twinkled in the sunlight and a grim smile was on his mouth. "That's right, Rafe. You would owe the Derringtons absolutely nothing."

"You realize that no one in his right mind would believe you'd do this without some strings attached. You're too shrewd a businessman for that."

"You forget that the Derrington family will benefit, even though your half of this enterprise with Parker Judson stays in your name."

Rafe was cautious and faintly amused by it all. He had no intention of cooperating until he got what he wanted—Hanalei. He also intended to keep his share of the plantation Parker wanted to call Hawaiiana, after a new granddaughter. Rafe was thinking that his plans for a showdown with Ainsworth concerning Jerome and Rebecca might never need to see the light of day. If he could get back Hanalei without a confrontation, there would be no reason to risk hurting Eden.

But what did Ainsworth have on his mind?

"You haven't explained yet what it is you expect in return," Rafe said. "Obviously you want something other than to simply express some charitable deed of kindness toward me after all these years."

"Yes, I regret that I didn't do it sooner, Rafe. I'll be honest with you. You provide the family with something that I unwisely didn't recognize during the years you were growing up on Kea Lani. I always thought you an intelligent boy but one headed for trouble. You didn't seem able to accept your father's death or your mother's marriage to Townsend. You had a chip on your shoulder. I was wrong, however. I shouldn't have permitted Townsend to bully you as he did. He's treated your mother cheaply, and the older I get, the more troubled I am about it."

Rafe wondered if he were sincere. Ainsworth looked genuinely concerned, and while Rafe had no sympathy for his smitten conscience at this late date, he had never felt that Ainsworth was as much to blame as his own stepfather.

"And now you've suddenly changed your opinion of me, is that it?" Rafe asked, trying to keep his cynicism from seeping into his voice. He admired much about Ainsworth, even as he did Parker Judson. Both men seemed to possess an uncanny sense of where financial success could be found. It seemed crass of Ainsworth to want to form a union with him now that there was little risk.

Rafe sighed and folded his arms. "I don't know. You see, there's really only one thing I want from you, Mr. Derrington."

They had turned and were looking off toward the road and parked carriage. Eden came walking across the field, the breeze blowing her skirt. She held her hat in place and did not look in their direction. Rafe frowned, finding her a troubling distraction, one that he had already made up his mind not to be greatly damaged by. Yet he was still bothered over her indifference and her quick judgments to doubt his motives for almost everything he did. When she arrived here today she had already assumed that he had wrecked the mission church and run roughshod over Ambrose and Noelani, clearing away the house as though it were rubbish.

"I want Hanalei back, sir."

"Hanalei. Might as well ask for Kea Lani, Rafe. I've no jurisdiction over Celestine's wishes to leave it to Townsend to manage."

"Townsend will do exactly as he is told. You know that. You can convince him he has nothing to gain by keeping it. Turn it over to me in thirty days, and whatever it is you want from me you're likely to get."

Ainsworth frowned. He shook his head, using his walking stick to turn over some clods of earth. "No, no, I can't do that."

Rafe held down his rising anger. "You'll have to. If you want to make a deal."

Ainsworth's brows bristled. "Then I'll gain Parker's cooperation in this pineapple venture. There are ways to put the pressure on him to let me buy in. If I must do it that way, Rafe, I'll work to eventually squeeze you out."

Rafe gave him a quiet, measured look. "Yes, I think you would try it."

"Not that I'd like to do so. Don't get me wrong. I'm finding that I like more about you than those stubborn characteristics that are so troubling."

Rafe smiled. "I think you have that backward. It is you, sir, who is stubborn, with a bent toward greediness."

Ainsworth's eyes flashed with temper. He looked as if he were about to say something sharply, then stopped. He drew in a breath as if to allow things to settle for a moment and turned again to look over the miles of rich land.

"Like I say, Hanalei I cannot give you. Townsend has his mind set on it. He's ambitious when it comes to those Kona coffee plants."

"So am I. I remember when my father planted them. I intend to own what my father built with his hands, what he intended should be left to his only son. Whereas Townsend will inherit your work, Kea Lani."

"No, he won't," he said quietly. "I'm leaving him only what he's capable of handling. The same goes for Zachary and Eden. It's Rozlind who will inherit. And that is my bargain with you. Marry Rozlind and I'll leave you Kea Lani. You can't say it is less than Hanalei."

Rafe looked at him. He could see the older man was deadly serious.

"Think about it, Rafe. Think about it carefully. Come see me next week with your answer. In the meantime I'll be talking with Parker, if not you. It's really your choice."

"I'm not in love with Rozlind."

"You can learn to love her. In the old days marriages were always arranged by parents and grandparents. The marriages that were made lasted. They were the lifeblood of the land, strengthening the country. Rozlind is a fine woman, intelligent and attractive. She'll make you a good wife, a fine mother of your children. In return I'll get what I need in you, that which is sadly lacking in either Zachary or Townsend. I may even live long enough to see a few great-grandchildren begin to grow up on Kea Lani."

Rafe folded his arms across his chest, using one finger to rub his chin as he looked at him. "You actually mean this."

"Of course. I wouldn't have wasted my time coming here otherwise."

Rafe looked over at the carriage. Eden stood with her back toward them. His lashes narrowed. He tapped his chin.

"I'll think about it."

"Good. Come see me on Tuesday of next week. I'll be waiting for you."

Rafe watched Ainsworth walk away toward the road, his shoulders straight with dignity and purpose beneath his jacket, his cane swinging.

He kept his gaze riveted on him until he got inside the carriage and Eden climbed in beside him. The driver flicked the whip and the Derrington carriage moved down the road, made a U-turn, and then started back toward the lagoon and the road to Honolulu.

Some minutes later Rafe was still standing there. He reached down and scooped up a fistful of red soil, squeezing it. At that moment he realized that he could get everything he wanted. All he needed to do was wait. A marriage would eventually give him control of Hanalei, even if he did not regain the plantation now. Marriage ties could only strengthen his position. Ainsworth was progressing in his final years on earth. Rafe could one day have Kea Lani, which he could use to manipulate Townsend and Zachary. He would also own half of Hawaiiana. Yes, in the future he could be as rich and politically influential as Ainsworth.

Rafe looked at the soil in his hand before allowing it to filter through his fingers. He looked up and saw his uncle Ambrose walking toward him across the field. In many ways Ambrose and Ainsworth were alike, yet also profoundly different. Both men had spent their lives working to accomplish what they believed was the best for Hawaii. One had everything; the other had almost nothing except his prized collection of theological books.

Ainsworth Derrington had invested his mind and soul in the great Derrington enterprise to the detriment of his children and grandchildren. And now, finding himself disappointed in their strength of character, he was searching for someone to safeguard his empire after his death. Ainsworth had failed because he had been so busy building a personal kingdom that he neglected passing on the real values to his own house.

Uncle Ambrose couldn't leave Rafe a kingdom nor a bank account, but he had passed on the principles learned from a walk of faith with God. He had given Rafe something far more valuable; he had participated in Rafe's life.

Now at the crossroads, Rafe remembered those long late-night talks at Ambrose's kitchen table in the little hut. He remembered the praise Ambrose had given when he had made a choice to obey the principles of Scripture in a tough situation. He remembered, too, that Ambrose had not always rushed to try to right his wrongs and injustices, but counseled Rafe to learn wise lessons from disappointments and hurts. He had taught him the value of standing alone when necessary. Nor would Ambrose rush to bail Rafe out of the trouble he'd gotten himself into when he had refused to wait on God's timing. Troubles and trials, disappointments and misunderstandings—all these things taught the greatest lessons of life: courage, perseverance, the need for patience, believing and trusting God.

Yes, Rafe thought as he walked to meet him in the field. There was a big difference between Ambrose Easton and the patriarch Ainsworth Derrington. And now he had a choice to follow the steps of one giant or the other.

Two men, two ways . . . both were strong, both were capable, both were getting on in the last years of their walk on earth. Now it was Rafe's turn to choose.

TWENTY-SEVEN

The lunch hour had long passed by the time Eden returned to Kea Lani with her grandfather. She had avoided any mention of Great-grand-mother Amabel's house on Koko Head during the carriage ride home. He had seemed satisfied with his discussion with Rafe but had said nothing of its outcome, and Eden could not bring herself to ask. Could Rafe possibly have any interest in a marriage arrangement with Rozlind?

The sun's golden rays appeared to scorch the waters of the Pacific before dipping behind the blazing horizon. During dinner Eden was preoccupied with a secret plan to visit Koko Head. Was Amabel's house the one she remembered in her dream? Would Zachary remember it? She debated whether she should mention it to him. She intended to go there in the next day or two, just as soon as she could do so without drawing the family's attention.

Great-aunt Nora was upset over Rozlind and hardly touched her dinner.

"I knew it would come to this," she said crisply to her brother. "You've expected too much of her, Ainsworth. She's convinced she's in love with that Hawaiian boy. A woman will give up the throne for a man she loves."

Eden took a bite of her stuffed chicken breast but hardly tasted it. She thought of Rafe. What did Rozlind think of Rafe Easton? What would her response be to Grandfather's arrangements? She remembered back to the diving contest when Rafe had brought up the black pearl. Rozlind had gone to the viewing stand to congratulate him. Eden had a fresh vision of Rozlind kissing him. She had seemed pleased to do it, and Rafe certainly hadn't avoided it.

"You needn't worry about her any longer. Eventually there will be a suitable marriage. Perhaps within the year."

"Griswold? She loathes him."

"No, to Rafe," Ainsworth said, satisfied. "I spoke to him about it today. He's quite amenable. Naturally, he'll become heir of Kea Lani."

A deadening silence settled over the table. Eden felt her heart drop to her stomach.

Townsend looked as though he'd been struck, and Zachary made no effort to disguise his jealousy.

Eden managed to lift her glass and sip her passion-fruit drink. As she looked up she found Great-aunt Nora watching her with a sympathy Eden hadn't realized was there.

"Well," Nora snapped at Ainsworth. "You do like to drop your little surprises, don't you? No matter that it may hurt the innocent."

Ainsworth looked surprised. "I can't see that anyone is hurt. What is important, my dear Nora, is that Kea Lani and Hawaii are best served."

"You wouldn't see the obvious if it were right before you," she said briskly. "Oh, never mind. . . . You might as well know that Celestine isn't the only one spending time away from Kea Lani. I, too, won't be staying on. Now that Liliuokalani is queen and I'm in full support of her reign, I'm making plans to move out in a few weeks. There's going to be a revolution," she stated, "and I won't live in the same house with kin that dare raise a finger against the legitimate rule of the monarchy."

Silence held everyone at the table.

"Looks like Father isn't the only one who likes to drop little surprises," Townsend said. "You're leaving for Hanalei?"

"No, my house at Koko Head that Mother left to me." She stood as though weary. "I have no appetite tonight. Eden dear, I will want you to come with me when I depart. Let us hope by the time Jerome comes home and you start your work at Kalihi Hospital the queen will have thoroughly established her rule."

Nora turned and left the dining salon, her gown fluttering behind her ankles.

Eden grasped at the opportunity. "Why, I never knew Great-grandmother Amabel had a house. No one ever mentioned it."

Her grandfather and uncle were silent, but Zachary, his eyes bright and animated, a twist to his smile, appeared anxious to discuss her question, to vent some of his frustration at his grandfather for making Rozlind heir.

"Great-grandmother never liked the mansion. She believed the Hawaiian witch doctors had cursed the place," he mocked. "She was afraid of the kahunas and of tiki heads."

Eden moved uneasily as she realized he must also be fuming over the matter of Grandfather and Rafe.

"Don't be absurd, Zachary," Ainsworth scolded.

"Absurd? What seems absurd is that the family never made use of it as a summer house."

Eden looked quickly at her grandfather and saw his frown.

"Amabel left it solely to Nora," he said.

"After all this time, I'm surprised she'd ask Eden to live there."

Eden felt the silence, as though it weighed heavily upon the hearts of everyone at the table. Her thoughts went rushing back to her dream. Yes, that had to be the house, the one she was beginning to remember, where she had fallen, and where she and Zachary had hidden beneath the daybed. Zachary's face looked strained in the lamplight as he talked about it. *He remembers*, she thought, *even though he pretended not to*.

Her grandfather stood with wearied dignity and looked at Zachary with an almost sad expression. "I've had a tiring day. I think we all have. Townsend, when are you leaving for Hanalei?"

"Tomorrow. I should have Rozlind back here in a few weeks."

"Good." Ainsworth turned to Eden. "Good night, my dear." He patted her shoulder and walked from the dining salon.

When he had gone, Townsend turned to Zachary.

"You'll gain nothing by goading him. I heard about the black pearls. Your thoughtlessness has only helped to convince him of the wisdom of choosing Rozlind. Now," he growled, "your stepbrother as well. Feast on that! Rafe, primary heir through marriage to your cousin!"

Zachary tossed down his dinner napkin with disgust and stood to his feet, meeting his father's gaze. At that moment, Eden could clearly see their similarities, both in mind and body. For a horrid moment she imagined them tangling in a physical display so prevalent among the Derrington men. But Zachary turned and strode out onto the lanai. He took the steps down to the garden and beach, bright under the rising moon.

Townsend looked after him, scowling. Eden didn't care for her uncle, especially after what Noelani had told her about the niece of one of the Hawaiian elders at the mission church. She would have excused herself and left the table, but since he had been the first one who hadn't seemed squeamish about mentioning the pearls, she took advantage of the opportunity.

"Why do you think Grandfather was so upset when he saw me wearing my mother's pearls in San Francisco?"

Townsend got up and went to the cabinet, pouring himself a glass of potent local liquor called *okolehao*, distilled from the ti root. "Anything connected with Rebecca's death disturbs him."

"Why should it trouble him any more than the rest of us?"

He looked over at her, taking a swig from his glass.

"Jerome was his favorite, his pride and joy. I've only disappointed him. . . ." He looked at his glass and took another defiant gulp. "When Jerome packed up and left after Rebecca's death, Father was moody for several years. But he eventually consoled himself with his beloved Hawaii and with Rozlind. Your mother's death seems to remind him of Jerome's absence, as though he were still grieving."

Eden had never considered this before.

"Grandfather told me my father is coming home sometime this year."

"Yes," Townsend said with self-incrimination. "The younger son is coming home from the far country. But this time, the *elder* son stayed home and spent his father's money on riotous living and harlots." He started to say more but hesitated, as though remembering to whom he was talking. "Well, I'd better pack my bag. If I don't bring Rozlind home to marry Rafe, Father will never forgive me." He strode out of the dining salon, and she heard his steps going up the stairs.

Eden sat alone at the large table sparkling with silver and Venetian glassware, the abundance of choice seafoods and fruits nearly untouched. Her heart was heavy, her mind troubled. She felt sorrow for them all. They had everything, yet they had so little that was truly worth living for. Townsend's excesses did not satisfy him. He was like a cup with a hole in the bottom that could never stay full.

"*He healeth the broken in heart*," she thought, remembering the words from Psalm 147:3.

Yes, the Lord could mend broken spirits and bring new hope and purpose to wasted lives. The divine Potter needed only the yieldedness of the clay to His touch as He molded a new vessel.

May it be, she prayed.

A few minutes later she got up as the servants came to clear the table. She went out onto the lanai and down the stairway to the court that led off to the beach to look for Zachary.

The February night breeze was cool for Hawaii, but pleasant, like spring in California, and the stars were glimmering. Zachary hadn't gone far. He was smoking his pipe, which glowed in the dark.

Eden removed her shoes. "There's a full moon tonight. Let's walk on the beach."

He knocked his pipe clean against his heel and stepped on some glowing ash, then shoved his hands in his trouser pockets, looking gloomy. They began walking on the warm, dry sand, which felt soft as it sank beneath her toes. The palm trees swayed gently as calm wavelets rippled along the shore. Her heart secretly wished that it was Rafe walking with her instead of Zachary.

"No one ever told me about Great-grandmother Amabel's house," she began.

He shrugged. "Like Grandfather said, no one liked it much."

"Were you serious about her fear of the Hawaiian kahunas?"

"Amabel was superstitious."

"Koko Head is a beautiful area. I'd like to go see the mansion. . . . Have you been there before?" she asked cautiously, not wanting to prod him but hoping he'd offer to take her there.

He looked at her, his face unsmiling in the shadows. "Yes, I've been there." He stopped, looking down at her.

"Would you take me there tomorrow, Zachary? I'd like to see it before Nora goes there. Do you have anything planned for tomorrow?"

When he did not respond, she walked on. All his bravado at the table with their grandfather had been purely a show. It seemed that Zachary feared Amabel's house.

"We could leave early in the morning," she said as he walked on beside her. "After Townsend leaves for the Big Island."

When he still kept silent, she tried her last ploy. "Well, if you won't go with me, then I'll have to go alone."

"You'll be sorry if you do" was all he said, and continuing in a dark mood, he turned away and walked back toward the house.

Zachary was afraid to go to Koko Head because of something he remembered, she decided. But what was it that troubled him? She wasn't getting anywhere trying to convince him. Perhaps it was better to go alone after all.

A few minutes later she saw his dark figure on the lanai silhouetted by the light from the dining salon. He went inside.

Eden was still standing on the beach by the palm trees when she saw a light go on at the third floor in one of the seldom-used bedrooms. While looking up at the lighted window she suddenly remembered something Zachary had once told her.

She ran across the sand and back toward the mansion, picking up her shoes and climbing the steps.

She walked through the salon into the outer hall. The house was quiet except for the servants moving about in the kitchen.

Eden took the stairway to the third floor, where Zachary had lit the lamps.

What had Rafe said at Chadwick that night? That she looked like Amabel? Well, she wanted to see dear Great-grandmother Amabel! And on the road here to Kea Lani that day years ago, Zachary had mentioned a different painting of her great-grandfather's sister. *"She was the family Puritan from the Congregational Church in New England. The one with the black dress and high collar. Looks like she's choking on a pickle, just like Rebecca. . . ."*

Those words had hurt, and Eden remembered them as though they had been branded upon her memory. She rushed to the hall and the little-used bedroom. There were other paintings there too, she'd been told. *There must be one of Amabel*, she thought. *Rafe said he had seen it.*

As she approached the room, the door was ajar and the lights burning, but there were shadows in the corners. She entered, glancing about for Zachary.

The large gallery had been shut up and smelled musty. Zachary stood below a large painting as though entranced. Eden picked up one of the lamps and walked quietly to stand beside him.

"That's Amabel's sister-in-law," Zachary said. "She didn't like Amabel. Can you guess why?"

Eden looked at the somber woman dressed all in black with a bit of white at the neck.

"Appearances are not always what they seem," she corrected. "Man looks on the outward appearance, but God looks on the heart."

Zachary took hold of her arm. "But look at this painting."

He led her until they came to another large painting of a young woman of perhaps twenty with ebony hair adorned in a mass of curls. She was strikingly pretty, with green eyes and a dimple in her chin, wearing an exquisite white frilly dress with a matching parasol.

"That, my dear, is our great-'granny' Amabel when she was a girl. It was painted long before she ever came to Hawaii, before Ainsworth and Nora were born. I've been madly in love with her for fifteen years. So has Rafe."

"Indeed?" Eden pulled her arm free of his grip and stepped back.

Amabel wasn't exactly the old-fashioned image that Eden had imagined all these years.

She stared at her for a long minute, then sighed. "Well, there's little to be learned from her picture."

"We used to come here when we were boys and make up stories about each one of the family members. Amabel was always our favorite."

That was something about Rafe she hadn't known before. "Did Rafe know about Amabel's house on Koko Head?"

Zachary shot her a glance. "No," he said too firmly, "he's never been there. Did he tell you he had?"

She wondered at his response. "No, I haven't talked to him about it. I only learned about the house today from Noelani, and tonight Great-aunt Nora mentioned it. What do you know about it, Zachary? There's more you won't tell me, isn't there? What don't you want me to know?"

"It's what Grandfather doesn't want you to know. Rebecca's buried in the cemetery near the house."

Eden didn't move. "That's not possible. I was told they never recovered her body from the sea."

"I was at the house staying with Nora when they laid her to rest." His mouth tightened. "I wasn't suppose to know, but I was hiding in the trees when they buried her without a funeral."

Eden's heart fluttered in her chest. "That can't be true. You must have been mistaken."

"Either what I'm telling you is true or it's not," he said stiffly. "It should be easy enough to verify. You'll be going there with Nora soon. Visit the old family cemetery there and see for yourself. Just don't tell them I told you about it."

He started to walk out, but Eden took hold of his arm. "You think Grandfather's trying to protect me from something?"

"Maybe he's trying to protect himself."

"My father's coming back soon. He should be able to explain everything. You must be wrong about all this."

His mouth tightened. "When you're satisfied, then I probably will be also."

Would he? she wondered. "What did you expect to accomplish with the pearls?"

"When I gave you those pearls I wanted Grandfather to know I knew something was wrong about Rebecca's death, something he wanted kept a secret. They provided me with some leverage, to gain what I wanted." He shoved his hands back into his pockets. "I admit it was pretty low of me. But Grandfather angers and frustrates me, though I care about him, probably more than he cares about me. Anyway, my scheme didn't work. And your coming home didn't change his mind either. He still favors Rozlind—and Rafe. The only chance we have now is with Great-aunt Nora. I don't think she'll leave her share of Kea Lani to either of them."

Eden wanted to put a quick end to anything he had in mind that included her.

"My plans are all made, Zachary. I'm joining my father in medical missions. I don't think Nora will appreciate any efforts you make to ingratiate yourself to her. In trying, you may alienate yourself even further."

She turned and walked from the room, leaving her cousin staring up at the painting of Amabel.

TWENTY-EIGHT

Eden made up her mind to act while she had the opportunity. She had asked the stableboy to ready a buggy and be waiting for her by early morning. Now she crept quietly down the stairs and slipped out the front door. She ran across the yard and, lifting her skirt, climbed up into the seat with the boy, who took up the reins. In a few minutes the gentle mare was trotting down the long palm-lined drive. Eden was on her way to Honolulu, to arrive while it was still early enough to hire a private boat to take her around Waikiki and Diamond Head toward Koko Head Crater.

Clouds were accumulating over the Pacific, reminding her of an invading army, and the wind was warm and damp with the feel of oncoming rain. Could she pay one of the fishermen to take her down the coast while the water was still smooth?

Arriving at the wharf, the stableboy helped her down, then reached for her bag. She thanked him and asked him to return the buggy to Kea Lani mansion. She walked along the wooden wharf to where boats, large and small, were anchored. The wind smelled heavily of the sea and fish. Shells were piled here and there along the beach where fishing nets were spread.

Eden stood on the wharf looking at the *Kilauea*, an older boat that was now being used for ferrying. There was a sign over the cabin that read *TICKETS*. Eden walked toward it. The boat appeared to be a one-man-operated business, perhaps coordinated with the larger inter-island ferry that ran only once a day.

Business hours were usually lax here, and the Hawaiians did what suited their fancy. If the day was pleasant and business good, the open-air fruit and vegetable shops could remain open until after midnight. During the stormy season, it was common to shut down at three o'clock, leaving the boardwalk empty and the pearl-and-coral shop boarded up. It struck her that once arriving at Koko Head, she may not be able to get a boat to return to Honolulu by evening. She might need to walk back up the coast on the Wai'alae Road or arrange to spend the night.

Eden looked about and saw fishermen attending their boats and canoes, but these Hawaiians with their bronzed bodies didn't appear to notice her standing with her bag at her feet. Her brave determination was slowly evaporating in the heat of the morning sun. When she left she had thought it better to go to Amabel's house alone—without Zachary—to try to remember more of that night when she'd hidden with him. Now she wondered.

Don't think that way, she told herself. *I'm sure it will work out. I can get someone to take me, and the dark mystery will soon clear up.*

She stopped beside the *Kilauea* and descended the narrow ramp, then boarded.

"Hello? Is anyone here?"

The boat creaked and moaned. Her eyes fell on a scribbled note. *Closed till Tuesday.* Her heart sank.

"You looking to go somewhere, miss?"

She turned at the unexpected voice coming from behind her. An old Hawaiian man stood in a flowered shirt worn over white pants cut off above the knees. Though strongly built through the chest and shoulders, he was wide about the middle. His friendly face was browned by the sun like dried sea kelp, and his deep-set black eyes gazed humorously from under a woven palm-fiber hat.

"I need to voyage to Maunalua Bay by Koko Head Crater," she explained, gesturing toward the ocean. Hawaiians had little use for terms like north, south, east, or west. She had grown up using Hawaiian terms of reference, which usually were place names, like "Diamond Head Crater," or hand directional signals, meaning "toward the mountains" or "toward the sea."

"My boat is tied up. Storm is coming."

"Then perhaps I could hire one of the sailors to take me. I'll make it worth their effort."

He gestured. "Those are not sailors. They are fishers."

"But I need to sail twelve miles down the coastline to a mansion on

Koko Head owned by the Derrington family."

His alert eyes responded with recognition. "Tamarind House?"

"I didn't know that it had a name. You know of it?"

"You're a Derrington too, aren't you?" He grinned. "Yes, I know Rafe Easton—and Keno too. Keno is a nephew."

Her mood brightened. "You're related to Noelani?"

"I'm a brother-in-law."

"I'll pay you well to take me there."

"Derringtons always do. They own everything 'round here—'cept the ferry. It's mine. You wanna go to Tamarind House? You come along." He gestured with his head. "I'll get you there in a little more than an hour. Need to hurry. See those?"

Eden followed his hand toward the distant silver-gray clouds.

"Strange weather this year. You pick bad time to visit."

"Yes . . . it's important to me, though. I was born and raised here and know what storms can do."

"I remember you," he said with a smile. "You change. Hair used to be down to here—" He put his hand at his hip. "And no shoes."

Eden laughed. "Why, you must be Kelolo. You used to help Ambrose at the pearl beds. And you attended the mission church sometimes."

He nodded. "And Rafe and Keno and Primo used to dive. Primo never make friends again with Rafe after that black pearl. Keno laughs at Primo, who still has promised that Kane will judge Rafe."

Eden didn't smile. "But Kane is not God."

Kelolo lifted a finger sagely. "But Rafe will tear down the church, so he is no friend of God; nor is he friend of Kane."

She knew there would be trouble over the church. Rafe couldn't tear it down! "The true God is the living God. And Kane is not living. So Kane cannot punish Rafe," she repeated calmly. "Maybe if more Hawaiians attended the old missionary church, Rafe wouldn't tear it down."

"They won't go because the kahunas say they do not like where it is. They believe in God, but also they honor Kane."

Eden tried to be patient and nodded that she understood their objection. "They know the Bible says we must love the Lord God with all our heart and soul and mind. They cannot serve the living God and the old religious ideas."

Kelolo smiled. "I understand, Miss Eden. They understand too. But many will hold to Kane too." He pointed toward the clouds. "We must hurry." He smiled again and, reaching over, picked up her overnight bag. "This way."

Kelolo launched the boat, raising and adjusting the sail as they began to leave the wharf. They sailed through swells and valleys of the dark Pacific, giving Eden a strong sense of unsteadiness. She clung to the side as the water parted beneath the rolling and pitching hull. Low, dark clouds scudded across the sky, and the sea breeze left her face damp.

She watched the green foliated hills on her left, which rose steeply out of the Pacific. The water was less rough as they sailed past Honolulu Harbor with the long Koolau Mountain Range in the background, which isolated them from windward Oahu. As they sailed past Waikiki Beach, Eden pointed out Diamond Head Crater towering above the coastline.

"The crater is beautiful from the ocean," Eden stated. "From here, I can get a view of the taller edge of the rim of the extinct volcano."

"It may be extinct now," Kelolo said gravely, "but the ancient Hawaiians called it *Lae Ahi*—means 'Cape of Fire.'"

When they sailed past Diamond Head into Maunalua Bay, she pointed. "That's Koko Head Crater in front of us?"

"Yes, Miss Eden. Tamarind Plantation is at end of bay, between Koko Head and Kuapa Pond. I will bring you on nice beach in one half hour."

Eden could see mounds of mist-shrouded hills covered with tropical growth and palm trees.

"It's on other side of bay." He pointed. "On clear day you can see top of Tamarind. It was first big house Makua Derrington build for his wife, Miss Amabel, but she didn't stay. Said there was evil spirits. So he moved to Kalihi and built Kea Lani House instead, on that good red volcanic soil. Good soil for sugar cane. The best. This area . . ." He shrugged.

Eden strained to see Amabel's mansion and caught a brief glimpse of its sloping red-tile roof.

"Was her fear of the kahunas the reason she wouldn't stay there?"

He looked at her thoughtfully, as though surprised she didn't understand. "She fell at Tamarind and hurt herself. They say she was just starting to plant hundreds of acres of cane. Some missionaries were there too. They built a bungalow church near the now-abandoned cemetery, but after she fell, Miss Amabel was afraid the kahunas had cursed her, Tamarind, and the bungalow church. The kahunas told her Kane did not want the Christian God there."

Eden clung to the side of the boat. To blame a simple accident on the magic spell of the kahunas seemed rather immature of her great-grandmother. Amabel couldn't have been much of a testimony to the omnipotent God if she had trembled before the kahunas and run away to Kea Lani. The Hawaiian priests must have thought their Kane was stronger.

Eden shaded her eyes to catch the last glimpse of Tamarind before the palm trees and vines overshadowed it on the hill.

When Kelolo brought the boat to the landing near Kuapa Pond at Maunalua, Eden thanked him for his help and paid him generously. The wind was rising and the palm fronds shifted and fluttered.

Kelolo looked anxious to be off as he scanned the Pacific horizon, straightening his hat. "Pardon, miss, but anyone know you come here?"

She preferred to ignore his question and asked instead about the route.

He pointed. "In Koko Head direction, you will find the small road. Stay on it until you come to the fork, turn left for graveyard and farther up about a quarter mile you will see Tamarind. You think Miss Nora is expecting you?" he asked doubtfully.

"No, I don't see how she could. She's not there."

"Not there?" he frowned. "But—"

"But I suspect there are servants keeping the house open and ready in case someone decides to come."

"There used to be a haole housekeeper there year-round. Her name was Mrs. Croft. Don't think she's there now. Sure you want to try it now?"

She smiled at his concern. "I'll manage, Kelolo, thank you. God speed you back safely."

"You want me to come back for you tomorrow? Or you can go by land too, on the road called Wai'alae."

She smiled, holding on to her hat now as the wind tugged more persistently. "I'll look for you. If you're not here, I'll remember the road."

His sharp eyes scrutinized her again. He scratched his gray locks. "I remember Miss Rebecca. You don't look like her, though. She did not have eyes like emeralds."

Eden's heart quickened. "You knew Rebecca Derrington? Did you know my father, Jerome?"

Kelolo did not answer her question. "Sea will get angry! Got to be going. Aloha."

Eden stood holding her hat, watching as the boat left the shoreline and struggled across the swells. Gripped by solitude, she experienced a momentary sense of anxiety, but it quickly faded. She turned away from the ocean and started across the sand, where rare seashells could be found, then walked toward the hill upon which she found a vine-tangled path and thickly growing palms.

Beyond the hill the path was rough in places. She thought of her great-grandmother Amabel. Sadness filled her heart as she realized that Christians often viewed tragedy that is beyond their control as not from the sovereign hand of God but from the forces of darkness.

"There's so much heartache and difficulty in this family. I know I can't solve their problems, but I also know that no problem is big to God."

As she walked, the weather worsened. She stopped on the path to open her overnight bag and pull out a scarf, tying it about her whipping hair. The wind was mild and humid and she did not need a coat.

She climbed the path until she came to thick ferns in rich, damp earth where orchids grew close to rocks in the calm shade. When she came to the fork in the path, she went toward the cemetery as Kelolo had told her. She followed this path for about fifteen minutes. The wind among the trees and rocks, the distant roar of waves crashing to shore, and the smells of ocean, flowers, and decaying bark saturated her senses.

Eventually the way grew dim with shadows as the heavy foliage and the trees shut out the cloudy sky. She had brought good walking shoes and kept a good pace, hoping the weather would hold so she could visit the cemetery. Had Zachary been right about her mother's burial here?

The shadows lengthened. The distance turned out to be farther than she had expected. The path wound its way to an open area where the ferns and vines disappeared. A blast of wind struck her as she sought for a windbreak by a cluster of palm trees. Eden turned back to catch a view of the ocean and the white sandy beach far below. The now gray and choppy Pacific waves pounded and splashed their spray upward and over the beaches.

Eden caught her breath at the splendid sight. Silver-gray clouds, in places nearly black, covered the horizon, and the sea fomented with energy, giving the impression that at any moment it would rise into a gigantic tidal wave and sweep over Hawaii. Above her head the gulls circled, catching the updraft as they were borne along effortlessly. Their mournful cry rode the wind, echoing back to the cliffs.

She turned away from the sea. Ahead lay the Derrington cemetery. She could see it now—unkempt, small, and very still. *Too still*, she thought as the storm seethed. She walked toward the little graveyard, the wind seeming to push her forward. The first drop of rain wet her face.

Mother . . .

At the border of the cemetery the wild green ferns, lush and almost smothering, grew tall like a dark fence. She walked through a small wrought-iron gate connected to a low wall made of lava rock.

Her eyes cast about her, seeing perhaps a dozen markers, all with crosses. No doubt most were missionaries and a few Hawaiian Christians who had lived here in the day of her great-grandmother.

Her steps quickened across the dirt walkway. She began the search, slowly at first, then more rapidly, as if she were driven to hurry.

" 'Hosea Derrington,' " she read aloud. " '1756–1820. Jesus is my Rock. All souls who read this dwell in the land of the dying. I have been summoned to the land of the living.' "

What was that intruding sound? The wind?

She turned and looked about her but couldn't see anything at first except darkened vines. Then, perhaps a hundred feet away, on the other side of the cemetery near the back wall, there was a figure in a knee-length dark raincoat and hood. She couldn't see who it was and tensed. *Probably just the caretaker for Tamarind,* she thought.

She was wrong. He put back his hood and she could see that it was Zachary who now walked toward her, unsmiling and looking as though he'd been without proper sleep.

"So you came," he called.

Eden's heart was still thudding. "How did you arrive before I did?"

"I decided to come late last night after everyone went to bed—just to make certain you'd be all right." He came up to her, his face somber. "I arrived earlier this morning. A Chinese brought me on the Wai'alae Road, but he's gone back. I thought we could take a sailboat back, but a storm is blowing in."

Eden let out a sigh of relief. "I wasn't expecting to see anyone here. You frightened me."

He pulled his hood forward. "I'm sorry I frightened you. It's about to pour. We'd better hurry."

"Have you been to the house yet? I wonder if Mrs. Croft is there."

"Mrs. Croft?"

"The housekeeper."

"I haven't gone there yet. Let's hope she is. If the place is completely shut up, we may not have any supper. Come along, my dear Eden, I've something to prove to you—that I've told you the truth when the rest of them didn't—including dear stepbrother Rafe. Not that it matters any-more about him. He's going to marry Rozlind." He smiled suddenly, as though the matter were settled. "You can't always trust *them*, but you can trust me," he said.

"Who is the caretaker?" she asked uneasily, glancing about at the wild, overgrown tangle of vines and ferns.

His thin smile flickered with irony. He gestured to the rustling over-growth. "It doesn't seem anyone keeps it, does it?"

"It does look forgotten. . . ."

"As is the house, this land. Come," he said again, "let's find Rebecca."

She reached to hold down the end of her fluttering silk scarf. "Not *find her*. My mother isn't lost. If it's so, that her marker is here, it can only hold her remains. She is safely in the presence of Christ. 'To be absent from the body and to be present with the Lord,' " she quoted from the New Testament letter to the Corinthians. "I don't believe that the dead loiter in the grave. They depart this world to spend eternity either with Christ . . . or without."

He smiled, but without joy. "Then you will feel comfortable here. When I was a boy I came here with Rafe. He showed me all the old mark-ers. They belong to the early generation of missionaries."

She looked at him, alert. "Rafe came here? He saw my mother's marker?"

"I'm sure he saw it. But like the rest of them he pretends that it isn't here. He's been prowling about for the last few years digging up old facts about Rebecca and Jerome. How much he knows, I can't say, but he must know about this marker."

And Rafe hadn't told her. . . . Why?

"The missionaries built a little church here too, like the one out on Rafe's property. But here there was also a school."

She was surprised but realized she shouldn't be. There was so much she didn't know. "Is the school still here?"

"What's left of it is over near the church. Lightning struck it. The wooden part has been burned away. Only lava rock foundations are left."

Eden felt the rain occasionally hitting her face as they walked. The wind whirled about, playing among the old markers.

Zachary stopped and gestured ahead. Eden looked and saw a stone marker and her stomach tightened. She half hoped that he was wrong, that the name would not be Rebecca Stanhope Derrington but that of some other woman he'd somehow mistaken for her mother's name when he was a boy.

Eden walked forward until she came to the headstone. Her heart quickened. Her mother's name was clearly inscribed with the dates of her birth and her death. She walked forward and stooped beside it, touching the rough stone with both hands and staring at its face.

Zachary had told her the truth. And the family, perhaps even Rafe as well, had kept it from her. But why? A hundred questions pounded at her mind.

The greatly anticipated moment of being here at last proved little as she examined the marker. It was only another headstone with a simple inscription. So simple, in fact, that it appeared to convey indifference. She frowned.

"What is it?" Zachary asked, noticing.

"I can't help wondering why my father didn't order words of endearment engraved on the stone." She ran her fingers across her mother's name. "There's nothing here but the bare essentials of Rebecca's birth and death."

"I can answer that. It wasn't Uncle Jerome who ordered the marker. He wasn't even here then; he had already left Hawaii. It was Grandfather who had the marker made."

Her father hadn't even troubled to have a headstone placed on her grave?

"That should tell you something of the depth of his feelings for Rebecca," Zachary said with an underlying suggestion in his voice that turned her heart cold.

Eden sat staring at the few words, feeling desolate.

"Let's go," he said dully. "I've proved my point. It's raining and we've almost a half hour walk. If Mrs. Croft isn't there, I'll need to get a fire going for the night."

She stood and faced him. "You've got to help me remember that night. You must try."

He closed his eyes and shook his head. "It's no use."

As they began to walk toward the house, Eden spoke of her own recollections. "I remember sitting in a carriage on a sunny day outside a big house . . . Amabel's? It was a sunny day, but clouds were moving in. I remember my mother running away . . . and someone chasing after her. I think I climbed down from the carriage to run after her, but someone stopped me. I was taken into the house, but I don't remember anything else except that night when the hurricane blew in. Nora said I came to her room afraid of the lightning. She read to me, and I fell asleep. She says that she left the room for a while, and when she came back I was gone. They searched for me but couldn't find me."

Zachary scowled. He shook his head and began walking more quickly.

"Try," she pleaded, following after him. "It must have taken place here at Amabel's house. We were afraid and hid. Do you remember a room upstairs surrounded with windows?"

"I don't remember that. You must have dreamed it."

"It did happen," she insisted.

He walked briskly up the dirt road beside the cliff's edge. Below, the waves pounded the beach. Eden rushed to keep pace.

"We hid under a daybed. Recently, I've remembered someone reaching under the dust ruffle to pull me out—"

"No. Absolutely not, Eden. If anything so dramatic happened, I'd remember. Good grief, I must have been all of fourteen and Rafe was twelve. He was here too. He'd remember that."

"Maybe he does," she said thoughtfully, troubled.

Zachary shot her a glance. "What do you mean by that?"

"I'm not sure. Except sometimes I think he remembers more than he'll admit. It's as if he's trying to hide something . . . or protect someone."

"Rafe?" he asked surprised. "If he is, I've no idea who it would be. He has no allegiance to Uncle Jerome, or any of the Derringtons for that matter. The only family he's ever cared about is you, Ambrose, and Noelani. And Ambrose and Noelani weren't there that night."

She looked at him. "Then you do remember something. You remember they weren't there."

His mouth thinned and he looked off toward the pounding Pacific. "Yes, a few things, but not hiding under a bed or a hand creeping under a dust ruffle. It sounds positively frightening."

"It was," Eden said, shivering, looking up the hill toward Tamarind House. "But to a child who's bewildered and frightened, it would be, even if that hand belonged to a friend."

"A friend? Now, why do you say that?" he challenged, an irritated gleam in his eyes. "I thought you said I was protecting you from something dark and sinister."

Eden sighed. "It doesn't make sense, does it?" she agreed. But there were times recently when she'd thought—but no, that couldn't be.

"No, it doesn't make sense," Zachary retorted, sounding somewhat mollified. "I'd rather not talk about this, if you want to know the truth. I came because I thought you might need me. And it looks as if I was right. We're going to be stuck here for the night. I wanted to prove my point about Rebecca's grave being here so you'd know I didn't lie to you. But I'd rather forget everything else you're trying to stir up. Let's just get to the house where it's dry. Hopefully there'll be some coffee in the cupboard and we can get a fire going."

He was right. While Rafe and the family all tried to hide the past,

Zachary alone had pointed out conflicting details about her mother's death and her father's quick disappearance from Hawaii. She wouldn't have known about her grandfather's bizarre reaction to the black pearls or about her mother's place of burial if it weren't for Zachary.

"You make the coffee, then," she agreed congenially. "I'm going to see if I can find that room I remember. Now that I know my mother's grave is here, this must be the house where it all took place, where I fell down the stairs."

"Look, Eden, are you sure you want to do this? I mean, maybe it's not a wise idea to go there."

"We've come this far. I'm not turning back now. If someone harmed my mother, I want to know." She looped her arm through his, trying to encourage him. "We'll help each other remember. I want to be free. Don't you?"

"I don't know," he murmured. "What if we remember something we want with all our hearts to forget?"

She thought about that, aware for the first time that Zachary may be choosing not to remember what happened out of pain rather than fear.

"Only when we face the truth and deal with it honestly before God can we truly forgive and forget. Then we can, with His help, put it aside forever."

"Can we?" he asked quietly, as if speaking to himself. "I wonder. I don't know. What if it's too terrible to forget . . . or for God to forgive." He looked at her, his gaze tormented. "Then what?"

For a moment she couldn't answer him as she saw the anxiety in his face. What did he know? Was she wrong to try to force the past from him? Was there any sin too dark for God to forgive through Christ? The worst thing she could think of was that her mother had been murdered and the family was trying to protect her father, or even Grandfather or Great-aunt Nora. But even Moses had murdered an Egyptian and buried him in the sand, and God had forgiven him. David had murdered Uriah by sending him to the front of the battle to be killed, and God had forgiven him.

"Through the work of Christ on the cross, all sin can be forgiven," she said to her cousin. Then, remembering the familiar words of the prophet Isaiah, she quoted, " 'Come now, and let us reason together, saith the *Lord*: though your sins be as scarlet, they shall be as white as snow; though they be red like crimson, they shall be as wool.' "

Zachary lapsed into silence. They trudged ahead with the wind resisting them, the rain becoming heavier.

"In this weather, we've no choice but to go through with it now," he said after several minutes of hearing little else but the wind in the palm trees and the roar of the sea. "When we're ready to get back to Honolulu, we'll have to hike to the main road, if the path around Kuapa Pond is not impassable."

The bushes, wild flowers, and shrubs began to hem them in, and the way grew dim with thick palm branches. Her skirt caught on vines and she stopped to pull it free, then hurried on after him.

Zachary surged ahead as if driven by nervous energy. Sometimes Eden had to run to keep up, her heart beating in her ears, the rain falling heavily, drenching her.

As she rounded the bend in the road, Tamarind House emerged fully into view, built on a terraced hillside with a wall of leafy tropical trees, ferns, and vines. It all seemed smothering to Eden, with the growth appearing to threaten the mansion, choking out the sunlight. Still, it was a magnificent structure. Though she couldn't make it all out in the descending darkness, she could see that it loomed wide and tall, perhaps three stories high.

Coconut and banana trees grew thickly along the road up toward the front entry. Through the rain and late-afternoon shadows she could make out the dark windows. No welcoming light glowed upstairs or down. Evidently the servants had not yet come to prepare for Great-aunt Nora's arrival in two weeks. Tamarind House looked deserted.

She sensed the same tension in Zachary that she felt. He did remember, and he wasn't looking forward to spending the night here in a rainstorm.

They reached the front steps, and Eden looked at the great solid door carved from native Hawaiian wood and stained black. She knew what she was seeking, and it was here—the bronze tiki-head door knocker with the hideous face that had frightened her as a child.

TWENTY-NINE

Zachary grabbed ahold of the tiki knocker, hammering loudly on the door of the house. When no one came to answer, he reached up to a ledge above the doorframe, where he knew a key was hidden. A few minutes later they stood inside a darkened hallway with the wind and rain blowing in.

"Doesn't look like anyone in the family's been here in years," he said gloomily. "I think we've made a dreadful mistake coming, Eden. I don't like this at all."

"Let's get the oil lamps lit," Eden insisted, taking charge and moving ahead of him as he lingered by the door. "A little light does wonders. And a fire in the hearth will cheer things up as well. Here—you light this lamp, and I'll light the others."

"It's musty in here. Nora can't possibly realize how things have deteriorated," he said. "It will take a month or more to ready this house if she really intends to move in."

"She must not have known Mrs. Croft was away. I wonder what happened to her," Eden mused as the lamplight began to glow and lighten the room.

"Probably died. I remember she was rather old even back then. Strange, though, that Nora didn't seem to know that last night when she mentioned coming here."

"Did you see Nora this morning before you left?"

"No," he said. "Did you?"

"No. She must have been asleep."

"Probably. I think this room is the parlor. . . . I'll go in and get a fire started. Let's hope there's some wood in the bin."

"I'm going to look around upstairs," Eden called. "Come up when you're ready," she said, taking one of the lamps. She walked toward a wide stairway with a banister of teakwood filigree. Her gaze followed the steps up into the darkness. She could just make out the third-floor landing. A sickening sensation crawled over her damp skin as she sensed that this was the stairway she had fallen down as a child. As if in a dream, Eden began to climb.

She would need more than her own feeble strength to wisely meet the emotional onslaught of the day, and as she climbed, she prayed. Concentrating on the presence of the Lord was comforting, and it bolstered her confidence as she ascended into the darkness of the past.

She stood on the landing of the second floor, her hand clutching the newel post, listening to creaks and groans as the wind and rain played havoc outside. She heard Zachary moving about in the parlor, presumably making a fire. She was still standing there minutes later, trying to find the courage to climb upward.

Finally, she slowly ascended to the third-floor hallway, where a table with a lamp stood against the wall. She fumbled, lighting the wick with shaking fingers, then walked on. She came upon another flight of steps, very narrow and steep, leading toward the roof. She was sure—though she couldn't say why she felt so—that she had been here before.

That night, that dreadful night of the hurricane. . . .

Unexpectedly alarmed, Eden drew back as mysterious emotions brewed in her mind. *Hide, hide!* The word repeated in her memory. At the same time, reason told her that she had little to fear.

Eden turned at the tread of footsteps. Zachary walked down the hallway toward her, unsmiling. An ashen look fell across his face, and Eden was convinced he was remembering.

She turned away from him and looked up the narrow stairway, taking in the soaring walls and roof, until her eyes rested high above. She remembered. . . . Absently, she touched the scar on her temple.

"The Round Room was Great-aunt Nora's art room. She liked it up here. Do you remember?" he asked, watching her.

"I should ask you that."

"Yes, I remember. Rebecca never came back after I saw her run away from you into the trees. Jerome went after her. You and I were afraid of the storm later that night. I brought you up to the Round Room, where we hid."

"Yes, I remember. You came into Nora's bedroom and said we must hide."

"Come, Eden, I'll take you up there." He looked at her quizzically, as if wondering whether or not she would go with him.

She wasn't afraid anymore. She held out her hand to him and managed a slight smile. "Let's light our lamps and chase away the darkness once and for all, shall we?"

Zachary appeared moved by her trust and took her hand tightly. "It's going to be all right, isn't it?"

"Yes, I think so."

They started up the stairs.

The Round Room waited, encircled with glass reaching to the ceiling. Eden sucked in her breath. *This is the room!*

Zachary's hand grew sweaty as he drew her inside.

"This is it," he whispered. "It's like facing my fears all over again. Even the rain and lightning are the same."

Eden saw artist easels, paint, turpentine—paintings—all of Koko Head Crater.

"They belong to Nora," he said. "The Round Room offers an extensive view of the island. During the day you can see the Koolau Mountain Range. The sun shines over Maunalua Bay. You can see everything from up here. Over there in that direction is the old cemetery, and over there the church."

Eden's heart throbbed in her throat as she looked out into the stormy darkness, seeing little except the reflections from their lamps . . . and from the glass, a broken expression upon Zachary's face.

"Oh, Eden, I'm sorry, I'm sorry. God knows I'm sorry!"

"Zachary," she whispered painfully. "What is it?"

"Back then, in my childish mind, I told myself I was keeping you safe. They were going to send you away after Aunt Rebecca died. I didn't want them to take you away. So I tried to hide you, the way a boy would try to hide a puppy that wasn't supposed to be in his room. I never thought it would end so tragically with you falling the way you did. I'm tormented if ever I think about it. Tormented by guilt. For years I managed to repress it, not think about it."

She stared at him, her heart pounding and aching.

He pointed across the Round Room to the daybed.

"We hid under there."

Yes, she recognized it.

"Grandfather and Nora don't think I remember. Neither does Rafe.

Actually, I didn't think about it until a few years ago. It made me ill for a time because at first I thought you had died."

He looked about the Round Room.

"Look! Lightning—just like that night."

Eden shielded her eyes from the blinding flash, then looked into the window glass and saw his reflection mirrored crisply, staring back at her. She had been afraid of a ghost!

"You were afraid of it. And the loud thunder. We thought the wind would break in the windows!"

Eden turned full circle about the center, remembering. He had been the ghost, she realized now, though Zachary had not known it. In her mind she saw the hurricane, heard the glass shaking as though it would crash all around them.

The past awakened and moved forward through the mist of childhood memory to the reality of the moment. She stood, remembering how they had crawled under the daybed, how the door opened and someone came in. She could see the candle in her memory flickering, casting serpentine shadows on the polished floor. *"Is that you, Mommy?"* she had asked.

A hand had thrust beneath the dust ruffle, reaching for her, attempting to help her out.

"Eden, come out from under there!" she remembered Rafe saying. *"You're in for big trouble this time, Zach. . . ."*

She turned now and looked at him. "And you scooted from beneath the bed."

"Yes."

"I remember Rafe's fingers releasing me quickly. There was a scuffle. Something crashed. The candle flame was snuffed. The room went into darkness."

"Yes," Zachary said painfully. "We were wrestling." He sank onto the daybed, dropping his head into his hands.

"I remember I crawled out past someone who lay crumpled on the floor," she said quickly. "Then I ran."

"Yes," he whispered. "I was so scared because I hit him with something. . . . I think one of Nora's vases."

"I ran past a taller shadow that reached out for me."

"That was me," he said, shaking his head again as though hating to think about it.

"I remembered you barely caught hold of my hair . . . but I got away. I ran out and down the hall. There were lights above me from the wall sconces. You ran after me."

"I didn't want you to tell my father that I'd clobbered Rafe."

"I could hear voices below the stairs."

"It must have been Nora and Celestine. They were looking for us but hadn't gotten up to the Round Room yet. Rafe had known where to find us. He came up because he found out you were with me. Then, when I was chasing you, Rafe had gotten up and come after me. He caught me again in the hall near the stairs. We had a big fight. He was strong because he used to swim a lot, and he almost got the best of me that time. I tried to get away, and . . . I bumped into you as you stood by the top of the stairs. . . ." He dropped his head, his voice breaking.

Eden's hands clasped tightly. "Yes, I think I remember. I backed away, losing my balance, and fell—"

"As a boy, I was afraid of getting into trouble with Father and Grandfather. I knew it was my fault—but they didn't want to talk to me about it, as if they thought I didn't realize what I'd done. And they sent you away, but I didn't know you were at Ambrose's place, because Grandfather and Nora didn't want me to know. They wanted to keep me away from you. For a while I thought you were dead and I knew I was to blame. . . ."

"But later on you found out I was alive," Eden said.

"Yes, but when we got older I was still burdened, afraid you'd find out. And I had a crush on you at the time, and I blamed myself every time I saw that scar. I thought you would think I pushed you, that you would hate me if you ever found out," he said through a husky voice. "Especially after your mother's death."

"If you thought I was dead, and that you were to blame for my fall, it's no wonder you became ill. Guilt is a terribly heavy burden to live with."

"Afterward I didn't want to remember. I kept pushing it from my mind. I denied that it ever happened. It was too painful to think about. I allowed myself to get sick. And they kept me in seclusion. I didn't even see Rafe. I remember that later, when I got well, he never said anything to me about it."

"He must have been trying to shield you. He thought you were—" She stopped.

"Yes, mentally ill. I don't think I am. But you don't know what living with this is like. . . . It just won't go away. There is no way for the guilt to go away! It doesn't matter what I do, it just keeps eating at me."

He looked at her, his eyes wet with tears. "Can you really forgive me for what I did that night?"

Her heart was moved. "Yes, Zachary, of course I can. Christ has forgiven me, and I'm told to forgive others. In the Old Testament, Joseph forgave his brothers even when they had malice toward him. He could leave all things with God because he knew God meant all things for good to those who love Him. You had no real malice toward me. I remember I was so confused because I couldn't find my mother and I was afraid of the storm, so I hid with you in the Round Room. And Rafe's hand—I thought it might have been the person who . . ."

His eyes grew troubled. "Yes, there's still that ugly matter, isn't there? And I vow I've nothing to do with that. Someone harmed her. And it wasn't me. Rafe and I were only boys."

She looked up at the rain thundering against the windowpanes. "Yes, God knows what really happened. I'm convinced I'm going to learn the truth about my mother too."

"Then you really mean it? This matter between us is settled? You don't know how grateful I feel." He took hold of her hand and squeezed it. "I've asked you to forgive me and you have. I'm in your debt."

"No, Zachary," she said gently. "When it comes to forgiveness between people, there can be no indebtedness. If I think you owe me something, then I haven't truly forgiven. The only one we are truly indebted to is Christ, who gave himself for us on the cross. Suppose that you really had pushed me out of anger, and that I had died as a result of the fall. You would have even more reason to be imprisoned with guilt for the rest of your life. As you now realize, people have no ability to eliminate guilt. That's the reason we desperately need to trust Jesus Christ, the only Savior of all men. If God is satisfied with the price Jesus paid for our sin, who am I to dare ask for more? You can ask Christ to forgive you of every sin and He promises to remove the burden of your guilt. I forgive you now, and we can be friends. You can let go of the past."

Zachary looked at her soberly. "You really mean all that," he said with awe.

She smiled. "Yes."

"I've learned a great deal from you that I won't forget. I remember going to church with Grandfather when I was a boy, and somehow I remember hearing all that, but it never took hold of my mind and heart. Eden,"—his eyes searched hers earnestly—"I want that forgiveness."

"Oh, Zachary, this is wonderful! This is what I hoped you would say. Right now, in this very same room where our first lies, fears, and selfishness began years ago, we can pray together. We can tell Jesus we turn to Him as our only hope of redemption and surrender our lives to Him."

"Yes, yes, I want that. . . ."

Eden quoted John 3:16 and led her cousin in a prayer of repentance and trust. Afterward, as the wind howled and the rain hammered on the windows, they looked at each other for a long moment and she sensed that the past was indeed fading away. He smiled, reached for her timidly, and then as Eden smiled and put her arms around him as a family member, he hugged her, laughed, and cried. There was only friendship in their touch. Eden sensed a new relationship being born, one that would bring them together as true cousins for the first time. She laughed through her tears and tugged at his arm. "Come," she said, pulling him up from the daybed, and they went down the stairs together.

Eden heard the wind and rain beating on the house.

" 'And the floods came, and the wind blew, and beat upon that house; and it fell not: for it was founded upon a rock,' " she murmured the words of Christ.

She looked at her lamp glowing brightly. All was not darkness. Even here at Amabel's house, there had once been a missionary church and a school. Light and hope and truth had once bloomed here. Songs of worship had once echoed in both Hawaiian and English in the church.

Light casts out darkness. And truth dispels lies and misunderstandings, she thought. *I'm glad my heavenly Father is Light and Truth. I've no reason to run away like Amabel, my mother, or Lana. I can face tomorrow.*

She looked at her cousin and saw a new joy in his eyes. *And now, so can Zachary.*

THIRTY

By dawn Eden was already up and dressed and looking out the window, hoping the storm would not impede their return to Honolulu. With relief, as the morning lightened, she saw that the storm had blown over. She opened a window with a clear view of majestic Koko Crater and the beach below, two miles northwest of Koko Head. The view was breathtaking in the early morning with white sand edging the rippling blue-green Maunalua Bay. The breeze was balmy even in February, and she whiffed the variant fragrances of warm, damp earth, sea, and flowers.

She thought she saw Zachary walking up from the beach toward the garden stairs that led up to the house, but as the form came nearer, she realized from the build and stride that it was Rafe.

How did he know I was here? Noelani must have worried after she told her about Amabel's house and must have then gone to Rafe about it. Eden ignored the sense of satisfaction she felt that Rafe had dropped everything at the new plantation to come looking for her. It didn't mean anything, she thought. He had hidden the truth from her, just like her grandfather and great-aunt. He, too, *must* have known about her mother's burial plot, yet kept it from her.

She left the room and rushed downstairs. The house was nearly dark, the drapes drawn. Zachary would still be asleep. That gave her time to talk to Rafe alone.

She went down the garden steps in the direction of the sandy shore, encountering the early-morning breeze.

At the edge of the hill Rafe was starting up the steps. When he saw her coming, he waited.

Eden hurried down, heart slamming, the wind fluttering her skirt hem about her ankles. She nearly reached the bottom before confronting Rafe.

The wet sand sank beneath her feet. The sun was a warm gold as the palm trees swayed and the wavelets rippled along the shore.

Rafe's energetic gaze briefly swept over her as if to convince himself she was in one piece. "I see you're all right," he said with a perturbed voice. "What did you mean by dashing off the way you did?"

Challenged to come forth with an answer, she now withdrew behind the safety of a dignified demeanor.

"I didn't dash off. My plans were well laid, and I had reasons to come and find the truth for myself. Zachary is here."

He looked up toward the mansion. "I suppose he's filled your mind with doubts and suspicions?"

"No, with the truth," she quipped. "That's more than I've learned from the rest of the family."

"The truth," he repeated in a contradictory tone. "And I suppose you think you've found it?"

"I've found out plenty; the most painful was discovering that everyone has lied to me."

Rafe flashed a look at her that made her cringe inwardly.

"Everyone. You're including me in that sweeping condemnation, I suppose?"

A catch caught in her throat, and she nearly felt bowled over by the emotional onslaught of his confrontation. No, she wanted to quickly assure him, yet how could she deny it? She could see that he was annoyed by more than her having come here alone. Was he upset because she hadn't trusted him?

The disappointment of having seen the child aboard the *Manoa* continued to stand between them like a fiery bulwark, though neither of them seemed willing to bring it up. Her own pride, and fear of what he might tell her if she did ask, kept her mute. Was she behaving like Zachary had all these years, repressing the truth because she feared to deal with it? The quiet resentment continued. There was also her grandfather's offer to arrange a marriage between Rafe and Rozlind, and Rafe's apparent willingness to cooperate and tear down the mission church.

Yet despite all of this, Rafe had come.

He went on in his calm, even voice that contradicted the blaze in his eyes. "Noelani told me you'd come here. I went to Kea Lani, but you'd already left. Why didn't you come to me? Why didn't you tell me your plans?"

"So you could stop me? Deny the reasons for my suspicions? So you could convince me my concerns were wrong?"

Rafe said in a very hard, dry voice, "Thank you, Eden, for believing my efforts were motivated to mislead you, to gratify my own selfish purposes."

She didn't believe that, not completely, and his accusation hurt.

"What do you know about my mother's death?" she asked.

She sensed that he understood far more than he'd ever been willing to tell her, but he didn't show the slightest response to her question.

"What do you think I'm keeping from you? A murder?"

His bluntness set her back a moment. She wasn't going to let him get by with disarming her so easily. There were red lava rocks under a cluster of palms farther down the beach, and he walked toward them. Eden followed, and when he sat down, scooping up some loose rocks as though giving them his full attention, she stopped, keeping her distance.

It was low tide and she stared out at the breaking waves. "I remember someone chasing her," Eden stated. "I've reason to believe it was my father."

Rafe tossed a rock. "Which proves nothing."

"I remember her running through the trees on the carriageway," she protested. "Zachary remembers too. He thinks my father may have harmed her, that the family has covered everything up to protect him, and that's why he's been gone for so many years."

"That's the danger of snooping about and uncovering a few unconnected details. That's what prompted Zachary to leave you that schoolboy note in the church two years ago and give you Rebecca's pearls to wear in front of Ainsworth."

"He's admitted all that, and he's sorry."

"So am I."

"Don't be so hard on him, Rafe. He thinks he knows what happened."

"But he doesn't. There are reasons for silence other than guilt. Pride is one of the biggest. The mighty Derringtons safeguard their pristine reputation so they can lead a revolution in Hawaii to unseat the queen. Whoever leads that revolution must convince the U.S. Congress to back the revolution. Ainsworth can't afford a scandal or mud on his face. He'll lose support if he does."

"There's no denying the evidence. I've *seen* it," she argued. "And I think you know about it too."

He watched her with cool speculation. "Then he brought you to the old cemetery?"

When she said nothing, he stood tossing aside the pebbles. "Zachary just keeps blundering! Of all the stupid things, he takes you *there*." He took hold of her hand and pulled her to her feet. "It's a marker, Eden, nothing more. No one's buried in that grave—least of all Rebecca."

"You expect me to believe that?"

"I had hoped you'd trust me enough to let me allay your fears and suspicions."

She shook her head. "They lied to me about her body being lost at sea. She didn't die in a storm. The boat didn't capsize. She was murdered."

Anger flickered across his face. "He was unwise to take you there. If he had doubts he should have come to me first to discuss it. He knows I'm aware of things. All he's done is manage to upset you and convince you of mayhem. It's a marker, put there by Ainsworth."

"Why Grandfather? Why didn't my father arrange for it?"

"Your father was too depressed to care about such details. He was consumed with grief and immediately went off on his first research voyage."

"Why did he run away? What was he afraid of?"

"He didn't run away. Come, Eden, I realize things look rather dark, but you can't mean that you really believe Jerome murdered your mother!"

"What am I to think? Why not? What do I really know about him? Or maybe Great-aunt Nora—or even my grandfather."

"Your grandfather!"

She pulled her hand away. "You know who it was, don't you? That's what you've been keeping from me all these years. Why else would my father go away?"

"Perhaps he had his reasons. He's a great man, Eden, a man of honor and sacrifice. He's a man you can be proud of, even if he wasn't here when you needed him."

She turned away, dismayed. "I was proud of him once . . . I wanted to follow in his steps. He's coming back to Hawaii, and I'd looked forward to working alongside him, and now . . . ."

Rafe took hold of her and turned her around to face him. "One day you'll understand him and you'll feel proud of his work again."

His conviction brought tears to her eyes. She wanted so desperately to believe in her father. But how could she?

"Why would Grandfather behave so oddly about those black pearls?"

"Because he understood Zachary's motives. That Zachary came here enlarging your suspicions proves Ainsworth's concern was justified. I told you in San Francisco what Zachary wanted. He expected Ainsworth to make you his heir. He's surprised even Zachary by turning back to Rozlind. There's not much Zach can do about that. He can't very well marry her himself because he knows she's a blood cousin. With you, he deceived himself into thinking you aren't."

"He knows differently now. We've gotten all that behind us."

"Has he? I'm glad to hear he's finally awakened to the facts."

"And what is this truth Grandfather so diligently wishes to hide, to keep from me? From the newspapers? I can't keep from thinking it's the suspicious circumstances surrounding my mother's death."

Rafe did not speak and for a long, quiet moment simply studied her face. Eden felt the heavy silence come between them again.

"Rafe, I've got to know. If you won't tell me, then . . . then I'll go to Grandfather, and Nora, too, if I must. I won't quit, not now. It's gone too far."

He seemed to make up his mind about something.

"I think you're right, Eden. It's time you knew. And I think you should go to Ainsworth and demand the truth from him."

She waited, but he said no more, and slowly her emotions spiraled downward, leaving her exhausted. He knew, but he wouldn't tell her.

"You were here the night I fell. Zachary told me. Why didn't you explain?"

"This may surprise you, but one reason is that I was concerned about Zachary. My mother insisted he might go over the edge if forced to accept responsibility for your fall. I never accepted that. I thought he'd do better if he owned up to it. But Townsend found out about that night. He was worried what it might do to Zachary's future in politics. He had my mother come to me and plead for my silence. I could see how distraught Townsend had gotten her. He used her when he couldn't accomplish things himself. Like when she got the black pearl from Ambrose. There's nothing as convincing as seeing your mother torn apart emotionally. So I vowed my silence for her sake—so Townsend would leave her alone. Then there was you. Even if I decided to break that vow, it would only have encouraged you to continue to think the worst."

"It was you who came looking for me that night. All that time I thought Zachary was protecting me under the daybed from someone with evil intent, but you were searching for me to help me."

"We were all looking for you, except Rozlind, who was asleep. Zachary found you first, but instead of going to Nora or my mother, he hid with you up in that room. He was possessive. He felt that you, too, would be taken from him. He was going to run away with you. I think he would have gone to Koko Crater once the hurricane subsided. I knew his favorite spot was that Round Room. He always went up there to be alone. I found you both hiding under the bed, but Zachary was bigger than me at the time. He struck me on the head with something. It stunned me but didn't knock me out. He chased after you. I followed a moment later and we got into a scuffle. That's when you fell."

She reached and touched the tiny scar on his chin. "You got that while trying to help me. . . ."

His fingers closed over hers. She looked up at him. A smoldering flame grew as they touched. Eden, afraid of what the future may not hold, refused to risk herself to the emotional encounter.

"No, Rafe."

"Don't tell me no when your eyes invite me."

His arm went around her waist, pulling her against him. "You're not fooling anyone but yourself."

She twisted free. "You've already chosen what you wanted, what you've always wanted. The only thing remaining to be decided is when, and under what circumstances, you will regain Hanalei. Well, I can tell you how. By cooperating with Grandfather and joining the annexationists. But you can't have everything your way. You may become another Parker Judson. You may even get Hanalei back by cooperating with my grandfather, but you can't have *both* of his granddaughters."

Rafe's eyes sparked with anger. He said nothing for a long moment, and she began to think he wouldn't respond at all.

"Maybe you're right," he said at last, his voice brusque. "I hadn't made up my mind about a lot of things, but I have now. I'd make one of the biggest mistakes of my life if I married a woman who not only thinks I'm covering up a murder, but also thinks I'm willing to sell out everything I believe in to fulfill my ambitions. Without trust and shared spiritual convictions, there's not much left. Certainly nothing that will help us weather the rough roads ahead." His mouth twisted. "And I can see that you and I would have plenty of them."

Stung by his response, she stared at him. She'd been so consumed with protecting herself that she hadn't taken into consideration how her mistrust and suspicion would hurt him.

"I'm sure you and Zachary can manage to get back safely to Kea Lani without my intervention."

Eden's heart ached, yet she felt emotionally bound and unable to show her dismay. She stood, transfixed, holding back tears that asked for release.

Minutes later, she was still standing there after Rafe had walked away and headed down the beach where a sailboat waited.

Run after him, her heart cried. *Don't let him get away. Tell him he's wrong, that you love him!*

Tears oozed from the corners of her eyes, and the wind chilled her damp face.

Eden sank to the lava rock, watching as the wind billowed the canvas of his boat. Rafe sailed away.

THIRTY-ONE

Rafe arrived at Kea Lani the next day after he'd left Eden at Koko Head. He walked up the steps of the white Derrington mansion with its wide green lawns carrying the journal that he'd given such time and attention to these last two years.

The Chinese servingman opened the front door and Rafe entered.

"Where's Mr. Derrington? Is he in?"

"In his office, Makua Easton. I'll tell him you come to see him."

A few minutes later Rafe entered Ainsworth's office and closed the door. The older man stood from behind his desk, looking pleased, as though he knew the reason Rafe had come.

"Hello, Rafe. You've made up your mind about my offer, have you?"

"Yes, sir, I have." He walked up to the large desk. "But before we discuss your granddaughter, there's something you need to know. It's all contained in this journal." He dropped it on the desk.

Ainsworth looked at him curiously, sat down again, and drew the journal toward him. "Something you've written?"

"I've been working on it for two years."

"Yes, I forget you used to work as a reporter. What's the journal about?"

"You'd better have a look. It will speak for itself, but first I'd like to tell you why I wrote it. I intended you should have it all along. It is yours to destroy if you wish, which I'm certain you'll want to do."

"I don't understand, Rafe."

"Mr. Derrington, even as a boy I always suspected about Rebecca and

Jerome. You see, both Zachary and I were hiding behind the trees watching when you 'buried' Rebecca."

As Ainsworth gasped at this revelation, Rafe sat down.

"There was no casket because there was no body—just a marker you had the caretaker put there in case you needed proof later on to convince the family a Christian burial had taken place. Zachary, always somewhat morbid, assumed the worst, which I did, too, as a child. But later on things were done and said, especially by Ambrose and Noelani, that convinced me a crime hadn't happened, but pride and fear of embarrassment had motivated you to save the Derrington name."

Ainsworth rose slowly and stared down at Rafe. "I think you'd better leave," he said, pale and shaking.

"No. Not yet, sir. I'm sorry, but we've got to see this through. I've investigated the entire matter and it's all down on those typewritten pages, including an interview with Jerome on Bora Bora, and again recently at his research camp in Brazil. There's also an informative interview with the Roman Catholic priest Father Damien on Molokai."

"I'm appalled you'd do this!"

"I had one intention," Rafe admitted calmly. "Until your recent offer—which came only after my initial success with Judson—I was an outcast in the family my mother had married into. I never expected to be treated as a grandson, so don't get me wrong. It was your plans with Townsend to monopolize my father's lands that hardened me as a boy. It eventually drove me to an ambition to get back what I justly believe is mine by right of birth. I came up with my own strategy—to exchange this information for Hanalei. I was going to threaten to go to the *Gazette* with it. I knew you wouldn't risk it, not at a time when you want to influence a revolution for annexation by honorably forging public opinion. I, too, believe you're the man to do it, but you're also a very proud man who uses secrecy to cover what you feel is shame. You've covered for Zachary all these years, and you've tried with Townsend, though he's unmanageable."

Ainsworth sucked in his breath.

"Don't worry. I wouldn't have turned it over to the newspaper. And I won't now, not because I care about the proud Derrington name, but because of Eden. It would hurt her. Not that I ever expected you to refuse me. I have you over the fire and you're too smart not to realize it. You'd cooperate all right, finding a way to force my stepfather to return what is rightfully mine."

The two men fell into silence as Ainsworth mulled over the devastating news.

Rafe watched Ainsworth's shaking hand open the journal, as though a venomous serpent might slither out and strike him. As he leafed through it, his expression turned from caution to consternation, then at last to grim defeat.

"The secret has gone too far. Eden thinks Jerome murdered Rebecca."

"What!" exclaimed Ainsworth.

"So does Zachary. Either explain, or I will."

"Are you telling me you—you're not going to the *Gazette* with this?"

"No. I have to live with myself."

"You realize you're giving up your one chance to get Hanalei back?"

"Some things you can only win by releasing them to the Lord, Mr. Derrington. I'll do the best I can out at Hawaiiana. That will have to be enough."

"You mean you're turning me down?"

"Yes, I've decided to stick with Parker Judson."

"You're making a mistake, Rafe. I can give you anything you want, maybe even Hanalei, if you'd marry Rozlind."

"I've an idea I'd make a much bigger mistake by accepting. I'm not ready to marry now. I've decided I like my independence, and I intend to keep it. If I were you, sir, I'd burn that journal. Just make sure you tell your granddaughter the truth."

Ainsworth looked up at him, startled, his eyes measuring him. "You'd let me do this and walk away?"

"Not for you, I admit. Certainly not for Townsend. At first I wanted Eden protected from this information, but I've changed my mind. She's already been hurt. She suspects something far worse than the truth. Zachary's shown her the marker at Tamarind. I would have told her then, but I felt it would be disrespectful to you. This is a matter that you should explain."

Rafe walked out and closed the door.

———

Eden had arrived home with Zachary earlier that day after Kelolo's ferry took them back to Honolulu. Zachary had gone to his room, and Eden, still emotionally dazed over yesterday's meeting with Rafe at Tamarind House, was resting in her room at Kea Lani when she heard a horse riding up the carriageway. She went to the window and looked out, seeing Rafe. He dismounted, carrying a leather satchel under his arm, and walked up toward the front porch. Eden vaguely recalled having seen that satchel with Rafe at Kalakaua's reception in San Francisco.

She smoothed her hair into place and checked her appearance, then went downstairs. The servingman told her that Rafe had gone into her grandfather's office. Eden slipped quietly into the parlor to wait, and when he came out, she walked to the doorway.

Rafe had looked at her but said nothing. Then she heard her grandfather telling the servingman to send for her. Eden noticed that Rafe had not carried the satchel when he left Ainsworth.

She walked to her grandfather's office. The door was open and she entered. Ainsworth was sitting at the desk with his head in his hands, and Rafe's journal was on the desk in front of him. She moved slowly toward the desk.

"What is it? What's wrong, Grandfather?"

"You'd better sit down."

She did so, slowly, cautiously, looking at the journal. Hadn't she seen it aboard the *Manoa*? And hadn't Rafe said something about writing an investigative story?

"Did Rafe write that?" she asked quickly.

"Yes."

Her heart was beginning to beat faster. "What's it about?"

"The truth about your parents." He looked at her, his face grave. "I have a confession to make. . . ."

Her heart jumped, and she felt breathless. "Yes?"

"Your mother is a leper on Molokai."

Eden sucked in her breath.

"Your father blames himself. He feels responsible for her catching the loathsome disease. He brought her to Molokai once to show her the pitiable situation. She hadn't wanted to go. Later on—he doesn't know how—she came down with it. We had to send her away to the settlement. It was the law! Jerome has spent these years combing the tropics for a cure. Having found none, he's an ill man, in more ways than one. I didn't tell you all the truth about his return to Hawaii. He may not be able to come at all. The obsession of his soul these many years has eaten away his vigor. Rafe visited his camp in South America on the Amazon and tells me how very ill he is."

No, it couldn't be true. Her mother *alive*, yet a leper! The pictures of lepers she had seen while studying tropical diseases at Chadwick came to mind in hideous detail. Imagining her in such a pitiable state all these years, abandoned on Molokai, unable to see her family, her young daughter . . .

Eden dropped her face into her palms and scalding tears wet her fingers and dripped down onto her lap.

Several days had passed since Eden learned the truth about Rebecca. It was Sunday morning, and she longed to see Rafe out at the mission church to apologize for misunderstanding him, as well as to discuss her mother.

The sunbeams filtered through the palms, illuminating the wooden cross on the small mission church that was still standing in an empty plot of reddish earth, in jeopardy of eventually being torn down. Eden sat beside Great-aunt Nora in the open carriage as it approached the field. Usually her great-aunt did not accompany her, but this morning Nora was upset over criticism of Queen Liliuokalani in the *Gazette*, and she insisted on talking to Ambrose.

There were no other haoles outside the church except for Ambrose, who had donned his frock coat to preach his morning sermon. He carried his Bible under his arm as he spoke to the small congregation of Hawaiians and hapa-haoles who had arrived two and three at a time.

"Ambrose! Ambrose Easton!" Nora summoned him, sitting beneath her pristine white parasol on the carriage seat.

Ambrose turned to see Nora and Eden. Saying something to the elders, he turned and walked across the field toward the carriage.

"Good morning, Nora, Eden," he called. "Are we graced to have your presence this morning for worship?" he asked Nora.

"First, I want to talk to you. It will only take a few minutes. I've no desire to interrupt your sermon time, though I must admit, Ambrose, I've heard you do run a bit long."

Ambrose smiled and came up to the side of the carriage, where Nora sat primly, her silver hair neatly arranged beneath a veiled hat.

Eden was trying to behave discreetly but anxiously glanced about for Rafe. Was he here? Would he accept her apology?

"It's about Liliuokalani," Nora was saying. "I know you've always supported the monarchy, Ambrose. If ever the queen needed all her friends who wish her well, it's now."

"I've heard from Rafe there's going to be a revolution," Ambrose said.

"I don't see how it can be avoided with all the rabble-rousers walking out of the legislature the way they did yesterday."

"Yes, so I've heard. Is it true the queen told members of her cabinet that her people are demanding a new constitution?"

"Well, what choice does she have?" Nora demanded. "The Bayonet Constitution was illegal anyway. The haoles will need to accept that and allow for some revamping for more native rights again."

"Now, Nora, you know very well that Ainsworth and the others aren't going to stand by and let the natives take over the government to their detriment. In their minds, they've made the islands what they are, from bringing western civilization to building an economy, and they're not going to pack their bags at this late date and go 'home.' This *is* their home. They have their allegiances and they won't surrender them."

"Gibberish, Ambrose. You know very well that all this fine talk about democracy and freedom is an appeal to the United States Congress to back the revolution to overthrow the monarchy. You know this is primarily about sugar. They want the Hawaiian sugar markets protected."

"I'll not argue that, Nora. But do give credit to some who actually care about the islands' destiny. They want it linked forever with the Stars and Stripes."

"Oh yes, yes, and if we don't get protection from America, we'll end up belonging to Japan, England, or Germany," she scoffed. "Scare tactics, that's all it is."

"I'm not so sure."

"Now, look here, how do you see this?" she asked impatiently. "You're sounding more and more like a dreaded annexationist. It's time we all became forthright about where we stand."

"I admit I'm walking a careful line between supporting the queen and looking somewhat longingly toward the United States. But you won't find my name on a list calling for a new declaration of independence, Nora. When I took an oath of allegiance to the islands, I became a Hawaiian. I meant it. And I'll not join forces to overthrow a legitimate government."

"Well, that's something. Can we count on you to stand with the monarchy?"

Eden saw the concern and regret in his eyes. Any move by the queen to oust the haoles from her government and replace them with liberal-minded Hawaiians would force the conservative Hawaiian League to counter.

"I spoke to Jedediah last night," Ambrose said of the legislator at Iolani Palace. "He came by to tell me of the growing trouble. He thinks Liliuokalani is determined to abandon these islands to opium, lotteries, and debauchery of many sorts."

"Nonsense!"

"I have my concerns, Nora. I'll need some assurances from Iolani Palace before I'll commit to making a public stand against the Hawaiian League."

"Then you'll get that assurance."

Eden was listening carefully. This was the first she'd heard of a concern that the queen would legalize opium dens and bring in casinos. Was it true, or just a ruse to upset godly men like Ambrose?

Nora reached over and patted Eden's arm. "I've good plans for Eden. As the daughter of a missionary, we intend to use her to speak for Liliuokalani. That should bring the wagging tongues to silence!"

Eden was sure her grandfather hadn't mentioned to Nora yet that he'd told her about her mother. Eden wondered about Nora's plans. Ambrose showed concern.

"You'd better make certain you know what you're getting into, Eden," he said, looking at her. "If there's to be a revolution, there will be risk and danger."

"Of course my great-niece knows what she's doing," Nora said energetically before Eden could respond. "We both do. And we're going to help the monarchy silence the newspaper and church critics." She held out her hand to Ambrose. "Help me down, dear fellow. I'm going to start my campaign by attending church this morning."

A thought crossed Eden's mind as she walked with Ambrose and Nora toward the mission church, where the strains of "Amazing Grace" floated to them in the gracious Hawaiian language.

Nora had taken a sudden interest in the little church. On the ride out from Kea Lani she had told Eden, "I think we ought to start a campaign to save the church, my dear—all in the name of Liliuokalani. After all,

it's those big sugar men who want to tear it down. Those of us who support the monarchy and the natives want to keep the church as a tribute
to the early pioneer missionary spirit." Nora had looked at her with a
gleam in her eye. "And it makes for a good newspaper story."

As Eden walked to the church she began to wonder. It did look as
though Great-aunt Nora was on a campaign. And as she had told Ambrose, she could use Eden to offset the stories about opium and lotteries. . . .

Eden sat down beside Nora on the hard pew and joined in the worship
of Christ as she sang praises to His name. Ambrose opened his Hawaiian
Bible and read in the native tongue.

Eden was thinking of those men who had come and translated the
Scriptures into Hawaiian. Along with Ambrose and the native congregation, she read Psalm 67, a missionary psalm.

> *God be merciful unto us, and bless us; and cause his face to shine upon us.*
> *That thy way may be known upon earth, thy saving health among all*
> *nations.*
> *Let the people praise thee, O God; let all the people praise thee.*
> *O let the nations be glad and sing for joy: for thou shalt judge the people*
> *righteously, and govern the nations upon the earth.*
> *Let the people praise thee, O God; let all the people praise thee.*
> *Then shall the earth yield her increase; and God, even our own God, shall*
> *bless us.*
> *God shall bless us; and all the ends of the earth shall fear him.*

After the prayer, as Ambrose began his sermon, Eden glanced cautiously about to see if Rafe were in attendance. She didn't see him and
wondered where he was. Noelani had entered unobtrusively in the back
and carried the young child Kipp.

Nora leaned toward Eden. "Whose child?"

Eden's face felt stiff, though she tried to smile. "Rafe Easton's."

Nora's brows shot up. "He appears to be about two years old."

Eden remained uncomfortably silent and looked at her Bible.

"Well," Nora said, "I wonder if Ainsworth knows about this. In matters where Rozlind's concerned."

After church, Eden told Nora, "I'm spending the day with Ambrose
and Noelani. You go on back to Kea Lani without me."

"Find Rafe," Nora told her. "Tell him I want to talk to him at Kea
Lani just as soon as he has time to spare."

Eden didn't think Rafe would align himself on the side of the monarchy now that he was among the sugar and pineapple growers, but she promised she would, mainly because it gave her the excuse she needed to ride out to Hawaiiana and locate him.

"Tell him I'm thinking of starting up a newspaper," Nora told her. "And I want Rafe to launch the editorial page with a scathing denunciation of the revolution."

"I'll tell him," Eden said, "but I wouldn't count on his cooperation. Things have changed since he got fired from the *Gazette* for supporting Liliuokalani."

"Rafe will do what he must for the good of Hawaii," Nora insisted. "You tell him what I said."

As Eden watched the carriage disappear down the road, she heard a friendly voice call to her. Turning, Keno gave a wave and trotted up to her.

"Morning, Miss Eden. Ambrose said you'd be coming in the buggy out to his place."

"Yes, I was thinking of it," she said simply. "Umm . . . is Rafe there?"

His alert glance caused her to straighten her hat in a nonchalant gesture as she glanced about her.

"He's there. He got in late last night from Molokai, but he should be up now. Wait till you see what else is going on out there. Groundwork's all laid now for the big plantation house. It's going to be a beauty. As good as Kea Lani for sure." Again his eyes twinkled mischievously. "Maybe better."

She said breathlessly, "Molokai?" and her heart beat painfully, yet with unsteady excitement. "What was he doing out there?"

"Didn't Ambrose tell you?"

"No! What didn't he tell me?" Eden confessed that she hadn't been able to speak alone with Ambrose since her return to Hawaii.

"It's about Rafe's work out there."

At first she was dumbfounded. Work? *Rafe's work?* "What work are you talking about, Keno?"

"Thought you knew, Miss Eden. Sorry . . . Rafe's been trying for months now—even before that—to get the Christians in the legislature moving forward on help for the leper settlement. He had this idea for the longest time of starting a missionary home there."

"Rafe?" she breathed. "Rafe wanted to do this?" *And for the longest time!*

"Well, he and Ambrose have finally done it! The legislator named Jedediah is receiving enthusiasm from somebody named Barker of the Independent Missionary Union. I don't know him, but Ambrose does. Mr. Barker's coming from San Francisco to talk with him and Rafe next month."

"Oh," she said, her voice higher than she intended and a bit silly. "Rafe wants to help the leper settlement. How interesting."

Keno cocked his head. "You all right, Miss Eden?"

"Oh yes. I'm absolutely fine. I want to see him. Not Mr. Barker, but Rafe."

"Ah . . . yes, sure. I'll help you into the carriage, then go see if Ambrose is ready. Looks like he's still talking to some of the elders. Say, here comes Noelani now, with Kipp." He started to walk away, but turned on his heel and looked at Eden, rubbing his chin. "Say—there's something you ought to know about that boy. At first we were worried about where he'd come from. But it's clear now he's healthy as you and me."

Eden tensed. "Where he came from?"

"Yes . . . ah, we sort of passed the word around that Kipp was Rafe's son. Just to keep the crew and anyone else from asking questions. I wanted to save my skin with Rozlind, not that it did any good. The Derringtons sent her away to Hanalei. But the baby ended up getting Rafe into the boiling pot." He glanced over his shoulder and walked toward her. He pushed his tanned fingers through his hair. "That's not Rafe's blood boy," he whispered.

Eden was absolutely still. The words sounded through her soul like the toll of a bell.

"Not his . . ." She stopped.

"Nope, just a baby from some poor woman on Molokai. From the looks of Kipp, he's all white. Maybe hapa-haole. It's hard to tell."

"Molokai?" she whispered, astounded. "But—"

"Yeah, I know what you mean. That was my fear too. But you know Rafe. So he wraps him up then and there and takes him with him. Naturally we had to come up with a story. So I did. He rescued him against my wishes, though I'd take him in a moment now. Nice kid—doesn't cry at night. Nothing like that. I think he's going to grow up to be an artist— maybe play the violin or ukulele. At first I was afraid to touch him. Rafe refused to help the woman on Molokai for the longest time, but when we got up next morning to leave on the *Manoa* . . . well, there was the baby. Rafe couldn't bring himself to leave him behind after he could see there weren't any signs of the disease. He said it would be like consigning the boy to certain death. Even so, I warned him his good deed would cause big trouble and I was right, wasn't I? Rafe does what he wants, though.

Always has. And got into the pot several times because of it too. If they knew, the government would take Kipp away. It was against the law to take that baby from Molokai. So you see . . . you mustn't say anything. Rafe will skin me if you do."

Eden lapsed into stillness again. "Why didn't he explain to me?"

He shrugged but looked at her knowingly. "Maybe he got his feathers ruffled because you didn't ask him about Kipp."

"Oh, Keno, thank you for telling me, for trusting me. Do you think I could see Kipp? Take a close look at him and see how his health is?"

"Sure. Here he comes with Noelani now."

"Does she know the truth?" Eden whispered as Noelani neared.

"I don't think so," Keno said in a low voice. "She might. She hasn't said a word. Neither has Ambrose. I can't believe they *don't* know the truth about Rafe."

Eden's heart beat warmly. She certainly owed Rafe an apology now. She had judged him wrongly about her mother and now about Kipp. What else might she be wrong about?

Before Ambrose arrived at the buggy for the ride out to Hawaiiana, Eden heard voices outside the church. Quickly she picked the child up as she heard Noelani call, "Rafe's here now. You want me to take Kipp?"

"No, Noelani, give me a few minutes first, will you?"

Noelani smiled and left. Eden waited, drawing in a breath. She heard Rafe walk into the small sanctuary, and holding Kipp in her arms, she walked out to meet him, enjoying the faint surprise on his face when he saw Kipp in her embrace. Rafe stood in a summer white jacket with the shirt open at the neck, looking handsome and rugged . . . and uncooperative. It was surely time for her to do the reaching out.

They looked at each other for a long moment. She walked toward him past the pews. Rafe held his riding gloves, drawing them through his fingers thoughtfully.

"You have a good-looking son," she said casually.

"I thought so."

"But he doesn't look anything like you."

His mouth moved into a slight smile. "What are you doing with my boy?"

"Looking him over," she said unapologetically.

"I see. Why?"

She shrugged. "Don't you know nurses always go around checking babies that belong to bachelors? I have to make sure you're feeding him well."

"No, I didn't know nurses always go around checking babies for malnutrition—or disease."

She looked at him.

"And what do you think, nurse?"

"I think you've done a fair enough job."

"Coming from you, I'm flattered."

"I think I deserve that. I've . . . umm, been rather difficult, haven't I?"

He flipped the gloves against his palm, scanning her. "Rather."

"Maybe I could make up for it?"

He looked at her, holding her gaze. "I don't mind your being indebted to me." He walked toward her.

Kipp smiled and reached both arms toward him. "Un'ca Rafe—"

Rafe took him and switched him to one arm, running a finger along the bridge of his small nose. "What do you think of her, Kipp?"

Kipp reached both hands to grab at her hair. "Nice."

"Smart boy."

Eden arched a brow. "My, you've grown into an expert at handling toddlers."

"Kipp is just the beginning," he said smoothly.

Eden looked away. "How did you manage onboard ship when you first took him from Molokai?"

"With difficulty," he said wryly, "I assure you. We cut a finger from a glove and tied it around a canteen opening. We picked up a nursing goat with a kid from Maui before we left for South America. Originally, I was delivering the baby to your father at the request of the woman on Molokai. Your father wasn't well enough to take him, however, and asked that I return him to Noelani."

Mention of her ailing father brought a moment of silence. Eden said, "Your idea with the glove finger was clever. I'm glad you didn't leave him to die on Molokai. . . ." Her voice caught, for she was thinking also of her mother.

He seemed to know it, and his eyes softened. "I'm sorry, Eden."

"I'm the one who needs to apologize. That's why I've come. Can we talk, alone?"

His alert gaze met hers. "I was wondering when you'd ask."

"And if I hadn't asked?" she said softly.

"Why do you think I came here today? I knew you'd be here on Sunday. I'll leave Kipp with Noelani and Ambrose and be back."

A few minutes passed and she heard the buggy drive away with Ambrose and Noelani. The voices outside were silenced and the noontide grew still. Rafe didn't return. She walked curiously to the doorway to look out. The reddish earth blazed in the noonday sun for miles about the small church in all directions. Keno and the elders were gone. For a desperate moment she thought Rafe had left; then she saw him tying the horse to the only place that offered shade—three lonely coconut palms standing where Ambrose's bungalow had once been. Eden left the church and picked her way across the clods. Rafe came to meet her, and they walked beneath the clear blue sky, feeling the sun pouring down.

"Who told you about Kipp?" he asked after a moment.

"Keno. I promise to keep your secret."

"I know you will. He could be confiscated."

"A dreadful thought. What would you do?"

He frowned. "I don't know. I've no plans to leave Hawaii. My days on the sea are gladly over. Let's hope I won't need to think about that."

She stopped and turned toward him. "Oh, Rafe, I'm sorry about what I said to you at Tamarind House on the beach. I was exhausted, afraid, and I didn't know what to think about things, especially my mother. Grandfather has since explained . . . not only about her, but about my father, about you and the journal. I realize you kept it from me because you didn't want me to be hurt."

"And because of Hanalei," he said evenly. "Eden, I had planned to use that information to hold your grandfather over the fire. I intended to force him to return what Townsend stole through manipulating my mother. I wouldn't want you to think otherwise. I went to a lot of trouble to get that story over a two-year period of my life."

She knew it had cost him. It was still costing him because he had allowed his work to slip through his fingers.

"And you surrendered it," she said. "Why? You could have won. Grandfather would have given you what you wanted to keep you from publishing the story. He would have made Townsend cooperate with you."

Rafe looked off in the distance, and his gaze came back to the church sitting alone in the field of rusty earth.

"If I had, Eden, I would have lost more than Hanalei. I weighed everything in the balance and decided there was something I wanted even more."

She dared not meet his eyes, afraid she'd give her heart away too easily. She concentrated on the mission church.

"What about Noelani—did she know of my mother?"

"Yes. But it was Lana who accompanied Rebecca in the boat to Molokai. I didn't put that in the journal, though. I didn't want to implicate Lana, because she's got a new life at Chadwick."

She told him that Lana was returning with Dr. Bolton to work at Kalihi Hospital. "Was my father with Lana when they took my mother to Molokai?"

"Yes, he kept you from running to your mother after you climbed down from the carriage at Tamarind House."

"My father was the man I remember in the dream?"

"Yes."

"But he chased her!"

"In your childish mind you misunderstood his intent. He only wanted to hold her again—but she feared she would pass on the disease."

Eden felt her throat tighten. She could feel the loss they must have suffered.

"Just as I mistakenly thought Zachary was my protector when we hid from you," she said.

"And what you thought was dismay on her face was really anguish because she loved him so much, and you. She was heartbroken that she couldn't kiss you good-bye. She couldn't take the chance."

"Oh, Rafe . . ." Though she tried to be very disciplined and businesslike, she could no longer maintain her demeanor. She began to cry as she had been doing on and off since that moment in her grandfather's office.

"Eden . . ."

He suddenly turned toward her and pulled her to him tightly. Her hat crumpled and fell off onto the soil and blew along the ground. "She lived there all those years," he said a minute later. "That was the real tragedy. It depressed me for a long time after I learned about it. That's why I insisted you take those pearls off at the reception. . . . It troubled me, just the same as it did Ainsworth, but for a different reason. He feared Zachary knew the worst, but I had just come from seeing Jerome in Brazil. . . . I saw what the tragedy had done to him. How he still loved her after all these years, how he labored on out of love and devotion, blindly hoping to find a cure—for a woman who could no longer be healed except by a direct miracle of God. There was no hope for her after so many years. Yet he couldn't accept it—he still can't."

She leaned her head on his chest, crying softly.

"That's what she meant when she returned the string of pearls to him. She would hold him in her heart forever—because she could no longer hold him in her arms."

Mama, poor Mama. A leper, forever separated from her husband and daughter...

"They couldn't tell you for the same reason they wouldn't deal with Zachary's problem. You see, Ainsworth and Nora both believed Zachary had deliberately pushed you down those stairs. They kept him away from social functions for over a year while they sent you to Ambrose, and covered up your mother's loss by declaring she'd drowned in the storm."

Because of pride, Eden understood. To be a leper was considered something to keep secret, to hide from society, the way a mentally retarded child was also considered a shame, as though God had visited the family with a curse.

"These ideas must change," he said. "Maybe someday they will. But not now."

"My mother . . . I . . . I must see her. . . ."

He frowned. "No, Eden—"

She clutched the front of his shirt. "Yes, Rafe, *I must.* I want to speak to her."

"You don't want to remember her as she is, dying of a disfiguring disease, but as she was in her best years—young, strong, and attractive, building this church with Jerome." He turned her around to face the mission church with the sunlight reflecting on the white cross against the sky.

Tears filled her eyes. In the victory of the Cross there was hope beyond the diseased, broken body, beyond the veil of death, all because of what Jesus had accomplished.

Slowly her tears faded and the longer she looked at the symbol, the more hope burned in her heart like a still, small flame. All was not lost. Yes, she would go to Molokai and somehow speak to her mother from afar. She longed for this fleeting chance that waited in the brevity of time. If God permitted, she would have it. Somehow in the near future she would seek to convince Rafe to take her there.

Eden let Rafe's words sink deeply into her heart. The story of her parents' love and devotion amid debilitating disease and hopelessness in this life moved her deeply. And to think this tragic love story had been considered something to be ashamed of by the Derrington family! Eden wiped her eyes on Rafe's handkerchief. She didn't think such a story of love and sacrifice was shameful, but noble.

"I'll always love her," she whispered. "I'll hold her in my heart, too, until one day I can reach out and embrace her in eternity."

Rafe drew her into his arms, burying his face in her hair.

After a few minutes he lifted her chin and kissed her lips very gently.

"How would you like to keep this church going in their honor?"

She smiled through her tears. "Oh, Rafe, could we?"

"Somehow. Someway I'll convince Parker."

"Even Nora wants to keep it open, but for her own political reasons."

"Yes, she hopes to use you. You'll need to decide in the not-too-distant future where you stand in this upcoming revolution. As must I." He stooped, picked up her hat, and placed it upon her head, tying the ribbon. He walked with her toward the little building and picked up a clump of rusty soil.

"See this?" he said. "It's worth keeping and holding on to, not just to grow sugar and pineapple, but to make sure the pioneer missionary movement of the past lives on for each new generation. We can best do this if we have freedom to own land and to hold ideals that represent God's truth. If we don't hold on to them, we'll lose them. Kamehameha was right about one thing. *Ua mau ke ea o ka laina i ka pono.* 'The life of the land is perpetuated by righteousness.' If Hawaii loses what men like Hiram Bingham and Titus Cohen gave us, we've lost everything."

Eden took the clod from his hand and stared at it as though it were a giant black pearl, precious and priceless.

" 'Declare his praise in the islands,' " she said, quoting the Scripture verse her mother had written in the front of her Bible.

She looked up at him and loved what she saw.

She smiled. Her tears had dried now. "Yes, Rafe, that's what I want. And I want to forget past hurts and reach forward to a future that God can bless. I want what He wants—not only for me, but for all Hawaii."

"A new beginning . . . for us as well?"

She reached up and once again, as she had on the beach at Tamarind House, touched the scar on his chin, her eyes warmly inviting his.

He drew her into his embrace, and as the trade wind blew against them, and as they stood before the mission church, his lips vowed that he belonged completely and only to her. Whatever the future of Hawaii might be, whether it rested with the monarchy or with the United States, they would be caught up together in the fulfillment of its God-given destiny.

The clouds of revolution were gathering above Iolani Palace. But whatever happened, Eden knew the best was yet to come. How could it be otherwise? she thought. They were the children of the *true* and everlasting King of Hawaii, even of all the earth.

AUTHOR'S
HISTORICAL NOTES

Many of the characters who appear in *For Whom the Stars Shine* are not fictional. Woven into the story of the Derrington family are real people who played an important role in the history of Hawaii in the nineteenth century. Here are descriptions of some of the more prominent players in Hawaii's colorful past:

Hiram Bingham, one of the first missionaries to Hawaii, who helped create the Hawaiian alphabet, which was used to translate the Bible into Hawaiian.

Titus Cohen, who preached as many as thirty sermons a week and was used of the Lord to usher in Hawaii's greatest revival.

Edwin Dwight, Yale student who led the Hawaiian Obookiah to the Lord and hoped he would return to his people as a missionary.

Obookiah, whose death during the winter of 1818 stirred many New Englanders to go as missionaries to Hawaii.

Father Damien, Belgian priest who was ordained in Honolulu and assigned at his own request to the leper colony on Molokai in 1873, where he died in 1889 after contracting the disease.

King David Kalakaua, who ruled over Hawaii for seventeen years and died in 1891; the second elected monarch and the first to visit the United States.

Princess Liliuokalani, the last reigning monarch of the kingdom of Hawaii, who was deposed in 1899. A musician and songwriter, she wrote Hawaii's most famous song, "Aloha Oe."

Lorrin Thurston, member of the Hawaiian legislature and a grandson of the pioneer missionary Asa Thurston.

Judge Sanford B. Dole, son of missionary Daniel Dole and a family member of the renowned Dole Pineapple Company, who played an important role in Hawaiian politics.

Claus Spreckles, the Sugar King from California.

James G. Blaine, the U.S. Secretary of State under President Harrison.

Minister Henry A. P. Carter, King Kalakaua's minister to the U.S., who negotiated the sugar and Pearl Harbor treaties, bringing greater American influence and control to Hawaii.

British Commissioner Wodehouse, who tried to keep the U.S. from gaining territorial control of the islands.

Walter Murray Gibson, King Kalakaua's controversial prime minister, who was eventually run out of Hawaii and died on his way to San Francisco.

William Ragsdale, the parliamentary interpreter who went willingly to the leper colony on Molokai, using his political skills to benefit the settlement; lived out his last years on Molokai with the self-imposed title of Governor.

Koolau, a Hawaiian from the island of Kauai who became an outlaw rather than join the leper colony.

The following men were encouraged to try their skills and exclusive "remedies," hoping for a cure for leprosy:

The Hawaiian priest Kainokalani; the Americans who mixed their own patent medicines; the Norwegian scientist Armauer Hansen; the Indian Mohabeer; the Chinese Sang Ki and Akana; the Japanese Goto; the German bacteriologist Eduard Arning, who got permission from King Kalakaua's government to implant leprous tissue in the flesh of a living subject, the condemned native murderer Keanu.